**YOUR FEARS AND HOPES,
YOUR DREAMS
AND NIGHTMARES—
THEY'RE ALL THERE
WAITING FOR YOU
IN THE ZONE....**

A BREEZE FROM A DISTANT SHORE—Long before death came to stay in the Danby household it had begun to take Tom's father away from him, and now he would never have a chance to say good-bye—or would he. . . ?

MY WICCAN, WICCAN WAYS—Cast into the future by her greatest enemy, the Grand Witch of England was about to find out whether there was any room for her old-fashioned kind of magic in a world full of witches. . . .

DARK SECRETS—Sometimes darkness is the least of what you have to fear. . . .

REALITY—Was it just a huge interactive sculpture, or was the mass of cogs, levers, switches, and metal exactly what its name implied—Reality. . . ?

These are just a few of the places you'll go and the people you'll meet as you journey through time and space and beyond to that special dimension known as the Twilight Zone. . . .

ADVENTURES IN
THE TWILIGHT ZONE

More Original Anthologies Brought to You by DAW:

JOURNEYS TO THE TWILIGHT ZONE *Edited by Carol Serling.* Sixteen unforgettable new tales—some eerie, some scary, some humorous—all with the unique *Twilight Zone* twist. Included is Rod Serling's classic, chill-provoking story, "Suggestion."

RETURN TO THE TWILIGHT ZONE *Edited by Carol Serling.* Eighteen new tales by such talents as Pamela Sargent, Robert Weinberg, Barry Longyear, Charles Grant, and Jack Dann. Included is Rod Serling's "The Sole Survivor."

ALIEN PREGNANT BY ELVIS *Edited by Esther M. Friesner and Martin H. Greenberg.* Thirty-six, all-original, imagination-grabbing tales that could have come straight out of the supermarket tabloid headlines. From the bride of Bigfoot to the discovery of JFK's skull on the moon to a surefire way to tell whether your coworker is a space alien, here's all the "news" that's not fit to print.

FRANKENSTEIN: The Monster Wakes *Edited by Martin H. Greenberg.* From a journalist who stumbles upon a modern-day descendant of the famous doctor ... to a mobster's physician whose innovative experiments might lead to a whole new kind of enforcer ... to the monster's own determined search for a suitable bride ... here are powerful new tales of creation gone awry.

ADVENTURES
IN THE
TWILIGHT ZONE

Edited by Carol Serling

DAW BOOKS, INC.
DONALD A. WOLLHEIM, FOUNDER
375 Hudson Street. New York. NY 10014

**ELIZABETH R. WOLLHEIM
SHEILA E. GILBERT
PUBLISHERS**

CONTENTS

INTRODUCTION
by Carol Serling

This is the third book in our *Twilight Zone* series. The first was *Journeys to the Twilight Zone*, the second, *Return to the Twilight Zone*, and now we have *Adventures in the Twilight Zone*. Here are twenty-three new stories, never before published, plus Rod's classic "Lindemann's Catch," and I feel that this is perhaps the most imaginative, compelling, and chilling book of the entire series.

The stories have an element of the bizarre in them, a certain tilt, in which ordinary people are thrust into fantastic situations. The stories aren't about bug-eyed monsters or space heroes, nor do they depend on the gadgetry of science fiction, but they do stretch the imagination because (as the *Twilight Zone* guru once said), "In the *Twilight Zone*, the ordinary laws of the universe do not apply."

... Read here then of rituals and deadly games replayed against the background of contemporary Athens, or experience a chilling glimpse around the corner into a future world where one lives by remote control.

... Or meet Jerry who watches murders night after night in his dreams, or the archivist who can't seem to count the collection correctly.

... And then there is the fanciful knight of Greenwich Village who *does* find the Holy Grail, and Abe, the young man who sees "home movies of a life that was never lived," and Caroline, whose phobia about nudity seemed to be messing up her afterlife.

... And, too, there is a touching story of a kiss from beyond the grave, and an account of a most unusual friendship between a kitten and a "hotfoot."

... And from the *Twilight Zone* master himself, a story of the toughest fishing captain out of Boston, who ran his ship and his men with an iron hand—right up until the day he netted a monster.

There are many other high voltage stories in this anthology, many from the true masters of the genre: Margaret Ball, Richard Gilliam, Billie Sue Mosiman, Lois Tilton, Adam-Troy Castro, J. Neil Schulman, Walter Vance Awsten, etc., all most unusual odysseys.

So read on ... and as Rod Serling once said:

"The stories will lead you to the shadowy tip of reality; you're on a through route to the land of the different, the bizarre, the unexplainable. Go as far as you like on this road. Its limits are only those of the mind itself. Ladies and gentlemen, you're entering the wondrous dimension of imagination."

Next stop ... *The Twilight Zone!*

THE REPOSSESSED

by J. Neil Schulman

He did not know until he found himself there Tuesday morning—half past six, as he pushed aside a leather sleeve to check his watch—that it was going to happen again. But here he was once more, this time sitting on a motorcycle parked in front of an expensive Spanish-style house on a quiet Beverly Hills street, and he knew there was nothing he could do to prevent it. Nor, if he was perfectly honest with himself, did he have any strong desire to prevent it. But that was part of the pattern, too.

Two things were different. Usually there was only one person to watch—and it had always been someone he knew. This time, however, there were two—and he did not recognize either of them.

He watched them from behind a parked car, several houses down and across the street. Both were men, large and well-muscled. One was clean-shaven, in his mid-forties, wearing a suit and tie. The other, ten-or-so years younger, had long hair and a beard, and was dressed in jeans and red work shirt. Though they were only a few hundred feet away from him, they had no idea that he was here, watching them. But that didn't mean anything. They never knew.

When talking about what happened in these encounters—sometimes to his wife, sometimes to the police, sometimes to one of his colleagues at U.C.L.A.—he had described the feeling as a lot like waking up with amnesia. He knew where he was, what he was doing, and how he was feeling—but that was *all* he knew. He recalled nothing before his appearance on the scene—nothing of who he was or how he had got there.

Perhaps as a necessary defense mechanism against being present at the scene at all, he had become completely detached during his own actions.

So here he found himself, watching the two men as they looked around furtively and then—trying one key after another—attempted to break into a recent-model Mercedes Benz parked in the driveway of a Tudor house.

Then he found himself kicking the motorcycle beneath him into life and speeding down the street. He found riding the motorcycle exhilarating, having no memory of having ridden a motorcycle before.

Pulling the motorcycle into the driveway to block the two men, he dropped the kickstand and dismounted casually. Neither of the men made any attempt to escape. Nor did either of them seem to be at all afraid. Perhaps they knew him, he considered. That would have been true to the pattern; often they did.

The older man wearing the suit said, "Good morning," and began reaching toward his inside jacket pocket.

Immediately—and it was always at this precise moment that he was the most detached—he found himself dropping into a crouch behind the motorcycle and drawing a Glock 23 semiautomatic pistol.

The older man said, "Relax, I'm just—"

But he wasn't paying any attention. He knew he wanted them dead. That was all there was to it.

Taking aim at the two men, he quickly shot each of them—the younger man in his chest, the older man in his stomach.

Even through their contortions of pain, he could see astonishment on their faces as they crumpled to the blacktop in front of the Mercedes.

He found himself walking calmly over to their fallen, bleeding bodies while lights began coming on inside the Tudor house. But he did not care whether anybody was watching. He aimed his pistol once again and carefully shot each of the men in the head.

He awoke suddenly, in a cold sweat as usual.

It always took a few seconds, after these dreams, to reorient himself. He was home, in bed. Everything was all right. He hadn't even awakened Michele this time; she was still asleep, next to him.

Two emotions flooded him immediately. The first was

an oppressive guilt for having just killed two men in cold blood. The second was an immense relief: *he* had been at home asleep, dreaming. *He* hadn't shot anybody.

He reached for the spiral notebook he always kept at his bedside to record his dreams and immediately checked the digital display on his clock radio for time and day. It was Tuesday morning—half past six.

Michele turned over and opened one eye. "Jerry?" she said.

"Go back to sleep," he told her, writing down the day and time in his notebook.

"Not another one?"

"Go back to sleep, honey. You don't have to be up for another hour."

Michele brushed blonde hair off her face and sat up suddenly. "Jerry! Who—?"

"Nobody we know," he said. "I don't even know why I was there this time. Maybe this one was only a nightmare."

"Oh, thank God," Michele said.

"Go back to sleep," he said once again. "I want to get this down while it's still fresh. You can read it at breakfast."

But he had said this only out of habit. Neither of them had ever managed to fall asleep again after one of his dreams.

Michele adjusted the pillow behind her and pulled up the strap on her nightgown. "Jerry, who was it this time?"

He sighed. "A pair of car thieves," he said. "They were shot by some guy on a motorcycle."

"You were the man on the motorcycle?"

Jerry nodded, half distracted already; he was busy writing it all down.

For maybe the fiftieth time since they'd been married, Michele asked, "Why are you always the killer?"

Jerry continued writing. "I wish I knew," he said. "I wish to God I knew."

The first of these "dreams" had occurred when Jerry Keller was thirteen, growing up in Natick, a town eighteen miles southwest of Boston—a small town as only Massachusetts can breed them. A town that in the early sixties had still not recovered from the dwindling of its

manufacturing industries and would not reap the benefits
of the computer industry until the next decade. A town
whose Army Laboratories had produced K-rations and
Space Food Sticks. A town whose favorite son was a local boy who played baseball for the Washington Senators.
A town with more banks than almost anything else—and
more churches than banks.

A town that wasn't expecting murder and didn't believe it when it happened.

The boy who had been killed—Billy White—had been
from a working-class family that had lived in the town for
over a century. Perhaps his parents were the only ones
who truly mourned him; Billy's ninth-grade teachers at
Coolidge Junior High School knew him as a troublemaker
and a terror to the younger boys. He had been suspended
from school once for beating up a seventh-grader in the
school cafeteria. But what school officials didn't learn
until after Billy's death was that the seventh-grader he
had beaten up had been a holdout from Billy's protection
racket, which had fifteen other boys forking over their
lunch money.

Jerry had been one of the fifteen.

It had happened on a school day one January while
Jerry had been home sick with the flu. Jerry had been
asleep, around eight a.m., when he found himself—in a
dream as realistic as his waking hours—behind the wheel
of a blue station wagon driving along Cottage Street. Seeing Billy White on the side of the street walking to
school, Jerry had found himself twisting the wheel and
accelerating directly toward the boy. The speedometer
read close to fifty miles an hour when he hit.

Billy's body broke like a doll's as it flew in an arc over
the wagon and landed in a heap on the street. The station
wagon continued speeding off ... and Jerry Keller had
awakened in a cold sweat, alone in the house.

His mother had come home from the bank, where she
worked as a teller, at her usual four o'clock, and had told
Jerry that she'd heard at the bank that his schoolmate,
Billy White, had been killed on his way to school that
morning by a hit-and-run driver.

Jerry had told his mother the dream he'd had that
morning—including the information that it was a blue
station wagon which had run Billy down—but she didn't

take it seriously; there had been no witnesses, and nobody knew what sort of car had done it.

Later that evening, Jerry repeated the story for his father just before the family turned on *Eyewitness News* to hear that Natick police had identified the hit-and-run vehicle as a blue Oldsmobile Vista Cruiser station wagon—owned by a man with several previous arrests for drunk driving.

But Jerry knew that the driver had not been drunk behind the wheel—and that the car had been aimed at Billy White *deliberately*.

Though his parents eventually came to believe that through some clairvoyance Jerry had witnessed his schoolmate's death, neither of them could accept Jerry's conviction that the boy had been run down deliberately, and Jerry's father forbade him to go to the police with his story.

The incident might have been forgotten entirely had not—six years later in Vietnam—Private Jerry Keller dreamed the fragging of his lieutenant through the eyes of some fellow private, only to be awakened with the news that Lieutenant Hall had been killed during the night by an enemy fragmentation grenade.

Three years after that, psychology undergraduate Jerry Keller—asleep in his dorm room one midnight—had been inside the heroin addict who mugged and stabbed to death one of Jerry's Columbia University professors. He remembered feeling rage against Professor Simon, even after he turned over his wallet, and a sudden, definite desire to see this smug motherfucker dead.

And U.S.C. doctoral candidate Jerry Keller had been unconscious in his car, after being rear-ended one night on the transition road from the San Diego to the Long Beach Freeway, when the next encounter had taken place. Once again, the murder weapon was an automobile; but this time when Jerry awoke—in Long Beach Memorial Hospital—he felt none of his usual disgust for the killer who had taken possession of his unconscious mind.

This time, the murderer was a union official taking the exit a minute or so after Jerry's accident. The murder victim was *not* the driver of the pick-up truck that had rear-ended Jerry, but the drunk who—wandering across a freeway exit ramp at eleven p.m.—had caused Jerry to slam on his brakes.

Jerry knew only this about the union leader's motives: The drunk standing on the side of the road looked a lot like a *scab*.

The frequency of the dreams had accelerated after that. There had been fourteen of them in the last five years. Until these car thieves, though—if it turned out the incident had actually happened—the pattern had always been the same.

The murder victim was always someone Jerry had seen at least once—a loan officer at the bank where Jerry and Michele had their checking account, a famed psychiatrist lecturing on the benefits of electroshock therapy at a symposium Jerry was attending, a third-grade teacher at his son's school whom Jerry had met at a P.T.A meeting.

The murderer—whenever he or she could be found—had always turned out to be someone familiar with violence from the wrong side.

And Jerry had always felt the *killer's* emotions, seen everything from the *killer's* point of view. He found himself inside the killer only moments before the crime, never had access to any other memories the killer had, and could never see anything not seen by the killer at the time.

Four years earlier, Jerry had decided to begin relating these dreams to the police.

Sergeant David Englander, a homicide detective with the Los Angeles Police Department, at first had agreed to see Jerry only because the man making these claims to impossible knowledge was a respected psychology professor from U.C.L.A. But since that initial meeting, Jerry had provided information that had led police to killers in five cases—and in two of them, information Jerry provided had caused police to reclassify as homicides what had previously been thought accidental deaths.

Of course, news of his abilities had eventually leaked to the press, and for a time Jerry had been besieged with phone calls from police departments all over the world for help with unsolved murders. Over and over again, Jerry had calmly explained that he had no abilities of use in investigating any murder he had not dreamed about, and he had no way to make himself a hidden witness every time somebody decided to knock off somebody else.

The only lasting significance of this press coverage was the tag that a national weekly tabloid had provided Jerry—and that colleagues in the psychology department used to rag him during faculty meetings. A clever headline writer—looking for a capsule term that would describe a psychology professor who could telepathically enter the minds of killers—had dubbed Jerry "the Psychopathic Keller."

He wished sometimes that he could witness the murder of that headline writer; to Jerry's mild regret, the man had remained unmurdered and in perfect health.

That morning, after Michele had left to drop the kids at school on her way to work, Jerry phoned Sergeant Englander. Thrown into close proximity over a long period of time, the two men had become friends. "I've had another one, David," Jerry began his call.

"Who, when, and where?" Englander asked.

"A motorcyclist shooting two car thieves grabbing a Mercedes, this morning at six-thirty," Jerry said, "on a residential street in Beverly Hills."

"Jesus Christ," Jerry heard Englander say softly.

Jerry's heart sank as whatever hopes he had of this latest one being just an ordinary nightmare faded away. "You've got one?"

"Can you drive over to my office?"

"No, I can't. My—"

"You have classes today?" Englander interrupted him.

"No," Jerry said. "But I've got office hours for students today between ten and noon. And my—"

"Expect me at your office at noon, Jerry," Englander said. "I'll buy you lunch."

"For Chrissake, David," Jerry said, "what *was* it?"

"Haven't you turned on a TV or radio this morning?" Englander asked.

"No," Jerry said. "The dream woke me at six-thirty, so I shut my clock radio off before it went on."

Jerry could hear Englander sigh over the phone. "At six-thirty this morning, Ray Laughlin, a five-year California Highway Patrol motorcycle officer, was—for some unknown reason—in Beverly Hills. He shot and killed two collection agents taking back a Mercedes."

Jerry couldn't manage to say anything.

"Yeah," Englander said, and hung up.

" 'Psychopath,' Ms. Webster," Jerry told the red-haired grad student sitting across the desk from him, with her legs provocatively situated, "is not the favored term anymore. 'Sociopath' is the preferred word nowadays. Of course, the media have given me a personal reason for disliking the older term."

Jeanette Webster barely smiled. "But, Dr. Keller," she objected, "isn't the real question whether either term has a scientifically verifiable meaning? Isn't psychopath—or sociopath, if you prefer—a useful word to describe a person who has never internalized society's taboos against killing?"

"I don't see that as a question at all," Keller said, "if by 'scientifically verifiable' you mean a proposition you can test in the laboratory. 'Conditioning' is a word we can test—either a rat will or won't, with predictable regularity, learn a maze given the proper reinforcement. I know of no way to test for behavior that—ultimately—is disdained when performed by private individuals for personal reasons, but which is perfectly acceptable throughout most of the world when performed by that same individual in an official capacity."

"Isn't that a rather value-laden viewpoint?" Jeanette asked.

"Is it?" Keller shot back. "I give you as example the federal agents who raided the Branch Davidians at Waco. The original Alcohol, Tobacco, and Firearms agents opened fire first on a house containing children. The FBI took over the operation and proceeded to torture these same children with the amplified sounds of rabbits being killed and endless repetitions of Nancy Sinatra's song 'These Boots are Made For Walking'—this last named is torture above and beyond the call of duty. Finally, either by deliberate intent or by criminal negligence, the tanks being used to insert CS gas into the house sparked the fire that destroyed them all. Both the government's agent and the so-called sociopath see their acts as justified—and consequently, feel no remorse about them. Both of them

see themselves as the disinterested agents of forces outside their control. Convince me—aside from our un-
derstandable personal preference that people shouldn't
randomly kill one another—that there is any *observable*
difference between the act of the official killer and the
private killer, and I'll consider 'psychopath' or 'sociopath' a useful scientific term."

Keller looked up and saw a large man in a somewhat
worn suit standing in his doorway. He rose, ending the interview. "I'd like to see if you can answer my objections
in your next paper," Keller told his student.

Jeanette Webster stood up, nodding, grabbed her book-
sack, and left.

Sergeant Englander walked into the office.

"How does The Source appeal to you?" the Detective
asked Jerry.

"Okay," Keller said. "But you're eating my sprouts."

They started discussing the case while walking across
U.C.L.A's lush Westwood campus to the parking lot.

"Jerry, this one just doesn't make any sense," Englander said. "We're not talking about a corrupt cop on
the take from a car-theft ring. Everyone who knows
Laughlin says he's a Boy Scout. That's not just a figure
of speech; the guy's a Boy Scout troop leader. The two
men he shot, they check out clean, too."

Jerry shrugged. "What does Laughlin say?"

"He doesn't remember anything after going on duty.
Says he has no idea how he even *got* to Beverly Hills."

"All I know, David," Jerry repeated, "is that it was deliberate. I *know*. I always know."

"Couldn't you be mistaken for once?" Englander
asked. "The way I had it figured, Laughlin follows these
two guys for some reason and sees them breaking into a
car—doesn't know they're repo'ing it. One of the repo'
agents starts reaching for his I.D., Laughlin thinks he's
going for a gun, and shoots without thinking. Possible?"

Jerry shook his head. "David, I *know* the desire he
felt—the determination to kill. And—if you don't want to
go by feelings—I *saw* him walk over to them while they
were on the ground and *shoot* each of them in the head."

"Christ." Englander sighed. "That's what one of the
neighbors said, too. But *why?*"

"You know I never know why," Jerry said. "I'm in there—God only knows how or why—I tell you what I feel and what I see. That's all."

"Yeah," Englander said.

They came to the visitor's section of the parking lot. "Where's your car?" Jerry asked.

"Right over there," Englander said, pointing to an un-marked Dodge. "But can we take your Porsche? I love riding in those things."

"I don't have it anymore," Jerry said. "I tried telling you on the phone this morning. I got four weeks behind on the loan payment and the bank repossessed it last week."

Sergeant Englander looked at Keller carefully. "That's the psychic link we've been looking for!"

Keller looked startled. "What do you—"

Englander rushed on. "Is it possible these were the *same* agents who took your car?"

"I suppose it's *possible*," Jerry said slowly. "It would make sense. I was wondering why this one didn't seem to fit into the pattern. Yes. Yes, now that I think about it they would *have* to be."

"Well, I'll be damned." Sergeant Englander shook his head ruefully. Then he thought another moment, glanced over to his Dodge, and said, "Listen, instead of driving over to The Source for lunch, how does walking over to The Good Earth sound to you?"

"Okay," Keller said. "But you're eating my sprouts."

It wasn't until the next morning at half past six, while he was shaving, that Sergeant Englander thought it was too much a coincidence that his friend Professor Keller had always met the victims he saw killed—and in several cases had good reason to resent them. Englander stopped shaving, with his old-fashioned, straight razor poised in mid-air in front of the bathroom mirror, while he realized that he was so long coming to this conclusion because it horrified him so much.

His horror was not caused only by the thought that a close friend might be a cold-blooded murderer, although that was certainly part of it. What really horrified Sergeant David Englander was his realization that there was no means in the legal code under which he operated—

from the United States Constitution on down to the daily
operating procedures of the Los Angeles Police Department—for investigating, indicting, trying, or punishing
a criminal who did not rely on *physical* means. If Jerry
could enter other people's minds and make them commit
murder, then how on Earth could a criminal
justice system which relied entirely on witnesses and
physical evidence do anything about it?

It couldn't, Englander concluded; and even more horrifying was Englander's knowledge that if Jerry Keller was
able to commit murders that society's legal system was
powerless to prevent, then it would be the duty of Sergeant David Englander to resort to extra-legal means to
stop a mass murderer: Sergeant David Englander would
have to become a murderer himself.

But there were even-more-horrifying moral questions,
Englander considered. If Jerry was *asleep* while he was
committing murder, then how could he be considered re-
sponsible for his own actions? And if Englander killed
Jerry to prevent him from committing further murders,
wouldn't he be killing a man who in his own conscious
mind was innocent?

Or would he have to leave out the moral question entirely, and kill Jerry the same way—and for the same
reasons—that one shot a rabid dog?

As he stood there before his bathroom mirror, David
Englander knew that what he was contemplating violated
every objective standard by which he had lived his life.
He knew that what he was considering was illegal. He
knew it would be viewed as immoral—that it might, in
fact, *be* immoral. He knew that there was a reasonable
chance that no matter how carefully he acted, if he killed
Jerry he might be caught, tried, convicted, and sent to the
gas chamber.

Sergeant David Englander also knew that he had already pledged his life to the protection and service of his
community. He knew that if he became utterly convinced
that Jerry was a mass-murderer, then it would be necessary for Sergeant David Englander of the Los Angeles
Police Department to set aside his badge—and his feeling
for a friend—and to execute Professor Jerry Keller.

"You're right, Jerry, you're right," Englander said
aloud to himself, as he recalled the conversation he'd

overheard the day before between Jerry Keller and his graduate student. "There *isn't* any difference between a psychopath and an executioner."

What David Englander had failed to take into account, as he spoke these words to his bathroom mirror, was that it was half past six in the morning, and Jerry Keller would still be asleep.

Thus, Englander was completely taken by surprise when he looked into his bathroom mirror and saw not his own face but Jerry Keller's.

Sergeant David Englander was only slightly more surprised when he watched his right arm, living its own life, drawing his old-fashioned straight razor directly toward his throat.

BALLAD OF THE OUTER LIFE

by Margaret Ball

A swarm of lime-green fliers bursts through the dark, dense emerald green of the canopy, shrilling their complex group song two octaves above the highest note my own ears can pick up. The tagalong lets me "hear" it through Spinne's brain, a weave of harmonies that makes me, no, makes Spinne leap and dance on its extensible, multijointed limbs.

The greenfliers scatter and skirl a sharp warning dissonance: a pithiva concealed among the looping vines has flicked out its sticky tongue and reeled in one of them for breakfast. We've analyzed the pithiva sap already. Yes, sap, not venom—it's a vine. Technically. A rootless, carnivorous vine whose sap paralyzes greenfliers and may possibly be a useful local anesthetic for humans, depending on how Ilona's analyses turn out.

The tagalong view of interlaced vines and treetops whirls, tilts, then steadies on a vista of gray scalebarks. Spinne must have dashed away from the pithiva. The tagalong gives me Spinne's increased heart rate, blurred vision, hypersensitivity to sounds and smells. All the sensory accompaniments of fear; I can almost feel the fear itself, my own heart racing in sympathetic accompaniment.

The greenfliers have wheeled away from the pithiva too, whistling and harmonizing above Spinne's head. Spinne crouches beside one of the scalebarks and watches them hungrily. All right, I don't *know* it's hungry, but I can feel the dizziness, the belly cramps, and my—Spinne's—eyes never leave the flock of greenfliers. I say Spinne is hungry.

The greenfliers are too smart to fly down within Spinne's range, but one of them makes another mistake now. They dive to perch along the writhing, scaled limb high over Spinne's head. Where the limb meets treetrunk, there's a dark blob, looks like moss. A greenflier lands there, and the mossy globule spurts out clear liquid whose tensile properties change in midair. Sprays like water, thickens like rubber cement as it lands and wraps around the greenflier. Before the bird can screech alarm, it's been compacted into a sealed bundle. No motion, no sound warns the other fliers. Spare drops of the clear gunk dangle from the parcel. Spinne rears up on hind appendages and its claws scrape against the tree scales, trying to reach the drops. They sparkle like faceted gems, emerald and diamond in green shade and sun.

A double blink of my eyelids and the helmet automatically moves away from my head. Sensortag connections peel loose with it, and I'm in the tower again. From here, through my own eyes, I can no longer see the bright dance of gold and emerald light that is Spinne's view of the rainforest. To human eyes it's a menacing jumble of dull brownish green scales and vines and oozing puddles. Not a place for human habitation. Not even, we've learned, a place for humans to explore. Carelessness with our sterile field cost us two of seven team members the first week on Tehuelche.

Three, if you count me.

Here inside the artificial light is cold and clear, surfaces are smooth and bright and clean. All the shiny reflections dazzle me after the shifting green lights of the rainforest.

"I've got a possible," I say, or rather, the voder says for me. Responsive to the slightest vibrations in my not-quite-paralyzed vocal chords, volume controled by the push of air from my still-functioning lungs, and programmed to produce the husky, sexy contralto of a long-dead actress. Want to talk? It's easy: just pucker up and blow.

Griff has been using the simscreen on the other side of the Tower to run computer analyses while I worked tagalong; now he stops and listens, nodding from time to time, while I describe the stuff I've decided to christen mossygunk. Could its secretions be a flexible glue?

Nadel strolls into the tower halfway through my description. Obviously, he's been picking us up on one of the other com units in the bubble. Equally obviously—and predictably—he disagrees. Probably not worth the cost of extraction. *Certainly,* he says with one of those glances I can't miss, not worth the cost of suiting up an able-bodied team member to collect a sample; rule is at least three samples within a ten-meter radius.

He has to say "able-bodied," as though I didn't know I can't be the one to collect the sample, as though I didn't know what a drag my disability is on the team. Why? I quit asking that question a long time ago. Could as well ask why three of us came down with a viral fever when we tore the first bubble and the other four never caught it, why Jon and Veeta died and I didn't—quite. A person could go crazy asking questions like that. Me, I work shift and read poetry. The brain still functions fine, though sometime I think Nadel doesn't believe it.

The Company's been generous—another fact Nadel points out more frequently than I like to hear it. Cost of my liftchair, modified from one used for advanced multiple sclerosis patients, seriously cuts into the profits the Company can expect to take out of Tehuelche in this first five-rotation shift. Unless, of course, we find a really good biopharmaceutical hidden in the rainforest—something like etoposide or vincristine or the other miracle drugs they took out of Earth's rainforests in the old days. Back when Earth still had rainforests.

We might make a find like that; you never know. Somewhere in that dull green, dripping, squishing mass of bioforms is the virus that put me in this liftchair. Somewhere out there must be a cure for it, some leaf or flower or bug that keeps native life forms like Spinne from demyelinating like me. Our biochemistries are similar enough; that's why the Company picked this planet as a likely research site. We've worked three revs of the five-rev contract; two slightly-longer-than-Earth years to go, to find a cure for my demyelinized nerves, or to pick up enough possibles that the Company will decide to extend our contract.

Nadel's grumbling on, trying to devalue my mossygunk

before we even collect a sample. Has anybody else observed this behavior? Hasn't this area been worked out? He's enjoying a thorough wallow in pessimism. Tehuelche was an impossible task for a seven-per team, let alone three.

"Four," Griff corrects.

Nadel doesn't argue, but he doesn't agree, either. "They're expecting us to analyze a world by remote control, from scratch, and come up with results as good as last century's medical botanists brought out of the rainforests on earth. Plotkin and Elvin-Lewis didn't have to go in cold," he grumbles. "Read their papers! Over and over they say, 'The natives told us how this plant was used ... When they understood what we were looking for, the natives came to us with their arms full of samples.' Where are the natives to unlock Tehuelche's secrets for us? Hmmm?"

"We've got more computer power and better chemical labs right here in the bubble than Plotkin and Lewis had in their entire lifetimes," Griff points out.

"And," I can't resist voding, "we have Spinne."

"Hah! *Die Spinne,* the spider! It's a description, not a name! Nonsapient six-legged tarantula! And you want me to use that—*thing* as a cue to what *human* biochemistry can utilize?"

Shahhh. I picture myself waving my hands in disgust, making a quick spin around to tell Nadel what I think of his team-politics games. But I'm not "in" Spinne now, and my own muscles can't pick up the message blocked and jammed by unsheathed nerves. It has to be conscious control now.

Resting my right forefinger on the sensor pad in the arm of the liftchair requires the concentration I'd once have used to solve a set of linear equations in six variables. The subtlest impulse in that finger sends the liftchair hovering down the corridor to my private cubicle; and sending that impulse tires me out as much as a session in the gymbubble used to. I don't have the energy to argue with Nadel today. Next shift I'll sensortag on Spinne again, see if I can influence it into going back to the mossygunk tree. Tagalong's supposed to be a one-way connection, but sometimes I get this feeling Spinne's picking up something from me.

* * *

"Und Kinder wachsen auf mit tiefen Augen
die von nichts wissen, wachsen auf und sterbern,
und alle Menschen gehen ihre Wege."

I've been using my eyes too hard, too many hours, to read now; but I have all of Hofmannsthal's poetry, and most of Rilke's, on disk. I can set the liftchair to horizontal—sleeping position—and listen to Hugo von Hofmannsthal's slightly demented vision, which is different from my own madness and therefore safe. "And children grow up with deep eyes / that know nothing, they grow up and die,/ and everyone goes on." *Die von nichts wissen.* You knew something, though, didn't you, Hugo? I think I'll rechristen Spinne. Call him Hugo. Think of it as your personal bit of immortality, my long-dead friend.

Ilona enters without knocking. I know why she doesn't bother; she said once that it was restful to know at least one person who wouldn't be doing anything private in his or her cubicle.

For Ilona, "private" means sex, and she means that she never knows whether Griff and Nadel are having another argument or are in bed together, and it makes her edgy. She doesn't mean to be cruel; imagining other people's feelings has never been one of Ilona's strengths. Of the four of us, I'm the only one who really likes tagalong shift, and Ilona's the only one who refuses to do it at all. She never could overcome her instinctive revulsion against the Spinnes, can't bear to sense Tehuelche through them and see beauty where our human senses perceive only mud and stink and a thousand kinds of nasty death.

I wonder if I'd have felt like that if the virus hadn't killed most of me. If I could still move in my own body, would I be so willing to tagalong "in" Spinne? I think so. I like to see things from a different angle—a dead poet's vision, an alien life form's senses—and Ilona doesn't. I tell myself that would probably have driven us apart in the end even if the virus hadn't struck, that my physical attraction to her would have been sated and we'd have become more than friends and occasional bedmates instead of passionate lovers interrupted before the fire could burn itself out.

I tell myself that rather frequently. Especially after a

tagalong shift, when the memory of how it is to run and dance and lust and eat is strong within me.

I don't protest Ilona's invasion of my privacy. She'd only tell me once again that I've no privacy left to invade, not when she already washes and turns my helpless limbs and fits me on the liftchair. I don't particularly want to hear it again.

I do protest, though, when she switches off my Hofmannsthal disk. "Hey," the husky voice that isn't really mine says, "do you mind? I was listening to that."

"I can't understand a word of it," Ilona says. "No, don't translate. I don't care what language you put it into, it doesn't make *sense*."

Ilona's our biochemist. She likes things neat, orderly, confined in test tubes and Petri dishes, turned to ash, their true nature revealed in flame and assay. If it hadn't been for my illness, she'd never have had to leave the bubble. Now she and Griff and Nadel have to take turns suiting up to collect samples. She never reproaches me, though. It would not be logical. She might as well reproach Jon and Veeta for having died.

"It makes more sense than all your chemistry manuals," I say, but lightly; I don't want to quarrel with Ilona. "Listen!" I quote from memory, translating as I go: "And sweet fruits ripen in the bushes / and fall by night like dying birds / and lie a few days and decay."

"Ugh," Ilona says. "Sounds like Tehuelche. Don't you get enough of that stuff on your tagalong shifts?"

I could try to tell her what Tehuelche is like through Spinne's senses, the play of fire and emerald, the rich thrusting interweave of life and death, the edge of constant danger.

"It's not good for you," she says before I can start. "You're working too much tagalong, Licia."

"About all I can do." I don't think the statement sounds self pitying; the voder isn't programmed to whine.

"And then you come in here and spend your off-shift poring over ancient texts. It's not healthy."

I wish the voder were programmed for maniacal laughter. What *is* healthy for a woman in my condition, Ilona? Shall we adjourn to the gymbubble for physical therapy? Up, down, up, down ... very good, now the *other* eyelid?

She means well; and I can't laugh, anyway. I can think a laugh, but the voder translates it as a low growl.

"How about some nice cheerful music instead?" She doesn't wait for my assent to switch the sound channel to the melange of pop tunes and light classics the Company programmed for our workbubbles. Supposedly some research, somewhere, has shown that these rhythms keep us cheerful, stimulated, and able to work eighteen-hour shifts. Have to maximize every one of our expensive hours on Tehuelche; Nadel told me once I don't want to know what it costs to keep this sterile bubble setup working for a five-year contract, and for once I'm in agreement with him. I don't want to know. If I did, I might worry about . . . all sorts of things that probably aren't going to happen.

Ilona shifts lightly from one foot to the other, catching the rhythm of the music, swaying like one of the white flowers that bloom in the night of Tehuelche and fade at dawn. Spinne can see those flowers, and so can I, but I've never seen any hint that they're good for anything, so I haven't mentioned them to the rest of the team. Have I? I can't remember now, with Ilona swaying closer and closer to my liftchair. I lie back and watch her; breath catches in my throat and I remember how it was. I've lost sensation as well as movement, can't feel her hands when she cleans and dresses me, but I remember. Oh, how I remember.

She bends over me, opening her mouth. I can see her warm moist lips coming closer, but the only way I know when they touch mine is that it's harder to breathe. If I could concentrate I could move my finger on the sensor pad, send myself spinning away from her in the liftchair, but equations are as far away now as the moons of Tehuelche and as little use to me. I've stayed cool so long, trying not to fall into this chasm of endless unattainable wanting, but today . . . Today I have danced in the emerald forest and I am drunk on an ancient poet's madness and I want, just once again, to feel a human touch on my skin.

She draws away, looking sad and lost. I wish I could put my hand to her cheek, make some comforting gesture, but the virus hasn't left me even that much.

"You really don't feel it, do you?" she asks.

"I can't," I tell her. "You know that." I don't tell her the rest, how much I still want her, how looking at her is making me feel everything inside that my nerveless skin can no longer know.

"You are so lovely, Licia," she says.

That's nonsense. Ilona is the one with the true beauty, the beauty of motion, freedom, action. What do I have? Anybody can draw a pretty face. Hell, Tri-D artists can draw a pretty face that smiles and kisses. That's a lot better than I can do.

"And so pure," she adds after a moment's awkward silence. "Nothing really matters to you, now, but your work and this poetry? I suppose it's better that way."

I'm told that blind people have to put up with this kind of crap too, being told how wonderful it is that they're gifted with some kind of extra sense to make up for their blindness, when the truth is it's no gift at all: They concentrate every minute and work damn hard to remember where things are, to pick up tiny clues that sighted people have the luxury of ignoring.

But at least blind people don't have to look at the idiots who are telling them about it.

"I'm rested now," I say, or rather the voder says for me, more gently than my own voice would have done it. "I think I'll see if I can pick up Spinne again, work a while longer."

Ilona shakes her head but doesn't try to stop me. It's dark outside, but Spinne can "see" in the Tehuelchen night. And we need the extra data. We've got three people collecting and analyzing where we should have had seven. Tagalong is the one thing I can do, and if I've got the energy to take another shift, she has no business telling me to stop.

Griff's working tagalong when I return to the Tower, lines of strain showing in his face. He's done a full day's work already, out this morning on a collection sweep and then analyzing samples in the lab, and he shouldn't be watching Spinne now. He removes the helmet and fits it on the back of my liftchair without argument.

"Nadel thinks we should forget the whole sensortag program," he tells me. "He says we aren't getting enough possibles from watching Spinne to justify the time it takes."

So he's been putting in extra hours with Spinne, a job he hates almost as much as Nadel and Ilona do, trying to help find possibles. I feel guilty and grateful and angry all at the same time. Lucky none of it shows in my face. It's good of Griff to put in the time, but I am so damned *tired* of thank you, please, so good of you, and all the rest of the phrases that fill my helpless days.

Griff presses the sensor tags down on my forehead, and all at once it doesn't matter: I leave this useless shell of a body behind in the tower and gallop with Spinne through the Tehuelchen night. The rainforest is gray and white and pearlescent to Spinne's night eyes, and the rain that would sting human skin is cooling shower to it. As if it knows and sympathizes with my needs, Spinne runs, leaps fallen trees, lopes fluidly over streams and through moss-lined gullies.

This is what we know about the spidery thing that Nadel christened *Spinne:* It seldom sleeps. Constant motion is its key to staying alive in the Tehuelchen rainforest. Other life forms use camouflage, secret hiding places, armored shells, or poison as their defenses. Spinne runs. That's one of the things that makes it an ideal recipient for sensor transmitters: It has to cover a large territory just to keep in motion. The second factor is its highly developed nervous system that feeds the transmitters a rich mix of sensory information about its view of Tehuelche. I mean, we could have tagged a greenflier, but the silly birds don't take in or use much information beyond the sounds of their own calls. Or we could have tagged a slomow and spent whole revs experiencing the inside of its burrow.

The other thing about Spinne was, we caught one early on, nosing around the bubble when it was first set up. So that's the third factor: It was convenient.

Right now Spinne is moving too fast for me to glean any information about other Tehuelchen life forms. I give myself up to the hypnotic shifting rhythms of the night run. Where is it going? For all the hours of tagalong watch, there's so much we don't know about Tehuelche, let alone about Spinne. We don't think it's sapient; it appears to live solitary; if it mates, we don't know how. Tonight I can add one infinitesimal datum to the accumulated notes on Spinne: It can run for an incredibly long time without collapsing. A piece of information that will be of no interest to the Company, though it may eventually make a footnote in the *Journal of Xenobiology*.

There's something wrong about this frenzied run, though, something desperate, irregular creeping into the rhythms of Spinne's body. It trips for the first time and I gasp in shock; then again and again, stumbling now, exhausted and in pain. I think this is pain, what the sensortags are sending me. It's been so long since I felt any, I have forgotten.

There's a circle of tall scalebarks, a marshy pond in the center, a stand of moonflowers in the center. There was an Earth vine called the moonflower, but I don't care; these are my flowers and I'll call them what I want. It's not as if they were good for anything anyway; Spinne has passed them before without a glance.

The water splashes around Spinne's thrashing legs. This is definitely pain, and fever too, burning Spinne's senses as the virus did to me and Jon and Veeta. I remember Veeta begging for water before she died, when the virus had numbed her mouth and throat so that she couldn't taste the water Nadel dripped into her open mouth. The real reason I don't like Nadel is because he tried so hard, that week, to keep us all alive, using every trick he'd learned in the parameds, downloading whole journals of xenomicrobiology to look for something that would halt the spread of the virus. He prevented me from dying, Nadel did. Do you want me to forgive him that?

I think Spinne is dying now. I don't particularly want to experience this. I've been through one death already—my own—and thanks to Nadel's efforts, I'll have to do the job again some day. Twice is more than enough. I blink the helmet and sensortags away and laboriously guide the liftchair back to my cubicle.

Ilona must be asleep by now; it's safe to listen to poetry. But I don't need the disk tonight. I've listened to this one so often I know it by heart. I cannot cry for Spinne, or for the vicarious world I'm about to lose; but I lie awake in the liftchair, communing with Hofmannsthal. "... run through the grass, / and here and there are lamps and trees and ponds / and all is empty, withering in death . . ."

If I'd written the poem, I could call it *Tehuelche: Requiem for an Alien Life Form*. But Hugo von Hofmannsthal got there first, and he called it *Ballad of the Outer Life*.

This morning I "forget" why I desensored last night. Go to the tower for a tagalong shift, find Griff packing away the sensor helmet and its computer. Not to mention everything else in the observation tower. Ilona and Nadel seem to be methodically stripping down the computer analysis equipment, piece by piece.

"The Spinne must be dead," Griff says, not meeting my eyes. Ilona and Nadel concentrate on the walls of simscreen and touchpad they're dismantling. "No sensor readings this morning. And from the notes you dictated last night, it's pretty clear what happened. I'm sorry, Licia."

"We can tag another one," I say. Voder doesn't translate the lump in my throat—just as well. Unscientific to get attached to experimental subjects, and even Griff would find the fact of my fondness for a Spinne perverse; I don't want to think what Nadel and Ilona would say about it.

Griff's lopsided grin lacks some of its usual sparkle. "Who you calling *we*, white lady?" He flips sealtape around the helmet's padded carton. It's as final a gesture, in its way, as the Old Earth custom of throwing dirt onto a coffin. "I'm sorry, Licia," he repeats, getting to his feet. "You might as well know—Our contract's been voided. We're being recalled to work another planet. They've decided this one is hopeless. Like Nadel said, we can't collect enough stuff blind, not working with all the sterile field precautions. And the tagalong project just wasn't producing results fast enough."

"They can't cancel us!" I protest, but I know they can. Any time, without cause. Contracts are all written by the Company law firm; who do you think takes the risk, us or them?

Griff looks sad. No, nervous. "Licia, they didn't cancel. We requested it. All three of us—Nadel and Ilona and I—we talked it over this morning when we found that the

Spinne wasn't responding. We're just not getting enough results to justify the program. We've poured three revs of work into Tehuelche and barely brought out enough biopharmaceuticals to pay back the Company, never mind any profit for the team."

"Give me time," I beg. "It's a biorich environment. There have to be more useful substances out there. We just have to learn to understand Tehuelche."

"Licia, we weren't just thinking of ourselves," Ilona tells me. "We have been seeing the toll this work takes on you. You've been working tagalong nearly every waking minute and withdrawing into depression the rest of the time. Licia, you still have a working brain, you're still a lovely woman. It is time to focus on what you have, not on what you've lost."

"It's time for all of us to cut our losses," Nadel puts in. "Licia, sometimes we must accept failure—just as I did when Jon and Veeta died."

My throat closes up for a moment, saving me from voding something unacceptable. "I . . . I see."

"There will be other projects, Licia."

But not for me. Even if tagalong were enough to compensate for what I've lost, I won't get another chance. When the Company writes the new contract, there won't be a place in it for an expensive cripple. Griff and Ilona and Nadel will go on to some distant star, and I'll spend the rest of my years in a nice sterile rehab facility.

Not acceptable.

If this is the end, I'll take it in my own way, not in theirs. No years in a comfortable padded liftchair for Licia, getting 'grams from the stars, pictures of the new worlds my friends will discover without me.

"I see," I repeat. "Would you excuse me? I, I would like to be alone for a little while."

They all nod solemnly. I think they're relieved to be spared a scene. What kind of scene did they think I could make with one finger and a voder? The voder isn't even programmed for a scream. Just as well. I think great sweeping bursts of motion; my right forefinger twitches a fraction to the left, then forward, and the lifchair floats me out of the tower.

But I don't go to my cubicle. The series of sterile bubbles leading to Outside are programmed to respond to voice command, so that people coming in with samples don't have to touch anything until they've been cleared to enter the living bubbles. Convenient. And I don't have to waste time suiting up, as Griff and Ilona and Nadel do; there's no way I can get a suit onto my useless, unresponsive body, no suit big enough to fit around the floatchair. Also convenient. I won't last long Outside, but that's no longer an issue.

The unfiltered air Outside makes my eyes tear up and burns my throat. The gusts of wind are something I hadn't counted on, as is the wall of tangled vegetation between the bubbles and the rainforest. Where our power beams cut a clearing for the bubbles, Tehuelche's gray-green sunlight streamed in and the edges of the clearing were almost immediately choked by walls of entangled vines. That's what you can see from the tower viewing wall, but it's never been real to me; my Tehuelche is the sun-dappled shade of the deep rainforest, where soaring scalebarks rise like the columns of a cathedral up to a green mosaic of hanging ferns and mosses and interlocking leafy branches. On the ground, far below those air-feeders, there is little undergrowth—not enough sunlight to feed it. There is room for Spinne to run and dance and leap. That is Tehuelche to me. This dense wall of greenery is an artifact, a problem we created for ourselves when we cut a hole in the forest.

But there must be some way through—or have they confined their "collecting" to snipping off samples of the leaves and vines that grow in this unnaturally sunny space around the bubbles? Jerks—no wonder we're not getting results. Can't blame them, though. They don't want to wind up like me. Even suited, they weren't about to venture into the true rainforest, where something might compromise their sterile suits, puncture their security, drip poison into their nerves.

I don't have to worry about that any more. The liftchair has power enough to punch right through the soft green tangle of vines. Some of them have thorns; I see the tears in my skin. In this light my blood looks gray, like everything else. I can't feel the thorns. There are some advantages to my condition. Nothing left to fear, and not much left to hurt. I'll go as far into Tehuelche as I can before the liftchair dies, and that'll be it. Quick—I've done

enough tagalong to know that whatever happens in this
dense, rich, moist world, it won't take long. By tomorrow
I'll be a mound of nutrients enriching the soil of Tehuelche.

In among the scalebarks now, sheltered by the canopy,
I can go as fast as my forefinger will twitch to guide the
liftchair. More pressure on the sensor pad gives me more
speed, swerving among the trunks, almost keeping up
with a flight of greenfliers overhead, almost as fast as
tagalong with Spinne on that last run. Until a fallen scalebark looms diagonally across my path and I can't tell my
finger to twitch fast enough to lift me up instead of
around. The impact is a blunted jolt, knocking me out of
the liftchair. I lie with my face half buried in soft rotting
scale mould. I think something got badly twisted in that
fall; if I still had a functioning nervous system, it would
be hurting like hell now.

Is this far enough? For the first time it occurs to me
that Griff and Ilona and Nadel might be fools enough to
come after me when they notice I'm not in the cubicle.
Especially Nadel. The damn fool never knows when to
give up: Look at what he went through to keep me alive
three years ago. Oh, *hell.* I wanted to kill myself, not anybody else. Should've found some neat clean way to do it
inside the bubble, where they could find my body and
wrap it up in another neat sealtaped package. Or pitch it
out to feed the soil of Tehuelche.

Can I make it back to the clearing, so they can see me
dead and know what happened? Not a chance. The
liftchair's three feet away, buzzing uselessly, running
down its power sources where it's jammed into the scalebark. It might as well be on the other side of Tehuelche.
I can't move my finger far enough to wipe off the drops
of sweat that are running into my eye, never mind trying
to reach the sensor pad on the arm of the liftchair.

There's a pithiva slithering in the vines above me, but
it doesn't seem interested; I'm far too big for it to digest.
Pity. That would be a quick and painless way to go—and
another thing occurring to me now is that death on Tehuelche may be quick, but it is not necessarily painless.
There's a lichen near my useless left hand; I can see it
from here. If it's one of the varieties that like to grow

through and feed on living meat, I may not feel anything,
but it sure won't be fun to watch.

The lichen has sprouted through the back of my left
hand now. I don't think it's used to taking in this much
hemoglobin; it's growing fast but looks weak and flimsy.
Yeah, I know I shouldn't look. But you see, when I close
my eyes I imagine another one, spores stirring in the
moist ground under my right eye, the one closest to the
ground . . . I still have some sensation in the eye muscles,
you see.
    This was an extremely stupid idea.
    I'm hot. And thirsty.

It's dark now. If Griff and the others looked for me,
they went the wrong way. If the last three revs have given
them any understanding of Tehuelche, they'll assume I
am dead by now, and they won't waste energy in more
searching. So I can stop feeling guilty about that, at least.
Whatever happened is over.
    What I can't understand is why I'm still alive. The li-
chen has spread over most of my arm; it looks as if my
skin is turning into scalebark. Every nerve that still car-
ries sensation tells me I'm burning up, even though the
sun's been down for hours, even though it never gets really hot under the shady canopy of the rainforest. Burning
and dry and thirsty, just like before. Nerves that have lain
useless for three revs twitch, legs trying to run and run
like Spinne on its last doomed gallop through the forest.
Instead of movement I get shocks of pain. A day ago that
would have been wonderful, sensation where there's been
none for so long. Now I think, what's the point? Why
can't Tehuelche just kill me without this added little *zotz*
of drama? Useless pain has never been my thing.
Should've done this the conventional way, sleeptabs in
the privacy of my cubicle, no fuss, no muss . . . I think
I'm delirious; the rainforest keeps fading in and out
around me. So does my train of thought. Death by free
association. "And children grow with deep eyes / that
nothing know, grow up and die . . ."
    Fever's up again. I think. And the thirst—it's the same
symptoms as the virus that paralyzed me. Back again to
take another crack at me. Must like human biochemistry.

But what's left for it to take? A few nerves. Brain func-
tion. When it paralyzes the autonomic nervous system,
I'll stop breathing. There used to be a giant snake in the
Old Earth rainforests that killed its victims that way, con-
tracting gently on each exhalation until the prey couldn't
draw a breath. Tehuelche is a serpent wrapped around
me.

The brain is definitely going. I think I see Spinne.
Well, they're curious; that's how we caught and tagged
one to begin with. But this one seems to have a gleam of
sensortags on its skull. That's not possible. My—our
Spinne, the tagged one, died in the marsh pond last night.
Griff said so.

A tearing pain in my left hand, the one with the lichen
growing through it. And hallucinations of motion now, I
feel like I'm flying, being lifted, carried, in the smooth
rocking motion I've learned from tagalong with Spinne
as it loped through the rainforest. Not a bad way to go.

Two blue moons and a forest of white flowers. And
mud in my mouth. I wish this delusion would stay con-
sistently pretty. But I'm thirsty, so thirsty that I don't
even mind the water and mud and God knows what else
slipping into my slack mouth. Swallow. Swallow again. I
should be gagging on the mud and slime, but the hallucinations are kicking in again: It tastes rich, nourishing.
Tehuelchen chicken broth.

Sun comes up over the marsh, and the moonflowers
fold in on themselves. And I'm still alive. But there's
something definitely wrong with my vision: Colors are
vibrant, emerald and diamond and piercing lime-green,
like tagalong vision through Spinne's sensors. Something
round and scaly moves, too close to my face, and I jerk
away from it. My God, I did move! I felt the splash of
marsh water when my head fell back! But the scaly thing
is still there. Panic. Thrashing, scrabbling backwards to
get away, it follows, follows . . . Dumbo, that's your own
arm.

And it moves. Oh, it moves ever so nicely. I lie there
in the marsh for a while, lifting my arm and rotating it
and admiring the way the brilliant green water swirls
off its delicate patterning of scales. After a long, long

time, it occurs to me that the other arm might move too.

I can sit up.

A pithiva slithers toward the water's edge, and I bare my teeth at it. Tehuelche, you better not kill me now; I haven't been alive in a long, long time, and I want to stick around to enjoy it.

I will, too. Spinne splashes through the water, frisking around me, extending and retracting its jointed limbs in a dance of delight. The sensortags flash bright on its skull. Why did Griff tell me Spinne was dead? Perhaps the virus is part of a lifecycle change; perhaps it caused Spinne to generate antibodies against the alien intrusion of the sensortags. So Griff would've picked up that null reading.

And whatever Spinne may have been before, it's definitely sapient now. Smarter than all of us—smart enough to run to the moonflower marsh when the virus struck it—smart and generous enough to drag another sick sapient to the same place.

I am beginning to understand. We don't adapt Tehuelche to us; it adapts us to it. When Nadel risked his life to bring Jon and Veeta and me inside the bubble for treatment, he also killed us. Alkaloids in the marsh water, something released by the moonflowers, necessary for the final synthesis. Nadel carefully put us where the water of Tehuelche couldn't touch us.

I can live on Tehuelche now. My eyes see the colors, my ears distinguish the slither of a pithiva from the innocent movement of vines in the wind, I can taste the sweetness of mossygunk secretions. Sitting in the marsh water, my body senses and tells me: This is poison, this is a food, this is a trap. And my memory of our work in the tower suggests that the poison is an alkaloid too complex for laboratory synthesis, possibly useful in small doses. That the moonflowers release something necessary to remyelinate the nerve sheathing, something that might help humans with MS.

I will bring the flowers back to the tower for analysis. And the mossygunk. And all the other leaves and roots and barks and insects whose uses I can now sense. Enough to save the project. If they haven't left yet, if the bubble is still there, I can bring them everything they need.

Everything we need.

"The natives came to us with their arms full of samples."

DESERT PASSAGE

by Randall Peterson

The first meeting took place in one of those sun-baked cantinas that maintains an unsavory symbiotic relationship with the reservation. On public land, just on the border, its cracked adobe facade and its dilapidated tar-thatch roof beckoned the stray alcoholic like the predatory lair of a wolf spider.

Inside proved to be just as confining and just as foreboding. Greasy ceiling fans wobbled, circulating the dank air and filth; a few tribals and illicit truckers sat at the bar watching a battered TV, its picture a mosaic of static from some far-off urban signal.

Maureen and I, a couple of scientists, hardly belonged here, but this was the place our go-between had suggested for us to meet Gil. And there he sat, in a dingy corner of the cantina nursing a Cuervo, chasing it with some Mexican beer. Maureen didn't like it. I knew that. But I was determined to get this dirty part of our project out of the way.

Gil, his only name, didn't bother to stand. The man with the patchwork face looked like a reject from an Ortega canvas, but he couldn't have been over forty. As we took our seats at the table, his yellow eyes monitored our expressions as if he knew exactly what we were thinking. Maybe he did.

"Do you have the envelope?"

That was blunt enough. A real business exec, this Gil. Reaching into my vest pocket, I pulled out a brown envelope and placed it on the table. He opened it, counted the roll of bills with a tobacco-stained thumb, then nodded.

A pause. "The map?" I requested, feeling that I had to state the obvious.

But he just sat there. Then he craned his head in what looked like slow motion, peering out from the shadows, as if he were hiding from something invisible. What the hell? Maureen caught my reaction.

Out of nowhere, a folded piece of parchment appeared on the table. The map. And a very old one at that. As though not wanting to contaminate himself, Gil nudged the fragile map toward me with his knuckles. He then reached out for the envelope, paused a second, looked up at something beyond our table, and crumpled the money in his hands and into his pocket.

That was the first meeting.

The second occurred a day later, this time in a trading post/diner, the kind of place that sells authentic Taiwanese Native American-style rugs, assorted jewelry that tourists want to believe is the real thing, and six-packs of Orange Crush. We sat down at a table amid dozens of hanging cheap trinkets, garish accordion-style postcards of the jackalope variety, rock candy displays, and miniature cactus gardens to send back home. It was in this atmosphere of utter artificiality that we met Corey Craig.

"And you must be Dr. Craig?" I asked, extending my hand with a degree of apprehension. Craig was a freelancer, much like myself and my partner, Maureen Sandler; but, along with his knowledge and expertise in carbon-14 and magnetic dating, he carried a lot of curious baggage—rumors, I supposed.

"Yes, that's what I answer to," Craig acknowledged, grasping my hand aggressively. "Aaron Wilkes, I presume?"

"Glad to meet you. And this is Dr. Sandler . . . Maureen Sandler." Maureen shook his hand, but I think Craig felt the tension and disapproval, palpable in their handshake and quite unmistakable in her eyes.

Not a momentous beginning for such an undertaking and one that, by its very nature, had to be based on mutual trust. But I figured that all scientific projects, those subsidized by foundations or universities or otherwise, began with the usual doubts, tentativeness, and social insecurities. So I pressed on. After all, we did share some common interests. Maureen and I, as specialists in dark-zone archaeology, had studied signs of ancient humanity in the dim recesses of caverns all around North America. My spelunking know-how and her skill in deciphering pictographs and other prehistoric art had provided for us a unique partnership.

But the fellowships, university grants, and the museum digs had too many governmental strings attached, and they had lost their luster; we now were in it for the kick, for the individual satisfaction . . . and, yes, for the bucks.

And Corey Craig? Well, let's put it this way. He had a rather notorious rep and an ego. But we needed him. Just as he needed us.

Craig's private van, unmarked by any institutional name, quite innocently parked outside the trading post, housed an archaeological dating lab sophisticated enough for any dig, anywhere. And now he'd agreed to be the third party in our project, that is, after we'd signed his agent's contract. That's right, a freelancing archaeologist with an agent. That should have been warning enough for us.

I should have listened to Maureen.

In a sense, there'd be no turning back. The tribal contact had been paid off—very well—and that had been the final obstacle. Map in hand, we surreptitiously made our way off the main highway in Craig's nondescript van. Thieves in the night, I thought to myself. But we weren't out to steal anything. At least *that* relieved my guilt. We were just recording a find—and selling the data to the highest bidder.

Of course, we soon found out that Craig couldn't have cared less about securing an illegal map of a sacred cave site in the middle of reservation territory, and still less about dealing with a totally corrupt and morally bankrupt tribal. All in all, this little excursion of ours spelled disaster, but in the heat of the moment, in the addictive excitement that can precede a great discovery, Maureen and I fell into a kind of trance of our own making.

After an hour or so of off-road driving, we came to immense rock formations jutting upward into the night sky. Looking like a planetarium projection, the sky of this late October night seemed almost too clear to be real, its diffuse stars spilling over the horizon like a billion eyes watching us.

Inside the van, we plotted the intersecting lines of the arcane map, and Maureen puzzled over the myriad of symbols that peppered the smudged margins. But the landmarks on the map were distinct representations. A few kilometers north stood the ruins of a rock and mud city carved into a huge cliff, home of the Ancient Ones. It was only vaguely visible in the starlight but nevertheless there, quietly resting for millennia. According to the map, the cave site lay on the monumental rock just ahead of us. That's where Craig parked the van.

"Do you hear that?" Maureen asked me, cupping her ear, as we approached the edge of the mountain foot.

"Hear what?"

"Nothing. The silence."

"Maureen, we're in the middle of the desert."

"Come on, Aaron. No insects. No animals. No ambient sounds at all?"

She was right. Not even a lone cicada. Then Craig turned to her. "What do you want," he said, "a delegation of coyotes to welcome us?" Maureen didn't answer, and she didn't appreciate his sarcasm.

We figured it would take most of the night and into the early morning hours to find the cave opening—a crevice, a fallen escarpment, or some kind of clue to its entrance. We were right about that. One likely opening turned out to be a mere indentation in the massive rock, another just a break from a thousand years of erosion. But another proved the map correct.

Maureen spotted it first. That is, she discovered the faint markings on the mountain, just about at shoulder level. All of us aimed our flashlight beams over the face of the rock directly in front of us. More markings. And then a vast pit of tumbled, smashed boulders, just around the perimeter. No sign of man, modern man. No footprints. No fresh graffiti. No vandalism.

Several meters across the pit we found an opening, a gash from rocks impacting but possibly a route to somewhere. Excited, we clicked into professional mode, lining up all of the cave gear—the helmets, lights, tracer string, radio beepers, special tools, video camera, small backpacks—everything we had always used in all of our other speleological explorations.

Having the most experience, I took the first descent. To my surprise, the floor of the cave's mouth was no more than a few body lengths downward. I signaled for the others to follow.

As Maureen descended, Craig held the guide rope taut from above. Then he followed. The extra light from their helmet lamps and flashlights now brought this initial chamber into perspective. Man had been here, to be sure. But not for many years, many decades. Yet the map existed, handed down through generations, down to Gil, its ignominious and final guardian. Was I to believe that we were the first ones to explore this cave? No one else? That's what bothered me the most. Was this a set-up? Were we a bunch of sitting ducks just waiting for a posse of reservation deputies to round us up for trespassing on sacred ground?

But all of these feelings of uncertainty I naturally kept to myself. Why raise the fears of the others, especially when we had a job to do? Craig impatiently kicked a few ridges of dirt, then motioned to Maureen, saying, "Clay pots, some shards. Nothing much."

"The mouth of the cave will be the habitation area," she replied. "That's hardly a surprise. We've found living quarters like this all over America."

"If this is where it all ends, then our job is finished," I said. And then my flashlight caught another surface, an adjacent wall. Another opening, a passageway. Now we had something of value. "Aha. Maureen. I've got something." She knew what I meant. She'd detected the same tone in my voice back in Tennessee's Jaguar Cave, just before we came across ancient footprints from four-thousand-year-old cave explorers.

Other dark-zone explorations had proven that aboriginal cavers had had the ability to negotiate extremely dangerous passageways over a mile from a cave's entrance. As we entered this corridor between two faces of massive rock, I noticed that we were still descending, but toward what? A burial site? A picture gallery? At this point, anything seemed possible.

Colder, much colder. As we maneuvered our bodies through the labyrinth of granite, we felt the very atmosphere change. And then, looming up from the shadows of antiquity, another chamber, only this one rivaled any of the huge caverns we'd encountered. Water, no, a pool, and falls from above—it was a veritable cathedral, a subterranean shrine!

After a few moments of silent amazement, Craig nudged me. "Okay, okay. Enough gawking. Do we have something that we can take back home, or just another natural wonder here?"

"Take back home?" questioned Maureen. "What do you mean by that, Dr. Craig?"

"I take it that we're here to *find* something, right?"

Maureen glared at me, as if I'd said it. Her green eyes were aflame with disgust, anger, you name it. Then she turned to Craig. "Look, all we're down here for is to document a possible discovery, record it, date it. And that's it."

"Sure. Return with nothing. Right." Craig nodded to himself, breathed in deeply, and wrinkled his nose. "Sulphur. I hate sulphur. And I hate bats. Where are the little buggers?"

"Bats," I said to myself. "Maureen? Bats."

She looked at me and read my expression. "Not a one. Not one bat. Nothing at the entrance either. Why not?"

"Well, so we've discovered something," I said, not knowing what it meant really. "No sounds outside. No bats inside."

"Bats? No bats? So what? I didn't take on this project to carbon date a damn bat." Craig stomped away toward the left edge of the pool.

Man-made or not, pathways cut into the cavern floor led directly around both sides of the exquisite pool and waterfall. Craig had now reached the halfway point. "Maureen, let him go. We'll cover the other side, to the right." She wanted to say something, but she didn't.

On closer inspection, the path indeed seemed to be smoothly cut directly in the stone floor, quite geometric, quite intentional. Maureen knelt for a moment, felt the walkway with her hand, felt its ultrasmooth texture, then shook her head. "Aaron? It's like satin, but every few centimeters—"

"Little ridges. I know. So . . . humans . . . won't slip."

"But how?"

"Got me." The echo of the cascading water created an unearthly effect, especially as we crossed around the fall, meeting Craig on the other side of the pool. Smugly, he stood there waiting, standing atop the first steps of a terrace of flat rock carved into the cave floor. "So much for just another natural wonder, Craig." He smirked, then ascended the prehistoric staircase as though it had been built for his convenience. Maureen and I held back, watching his shadowy figure dissolve into the inky blackness. We heard a few taps of a sharp tool against rock, then Craig's muffled expletive.

"Craig?" I called out. "Craig, what is it?"

"Get up here, you two! We've got pictographs all over the place. Tons of them."

That's all Maureen had to hear. She shot up those steps, screaming at Craig, "Don't touch anything! Don't touch a damn thing!" Craig remained silent.

Our collective beams of light lit up the wall and its gallery of symbols, some familiar, some not, but these drawings showed something else. They were unintelligible in places, but in others we saw a kind of progression, a story, beyond the usual tracings in damp, mud-covered dark-zone walls that we'd previously encountered. In fact, according to Maureen's hypothetical analysis, these drawings demonstrated a real attempt at communication. Almost Mayan in construct. Or Egyptian. Cross-cultural, eclectic. While the petroglyphs showed the traditional outlines of insects, animals, and what appeared to be god-like figures, Maureen found other symbols never before seen. Sun symbols, usual enough, but not just one—several suns with what looked like planets in elliptical orbit around them. And a web of curious lines intersecting the planets.

"Oh, my God, Aaron, you don't think—"

"Come on, Maureen. We're scientists, remember?" But that was all I could say. What could anyone say?

"Over here. Hey—" Craig had now uncovered something else. Encased in the lower part of the wall, he'd found a recessed area, built-in shelving. And he'd found more than that.

Turquoise, agate, obsidian. He'd discovered a treasure trove of objects, but not the usual arrowheads and beads. No, these artifacts served some other purpose, perhaps a higher, religious purpose. As if suddenly possessed, Craig clutched at them, exclaiming, "Now we have something to take back with us." He examined a perfectly cut piece of quartz, turning it under his flashlight. "At last, something of *real* value!"

"We take back nothing," answered Maureen. "That's not what we're down here for." Her teeth clenched, she jerked her flashlight directly into his face. "How many times do we have to go over this, Craig?"

He winced, retracting his lips, his eyes squinting in disbelief. "Oh, that's fine. That's not what *you* came down here for. But there's nothing in our contract that says—"

"To hell with the contract, Craig," she said. "We take back nothing. That's our policy. Aaron, can you get some video footage of these artifacts?"

"They're mine." Craig now held a gun in one hand, his flashlight in the other. "Understood?"

"Have you lost your mind, Craig?"

"Shut up, Wilkes. Just stand back." He began filling his pockets and backpack with an array of minerals, the objects of unknown design, now reduced to loot. Rising from the ground, he approached us, fixing me with a vindictive grin. "Lost my mind, Wilkes? Yeah, maybe. But I'll be a rich man. You'll be a damn fool." And then he brushed by us, to leave, to leave without us. He may as well have shot us both. Did he really think we'd survive? Almost a hundred miles away from any traveled road? Yeah, we were resourceful enough to hike that desert, but what would we do about it? Call the highway patrol, the Bureau of Land Management? Tell them that this bastard held us at gunpoint while we were illegally exploring a sacred cave site? Yes, Craig had thought this through. Premeditated.

"Damnatio memoriae," muttered Maureen.

"What?" I asked.

"Hatred for the past. An effacer of time. Craig's the type who'd destroy the memory of all of our predecessors if it paid him enough."

"Yeah. Looks like he'd destroy a couple of his contemporaries, too."

And then the rumbling, at first a low moan, and then a physical vibration beneath our feet . . .

"Quake?" screamed Maureen.

"We're not on any fault line—God, what's that noise?"
But before she could answer me, we heard Craig shout
out something. He hadn't even reached the pathway
around the great emerald pool when the whole wall—the
entire gallery—exploded with light. Each and every character of the ancient tableau glowed with some kind of an-
imated, fiery incandescence. Maureen grabbed my arm. I
pulled her away from the shimmering wall that now bris-
tled with life, pulsating with a mind of its own. A hissing
sound licked at our ankles, surrounding us from below.
Gravity itself seemed to escape. What looked like numer-
ical figures flashed across the face of the gallery wall and
then continued in an arc around us, enveloping the interior of the cavern with hallucinatory images of astronom-
ical calculations.

Craig, astonished, tried to scream. But he couldn't. He
couldn't move. We saw his body suddenly stretch upward
like some sick cartoon, and then he left the ground in a
hailstorm of light, snapping backward in a wild torrent of
unleashed power. He literally "fell" through the center of
the gallery wall, through its interior, to somewhere.

Maureen's auburn hair burst into flame. I felt the same
sensation, but no heat struck us. Just a shower of prickly
energy sizzling around our heads, feet, and then consum-
ing our entire bodies. Then gravity lost us, the two of us
washing away upward through a chasm of stars, of a million stars' light. And just as suddenly—total blackness in
a wrenching jolt. Maureen fell away from me. My arms
grasped the nothingness, and then I felt something shift.
My consciousness, or my entire world.

I felt my heart stop beating. And then start again. My
lungs refilled with air. My eyes opened to the inside of
another cave, but one of enormous proportions. I tried to
move forward, but something dragged with me. I raised
my hands to my face. My arms, head, my whole body
now inhabited a corrugated life support system—a spacesuit!

I could hear each breath I took, each breath I exhaled. Frightened? To say the least. But somehow I
coped. Something told me to move ahead. I did so. No
voice, just an instinctive knowledge. I searched for
Maureen. But I could see no sign of her. Only the immense cavern walls, incredibly high. Laced through

them I could perceive just an inkling of what this place might be. Machines behind clear portals within the walls blinked and wavered in a mirage of symbols projected onto the windows of each chamber. An underground city, or a network of computers? I could not make it out.

Turning around, I could see that the cavern narrowed, a pinpoint of light emanating from what could be an outside escape. That's the direction I'd take. Possibly Maureen had found her way to the outer chamber, to the entrance/exit of this place. My attention diverted to the periphery of my vision. Undulating shadows played upon various surfaces, like a puppet show of unseen entities. As I'd turn, they'd vanish. Movement. Shadows. Nothing.

Downward, to my left. An expanse of gray rock projected out with a different kind of surface from the others. Dimly lit, so I had to edge over for a closer look. Now I could see more detail. It looked like a beehive, or some kind of colossal storage area. And in it, high atop, stuffed inside a cubicle, his face a twisted mask of unbearable horror, lay the contorted body of Corey Craig. No spacesuit. Naked and dead to the world. To this world. Stuck. Frozen.

In revulsion, I quickly turned away and continued my search for Maureen. Drumbeats, the sound of my heartbeat, a pounding, surging percussion blasted through my spacesuit. How could I be hearing this? How was it possible? What rational explanation could console me? It grew louder. And then a voice, and more, a chorus of chanting, alien voices met the drumbeats. "Maureen! Are you in here?" Helplessly, illogically, I screamed for her. Placing one foot in front of the other, maintaining my ability to think, by force of will, the spacesuit progressed forward.

A movement. Maureen? A shadow swept across the expanse of the upper cavern. And another. A great silhouette of a man, a dancing man. No, a bird. A man or a monster. A dancing, twirling creature and a howling chant in a cacophony of pounding, smashing . . .

A laugh. A human one. A giggle of delight. A woman's response. Maureen? Could it be . . . Something propelled me forward. Lunging as fast as the environmental hulk that encased me allowed, I finally met with that pinpoint of light.

An exit? A way out? The ground now revealed itself. It was a red rock-strewn blanket of dust, a fine powdery dust, as if a billion years of erosion or geological forces had pulverized the surface. The outer light grew more intense. Emerging from the cave's entrance, my visor darkened to accommodate the bright sky, a sky of dramatic hues of red and orange.

I had found my way out, out to a landscape of stark desert, of solitary, alien formations on an altogether inhuman scale. Out to the arid, red terrain of what could only be that of . . . Mars.

"Mars?" I whispered to myself. "Mars. Dear God in heaven. Don't leave me here. Take me back. Take me back. Take *us* back! Please—"

"Dr. Wilkes? Dr. Wilkes?"

My eyes opened to a watery, out-of-focus image of a Native American's face. Coming clear, the face smiled down at me. I relaxed.

"Dr. Wilkes? You are in a hospital. Flagstaff. You are safe."

"Yes. Safe," I repeated.

"My name is Dan Masipa. Sheriff Masipa." He tilted his head toward a large man dressed in white. "And this is Dr. Lawrence." With an air of assurance, the medical man winked at me and nodded.

"Was anyone with you, Dr. Wilkes?" asked the sheriff.

"Yes. Maureen Sandler. And Corey . . . Dr. Corey Craig. But he's dead. At least I think he is."

"You say that Maureen Sandler was with you?"

"Yes. How is she, how is—"

"We found no one. No one in or out of the cave. Except you, just lying in the middle of the desert. The van was empty."

"The van?"

"Dr. Wilkes. We know who you are. You're an archaeologist, but you had no permit, no guide. The cave is off limits. It's dangerous. How you ever found it . . . it's considered to be sacred. Not even a tribal chief can enter it, yet you just break the rules and—"

"Sheriff," the doctor interrupted, motioning with his hand, "please let him rest. Your questions can wait."

* * *

Questions can wait. Can wait. And now I come to the end of this document. It will vindicate me. It must be said that no matter what any psychiatrist may tell you, that no matter how many times the spirit of Maureen Sandler contacts me in the early hours of the morning, that the truth of my experience will finally be told. That, illusion or not, the unearthly dangers of that cave, the thing that defies time and space, the alien machine—it must not be tampered with. It must not.

I'm a rational man. I'm a scientist. I'm an explorer of the dark zones, of the inaccessible wet clay passageways, of those regions beyond the light of day. And I tell you that this document must persuade someone of my sanity.

For I am not insane. This man in this ward, in this secured room, will somehow find his way out. In one interval between the ticks of an early morning's clock, Maureen will visit, and she will show me the way out, the way out to salvation . . . or oblivion.

A DEATH IN THE VALLEY

by Robert Sampson

At the crest of a shallow rise, Donovan stopped and squinted back toward the black smoke smudging the sky. That marked Winchester, now some three miles behind.

He was only a little scared. Along the dirt road, a few hundred yards away, straggled men in blue uniforms. Beige dust blurred the May air.

The roads and fields beyond were clotted with the debris of flight: cast-off blankets, clothing, knapsacks and rifles. A wagon hunched over its broken wheel. Barrels strewed the dusty field grass. It was an extended junk heap.

"No Johnnies chasin' us yet," Donovan said. "You sit a minute, Miller."

"I'm fine," Miller said. But he sat quickly enough, his face yellow-brown under the beard. Bloody cloth wadded the side of his neck.

He stared intently at the bushes lining the bottom of the hill. A soft puffing sound had just shaken them hard, and a dust film was hazing up.

"Lookit down there," Miller said in a soft, angry voice. He cocked his rifle.

Donovan had dropped his knapsack and rifle when they stopped. Now he snatched his weapon up, moving fast for such a massive man. He watched as a figure clambered out of the bushes below.

"Civilian," Donovan said sourly. "Don't he look like famine."

The civilian trotted up the rise toward them, waving both arms. As he approached, they saw he was barrel-shaped, dressed in neat dark clothing. A massive belt buckle, the color of soot, showed under his open coat. His shoes gleamed brightly.

"Point your guns away, boys," he called. "I'm for the Union."

Miller showed his teeth, said: "He's retreating too."

The heavy man came puffing up to them, his face ridged with smiles, staring ravenously, as if the sight of two sweating infantrymen in dirty uniforms were something wonderful. "I was sure afraid I might get here too late." He grinned at them, a private joke bright in his eyes. "It's hard to hit the precise time."

"You'd best hike yourself along," Donovan told him. "A man might get hurt out here."

"Yes, indeed. Yes, a man could. Exactly why I'm here. Exactly." He patted his hands together, acting drunk with pleasure. Then, ignoring the rifles angled toward him, he tromped past to the hill crest and looked off toward the road.

He said: "There it is. The Valley Pike south to Winchester. And the field. And there's the rail fence, right at the bottom of the hill, right where it's supposed to be."

He swung to face Donovan. "Did you know it's exactly 216 yards to that rail fence?"

"Don't give a damn," Donovan said.

Miller, looking sick and narrow-eyed, said, "Mister, I do suggest you git while you can git."

The fat man faced them and smiled and smiled. He was full of delight. "I got to catch my breath," he said. But he didn't stop talking. "So here we are this nice day in 1862. Yes, sir, 1862, if you'd believe it. And I know lots who wouldn't believe it, you'd better believe that, too."

He wiped his sweating face and grinned all over, pure happiness. "You know, there'll be a plaque on this measly little hill some day. You know what it'll say? It'll say, 'From This Hill, Stonewall Jackson Was Shot Dead, May 25, 1862.' "

He swelled with pleasure, beaming and rubbing his hands. "What do you say about that, boys? What do you say?"

Donovan shuffled uneasily. His eyes rolled around at Miller. "We best be hikin'."

"Another minute," Miller said.

"Another minute and we like to see some rebel horse come flyin' up on us."

"Not yet," the fat man said, very sure. "We got a few minutes."

Donovan looked at him, a distant, empty look that dimmed the smile on the fleshy face. "You fixin' to talk at us till they come?"

"You misunderstand," the fat man said. "I can't blame you. Let me introduce myself. I am Associate Professor Dr. Winston Smith. From the Zanesville State University in Ohio."

"Ohio's a hell of a long way off from Virginia," Donovan said.

"Long walk in those shoes," Miller remarked.

Smith smiled again. "I got a little piece of information, boys. Just one little piece, but it's worth a ton of gold. It's going to shorten this war by a year."

He beamed triumphantly at them. "Maybe more than a year. But a year for sure. Yes, sir."

"Maybe you better talk to General Banks," Miller said. "Always supposing you can catch up with General Banks."

Smith advanced on Donovan. "Are you a good shot with that gun? Can you hit where you want?"

"Sometimes."

"Can you kill a man at 216 yards? Could you? Easily?"

"Yes," said Donovan, glancing over at Miller.

"Good. That's very good. Because shortly, a very few minutes from now, Stonewall Jackson will be standing by that rail fence. Stonewall Jackson, himself. Two hundred and sixteen yards away. You take one shot and the war's shortened by a year. At least a year."

"You a Pinkerton?" Miller asked sharply.

"Not me. Just an unsuccessful professor. Associate professor. There's a difference." The smiling surface of his face stiffened just for a moment, as if a delicately transparent skin of ice had flashed beneath the sweating smile. "Unsuccessful till now. Till I happened to see a way to change history—with the help of the present company, of course. And with a little bit of experimental lab equipment I happened to borrow, just for a minute. So it's going to end before it starts. No holding the line at Antietam. No holding the right at Fredericksberg. No flank march at Chancellorsville. The best of the Confederate generals, Lee excepted. Dead in a field north of Winchester. Courtesy of Dr. Winston Smith."

The smile grew all over his face. He patted his oversized belt buckle and his voice rushed on, disagreeably pleased with itself. "This is going to change the world, boys. Change the world. Not your world, maybe, but I know of one that'll change."

Miller said, "You get rid of the shooting and this one suits me fine."

"Not me," said Smith. "Let it change. Maybe it will and maybe not. The world's not been so fine to me. Let it change, and the hell with all of them." He looked up at Donovan. "You can do it all with one shot."

Donovan said: "Sure. Just a shot."

Turning away, he stepped to the crest of the hill and stared off toward the road, and they heard the breath hiss in his mouth, as if he had been hit hard in the stomach.

"Cavalry!"

Smith darted up beside him to look. Snarling, Donovan threw the fat man down and hurled himself flat into the long grass. Smith yelped, tried to rise.

"Down, you damn fool."

Smith thrashed over on his side, fingers clutching at the big belt buckle, caressing, patting, fumbling. After a moment, relief eased his face.

"Easy now," he whispered. "The equipment's pretty delicate for field use. Got to treat it easy." Secret amusement twisted his mouth.

"Quiet," Miller snarled.

Donovan bent toward Smith, saying in a low, hot voice, "Stay down. The Johnnies blow a hole in you size of a wagon."

"I wanted to see Jackson."

"Jackson, hell," Donovan said.

"Quiet," Miller said again, sounding as if he meant it.

Donovan inched his big frame forward. Fat sweat drops greased his sun-reddened skin and concentration grooved his face under the beard.

He began to part the grass, pressing aside each blade with slow precision, as if no other occupation interested him so much as the methodical movement of his fingers.

He sighed faintly. "Six on horses. Some artillery along the road."

"Let me see," Smith hissed urgently.

Miller said: "Stay put."

"I came a long way to see," Smith said sharply. "Longer than you know. I have to see."

He started to rise, craning his neck. Miller extended his rifle, and the muzzle dented the pale skin below Smith's ear. "Lay easy," Miller said.

Smith's eyes bulged. He looked defiant, contemptuous, surprised.

"Okay, okay," he said.

"Stoppin' by the fence," Donovan reported. "Gettin' off the horses." He spoke with extreme care, as if his words possessed the disagreeable characteristic of becoming visible.

"It's 216 yards," Smith whispered. "Jackson's the tall one with the dark beard."

"Billy," Donovan said in that careful voice. "If he keeps talking, use your knife."

"Please," Smith begged. "Please. Is it Jackson?"

"They all got beards but one," Donovan said after a long while. His fingers tenderly pressed back another tuft of grass. He squinted across the easy roll of the countryside back toward Winchester. Yellow-gray dust rose against the smoke smudge from the town.

"More horse comin'," Donovan announced. "Not many. Maybe half a mile."

"You hold them," Miller said. "I'll flank them." He laughed quietly, showing yellow teeth.

"Let's both flank 'em," Donovan said. With slow care, he let the grass close and edged carefully backward, moving like some dull blue shadow across the grass. "Time to skedaddle."

Miller nodded and winced and touched his neck. "I do hear the captain calling so sweetly." He began to work down the slope, grunting softly.

Smith stared at them, astounded. "Where are you going?" He came up on one elbow.

"Away from here," Miller said.

"That's Jackson down there. Stonewall Jackson. Two hundred and sixteen yards away. Easy shot."

"Come on," Donovan said.

In an urgent, furious voice, Smith said: "Listen, I know it's him. It's Jackson. Get him now. You got to. You'll cut a year off the war."

"Your mouth'll kill us," Miller snarled. One hand reached out toward Smith.

Smith tumbled back away from Miller's fingers. "You know what comes next? Second Manassas, Antietam, Chancellorsville. Jackson at every one."

He lifted his staring face above the grass.

"It is Jackson, by God. Give me a gun. I'll do it myself."

His voice rose. He came scrambling through the grass toward Donovan, who said, "Aw, now," and hit Smith high on the cheek.

Smith sprawled back on his side. Donovan hurled himself across the fat body, feeling it twist frantically, like a rat under a board. His own head had risen above the grass, so that he looked directly down upon the men and horses scattered along the rail fence.

A tall man, lean and bearded, in loose, faded clothing, stood apart from the rest. He was peering intently up the hill. Looking directly into Donovan's eyes. He jabbed one long arm up toward the hill top and came away from the fence, calling to the others. His extended arm jabbed again toward Donovan, who felt his insides grow hot and small.

"Charge with horses," he thought. He tried to flatten out into the grass, felt Smith writhe free.

At the same moment, the group by the fence broke into confused movement, closing protectively around the tall man.

Donovan rolled off the hill crest and went scrabbling on the seat of his pants down the slope. Just below, he saw Smith groping in the grass by the knapsack. Miller threw himself against Smith, who fell back on one knee, a protective arm thrust out.

"Jackson," he cried frantically. "Kill him."

Miller's eyes touched Donovan's rigid face.

"Crazy man, by God," Donovan said, sounding faintly shocked.

Smith grabbed for the rifle, and Miller kicked him in the chest. The kick made a dull, thick sound, quite horrible, and Smith fell into the grass, his hands and legs flopping. Miller tried to get at him but fell, sprawling over the knapsack.

Donovan swept up his rifle, poised the butt over Smith's wet face.

Smith stared blindly up, both arms clutched around his thick chest. He looked completely amazed, like a slapped child.

In the instant between seeing and striking, Donovan changed his target. There was no way he could strike that helpless face. Instead, he drove the rifle butt into Smith's stomach, slamming the edge of the belt buckle.

The buckle popped crisply, as if dry little sticks snapped.

A bright spark sputtered up. The spark became bluish-white, an intense, hissing point at the center of Smith's body.

Smith made a thin, desperate noise and kicked. The light became large and violent, and there was stinking smoke. Behind the smoke, they saw Smith flopping, and then disagreeable things happened as his body came apart. They had seen that before in combat, but it was nothing you ever got used to.

Donovan choked and swore. Jerking away, he sprinted to the hill crest, threw himself down, his rifle barrel jutting toward the fence. He expected to see the slope full of horsemen plunging at him.

Instead, the Confederates were cantering off across the field.

Incredulous delight lifted in him. He felt hollow, light, dizzy. He had not expected to be alive in five minutes. Miller thumped down in the grass beside him, rifle ready. Together they watched the horsemen go. More pale dust rose above the distant road.

"We might better hike it," Miller said.

Donovan squirmed into his knapsack harness. The odor of burning was strong. Both men tried to breath shallowly and not look toward Smith.

Donovan asked, "What was that fire, you suppose?"

"Photographer's powder, maybe."

They moved down slope, the sweetish-greasy stench of burning following them. Once in the valley, they fell into the easy stride of the foot soldier, packs riding high, rifles balanced.

For a time there was no sound but the swish of their passage through dense grass. At their left, the green mountain wall angled north, becoming pale blue in the distance. The sun was hot.

"Where's Chancellorsville, you reckon?" Miller asked at last.

"Never heard its name."

"You suppose that was Old Stonewall, himself."

"Out in front like that? Like hell. How could it be?"

Miller sighed and felt the bandage at his neck. "Oh, Lordy, this campaigning do be so much fun."

They slouched left across a cedar-strewn slope and were lost to sight.

From the hill behind drifted a small amount of smoke. But not much.

THE SACRIFICE OF SHADOWS

by Billie Sue Mosiman

When Gregori Thanopolis came into the Maklos Club in
Athens that young spring night, all heads turned to watch
him. Even his enemies could not stop themselves from
giving Gregori the attention he so easily commanded.
Part of the public's fascination with him had to do with
his international fame as an architect, but the greater part
of it had to do with Gregori's dark handsome features—
the bronzed skin, the hair the color of a moonless midnight, the finely chiseled nose and lips. He was tall,
dressed impeccably, and when he smiled, though it was
seldom, his face could light a room.

Paul Carpon, a society columnist for the city's largest
circulation newspaper and Gregori's harshest critic,
watched him thread his way through the tables, stopping
here and there to shake a hand, to kiss the upturned cheek
of a woman, to spend a moment with old cronies. *If he
comes near me, I'll cut him cold,* he thought.

But Gregori did not approach Paul that night. He dined
alone, ordering the salad with the small boiled potatoes,
greens, goat cheese, and black olives, drank a bottle of
fine wine, and left, again being hailed as if he were a king
as he moved toward the exit.

In the next day's edition of Paul's paper he wrote,
"Gregori Thanopolis was seen last night at the Maklos
Club. Since the excavation work has been completed on
his newest addition (atrocity) to our city skyline, it would
seem our resident genius might celebrate with a beautiful
lady, but Thanopolis dined alone and appeared rather hag-
gard and careworn despite the Armani suit and Jerselia
shoes gracing his person."

Paul leaned back away from the computer terminal and took up the slim black cigarette smoldering in the ashtray nearby. What more could he say that he had not already said about the man who had turned the historic city into his own private version of a tortured futuristic scene from a fevered, some said *sick,* imagination? Commissioned by the city fathers, Thanopolis had designed and erected a community theater that featured black granite columns and triangular protrusions into the sky that gave the impression of teetering over the streets surrounding it. Though Paul frequently railed against the monstrosity (it frightens passersby, it has no structural integrity, it diminishes the other buildings around it, there is no subtleness in this man's vision), Thanopolis went on to build the horrid red brick pyramidal structure now housing the new library.

And now he was building a giant dome-shaped *thing* that was supposed to be a common market where tourists could browse and spend their money. The publicity drawings of the plans printed on the front page of the paper months ago could by no means be called graceful or elegant. It looked to Paul like a cabbage lying in a field of wildflowers. He despised it from the first, as he had all the other Thanopolis creations, and made his vitriolic views known every chance he had. If only the populace would pay attention to him!

But they seemed to adore their native son who had traveled the world, stayed in palaces and the rooms of presidents and prime ministers. He was their celebrity. He would bring people to Athens to help bolster its depressed economy. Merchants were thrilled with him. Government officials gave him building permits and generally kowtowed in his direction whenever he came asking for favors. Almost everybody loved him.

Paul stubbed out the butt of the cigarette and finished up his column before deadline. He was doing all he could to stop the defilement of a once great city. The ghosts of his ancestors could not complain on that score.

In the Cafe Camellia Paul was finishing up a particularly delicious baklava when he glanced up to see Thanopolis heading his way. He frowned and set down his fork beside the saucer.

"Mr. Carpon?"

"Yes."

"May I sit down for a minute? I'd like to discuss something with you."

"By all means." Paul shoved his dinner plate and water glass aside. He felt an inner smile forming and held it from reaching his lips. He's come to beg me to like his work, he thought. Not that it will do him the smallest bit of good.

"I've been reading your column for over a year now. I wonder if you could tell me what it is about my architecture that offends you so completely? Or is it something personal about me that you don't like?"

Paul shook a cigarette from a pack in his pocket, lit the tip with a gold lighter. He inhaled deeply, then blew out a plume of smoke that sailed across the table directly in front of his guest. "I just don't like what you do," he said. "It's really nothing personal."

"By *do*, I assume you mean my buildings in Athens."

"They mar the city. They belittle the people. They vie for attention and take it away from the Acropolis, the Temple of Olympian Zeus, the National Garden, the tomb of Herodes Atticus. In other words, Mr. Thanopolis, your work is a disgrace and a disfigurement of what was a great and beautiful ancient city."

"As an architect I understand your feelings about the historical landmarks, but we live in modern times. There should be room for both the old and the new."

"Not as far as I am concerned. I'm sorry." He wasn't really, not sorry at all, and in fact he was having a joyous time debating his position in person with the man he had run down so many times in print.

Thanopolis sighed. Paul, who had carefully kept his gaze fastened on the bar across the room, glanced from the corner of his eyes at his table guest. He looked away quickly before he was caught. He meant to keep his haughty composure, and he would not lose the advantage by looking at the man directly.

Thanopolis said softly, "I had thought we could come to some kind of understanding, Mr. Carpon. It's obvious that's not going to happen. Would you, however, do me a favor? It would be the last I ask of you."

"And what would that favor be?"

"I will be placing the cornerstone for the market dome building tomorrow evening. I wonder if you would meet me at the construction site, only for a few minutes, around two tomorrow?"

"Why should I do that? I don't expect to commemorate a building I find repulsive in the extreme."

"I have something to explain to you about its construction that I think you'll be interested to know, but I can only explain it at the site."

Paul flicked the ashes from his cigarette, immune to the fact they had already fallen onto his clothes, and this time he looked right at his companion. "You might find this request will backfire, Thanopolis. I will write in my column *exactly* what I think despite any sort of explanation you choose to make."

"If you'll meet me there tomorrow at two, you can write whatever you want about it. I won't bother you again on the subject."

"Done."

Paul watched Thanopolis leave the cafe, his presence causing the malingerers at the bar to turn their heads and whisper behind their hands. That there went the Great Man, no doubt. The Marvelous Designer. The Gorgeous One who was bringing Athens into the twenty-first century all on his own.

If he had not been so disgusted, Paul might have found some humor in Thanopolis' reputation. And besides, no man had the right to look so good so early in the day.

Paul wiped down the ashes trailing his shirt front, leaving gray streaks down the white poplin, and decided that finishing his dessert now wasn't worth his time. He had a column to write.

The domed building was to be raised on Patission Street across from Kaningos Square and next to Omonia Square. Paul knew that from having to drive past it every day on his way to work at the paper. Each time he passed it by, he kept his gaze steady ahead on the traffic. He did not want to see the great gouged hole before they poured the cement foundation, he would not watch the girders rise skeletal in the air, nor would he visit the place once it was completed and opened to the public.

He stood in the sweltering heat of afternoon sun near

the site now, waiting and watching for Thanopolis to arrive. The travesty of this place made his heart sink. Sweat rolled down his forehead into his eyes, and he brushed at it with his forearm. Workmen roamed the area, hardhats glaring silver in the sunlight. Where was he? If he didn't show up in the next two minutes, Paul was leaving.

He heard a car motor behind him and turned, shielding his eyes to see. It was a black Mercedes. It slowed, parked, and Thanopolis exited from the driver's seat, clean and neat and unruffled in a pair of dark blue slacks and a crisp pale blue shirt. He wore a tie printed in colorful paisley. He looked like an insurance salesman. A very successful one.

The son of a bitch looks refreshed and I look like a soggy transient, Paul thought with a fury that surprised him. He turned back to the site, waiting.

"If you'll follow me over here ..." Thanopolis indicated a worn path that circled the building's foundation. Paul traipsed behind him, wishing vehemently he had not bothered to come out to this ugly place for any reason at all. He owed this man nothing, not even the time required for some kind of explanation of his methods.

Thanopolis paused and pointed his finger at a large smoothly carved stone. "My cornerstone," he said. "It will be the first laid, the one that supports all the rest."

"What does this have to do with anything?" Paul tried to keep the peevishness he felt out of his voice—he wanted to appear cool and unaffected—but it had crept in anyway, and that tone caused Thanopolis to raise his eyebrows.

"Indulge me, Mr. Carpon. Would you step over here next to me a moment? Yes ... right here, close to where the stone sits."

Paul moved closer until his shadow fell over a spot right beside the cornerstone. "What is it?"

"Just stand there a moment. This won't take long."

Thanopolis put two fingers into his mouth and whistled shrilly. The sudden sound jarred Paul. He saw a crane across the site turn and lumber on its monster tracks toward them. It came closer until the crane's jaws hung suspended high above the cornerstone. Paul craned his neck, looking up, fascinated by what Thanopolis had up his sleeve.

Thanopolis waved and the crane lowered the now opened huge jaws of its cradle, slowly, gently; and like a woman taking up a lead-crystal glass, it locked itself around the cornerstone, lifted it barely a foot from the ground, then very slowly moved it two feet to the left and deposited it again. Paul felt a cool breeze slip down the back of his collar and caress the sweaty skin of his back. He shivered.

Thanopolis waved again, and the jaws loosened, lifted, swung away. The massive crane backed across the lot, the sound of its motor a deep hum that vibrated the air. A dust cloud hung suspended, filtering out over the office trailers and disreputable pick-up trucks. The air was dry, untinged here by any scent of the Aegean Sea.

"What was that all about?" Paul stepped back, wiping sweat from his brow again. "I really don't have time for things like this. I can't say I'm all that interested in your cornerstone for what I consider to be a blight on the landscape, Thanopolis."

"I am sorry to report to you, Mr. Carpon, that within the year you will now die."

"What?" Paul rubbed at his right ear. He couldn't have heard correctly. It was the whine of the crane that was jumbling the architect's words.

"I just had you stand here so that your shadow fell next to the cornerstone."

"Yeah, so?"

"Then I had the crane lift the stone and put it over your shadow."

"Why don't you get to the point and tell me what this is all about and why you wanted me out here."

"Mr. Capon, in the past, that ancient past you hold so dear, it was the custom of builders to kill a cock, a ram, or a lamb and to let its blood flow on the foundation stone for a new edifice. Then the dead animal was buried under it. Today it is acknowledged that a more efficient way is to entice a man to the cornerstone, secretly measure his shadow, and bury that measure under the stone. Or he may, as I have done, bury the shadow itself underneath the stone. This is a sacrifice. Only the best of us who design and build the greatest buildings know about it. It insures that the building will stand unharmed. Each of my buildings has someone's shadow beneath it upon which it stands solid."

"What a crock."

"It also insures that the shadow's owner dies within the year. This way I have accomplished two objectives: My work will be safe, and my worst critics will be finally and forever silenced. Had it not ever occurred to you that you were a lone voice in the wilderness when you criticized my work? Where do you think all the other voices vanished to? We might have avoided this if you'd listened to reason the other day, but alas . . ."

"Thanopolis, you're a raving maniac. And I'm going to say so for every reader in the city." Paul stomped off, infuriated that he had participated in a conversation that amounted to nothing more than superstitious browbeating. If the man thought he could scare him off, he had better think again.

It was a month before the pains began. Paul hurried to his doctor complaining of the cramps in his stomach. After several diagnostic tests that were just as painful as the cramps, he was told he had cancer. That it was spreading. *Metastasized,* the doctor said sadly. He did not have long to live.

Paul fainted in the doctor's office and had to be revived.

Sitting alone in his room in a beautiful old boarding house on Kipselis on the outskirts of the city, Paul clenched and unclenched his fists. Soon he had his reference books spread all over the bed and the floor at his feet.

He was not looking for information on cancer. Nothing could be done about the death sentence, and he knew that.

He was looking for a way to kill Thanopolis just as Thanopolis had obviously killed the only critic of his work left in all of Athens.

Paul met the hunter outside the city in a tavern called the Golden Quail. "I'll give you this gold and diamond ring if you will bring me a wild boar and three doves. The boar must be dead and the doves alive."

"This ring?" The man turned it over in his palm. It was

a man's ring, heavy gold, with a solitaire of a half carat and twenty-four smaller diamonds encircling it. "It's worth a lot. I'll do it. When do you want them?"

"Can I have them by the weekend?"

"Certainly. By tomorrow night, if you want."

"Saturday will be soon enough."

After putting his column to bed at the paper that Saturday, Paul lugged the heavy, cumbersome cloth sack containing the small wild boar in it to his room. His landlady was absent shopping, so no one saw him. He went back to the car and retrieved the three wild doves in the cage.

In his room, with the door locked, he slit open the boar and pulled out the innards. It made a terrible mess and made him gag, but he persevered. Then he caught the doves and one by one held them inside the boar's cool empty cavity. Afterward he put them into the cage again, except for one. This one he promptly killed by wringing its neck.

He disposed of the boar, its insides, and the dead dove in the trash container behind the boarding house. He then called Thanopolis' office and left a message asking that he meet him at the Maklos Club that night.

When the architect entered, Paul saw that the spell was working. His hair was as dull as the coat of a starving dog, his face shone with a sheen of sweat, and his eyes looked out from blue hollows. People whispered as he moved across the room, and this time, Paul thought, they aren't saying what a genius he is or how handsome, they're saying he looks sick.

"Not feeling well?" he asked as Thanopolis sat at the table. "Should I order you a drink?"

Thanopolis winced. "I don't want anything. Why did you want to meet with me?"

"I'm dying of cancer. Stomach cancer. I live on water and baby food. And I used to love to eat. It's certainly a pity, isn't it?"

Thanopolis looked away guiltily. "I take no credit for the method of your demise."

"No? Just my death itself, you mean?"

"Look, what is the point? You tried to thwart me. I had no choice in the matter."

"Nor do I."

"What does that mean?"

"You'll see."

"I haven't time for your riddles. Don't call me again. Whatever happens to you is of your own doing." Thanopolis stood, too quickly it seemed, for he swayed on his feet, and a woman at a table nearby gasped, thinking he would faint.

Paul sat watching with clinical detachment. The blood rushed back to Thanopolis' face, and he turned and left the club without ordering.

Now that Paul had seen evidence killing the doves did indeed kill off one's enemy, he hurried home and quickly dispatched the second dove while saying Gregori Thanopolis' name. If this worked, then all the gods in heaven were on his side. And Athens would be spared any more of those fantastically hideous creations from their favorite architect.

The stomach pains moved. They traveled like wanderers in a strange land. One hour it might be his right shoulder blade that ached to the point of bringing tears to his eyes, or one side of his chest, or a kneecap, the back of his neck, the crown of his head. He hadn't much time to finish his revenge. Fevers attacked him now and led him into delirium where he hallucinated monsters with two heads, dead-eyed killers with stilettos, earthquakes that shook the city and swallowed it whole. He could not sleep. He could not eat. He cursed Thanopolis every second he breathed.

Two nights after the killing of the second dove, he took the third one carefully from the cage and stuffed it into a pillowcase. He drove to Thanopolis' home. It was not necessary for the victim to be present when he killed the third dove; Paul simply wanted to be there when it happened. To be sure. To make certain. To *witness* the death of a malevolent being. His own hatred and reportage of some of Thanopolis' building schemes was petty compared to visiting upon a man his death before his appointed time.

Black wrought iron gates swung wide on a winding white gravel drive. Moonlight showed bougainvillea that climbed over high walls, painting them vibrant pink. A fountain standing just before the house threw sparkling water through colored lights. At the double walnut entrance doors, Paul had to wait to catch his breath from the

onslaught of pain wracking his thin body. He leaned his
forehead against the gargoyle door knocker and panted
like a man who had just run a marathon race. He managed to step back and rap with his knuckles. He would
not touch the twisted face on the knocker. There had been
enough bad luck visited upon his person.

It was a maid who answered the door. She tried to keep
him from entering, but he pushed past her into the hall.
"Where is he?"

"He's resting in the library. He can't be disturbed, he's
been ill."

"I know he's ill. Now get out of my way. He's expecting me."

He threw open the door and staggered, beset by new
bright pain, across the lovely rose-patterned carpet. He
found Thanopolis slumped in a chair facing a dead
hearth. He was asleep, chin on his chest. Or so Paul
hoped. He would not be cheated now that he had the last
dove in his possession. It fluttered its wings against the
confinement of the pillowcase, perhaps knowing its fate.

"Thanopolis, wake up!"

The maid came into the room after him, wringing her
hands. Thanopolis came to groggily. He focused his eyes
on Paul and then the maid. He motioned her to leave
them.

"You've done something to me," he said. "I feel like
I'm dying."

Paul chose another chair where he could watch his
nemesis, see his every emotion reflected on his lean Gre-
cian face. "I most certainly have," he admitted. "But no
more than you've done to me."

"Ah, enemies who return fire. I've never had that happen before. How odd it should be you who returned the
deadly volley," he said.

"You underestimated me, that's all."

"It is indeed the truth that I have. So why are you here
now, to gloat?" Noticing the movement in the bag at
Paul's side he added, "What's that?"

Paul held up the pillowcase. The dove inside fluttered,
fluttered. The rustle of its wings was the only sound in
the room.

"It's the last dove," he said. He felt a wave of dizziness

sweep through his brain, and he put his free hand to his eyes.

"Dove? Why do you have a dove with you?"

Paul came out of the vertigo and in its passing felt the chill it left behind like a caul over his face. "There is another Greek ritual," he said. He dug into the neck of the pillowcase and caught the dove. He drew it forth and rubbed the dove's soft head against the skin of his clammy cheek. "This ritual involves taking three doves from a wild boar. As the doves are sacrificed, the enemy is killed."

"I don't believe ..." Thanopolis hesitated and understanding came into his sunken eyes.

"You don't believe what?" Paul asked, cocking his head. "That shadows can be stolen, that buildings can be consecrated with blood, that death comes to a marked man, that doves can *kill* you?"

"I've done so much wrong," Thanopolis said, hanging his head as if its weight were too much to carry on the stem of his neck any longer. "I wanted only to create the most beautiful architecture the world has seen since the great temples were erected. I couldn't do that if there was a furor in the press, if critics destroyed every idea I tried to bring to fruition."

"And your pride knew no boundaries." Paul caught the dove's head with one hand. He began to twist it slowly, in increments, the way he might turn the lid of a jar.

Thanopolis jerked upright, and his hands flew to his throat. "Don't ... kill ... me!"

"This should have been done long ago."

Paul finished the twist with a violent wrenching movement and watched as Gregori Thanopolis fell forward to the library carpet, dead.

When he left the house, he drove directly to the site of the dome that would stand nearly forever upon the cornerstone of his soul. He slipped in the darkness to the place where the stone stood, one of many now, buried beneath walls rising and curving into the night sky. He knew it was the right stone for Thanopolis had had it engraved: PARTHENIAN MARKET.

He lay the wrapped sticks of dynamite near its base and strung out the fuse about three yards away. Then he felt for his gold lighter and discovered he had not brought it. He searched in his pockets and came up with a match-book from the Maklos Club. He smiled, struck a match, and lit the fuse.

While he watched it snake its way to the explosive, he quickly popped a slim black cigarette into his mouth and lit it with the last of the match flame. He might have one good draw coming before the world turned to fire and rained down rock onto his head, burying him beneath the rubble of the last Thanopolis' building ever to debase the pleasant skyline of the historical city of his birth.

DARKENED ROADS

By Richard Gilliam

Most dark roads look the same when you're not bothering to go anyplace that matters. I'd been going there for years. Same old roads. Same old choices. Life on autopilot. The pretense of caring. The emptiness of not believing in anything, least of all believing in myself.

Evan changed that, though he didn't mean to. Evan and what happened. What happened to him and to me. The night Evan tried to make his comeback.

The night was dark, real country dark. We drove much as we had in the old days, back when we lived in Drake's Crossing, in the days before the Boss had built his machine, long before television began deciding elections. Days when the only way to get votes was to go out and work for them, attending rallies, shaking hands, and making deals that would get you much more than just a look behind door number three.

The LTD we rented was a far cry from the many Lincolns in which I had driven Evan over the years. Unlike the messy Decembers of Tennessee, the New England weather was cold but clear. The heater helped greatly, though the badly warped linings around the windows caused a draft that never quite allowed us catch up with being comfortable. I could see well ahead, though nothing distinguished one side of the road from another. The rear was not so well lit, and I had to strain as I looked into the mirror to see the trailer we pulled.

Evan sat to my right, his silence an unnatural state for a politician. At least he knew our destination.

When I had asked Evan about the trip, his answer had been noncommittal. "We're heading for the most evil

place in all the fifty states," he'd said, though I knew by
his grin that this was a joke. "Of course, you realize," he
added, "That Washington, D.C., isn't in one in one of the
fifty states. Actually, this is only the second most evil
place in the country."

I laughed, as I was supposed to. Not much else for me
to do these days. Just drive and laugh. The Boss had gotten mean in his old age. Laughing at his jokes helped.
Laughing and doing what I was told.

We had the Boss' wife in the back of the car, in the
trailer, frozen. Susie had been dead twelve years now, to
the day tomorrow. Cancer had eaten her away, slowly at
first, later too quickly for any treatment to have helped.

The only thing that had done any good was the morphine. Even if her cancer had been cured, she'd have
been an addict. Everyone knew Susie wouldn't live when
they gave her the drugs. The Boss knew, too, as much as
he wanted her to recover.

She'd been twenty-four when it first hit, before Evan
first ran for office. They'd been married only a couple of
years and hadn't had any children. The surgery had
"cured" her, though she was left barren. I suppose the extra thirty years of life it gave her was pretty good, but
she'd spent it in constant fear the cancer would return,
and finally it did. Funny how many different ways there
are that people will react when faced with death. Susie
was one of the ones who went to pieces. The morphine
had handled her hysteria along with her pain.

I looked in the mirror again. The trailer was still there.

"You're thinking about her, aren't you, Billy?" Evan
spoke.

"Yeah, Boss. Hard not to when I gotta watch that
trailer we're pulling," I replied.

Evan nodded. "You never approved, did you, of freezing her before she died?"

"Not my call to make, Boss. She signed the papers and
the doctors approved. Not my place to judge."

"Her only chance. I owed it to her. Owed her a chance
to live again. To live better than I let her live the first
time."

I nodded. Like I said, it wasn't my place to judge.

"I never was really the same after she died," said Evan.
"Won the next couple of elections, of course, but never

really felt comfortable again. Started making mistakes.
Got careless with that TV thing."

"TV changed things for a lot of people, Boss."

"Those bastards. Reporters aren't interested in the
truth. Just in becoming famous reporters." Evan scowled.

I laughed. "That's real true, Boss."

"Those sons of bitches have gotten smarter, too. They
know when to break a story—like the week before the
election. Even if it's not true, there isn't time to repudiate
it. Scandal sticks in a voter's mind. There are just too
many votes out there to buy enough to matter, nowadays."

"Not like the old days," I said.

Evan smiled but did not respond.

"You always did well up here, Boss. Never got less
than 30% in any of the primaries."

"It wasn't enough. I lost."

"You should've been President, Boss. This country
needed you."

"Maybe I will be yet, Billy. Maybe I will be yet."

I smiled. "Sure was a nice plane that brought us into
Providence. You got a new backer, Boss? We gonna run
again?"

"Maybe," he said. "Need more than one backer,
though. Need a lot more than just one friend with a small
jet."

"Before we get too old?" I asked and knew I shouldn't
have.

"We're already too old, Billy. Time moved on without
us. Would take a special kind of comeback. A very special kind."

"And Susie, too?"

"Maybe" he said, yawning. "I want to rest for a while.
Just keep driving north. I'll let you know when to turn."

As we drove from the city, I continued to grow curious,
not to mention a little scared. The weather had been clear
when we landed, and I hadn't noticed sufficient clouds
forming to cause the coal-tar sky which loomed above us
now. No light, whether streak or haze, penetrated the ap-
parent void.

The monotonous sound of the drive and the sameness
of the view made me wonder whether the road moved
with us through the night as one, instead of us along the

road. I assured myself unconvincingly of the natural origin of the sky, and as I did, I wished for a glimpse of the stars and for the light that would allow me to see the features of the land around me.

If we had driven as far as it seemed, we would have been in Canada by now; yet despite the absence of highway signs, I was fairly certain we had not left Rhode Island. I had never realized it was possible to be bored and frightened at the same time. I knew my place, so I just drove.

After a time, Evan broke the silence.

"It came to me one night a week ago, how I was going to make my comeback and have Susie again as well," he continued, never really looking toward me as he spoke.

"You know when I had her preserved, I'd always figured I wouldn't try to wake her until they'd found a cure. You never believed it would work, but I appreciate that you stood by me anyway. Doesn't make much difference now one way or the other, which of us was right.

"I never thought there could be any other way to do it." He paused, and the silence lasted more than a moment. Then, as suddenly as he had stopped, Evan cleared his throat and began once again. I knew he would ramble for some time, falling into a habit I'd found common among people accustomed to making public speeches.

"There was this rustling noise that woke me the other night, though as badly as I sleep these days, I couldn't swear I didn't just wake up and imagine the sound because of what I saw.

"A small brown furry thing stood to my left. It was larger than most cats but not by much, so my first reaction was that a stray had wandered in from the cold. I waved my arms at it, but I was so drowsy, I doubt if I moved quickly enough to startle the thing.

"Turns out I was the one who was startled when the creature spoke and announced himself to be a *familiar*. Do you know what a familiar is, Billy? It's an emissary from a spook. And not a lawyer from an N-double-A-C-P spook mind you, but something from a real live spook, 'cept I don't know whether this kind of spook is really alive or not."

As he talked, the clouds parted and the moon, full but still low in the sky, found a small hole through which to shine. I breathed a sigh of relief, although in retrospect the bleak landscape was no more cheerful than the blackness that had so recently encompassed us. Even for winter, the barrennesss of the countryside was a surprise. Solitary trees stood sparsely with little vegetation between them. No animal could be seen or heard, nor could I sight any building.

"There was the slightest twang of Yankee in the creature's voice," Evan continued. "Of course, that might just have been my imagination. Don't think so, though. We'll find out soon.

"As I watched, the familiar raised himself upright on his hind quarters and reached into his fur. He tossed onto my bed the body of a small, common looking bird. Don't know what type," he paused. "I never learned all those names.

"He told me to look, and I was afraid not to."

Evan paused again, glancing toward the mirror.

"The bird was still warm. Don't know why I picked it up. The thing, this familiar, reached into his fur and produce a jar, slightly larger than the bird. He thrust the jar at me, and I took it, setting the bird aside. The jar contained a blue oval rolling in a thick green paste. I was too scared to be bewildered. The thing gestured, and I set the jar on the floor. He grabbed the bird tightly and squeezed until a trickle of blood fell into the jar. I watched intently as within the jar a new bird formed—identical to the carcass on the floor.

"Even more amazing, the bird began to move. It struggled from the jar and flew low across the room until it came to rest at the foot of my dresser. Only a pile of dust remained where the body of the first bird had been."

Evan paused again and picked his nose. That was a sure sign he was nervous. He had been caught at it more than once by a camera. Some people think that shot CBS took of him entering the convention may have cost him the '72 vice-presidential slot.

"It seems no matter what age the donor is, the result will always be a replica that approximates a young adult in every respect. Not only that, the memory stays intact! I guess you know what I'm thinking. The familiar says it will work on Susie and, of course, on me too."

"That's great, Boss." What else could I say? I was

scared, and I didn't want him to know. "I'm sure it will work. Is that why we're here?" The words hung heavy for a moment, then he spoke.

"The jars needed to replicate humans are too large to transport easily. They'd have had to have brought three. I'm gonna need you around for my comeback."

"Not me, Boss. I don't want to."

"Of course you do. I've got it all figured. Right down to new identification. There was a good piece on *60 Minutes* about it. Showed everything. You check out some cemetery and find someone who would be about your age if he hadn't died as an infant. Then you go request the birth certificate as if it was your own."

"I don't think so, Boss. At least not until after I see how you and Susie turn out. Besides, won't people get suspicious when they notice who we resemble?"

Evan turned his head slowly. "What you've got to remember is that we'll look like we're around twenty-one. Not many people remember what I looked like then. There's a lot of changes in a man in fifty-five years. By the time we grow older, so much time will have passed that it will just be a coincidence no one will notice anyway."

After that, we didn't talk for a while, which was all right with me. I just kept on driving.

He had said the mind would stay intact, and that meant the personality with it. The bitterness of the recent years would be there, only the hatred would be stronger. That's what really cost him the nomination. All the hate that was carefully coded inside his talk about states rights and keeping the criminals in jail. Afterward, I had only stayed with him out of habit, too old and too tired to change.

I thought a lot about being young again, and I thought a lot about staying old, too. It had always seemed to me there must be some good reason why folks grow old and don't grow young again. Sort of a natural order to things. Whatever fate had dished up for me, I felt like leaving that way. I wasn't too proud of how I'd spent my life the first time, and I couldn't see how if I stayed with Evan, I'd do any better the second time.

Evan broke the silence. "You'd best turn up here," he said, indicating a house far off to the left.

I hadn't seen the thing. As we drew closer, I could tell

it was an anachronism in an area where colonial structures are common. The house had every feature you could want in gloominess. Entering the long driveway, I could see the moon begin to show behind the outline of the roof. No wires ran to any section, and I doubted the house had a generator. A single light seeped from one window, its flickering strengthening my fears.

We passed a mailbox, but it bore no name that I could find. I was strangely comforted to see the house boasted not the traditional seven gables but a mere four and, insofar as I could determine, no unusual marking on its exterior. I halted the car, and without a word the Boss opened the door and motioned toward the house. The porch had stone steps and large oaken doors at the center. Evan walked maybe two paces ahead of me. I followed, shivering in the cold.

While the driveway had been strewn with leaves and twigs, the porch was distinctively clean, and the dirt from the Boss' shoes was visible upon the unvarnished surface.

I hurried up the stairs to join him. Without knocking, he opened the doors and entered what had once been the great hall of the manor. Ahead some ten paces a door was ajar, and from it came the light I had seen as we approached. Evan took sure steps as he moved. Mine were less confident.

Suddenly, a brown creature scuttled across the floor. It entered the room ahead of us, and I saw a figure there bend and hold the furry thing at his waist. Regardless of my earlier doubts, the Boss' story seemed credible now.

The figure stepped back as we entered, positioning himself near the center of a large rug that lay across the rear two-thirds of the floor. The walls held no pictures, and the furniture was sparse, although a large, ornate chair sat within reach of the figure. Behind the chair were three huge jars, each large enough to hold even the tallest person, and a stepladder, obviously needed to reach the rims. Across the stepladder lay a heavy rope. Although it was coiled, I could see large knots spaced along its length.

"Welcome, gentlemen," said the figure. He wore a robe of deep brown, its hood covering his head but not so much so as to conceal his face. The familiar rested in his right hand, purring while he stroked it with his left.

I was afraid. I stopped at the edge of the rug, careful to remain on the wooden floor, although I had no specific reason not to step onto the rug. The Boss continued until he and the figure were face to face, about two feet apart.

"You're the Devil, I presume," said the Boss.

"You presume much," said the figure. "Assuming I am a representative of the organization of which the one you name is Master, why do you honor yourself to think that he would find it necessary to occupy his time with one as trivial as you?"

Evan lowered his head. "I didn't mean to offend you." He spoke in the manor of a supplicant, subservient in a way I could never recall having heard him before. Silently the figure stood, much like a judge considering a verdict.

After a moment, Evan continued. "Look. This means a lot to me, and not just my comeback. I want to do it right this time. Live life over with Susie. You've made me think about things. I only dreamed there could be another chance. And I didn't come to you asking you to do this. You sent that thing to me with an offer." Evan pointed at the familiar, but neither it nor its master gave any response.

Sweat formed on Evan's brow as he tried again. "All right, then what is it you want? My soul? Isn't that the standard item of exchange?"

"Again, you overestimate yourself," said the figure. "Just because each of you begins life with a soul is no reason to assume it invariably remains with you throughout life. Yours seems to have become lost quite a long time ago."

"Well, what then?" said Evan, sounding impatient.

"Actually, there are many of us who admire you. All those fiery speeches, the riots they caused, the bombings, the bigotry. Made our jobs a lot easier. When you come right down to it, you're just our kind of guy. You know— The People's Choice."

Evan was silent. Clearly he wasn't in control. His right hand flicked at his nose, while sweat poured from his forehead. Had he glanced to his rear, he could have seen the sweat on mine.

The light dimmed, or maybe it just cast itself away from our direction. I still had little idea of the source, and

I didn't want to look around much since I probably would have seen something even more unsettling. Only portions of the face within the hood were visible now, and not the mouth at all. Then I realized I didn't really remember much about the face and how it had looked before the light had been lowered.

"You have seen the procedure. Take these forceps and go to the body of your wife. Tear a small piece of her flesh. Make sure you are well under her skin, since her outer layer may not have been preserved. Return to this room and place the tissue into one of these three jars. It matters not which you choose. When she is formed, use the rope to help her from the jar. Repeat until you have each been restored. You will then have your desire."

With that the figure faded. The Boss remained silent as wisps of smoke curled around the spot where the figure had stood. When the smoke cleared, Evan turned quickly and headed for the outside, the forceps in his hand. I hadn't seen him take them, but no matter, they were there.

I was relieved to reach the porch and proceeded to the trailer. It opened easily. The artificial coldness of the interior clashed with the coldness of the night and mingled badly, like two women wearing the same dress at a party.

On a stretcher amidst the refrigeration tubes lay Susie. Evan wouldn't let her rest in a container—too much like she was in a casket he said.

I hadn't give her much of a look when we loaded her into the trailer, but I couldn't help it now. A thick layer of frost coated her, just like a slab of meat that's been kept in a freezer too long. Her hair was brown with a strong suggestion of gray, and it was short and unkempt, as was the hospital gown she wore. Once a robust, athletic woman, she now weighed only eighty pounds, her body ravaged before the end, if it had been the end.

I looked at my watch. It was almost two A.M., and I was glad the drive alone had taken us past midnight.

"Let's wait until dawn, Boss," I asked, trying not to sound like I was pleading. I've never been superstitious, but a little caution here seemed appropriate.

Evan neither waited nor answered. Instead he climbed into the trailer and eagerly plunged the forceps though the folds of her gown.

"Damn!" he shouted as he failed to penetrate her abdomen. "She's frozen!" I really wondered what he expected her to be.

He gouged for a moment longer, then, frustrated, said, "Come on. We've got to unhook her and get some of this flesh warm enough to tear."

The trailer was too small for us both to enter, so I waited while he undid the straps holding her. He crawled out, rear first, dragging Susie by the feet as he came.

"Let's get her to the car. Put her by the heater in the front seat." I did as he commanded, although the thought of touching the corpse sent a wave of nausea through me. Evan still had her feet so I took her head. Her hair was brittle, and it crackled as I placed my hands underneath it. Her twisted face looked at me, eyes and mouth open as she had been when the preservation took effect. My hands were painfully cold.

Evan removed his coat and used it to gain a hold on Susie. He began shoving her into the seat, her small body fitting upright into the front passenger's side. Since I had the keys, I went around to start the ignition.

She was still on the far side of the seat, and that suited me okay, but Evan shoved her toward me, giving himself room to enter. She rested between us, inclined against the divider, her legs underneath the radio. The car's motor was still warm; we hadn't been in the house long enough for it to cool. I channeled the heat through the car's upper vents, the ones designed for the air-conditioning system.

The Boss stared deep and long at her. I almost expected him to talk to Susie, as if soothing her spirit would make her rebirth easier. Instead, he reached into his pocket for his cigarette lighter. He tried to lift her still ice-laden gown, holding the flame near the point he had tried to enter earlier.

"I should've thought of this lighter before. We wouldn't have had to move her in here," he said excitedly.

I watched the frost melt, then the flesh glow red at first, then darken. He extinguished the lighter and took the forceps, this time successfully penetrating the skin.

Evan went deep, as the cowled figure had told him to do, and I became sickened as he removed the forceps with the bloody tissue at its end. I sat dazed, but for only a moment as the shutting of the car door brought me back to reality. Susie's corpse bowed at the waist, her face resting in the direct flow of the heater's exhaust.

Evan walked quickly and purposefully toward the house, taking care that the flesh would not be jarred from the grasp of the forceps. I had no intention of following. I had followed Evan for too long.

The car was quite hot. Susie's face was beginning to thaw, enough that her jaw hinge worked and her mouth closed. The corners of her lips curled up slightly, with more than the suggestion of a smile. I didn't know what to do, so I just looked at her.

And then she dissolved. A powdery white dust floated as the heater current blew through the car. I felt as though I were inside a Christmas toy. One with the glass filled with water and inside it a house in a woods, with the snow settling around after you shook it. The kind Charles Foster Kane dropped as he said "Rosebud."

The dust made me cough. As I opened my door, a terrible retching noise came from the house. I looked quickly. No longer did the light flicker from the shaded window. I heard the heavy sound of desperate feet moving rapidly across the wooden floor. A second more muffled tread followed, until the two merged. A deep low-voiced scream filled the air. In the light of the now risen moon, I saw a hideous, diarrhoeal mass gather itself and emerge from the door.

The shape was mostly brown, roughly like that of a human, with four appendages attached to a torso and topped by a lump that was not a head. The two upper appendages held the dead body of what had been the Boss. His mangled remains were being absorbed into the ooze at an unbelievably rapid rate.

Given the choice of facing that or having to breathe Susie's dust, I jumped back into the car and slammed the door.

The motor was running, so I pushed the LTD into drive and spun it around, roaring from the house. I hit the mailbox head on as I took to the road in the direction from which we had come.

Evan had found his destiny, and, perhaps, like Jimmy Hoffa, his disappearance would fuel rumors for decades to come. No one would guess the truth. How could they?

I could only guess, myself, what went wrong. The first thing I thought of was Susie's cancer. But Evan had burned the flesh with his lighter, so maybe it wasn't the cancer at all. Really I didn't care. The old days were over. Evan was dead, and I had the rest of my life to live. I thought I'd go back to Drake's Crossing. Start over as much as I could. Find myself again.

The road didn't look so dark and empty any more.

DEAD AND NAKED

By Pamela Sargent

Caroline had more than her share of phobias, anxieties that went far beyond those of normal people. Even other phobics might have found her fears hard to understand.

How could she explain, even to a psychologist, that there would inevitably be mornings when she got up on the wrong side of the bed? Her bed was up against the wall, a necessity given the size and dimensions of her bedroom, which meant that she had no choice about which side to use, a fact that could drive her to distraction. Too often, she knew without a doubt that she had gotten up on the wrong side of the bed, even though there had been no alternative. Once she was off to the wrong start, Caroline never regained her momentum; her day was always a total loss after that. Nothing to be done, she supposed, but to accept her fate and hope for a better day tomorrow; but it niggled at her that there would always be a wrong side of the bed. Sometimes, overcome by her powerlessness, she could not bring herself to get up at all.

Normal people, when shopping, worried that when they used a credit card, it might be rejected and the clerk and everyone else in the vicinity would know they were maxed out. Caroline fretted over that, convinced that fellow customers would consider her a potential bankrupt and a careless recordkeeper at best. But she also suffered agonies over what the clerk and everybody else around might think of her purchases, to the point that she often went miles out of her way to shop at stores where she had never been and was unlikely to return.

If Caroline dialed a wrong number, the thought of apologizing to a person who might have stumbled to the

phone from the shower, been in the middle of the first un-
disturbed family dinner he'd had in weeks, or who might
be waiting for the doctor to call and tell him whether or
not he had cancer, filled her with such a sense of inadequacy that she usually could do no more than let out a
shriek before hanging up. She had long ago given up eating in restaurants, since every dish on the menu seemed
a minefield of potential etiquette disasters. Accepting dinner invitations was out as well; what would she do if her
host or hostess offered a repast of such foods as French
onion soup, tacos, spareribs, fried chicken, corn on the
cob, or boiled lobsters ready for a messy dissection?
Safer to stay home and mutter excuses about diets and
cholesterol levels.

But her most overwhelming fear, one so strong that it
went beyond mere phobia to obsession, involved nudity—
her own nudity, as opposed to that of others. Just the
thought of being naked, or even mostly undressed, in the
presence of another human being was enough to throw her
into a panic. On the few occasions when she had allowed
herself to be swayed by an amorous suitor, she had retired
to her bedroom to don a Mother Hubbard nightgown before allowing any intimacies, a habit that did not encour-
age men to call on her again. She rarely went to doctors
and then only when the whole examination could be conducted with Caroline covered by both a hospital gown and
a sheet. To go to the beach in what passed for a swimsuit
or to lounge about at poolside was an impossibility for
her. At times she deeply regretted that she could not find
it within herself to become a Muslim, so that she could go
through life completely covered in public.

Caroline did not know how she had acquired this particular fear. She might be an unlikely candidate for *Sports
Illustrated*'s swimsuit issue, but she would not have taken
first prize in a dog show, either. Anyway, she was enough
of a feminist, despite a terror of participating in any orga-
nized political activity, to know that women should not be
judged by their bodies. Her parents were not abnormally
prudish, and she could take a healthy interest in male
strippers strutting their stuff on *Donahue*. It wasn't sex or
being around scantily clothed people that bothered her
but the thought of being stripped, defenseless, unshielded,
with all her flaws only too evident.

Now her phobia had acquired a metaphysical aspect. Were people nude in the afterlife? That notion had come to her at three in the morning, always a bad time to dwell on anything metaphysical. What if, when you died, you had to live out whatever spiritual existence you were granted buck naked? Maybe the afterlife was like that painting of damned souls she dimly remembered from a college art history course, souls that had to suffer their torments in the buff. Not, of course, that she actually believed in Hell; Caroline leaned more toward the rushing-through-a-tunnel-toward-light-and-being-greeted-by-dead-loved-ones hypothesis. Still, she might emerge amid the assembly of welcoming souls stripped of everything, ready to die all over again of total shame and embarrassment.

It wasn't logical to worry about being naked when dead, but she could not keep herself from obsessing on the subject. An undertaker would probably have to disrobe her body, but since she wouldn't be there any more, she wasn't particularly upset by that. It was the nakedness of her soul that tormented her, the possibility that when she left this world, she would be, in some sense, totally nude in the next. Sooner or later, her number would be up and her spiritual ass bared, and there was nothing she could do about it.

This fear tortured Caroline to the point where she could not sleep and could hardly get through her days at the office. Monster migraines, brought on by her terrors, often kept her in bed for hours. She went from doctor to doctor, accumulating prescriptions for Percodan to dull the migraines, Valium to chill out enough to get her work done, and Seconal to help her sleep. Sometimes, when she was especially panic-stricken, she followed the Valium or Seconal with a Scotch. Don't let me die, she prayed, hoping there was a God on the receiving end of the prayer to hear her.

A morning soon came when Caroline no longer had to worry about getting up on the wrong side of the bed because she was unable to get up at all.

Well, I'm finally dead. That was Caroline's first thought as she floated toward the ceiling, then looked back to see herself still lying in bed. She must have taken

some extra Seconal without knowing it, and she probably
shouldn't have had all that Scotch after dinner.

Her next realization was that she—that part of her
floating around the room, not the stiff in the bed—was
wearing a long white robe. Did that mean that there truly
was a Heaven and that she was on her way there? Caroline, overcome with relief at finding herself clothed, did
not much care where she was headed as long as clothing
was part of the deal.

The wail of a wind rose around her; the bedroom suddenly disappeared. She was being drawn through a long
tunnel toward a distant pinprick of light. She was still in
her robe, but maybe that was an illusion. Life after death
might be like one of those movies where a guy could
change into a werewolf and still have his clothes on when
he changed back to human form, even though logically he
should have been nude. The pinprick of light was rapidly
increasing in size, and the wind was deafening. Just as
Caroline was beginning to wish that there were Valium in
the afterlife, the wind died and she came to a stop, landing lightly on her feet.

She seemed to be standing in a cave, gazing out at a
vast ballroom suffused with a soft golden light, a room so
huge that she could not see any walls. Above, hanging
down from an impossibly high ceiling, were colossal
chandeliers that resembled the mother ship in *Close Encounters.* People in small groups greeted one another or
stood around talking as if they were all at a cosmic cock-
tail party. She might have been looking at a gathering of
United Nations delegations, except for one feature that
would definitely not have been part of such a social func-
tion: All the people in the ballroom beyond were nude.

Caroline took a step toward them, then clutched at her
robe, afraid she might lose it. Maybe the rest of them had
been in robes while coming through the tunnel, only to
get stripped later on. She took another tentative step and
met an invisible barrier.

A few people were coming toward her. One gray-
haired man looked familiar, and at last she recognized her
grandfather. The others were probably departed relatives
as well, but it was hard to be certain since she had only
seen them before with their clothes on. Apparently people
who had just died were greeted by loved ones, although

it surprised her that the dead seemed to have the same bodies they had worn in life. Somehow she had assumed that you got a good-looking youthful body—or a good-looking, youthful soul container—in the next world.

A red-haired woman left the others and came nearer. "Hello, dear," the woman said. "Don't you recognize me?" Caroline shook her head. "Why, I'm your Great-Aunt Sarabelle."

"Sorry," Caroline said, "but I was only seven when you kicked off—er, passed on." A memory was coming to her; Great-Aunt Sarabelle had always had a weight problem, and being dead hadn't trimmed her down. Sarabelle's melonous breasts bobbed above a large, rounded belly, and her thighs were huge. Yet she moved as gracefully as one of the dancing hippos in *Fantasia*, and there was something comforting about her bulk.

"You just wait there, dear," Sarabelle said. "I'll come out."

"I don't see Cousin Joey," Caroline said, relieved that she didn't. "Guess he must be circulating."

"I'm afraid he isn't here at all," Sarabelle said.

"Oh." Maybe, Caroline thought, there was a Hell after all. That would explain Joey's absence since he had richly deserved to end up there.

"We've been waiting for you." Sarabelle waved her companions away, then sat down. "I hope my being buffo doesn't bother you." Caroline shook her head. "Anyway, since you can't come in, I'll have to talk to you out here. Do sit down, dear."

"But why can't I come in?" Caroline asked.

"Becasue you're not dead."

"What do you mean, I'm not dead? I'm here, aren't I?"

"But you're not dead," Sarabelle said. "You're still in your robe, and that means you haven't shed wordly things, that you're still tied to your body in some way. We have to bare our souls here, Caroline. I think it has something to do with moral cleansing or whatever, but theology was never my strong suit. What I mean is it's sort of like getting ready for a shower and then finally getting clean."

"And I've got to strip down for this cleansing moral shower or whatever."

"Well, yes."

"I can't do it."

"Of course you can," Sarabelle said. "Everyone does. Granted, some souls find it a bit unnerving at first, given their customs—not that I mean to criticize anyone else's way of life. You do get over it, though. Once you're bare, once you've rid yourself of all that worldly clutter, it's quite nice here."

"Oh, God," Caroline said, before realizing that this was not an expression to use lightly under the circumstances. "I thought—"

"That we all went around in robes? Maybe you expected harps, too."

"I didn't mean that. It's something else. You see, I have a real thing about my body, about showing it. I can't even wear a pair of shorts in the summer when I'm alone in my apartment. I know it's crazy, but—"

"Really, Caroline." Sarabelle shook her head. "This isn't your body. Your body's somewhere else. The form you're in now is—well, I'm not sure what you'd call it. A manifestation, maybe. Anyway, you'd save yourself and those you left behind a lot of trouble if you'd step through this entrance right now instead of waiting until your earthly body fails. You're going to be naked sooner or later."

"You don't understand," Caroline said. "I can't."

"Maybe you'll change your mind when you see yourself."

The cave and ballroom vanished. Caroline was sitting with her great-aunt in a room with green walls. Her mother, her father, and a balding man in a white coat were standing around a hospital bed. Caroline slowly rose to her feet. A thin, pale woman with long brown hair lay motionless in the bed, with tubes in her nostrils, an intravenous needle taped to one arm, and the end of a respirator attached to the hollow of her neck.

"Well," Sarabelle said, "there you are."

"There's no chance your daughter will ever regain consciousness," the balding man was saying. "She could be in this coma indefinitely."

"We can hope for a miracle," Caroline's mother murmured, tears in her eyes. "Can't we?"

"Honey, accept it." Caroline's father took his wife's

hand. "Maybe we should let her go. Do you think our girl would want to go on in that state?"

"Yes, I would," Caroline shouted. "Keep that respirator going! Don't pull the plug on me!"

"Seems to me," Sarabelle said, "that you're carrying this phobia of yours a bit far."

Caroline moved toward the bed. That body would last; she would will it to last. She was not about to spend eternity in her birthday suit.

Caroline had never taken the time to draw up a living will. She had always meant to do so but was now relieved she hadn't. Her parents, because of that, would need a court order to get her off the respirator, and soon a local right-to-life group entered the fray in her body's defense. The legal battle was likely to be protracted, which meant that Caroline had a reprieve, so to speak.

She spent her time, if there was such a thing as time in the afterworld, greeting new arrivals before they shed their robes to join their old friends and family in the ballroom. Occasionally others whose bodies were also comatose stayed with her to schmooze until their bodies gave up the ghost or somebody pulled the plug. Caroline might not be able to enter the ballroom, but her afterlife was pleasant nonetheless. Other dead relatives besides her cousin Joey had apparently not made it to the cosmic party, but those who were there often visited with her. She met a lively group of vacationers who had been on their way to a Club Med until their DC-10 ran into trouble. A couple of old friends who had always neglected to fasten their seat belts came through the tunnel and hung around the cave to reminisce even after shedding their robes.

Caroline had only a moment of panic after the Supreme Court decided in favor of her parents. The respirator might be gone, but the feeding tube remained, and it looked as though the right-to-life group would fight hard to keep that from being removed.

"You could save yourself and everyone else a lot of trouble, dear," Sarabelle said to Caroline during one visit. "All you have to do is drop that robe and come through starkers. That body can't last much longer—you're all that's keeping it alive." The red-haired woman shook her head. "I've never heard of such a thing. We've had folks cooling their heels here, impatient to ditch their robes and get on with it while some fool doctor's messing around with their body or some idiot lawyer's getting court orders, and you just want to sit here." Sarabelle did not approve of the right-to-life groups and their efforts, and Caroline had the distinct impression that few others here did. That probably made sense, given that everyone here was dead.

"That body might last longer than you think," Caroline said. "Medical science is making all kinds of advances." She had spoken to a couple of people who had been cryonically frozen just after death. Since they had come through the tunnel and quickly passed into the ballroom, it was clear they had wasted their money, but they had every hope that future cryonauts would be more successful. Science might find a way to keep the human body in suspension indefinitely, which meant that Caroline might acquire a lot of companions in her cave.

Her great-aunt and other relatives were soon sending the souls of psychologists, psychiatrists, psychiatric social workers, and shamans her way. The problem was that Caroline had even less reason to struggle with her phobia and overcome it here than she had in her earlier existence. Even at the edge of the ballroom, she could still be part of the party; indeed, she was becoming quite an attraction and rarely lacked for company.

She clung to the hope that her body could be kept going long enough so that someone might decide to freeze it. Sooner or later, it had to occur to the right-to-life lawyer fighting for her life that cryonic interment was a logical extension of his views. If God meant for someone to die, putting the person in a vat of frozen nitrogen wouldn't stop Him, and in the meantime, that person's right to life would be maintained.

Whenever she stopped to consider the matter, she realized that she had the perfect existence. She had made a lot of new friends. She did not have to worry about eating in front of others, since there was no food in the afterlife. She would never again get up on the wrong side of the bed, since she no longer had to sleep. She would be modestly garbed for all time.

It was too perfect to last. A sudden weakness in her

limbs, as if she were a puppet whose strings had been cut, told her that her earthly body had finally failed. A nurse, touched by Caroline's plight and that of her grieving parents, had smothered her with a pillow.

She was about to lose her robe; Caroline could not bear it. She huddled against the cave wall, hugging herself with her arms. But her robe still covered her, and when she looked up, several friends and relatives had gathered near her.

"I'm still here," Caroline said as she stood up. "Does this mean I can come in there in my robe after all?"

"No," her grandfather replied.

"You have a lot to work off, dear," Sarabelle said. "I'm afraid you can't come in at all, with or without your robe, and you definitely can't stay there."

"What do you mean, I can't come in? I'm dead now, aren't I?"

"The problem is," her grandfather said, "that your phobia's caused a lot of trouble. My son and his wife went through financial and emotional hell—you should excuse the expression. A lot of money was spent on you and on legal fees. A lot of people were dithering over what to do with your carcass when they might have been doing something more constructive and meaningful. Now a nurse whose only crime was taking pity on you has to go before a grand jury, although the grapevine tells me that they probably won't indict her. You have a lot to answer for, girl, and all because you just can't bear to take off your clothes."

"Probably a sign," Sarabelle murmured, "of some spiritual lack. You can't be a good person unless you're honest with other people, and you can't be much of a soul until you get rid of stuff you don't need. You're not ready to join us, dear."

Caroline's heart sank. One of her minor phobias had been an aversion to the smell of charcoal briquets when her neighbors were having a cookout. Now she would probably have to get used to such odors and worse. She was likely to run into Cousin Joey, who had made her family's holiday get-togethers so miserable, and she would have to suffer through it all in the nude.

"What's going to happen to me?" she asked in a faint voice.

"What happens to everyone who isn't ready," Sarabelle said. "You have to go back and try again."

Before Caroline could protest, a wind was sweeping her into the tunnel, away from the light. I should have worked things through with one of those dead shrinks, she thought just before her fear seized her completely. She would have a little time to wrestle with her phobia in the womb, to think about what it would be like to be born again, naked.

MY MOTHER AND
I GO SHOPPING

by Lawrence Watt-Evans

My mother always knew all the best places to shop, all the tricks and bargains. You could send her out with ten dollars and she'd come home with stuff you swore would cost a hundred or more. When I was a kid, I was slow learning how money worked because it seemed as if my mother could stretch it as far as needed, no matter how little there was; as a result, I had trouble with concepts like "broke" and "unaffordable."

I never knew how she did it; I thought shopping was dull, and I seldom went along.

She did it, though. After I grew up and went off on my own, she kept on in the old home town, bringing home bargains and somehow living on my Dad's pension. I got married, and divorced, and married, and divorced, and she kept on at the old homestead.

I stopped in sometimes when I could, but she didn't seem to need me around, so I didn't make it a regular thing. It wasn't as if we'd been all that close, as these things go.

But Mother was getting on; she'd been on the far side of eighty for a couple of years, and she couldn't get around as well any more. Her eyesight wasn't good enough to drive, and she'd lost her license. Usually her friends took care of her, but the day inevitably came when no one else was around, and she needed to pick up a few items, and I was nearby, back in the area on business.

So my mother and I went out shopping—and I must

admit, despite years of listening to her and even following her around as a kid, I'd never quite figured out how she found the bargains she did, so I didn't really mind a chance to see her in action again. I assumed it would mostly be boring beyond belief, but I thought I might learn something.

I did.

The first thing I learned was that my mother still wasn't taking any sass from her youngest, even if I *was* forty years old.

"Do you want to go to the mall, Mother?" I asked, as I helped her into the car. "It's a nice place . . ."

She snorted. "It's a den of thieves," she snapped. "You just go where I tell you."

"Yes'm," I said; I kept the sigh in until I'd closed the car door.

I got in the driver's seat and asked, "Where to, then?"

"You just drive," she said, making brushing gestures at me. "I'll tell you where to go."

So I drove.

We headed in toward town, and I thought we were headed for the big old department stores downtown, maybe for the bargain basements, but then Mother snapped, "Turn right at the corner."

I turned right, onto a street I vaguely remembered but couldn't name.

"Left," she said, and we turned into the potholed alley behind a row of shops, and then right onto old brick pavement, and right again, and we were on muddy gravel between two smoke-blackened brick walls, and I'd lost my bearings completely. I was pretty sure that wherever we were, I'd never been here before.

It didn't look like a very good neighborhood, either, and I was a bit worried—Mother had been coming *here* to shop? Where was there to shop here, anyway? Warehouses, maybe? All I could see was brick walls, boarded windows, and padlocked doors.

Maybe it was just a shortcut.

Then we turned another corner, and another, and there *were* shops, quaint little ones, a row of them on either side of the street—such as it was. The street here was just mud, without even a leavening of gravel, and it ended in a T intersection with an alleyway at the end of the block—if I went straight ahead I'd run smack into a sagging wooden structure that might have been an old garage or an old barn.

"Here we are!" Mother chirped cheerfully.

I hadn't heard her speak that way in years—decades, really. Startled, I turned to look at her, and she glared back. "Just park the car, Billy boy," she said.

I looked at the street, with its bare mud reaching from doorstep to doorstep across a width of maybe twenty feet, with no sign of sidewalks or curbstones, and decided that one place was as good as another; I stopped the car where it was.

It wasn't as if there were any other vehicles in sight. There weren't.

I thought I could feel the car sinking into the mud when I shut off the engine. Certainly, when I got out, *I* sank into the mud—right to the tops of my shoes.

I'd wondered why Mother was wearing boots when it wasn't raining or snowing; now I knew.

I looked around, and I suspect my jaw dropped.

I'm sure you've seen those little mock-colonial neighborhoods, with the mullioned bow windows and the gas streetlights and the brick sidewalks and a bunch of overpriced fake antiques inside, with stick candy in a jar by the cash register. They're big with the tourists; you'll find them all over New England and scattered through a few other places along the eastern seaboard as well.

I'd thought that was what this place was when I was driving in, but now that I had a good look—the roof on one shop was *thatch*. There weren't any streetlights; the lanterns over the doors had candles in them, candles that had actually been lit, going by the smoke-stained glass and the blackened wicks. There weren't any sidewalks, but some shops had planks out to help customers across the gutters. Paint was peeling, bricks were smoked and dirty, glass was cracked—if this was a tourist trap, it was the worst-maintained one I ever saw.

And the signboards, the stuff in the shop windows—it looked *real*.

"Where *are* we?" I asked.

"Old Town," Mother said. "Come on." She stomped off at her best pace, which wasn't very good, and headed straight toward a shop whose faded signboard read APOTHECARY.

I slogged along behind her; at least I didn't have any trouble keeping up. That would have been embarrassing, given her age.

She scraped her boots on an iron gadget by the shop door; I tried to do the same, but I didn't quite have the hang of it and damn near pulled one of my loafers off. By the time I had my balance again, she was inside and headed straight for the counter, past cabinets full of bottles and displays of weird chemical apparatus.

I hurried after her, across a plank floor that was absolutely black with accumulated grime, and stepped up beside her just as a white-aproned fellow stepped out of the curtained-off back room, took one look at Mother, and said, " 'Tis Old Mag, is it? A good day t'ye!"

The phrasing was good old Irish, but the accent wasn't; it sounded almost southern.

"And to you, David Coleman," my mother answered, but she wasn't looking at him; she was rummaging in her purse.

"You've more of your remedies, then?" the man asked, leaning forward.

"More of the same, Mr. Coleman." She pulled a little plastic bottle out of her purse, a bottle of big white pills; the label had been peeled off, leaving just a patch of gummy white residue.

"Mother," I whispered, "what *is* that?"

"It's aspirin, Billy boy—now shut up," she whispered back.

"And is the price the same?" Coleman asked.

"Unless you'd pay more," Mother snapped back.

"Nay, Old Mag, none of that! I'll pay you a fair price for your witchery, but I'll not be cheated."

"And I won't cheat you. Same price."

Coleman nodded and reached below the counter. Mother set the bottle on the polished wood but didn't let go of it.

I didn't know what the hell was going on, so I just watched, and I hoped that stuff really was aspirin. I'd have hated to find out at this late date that my mother was a drug dealer.

Coleman brought up a handful of little round lumps of

something and began counting them out onto the counter. At twelve he stopped.

"And there you have it," he said. "A dozen scruples of fine gold."

"Thanks," Mother said, as she carefully scooped up the gold doodads.

"Would you have aught else of me this fine day?" Coleman asked.

"Don't think so," Mother said. "Been a pleasure doing business with you."

I could just barely keep my mouth shut until we were out the door.

"Mother," I hissed, "why are you selling that man aspirin?"

"They don't have it here," she answered placidly.

"How much is a dozen scruples, anyway?"

"Half an ounce, ninny—didn't anyone ever teach you that in school?"

"No, they . . ."

I stopped in my tracks. "Mother," I said.

"What is it, Billy?"

"Half an ounce of gold is about a hundred and fifty dollars, isn't it?"

"About that," she agreed. "Except this is avoirdupois, and they figure gold in troy. Figure a hundred and twenty."

"For a bottle of *aspirin?*"

"They don't *have* it here, Billy. Now, come on."

Utterly confused, halfway certain I'd just seen my mother sell a hundred tablets of cocaine or something equally illegal, I followed her across the street to the car. I opened the door for her but then asked, "Where *are* we, that they don't have aspirin?"

She shrugged. "I told you, Billy," she said, "Old Town."

Before I could say anything else, a voice cried, "Old Mag!"

Mother turned, and so did I.

There was a woman standing in the street, hands on her hips, glaring at us. She was a handsome creature, rather gypsyish—dark-haired, medium height, medium build, hair pulled back in a long, thick braid, wearing a white blouse and brown ankle-length skirt. She could have been anywhere from twenty-five to fifty.

I stared, I admit it. She was worth staring at.

"Jenny McGill," Mother said."What do *you* want?"

"You know what I want, Old Mag," the woman answered. "I'd have seen the last of you, that's what I want!"

"Oh, come on," Mother said. "I'm eighty-three years old next month, I'll be dead soon. You can't let me do a little business here while I last?"

"Ha!" The McGill woman tossed her head theatrically. "*Your* kind can't be trusted to die a decent death, and I've had enough of waiting!"

"So don't wait. I come here what, once a week, and sell Davey Coleman a few things?"

"Mother . . ." I began.

"Shut up, Billy," Mother muttered.

"Old Mag, I told you when last you came, there's no room for two witches in Old Town, and 'tis *my* place, not yours! We need no outsiders here."

"I've been coming here sixty years, since before your mother was born, and you call me an outsider?" Mother called back. "Jenny McGill, you mind your manners! Your mother never spoke to me like that, rest her dear soul." She climbed into the car.

I hesitated, looking at Mother, then at Jenny McGill.

"Close the door, Billy. Let's get going," Mother said.

I shut the door and started around to the driver's side, but before I got there, Jenny McGill came striding up.

I started to say something, to apologize for my mother, but before I got a word out, she put a hand on either side of my head and pulled me down and kissed me.

Wow.

I've been married twice and had a few flings, and I figured I knew the basics, but I had *never* been kissed like that. I mean, I popped right to attention, so to speak, thought I might tear my pants, I was sweating and trembling and half-blind, couldn't see anything but those dark eyes . . .

"Take your hands off him, Jenny," my mother called, leaning out the car window.

Jenny stopped kissing me, but she kept her hands right

where they were. "Never before were you so foolish as to bring a *man*," she called back. "You know where my powers lie, yet your chosen companion this time's a man in his prime—you've grown old and foolish, Old Mag, and I've got you this time."

"Jenny McGill, you take your hands off my son," Mother called.

She had been bringing her lips up for another kiss, but at the word "son" she froze and stared up into my eyes.

I wasn't thinking any too clearly, but I had an armful of woman, and I did the natural thing—I started to lean down to meet her halfway with that kiss.

She screamed and tried to pull free, my hands slipped, and she plopped backward into the mud.

"Your *son!* she shrieked. "You ... I ... Old Mag, forgive me, I didn't ..."

"Get in the car," Mother snapped.

I got in the car.

"Drive," she said.

"But she's still in front of us."

"*Drive,*" Mother said, in a tone of voice I remembered from childhood—remembered with considerable dread.

I drove.

Jenny McGill rolled out of the way, and by the time I realized I was heading toward that T intersection at the end of the block, she was on her feet again, dripping mud, shouting after us and waving her fist.

"It's going to be tough turning around here," I said. "The street's pretty narrow ..."

"Are you crazy?" Mother asked. "We're not turning around. She's still back there, and any minute now she's going to realize that even if you *are* my son, you don't have any more of the Talent than a cabbage. If you did, she'd have felt it when she kissed you."

"But then where ..."

"Through there," Mother said, pointing.

The door of the garage, or barn or whatever it was, was opening.

I didn't know what else to do; I drove though.

The interior was dark; I could just barely make out a dusty interior, strange machinery like antique farm equipment along either side, and a ramp straight ahead that ran down out of sight, down into more complete darkness.

I headed down the ramp. I turned on the headlights and saw nothing but hard-packed brown earth, underneath us and to either side. Whatever was above us was invisible in the gloom.

"Where are we going?" I asked.

"Down," Mother said.

That wasn't much help, but I drove on in silence for a moment. The ramp kept going down, between those two walls, deeper into the darkness.

After awhile I'd had enough, though. "Mother," I said, slowing the car a little, "What the hell is going on?"

"I'm trying to get a little shopping done, that's all," Mother said defensively. "It's not *my* fault Jenny McGill's got too big for her britches, wanting to keep Old Town all for herself."

"She said you're a witch."

Mother shrugged.

"Mother," I said, "what is this Old Town place? I never heard of it, never saw it before. How can they have witches there? Nobody believes in witches any more. Why don't they have aspirin?"

"Never invented it, I guess," she said.

"And witches?"

She shrugged again. "I know a few things," she said. "They want to call it witchcraft, what do I care?"

"But what *is* Old Town?"

"It's a place, all right? You think every place there is gets on the maps, every place has TV and telephones?"

Well, in fact I thought exactly that, but I decided not to say so. "It seems kind of backward," I said.

"It's different, all right," she agreed—if it *was* agreement. "Good place for leather goods and ironmongery, and I can usually do someone a favor there for a little spending money."

It was getting stuffy in the car; I flicked on the air conditioning. I thought I saw a faint orange glow ahead, though it was hard to be sure with the headlights on.

"Listen," Mother said. "We're going to come out in a big cave in a few minutes, and when we do you want to take the second tunnel on the right—got that? Second on the right."

"Yes, Mother," I said.

She hadn't mentioned that the cave would be so swel-

tering hot that the air shimmered and the windows were
hot to the touch. The car's air conditioner was struggling
along as best it could, but I was sweating and the steering
wheel was sticky.

She also didn't mention the bright orange glare that
came from somewhere off to the left, down below the
road, where I couldn't see whatever produced it. She
didn't mention that we'd be on a narrow road along
the top of a cliff, with no railing, just a sheer drop. And
she didn't mention the *things* that were watching us from
niches in the far wall, on the other side of the chasm.

If Mother hadn't said anything I'd have taken that first
right, to get the hell out of that place, but I held on another hundred feet and took the second right, into the
welcome darkness of another tunnel; this one, thank
heavens, was heading upward, rather than further down.

Unfortunately, it wasn't as nice and straight as the one
that led down from Old Town. It wiggled and wound its
way upward, and twice I heard metal scraping on rock as
I squeezed the car around those narrow turns.

"I don't usually come this way," Mother remarked.

"I can see why not," I said, as I negotiated another
curve.

"Mary's Cadillac won't fit through here at all; I'm glad
you've got a sensible car."

Mother's friend Mary has a '73 Eldorado. "I like to be
able to park," I said.

Then the tunnel ended—the headlights illuminated a
pair of heavy wooden doors instead of more rock. I
barely stopped in time.

"The bar's on this side," Mother said. "You'll have to
open them."

I squeezed out of the car, lifted the bar, and pushed the
doors open; sunlight poured in. I blinked and looked
around and saw forest. "Where *are* we?" I asked.

"Come on, get in the car," Mother called.

We got rolling again, down a dirt road that wound
through woods, past some of the biggest trees I've ever
seen in my life—not giant redwoods or anything, but
oaks and chestnuts that would've considered a sixty-
footer a hopeless runt.

"I wasn't planning to come this way," Mother said,
"but as long as we're here, take a left at the fork."

I took a left, and then . . .

Then I don't remember what happened next, but I was driving through the woods again, the sun was lower in the sky by at least an hour, and there was a bolt of fabric on the back seat.

I looked at Mother, at the fabric—lovely stuff, patterned silk—and then at the road, and decided not to ask about it.

"Where now?" I asked.

"Right," she said, pointing, and a few minutes later we came out of the woods onto the shoulder of the interstate a mile outside town. I got on the highway.

"D'you know where Stilson Jewelers is?"

"I *think* so," I said.

"Well, go there—I'm going to sell Mr. Coleman's gold, and then you can take me to Aubrey's Foodliner and we'll get the groceries."

I waited in the car while she sold the gold, and while I waited I thought about it all. This had been, without a doubt, the weirdest day of my life—but it was fascinating, too. That forest was beautiful, and I had a feeling that whatever I didn't remember there had been pleasant, and driving the tunnels was exciting, and Old Town had a certain charm to it.

A large part of that charm was Jenny McGill, I had to admit. She was a fine-looking woman, no question about it.

Of course, she was apparently ready to kill my mother and me on sight, but still, remembering her had a certain thrill. Maybe it was witchcraft, or maybe I just hadn't been kissed by enough pretty women lately.

And of course, there was the mystery of where those places *were*. They didn't seem to connect. There weren't any woods like that along the interstate, I'd have sworn to it, and I never saw anything like Old Town before. Remembering the route, I thought we should have come out behind the old railroad station, not on a block of shops left from some other century.

But did I think every place there is gets on the maps, that every place has TV and telephones? I'd always loved stories of secret rooms and hidden passages when I was a kid—maybe I'd just found the grown-up equivalent.

"Mother," I asked, when she was back in the car, "how'd you find these places?"

She didn't pretend to misunderstand. "You've just gotta know how to look, Billy boy," she said. "And I've been at it a long, long time. Since before you were born."

"Why'd you never take me along?"

She sighed. "Two reasons—maybe more. First, a boy child's a little too valuable in some of them, a little too tempting. You wouldn't leave one of those boomboxes on the car seat down on East Main Street while you were shopping, would you?"

I had to admit that I wouldn't.

"Second, I didn't suppose you'd appreciate it. You were always such a sober little kid, no sign of the Talent at all. Why confuse you with a bunch of places you'd probably never see again?"

I could see that. I didn't think it was right, not really— but I was never the life of any party, never had much of a creative flair for anything. Whatever fantasy life I might have never showed much—I never let it. Hell, my first wife left me because I was boring. I've known for a long time that people didn't find me fascinating.

Even my own mother.

I thought about that while I pushed the cart through the supermarket for her.

I wasn't as boring as all that. I had an imagination. It just didn't show.

And this Talent that Mother talked about—what *was* it?

Did I have it after all, maybe? That kiss might have told more than Mother knew.

"That Jenny McGill . . ." I began.

"That bitch," Mother snapped. "See if I go back *there* again! Someone *else* can bring them their aspirin and penicillin from now on!"

I thought about *that* on the way back to Mother's house.

By the next week, I was back home and Mother's friends were driving her again.

But a month later I wangled a transfer to Boston. I said I wanted to be nearer Mother, in case her health went, and the home office didn't mind. I bought a condo a mile from Mother's house and commuted into the city five days a week.

On weekends I just drove around town. Alone, not with Mother.

It took me six weeks and a dozen tries before I found Old Town again. It took me an hour of fast talk and dodging before Jenny McGill would listen to what I had to say.

Finding the place got easier every time, though, and really, Jenny can be perfectly reasonable when she wants to.

She doesn't think I'm boring. I courted her for six months, and at last she gave in. We've posted the banns, and she and Mother have declared an armed truce. Mother still won't go back to Old Town, but I've brought Jenny to dinner a few times. Maybe I'm under a spell; if so, I don't care. Witch or not, she's a fine woman.

And I've found a few shortcuts. There are a *lot* of places that aren't on the maps.

Whatever happens now, it won't be boring.

Mother always did know the best places to shop.

THE KNIGHT OF GREENWICH VILLAGE

by Don D'Ammassa

The dragon soared with outstretched wings above the
Empire State Building and disappeared behind the rising
tier of skyscrapers just beyond. It wasn't really a dragon,
of course, any more than the spires and pinnacles of Manhattan were the abutments of a gigantic, sprawling castle.
But to Albert Lance, the airliner was a mythical beast and
the entire city a land filled with enchantment and wonder,
the source of endless heroic adventures perceptible to Albert alone, his personal Camelot.

A few minutes earlier he'd dealt with the ogre that
lived in his building, its den strategically placed across
from the main entrance. To everyone else, Rocco appeared human, but Albert saw his true soul, a small con-
voluted knot of self interest and pointless cruelty.

"Lance! I've been trying to catch you all week. That
goddamned mess of yours downstairs has got to go. Either you take care of it, or I'll hire someone and add the
cost to your rent. You hear me?" Rocco was short and
squat, but his shoulders were so broad that Lance marveled he was able to get in and out of his apartment without turning sideways.

"But no one else is using that space." He'd been Sir
Albert on the elevator ride down from the eleventh floor,
but now he felt the persona slipping away. "There's
plenty of room left."

"Maybe so, but it's not *your* room. The other tenants
have the same rights as you do, you know. They're just
goddamned books, Lance. You must've read 'em all by

now. What do you want to keep 'em around for? Throw 'em in the incinerator, why doncha?"

If there'd been any doubt about Rocco's ogrish nature, it was banished by that unholy suggestion. "I couldn't do that! I mean they're ... they're *books*."

Rocco shrugged. "Whatever they are, they go tomorrow or else."

"Give me a break, Rocco. I'm really busy this week. I'll take care of things Saturday, I promise."

"All right, Saturday then. But this is the last time I'm gonna talk to you about it. You hear what I'm saying to you?"

With the ogre outmaneuvered for the moment, Albert had left the building. The crisis remained unresolved; there was just no possible way to fit the overflow from his library back into the three small rooms he occupied. But at least he could delay dealing with the situation for a few days. Some solution would offer itself, as had always happened in the past. Sir Albert had never been defeated by a challenge, large or small.

On the way to the subway, he helped an elderly woman cross the street/rescued Lady Guenevere from a crumbling cliff by carrying her across a tightrope stretched above a bottomless abyss. Two blocks further on, he evaded Cerberus himself, a foul tempered terrier fortunately restrained by a short leash. Harpy pigeons fluttered around his head as he broke into a jog, realizing that he was in danger of being late to work again. Pedestrians called out in anger as he brushed past during his descent below street level, but he ignored their crude remarks. Peasants never understood the requirements of chivalry, the weight of obligation pressing down on those selfless defenders of civilization.

A giant serpent rushed out of the mouth of a subterranean passage and obediently came to a stop. After a great struggle, Sir Albert had managed to bend the king of these creatures to his will, exacting as its life price the promise of safe passage within their bellies to wherever in Camelot he wished to travel. He stepped inside, and the serpent flowed forward into its lair.

Albert reached the front entrance to Bidwell and Carter only a minute after he was supposed to be sitting at his desk, and he briefly entertained the hope that he might reach that sanctuary undetected. But Mrs. Criswell had been watching for him, and even as he took his seat and typed his sign-on, she moved swiftly down the row of data stations to stand directly behind him.

"Late again, Lance? That's the third time in two weeks."

Sir Albert gritted his teeth, knowing that capture by the slaveholders was a necessary test of his courage and that by the end of the day he would have inspired his fellow captives with the will to revolt. But for the moment, he must bend his neck to the lash of the chief overseer's cruel tongue.

"I'm sorry, Mrs. Criswell, but an elderly man collapsed in the street, and I had to find someone to help him." He had no compunction about lying to the overseer; even noble slaves were entitled to mislead their captors.

She had moved to one side so that she could watch his profile. Albert carefully kept his eyes on the screen, which had already changed to the data entry program he fed every day. "I see," she said quietly. "And last Thursday you witnessed an automobile accident, and Monday it was a purse snatching. What will it be next week, I wonder? Armed robbery? A volcano in Central Park? Or perhaps Martian invaders immobilizing the subways with their death rays?" Albert knew it had been a mistake to let her see him reading a science fiction novel at lunch that time; she'd been making sarcastic references ever since.

"I'm really very sorry, Mrs. Criswell, but you know that my performance is above average. I'll work through the morning break if you'd like, to make up for being late."

Criswell smacked her tongue against the roof of her mouth, a coarse, impatient sound. "That's not the point, Mr. Lance. Everyone else here manages to get to work on time, every day, and without being diverted by petty disasters, real or imaginary. I expect you to do the same. Do you know what the job market is like out there today?" She gestured toward the row of windows at the far end of the room. "I could have six data processing *managers* begging for this job in an hour, if I wanted. So either straighten out or get out."

"Yes, Mrs. Criswell." But he was speaking to her rapidly receding back.

Despite the morning's upset, Albert was able to drop into input mode with practiced ease, converting hard copy of the previous day's polling information into electronic statistical data. At first he'd found the work interesting in itself, trying to imagine the personality of an interviewee from the pattern of answers displayed on each survey. But the randomness of it all bothered him after a while. There was no correlation between educational level and philosophical orientation, income and political stance, and little consistency even within the same sample. Faced with the growing possibility that it was all just random after all, he disengaged his mind and began processing the data mechanically, allowing himself to concentrate on his secret life.

The morning passed quickly after that. After a meager meal of bread and water/tunafish salad and lemonade, Albert left the company cafeteria where, as always, he had remained alone in an isolated corner. He consulted the water cooler oracle on the way back to his station, deftly changed routes when he spied overseer Criswell ahead, and spent the rest of the day dreaming of dragons and beautiful princesses and assorted derring do.

The slaves revolted right on schedule, streaming out of the ravaged gates of Bidwell and Carter into the freedom of early evening. Rather than brave the crush on the subway, Albert walked two blocks downtown and bought himself a simple supper from a street cart/itinerant farmer, eating it quickly while window shopping at a series of novelty shops. He ignored the efforts of an older man in disreputable clothing to extort his extra change, briefly fingering the broadsword he carried disguised as a ballpoint pen in his jacket pocket. When he finally returned to his apartment building in lower Manhattan, he was carrying a small plastic bag that contained three new paperback novels, even though his unread backlog had already grown to well over two hundred.

There was a message from his mother on the answering machine.

"Albert, this is your mother calling. God, I hate these things! Listen, Albert, I want you to call me back tonight. No excuses this time. Your father and I deserve better than this. We didn't mortgage the house to put you through college just so you could fritter your life away playing with computers for minimum wage. Dad's been asking around, and Mr. Stoughton at the bank is looking for someone to help out with the new system they're putting in, and your father put himself out to mention that you had a real talent for things like that and Mr. Stoughton has agreed to talk to you about it if . . ." And that's where the tape had run out, long before his mother's breath did the same.

He hastily rewound and reset the machine. His parents had long since fallen under the influence of the evil sorceress Morgan Le Fay, and he had yet to devise a method of freeing them from this vile bondage. After scribbling "Call Mom" on a post-it note, Albert stuck it on his message board, where it joined a dozen others with similar messages.

Albert remained restless and upset despite several futile attempts to lose himself in the book he'd been reading, so he decided to go for a walk. Ignoring the siren calls of disturbed automobile alarms, avoiding the ever present wild boars with their characteristic bright yellow coat and checkered crests, Sir Albert strode courageously out into the growing darkness.

Washington Square Park was a place of great enchantment for Sir Albert, and he drew strength with each breath as he stood leaning against the boulder from which he had once wrested an enchanted sword. Bands of elves and gnomes were scattered about the park, carrying boom boxes and dressed in garishly designed clothing. As a knight of the realm, Sir Albert's primary responsibility was to human beings, but he had extended his zone of tolerance to the little people as well, even if their mischievous nature often disturbed him.

But tonight there were too many unsettling thoughts running through Albert's head to allow him to sit passively and watch. It was only a matter of time until he lost his job at Bidwell and Carter; it was well known that Mrs. Criswell never let up on anyone she disliked until she'd driven them out. Nor could he continue to avoid dealing with his parents forever. They had already threatened to drive into the city to visit, and he'd only put them off by promising to be better about keeping in touch. Nor had he admitted to them that Gwen, the girl he'd supposedly been dating for the past year, was no more than a product of his imagination.

Albert rose and started off toward the Village with no specific goal in mind, knowing that he would find adventure no matter where his feet led him, that there was danger and challenge on every block.

But for once his imagination seemed to fail him. College students and panhandlers remained exactly that, and try as he might, the grills of passing taxis refused to curl into tusked mouths. When he passed the Black Goat Tavern, the facade remained neon and glass, and the sign continued to flash "HERLIHY'S PUB," flickering and buzzing.

Impatiently, Albert turned left, walked down a dimly lit alley and continued toward the east side. This wasn't a route he'd traveled often, and the nature of the businesses behind the individual store fronts changed so often that each trip had been a journey of discovery.

A few minutes later, Albert knew that fate had directed his footsteps this evening, that the trials of the day had been designed to lead him to the greatest challenge he had ever faced. He was standing in front of a Greek restaurant whose specialties appeared, paradoxically, to be beef stroganoff and veal parmigiana, when he glanced across the street and picked out the nondescript sign identifying a dimly lit bar.

It was called *La Sangreal,* and Sir Albert turned the head of his tall white charger toward his destiny.

If anything, it was darker inside than on the street; the decor was hardwood with slick, synthetic coverings, browns and blacks and brass studs that glittered weirdly in the light cast by scattered red bulbs. Albert needed little of his imagination to superimpose an infernal overlay, peopling the shadows with imps and goblins and diminutive demons. Narrow booths divided the left wall, and far in the back a small, cavelike room was dimly visible through half-open sliding doors. A lair of trolls, no doubt.

The only conventional illumination was behind the bar, an oval of small bulbs flashing in sequence to counterfeit a constant clockwise flow. The oval was set around a narrow shelf on which a single object sat, perfectly centered, positively glowing. It was a wide rimmed cup with two delicately sculpted handles set directly across from one another. The design was simple, the lines clear and clean, and Albert knew what it was from the outset.

The Chalice, the Holy Grail, the cup from which Jesus drank at the Last Supper, spirited away by Joseph of Arimathea along with the spear that drew Christ's blood, protected through the ages by sinless guardians until one of them suffered a lapse and the holy objects were lost forever.

Or perhaps not forever after all.

He stepped through the door, his eyes sweeping from side to side. The bartender didn't even look in his direction, a tall, spindly man wearing a turtleneck, with unruly black hair that fell to his shoulderblades. There were few customers in view; only three of the eight booths were occupied, and the small, sexless figure slumped at the far end of the bar seemed to have fallen asleep.

Sir Albert entered, his sword concealed within the folds of his purple cloak, and approached the tavern keeper.

"What can I getcha?"

He sat at the bar, waiting for the head to settle on his mead, trying to act casual as his eyes hungrily caressed the shape of the Grail. Despite its simplicity, it was the most beautiful object he had ever beheld, and Sir Albert knew that he would not be able to rest until he had liberated it from this den of thieves and infidels.

By the time Albert accepted a second drink, the bar was considerably more crowded and noisy. The sleeper had stirred and shuffled out into the street, still not betraying his or her gender. He rarely touched alcohol and sipped diffidently, so intent upon his veneration of the sacred object suspended before him that he almost failed to notice when a familiar face entered.

It was the Black Knight, his deeply scarred cheek unmistakable even in the garish light. Although Albert didn't know the Black Knight's real name, he had from time to time noticed Rocco speaking to him in the lobby, and a short while later bored looking young women paid his landlord short visits. Albert had also seen him passing small packages to other unsavory looking individuals on the street. He was a large man, with hard eyes but a soft body, flesh that hung loosely from jowls and clutched him tightly around the waist.

His presence here only served to confirm Sir Albert's conviction that he had been drawn to this den of evil for a purpose, to rescue the Grail. He shifted slightly in order to study his presumed opponent and only then realized the Black Knight was not alone. A young woman stood at his side, long blonde hair, lightly freckled face, relatively plain features neither pretty nor unattractive, quite obviously not old enough to be legally served. She stood awkwardly, clearly uneasy, fingers clenched tightly around the straps of her shoulderbag, blinking in the uncertain light. There was a lack of focus in her eyes that made Sir Albert believe she'd been drugged.

A fair damsel to rescue as well as the Holy Grail. It seemed too good to be true. In fact, Albert's innate caution began to stir under his knightly persona, a silent plea for discretion that Sir Albert decided to heed. For the moment.

The bartender and the Black Knight spoke in hushed tones, and the few words Albert was able to overhear did not convey any real sense of what they were talking about, although the young woman was clearly part of it. A wooden cutting board with a small loaf of bread and a bar of pale cheese appeared; the Black Knight accepted it, then led his companion by the arm into the dark room in the rear. The bartender deserted his station long enough to slide the fanfold door shut, and Albert hastily turned his head to avoid being caught staring.

After a reasonable interval had passed to avert suspicion, he asked about a restroom and was directed to a small archway just this side of the partition. Although he lingered there for a few seconds, the rumbling conversation from the booths was loud enough to prevent him from hearing any sound from beyond the barrier, and the discovery that he really did need to relieve his bladder turned his attention elsewhere.

Sir Albert descended into the lower levels of Hades, avoiding a mop and bucket sitting on the landing; ignoring the magical incantations scribbled all over the walls, he reached the foot of the staircase. There were four doors here, all closed, and he opened the one marked "Hombres." It was a filthy hole, obviously used to imprison recalcitrant slaves or perhaps some monstrous ghoul or other inhuman beast.

He hesitated at the foot of the stairs. Two of the other doors were unmarked, and the first was locked as well. But when he tried the second, he found that it opened immediately. It was a closet, with a single bare lightbulb set in the ceiling, filled almost to overflowing with cartons of toilet tissue, paper towels, mops and brooms and other cleaning supplies, a complete porcelain sink with a large crack in the side, and a jumble of unrecognizable boxes, bags, and miscellany.

The sliding door was still closed when he returned to his seat at the bar, and it remained that way for the next two hours. Albert was working on his sixth beer; he didn't realize how lightheaded he was getting until he slid off the stool and almost lost his footing. This earned him a pointed look from the bartender, but he smiled and pulled enough cash from his pocket to cover the tab and a generous tip, dropped it on the bar.

"Guess I'm done for the night. One last visit before I go." He nodded toward the stairway.

The bartender shrugged, made the money disappear, and turned to another customer.

Albert had to brace himself with one hand against the wall on the way down, moving his feet slowly and methodically. His lack of experience with alcohol was taking its toll, and he felt incredibly sleepy. In Hombre territory, he stood with his forehead pressed against the wall while he used the urinal, then spent an unnecessarily long time washing his hands so that two other patrons had returned upstairs before he moved as quickly as possible to the storage closet and slipped inside.

The light went off as soon as the door closed, but Albert managed to reach the rear of the small room without making too big a racket, then sat down on the floor behind a block of crumbling cardboard boxes. Although he intended only to remain there quietly until after the bar was closed and everyone had left, he drifted off to sleep instead.

What woke him up was the clatter and bang when the mop and bucket were thrust inside the door. The wash of illumination barely registered before it was gone, the door slammed shut, and Albert sat in the renewed darkness, trying to remember where he was and why. Then Sir Albert reasserted himself.

There was no sound from outside, and the door opened easily. After a moment's thought, Albert paused to unscrew the mop handle, testing its balance. A crude staff at best, but it would have to do.

Although he'd planned to wait until the bartender was gone for the night, it occurred to him now that the bar must have a security system and he might well find himself locked in if he waited that long. So he crept cautiously up the stairs.

The sliding door was partly open, and there were voices from beyond, low, indistinct. The bar seemed otherwise deserted; only a single short fluorescent mounted above the front door was still lit. He moved silently across the floor, slipped behind the bar, and lifted the Grail down from its resting place with swift, smooth motions. It was cool and hard in his fingers, which tingled electrically, although that might have been his imagination.

The outside door was tantalizingly close, but Albert was cautious. He grabbed a towel from its hook behind the bar and gently wrapped the Chalice, tucking the ends in so that it made a tight bundle, then carried it around to the front of the bar, still listening for any sign that the voices from the rear might be coming closer.

And that's when he heard the young woman's voice.

It wasn't a scream, more a cry of protest, but the sound stirred Sir Albert's memory of the fair maiden he'd seen languishing in the clutches of the Black Knight. Without making a conscious decision to act, he set his prize down on the bar and approached the sliding door.

"C'mon, kid. You can't back out of this now." It was a deep, gravelly voice. The Black Knight.

An inarticulate response, low and intense, then louder. "Let go of my arm!"

Laughter, two men. Albert reached the edge of the door, slowly turned to look inside.

There were four round tables more or less evenly spaced around the room. The chairs were upside down on top of three of them, legs pointing toward the ceiling; the floor glittered wetly where it had been freshly mopped. Three figures sat at the fourth table, the Black Knight, the bartender, and the fair maiden. She appeared to be attempting to rise, but her forearm was held pinned by the Black Knight.

Sir Albert ignored the thin voice of panic and stepped around the door, the mop handle concealed behind his back.

"Let her go!" It would have been more effective if his voice hadn't wavered, but their reaction was immediate, three sets of eyes turning in his direction.

"What the . . . ?" The Black Knight was surprised, perhaps even amused, the woman confused; but the bartender was actively angry. He rose and stepped around the table, both hands clenched into fists.

"This little asshole was here earlier," he said hoarsely. "I wondered why I never saw him go out."

He kept coming, moving quickly, and Albert fought an automatic impulse to step back or, even better, turn and run. But Sir Albert overruled him and, just before the other man could strike, he pivoted and swung the mop handle in a short, vicious arc. Although the bartender attempted to duck away, he wasn't quick enough, and the shaft landed across forehead and cheek with a satisfying loud crack.

Albert moved forward as his opponent staggered back against one of the tables and jammed one end of the stick into the unprotected midsection. The table tilted to one side, and the bartender crashed to the floor, groaning.

All traces of amusement were gone as the Black Knight swore softly and rose to join the battle. Albert noticed that his staff had split with the second impact, but he raised it anyway, wondering whether Sir Albert had finally gotten in over his head. The heavier man approached cautiously, removing something from his pocket that clicked and then glittered in the dim light, the smooth edge of a highly sharpened blade.

"I'm gonna open you up, boy."

Albert was prepared to meet his own fate when someone else took a hand. The young woman had quietly gotten to her feet, lifted a chair above her head, and now she brought it crashing down against the Black Knight's back. It wasn't a disabling blow; she lacked the strength to do much direct damage. But it caused him to lose his footing on the slick floor, and he stumbled forward awkwardly.

Albert slammed the mop handle down across the crown
of his head and followed up by driving a foot directly into
the villain's groin. A foul blow, perhaps, but there were
so few vulnerable spots in a knight's armor, one took advantage of whichever offered itself. The Black Knight
was down, groaning, experiencing unfamiliar pain and
defeat.

"Let's get out of here!" It was the woman, her eyes
filled with concern, one hand on his arm. Conflicting
emotions whirled through Albert's mind—triumph, surprise, fear, wonder, confusion—and he made no effort to
resist as she pulled him out of the room.

But he did retain the presence of mind to grab the Grail
before allowing himself to be led out into the street.

It was cooler outside, and windy, and the change
brought him back to himself. "Where are we going?"

She shook her head, long blonde hair brushing her
shoulders. "I don't know. Away from here."

Albert nodded, to himself not the woman. "Where do
you live?"

"Nowhere. Not yet, I mean. I just got here a couple of
days ago."

"Got any money?"

"Some." Not enough, he guessed. Desperate, or a runaway, or perhaps just a dreamer Albert realized. He knew
about dreamers. Available prey for a fast-talking pimp, a
dose of some come-hither drug slipped into a free and
badly needed meal.

"I've got a place," he offered. "Not far from here."

She stopped, turned to face him, and he felt the touch
of her eyes searching his face, suspicion written broadly
across her own.

"There's a couch you could use," he added, though it
would need to be cleared off. "Until you find something
better, I mean."

The wariness didn't disappear, but it softened. "All
right. Thanks. What's your name?"

Sir Albert began weaving a new script, trying to decide
what happened *after* the damsel was no longer in distress,
but unbidden memories interfered—his inability to func-
tion at work, to deal with his bullying landlord—and for
the first time Albert resisted, and the knight shrank back
into oblivion.

"Albert. Albert Lance. Come on; it's this way."

But they made one brief stop first. As they were passing a row of trash cans set out for the morning pickup, Albert paused, weighed the Grail in one hand. Except it's not the Grail, he told himself, it's just a fancy glass cup used to decorate a lowlife bar. "No more fantasy," he said aloud, then smashed the bundle against the side of one of the trashcans. The glass shattered noisily and made a brittle sound when he dropped it in with the garbage.

Two hours later a homeless drug addict named Bohort was searching the garbage for anything he could salvage for use or sale when he found a fancy cup wrapped in a heavily stained towel. It was a real find, since the glassware seemed to be in perfect condition, without so much as a chip out of its many-faceted surface.

Bohort placed it carefully inside his grocery cart and walked off, taking the first steps on his own personal path to redemption.

PEACE ON EARTH

by Wendi Lee and Terry Beatty

Claude Meeks sat in the very last booth at the back of the dimly lit bar and stared glumly into his scotch neat. Through a blue haze of smoke, he watched Wally, the Triangle Tap's bartender, pour a whiskey on the rocks and shove it across the bar to the thin, fortyish waitress, who brought the tumbler to an occupied table up front. An anemic version of "Hark! The Herald Angels Sing" played over and over again on the jukebox, which only depressed Claude even more.

"You haven't even touched your drink, Claude." He looked up into the face of Joy, the waitress. She had not been aptly named, he thought. Her frosted curls sprang out from her head, independent of one another. Her bony shoulders seemed more like a clothes hanger for her blouse. But her smile was kind.

Claude tried to smile back. "I hate this time of year."

"Most people do," she replied, shifting her empty drinks tray from one hip to the other. "There isn't much happiness in the holidays anymore."

"Is your kid looking forward to Christmas?"

A troubled look flickered across Joy's face, but she covered it with a sad smile. "I hope so. You know that Joe left us last month." Wally signaled to her, and she excused herself to wait on a new customer.

All the regulars knew Joe, Joy's fourth husband. He'd been a Triangle regular too, before he married Joy. Claude himself was a bachelor. He would have liked to have gotten married, but the right girl had never come along. Now he was too set in his ways for any woman to put up with him. But it meant loneliness for him as well.

When his mother became sick, he took care of her until she passed away last year just before Christmas. Now there was no one, no sisters or brothers, not even a cousin or aunt, for Claude to spend the holidays with.

Several years ago, with the onset of the recession, he had lost his bookkeeping job and had been doing temp work ever since. It paid the bills, but just barely, and there was precious little left over at the end of the month. Still, he managed to scrape together enough coin to stop into the Triangle now and then. At least when his mother was alive, her social security check had supplemented his meager income.

Claude had nothing to look forward to this holiday except a can of baked beans and a small ham. He wondered what Joy and her kid had to look forward to—she couldn't make much money working in a place like this.

Claude glanced at the TV that was perched in a corner of the ceiling above the bar. More depressing was the network news that showed footage of one of the civil wars that had broken out in Eastern Europe, people being shot, people being herded into a concentration camp, families torn apart and left homeless and hungry. He shook out a cigarette and lit it, watching the blue smoke curl up and join the stale air that had hung there for decades.

Joy had come up to his table again. He looked at her. "Jesus, I'm tired of hearing about people behaving like that," he said, pointing at the TV screen. "It's no better here, with people robbin' and killin' each other. Why *can't* we have peace on Earth? What would it take anyway?"

She shook her head, a small smile on her face. "Claude, you're a dreamer. Want another scotch?" She knew he never drank more than one, but she asked out of habit.

He shrugged. "I just wish I had a simple solution to all our problems." Smiling and shaking her head, she went away. Claude hunched over his drink and took another sip, savoring the feeling it gave him when he swallowed. Liquid warmth.

A double scotch was placed next to the one he was enjoying. Claude looked up to see Joy standing beside his table again. He knew Wally was not a guy who bought his customers drinks on the house, even though it was almost Christmas and even though Claude was a regular. He also knew that Joy had to pay out of her own pocket for any drinks she wanted to give to the regulars.

"Joy, I appreciate the gesture, but—"

She held up her hand to silence him, then jerked her thumb in the direction of the bar. "I only wish I could take the credit," she replied with a slight smirk. "It's from the guy in the white suit."

Raising his eyebrows, Claude thanked Joy. Taking advantage of his sudden good fortune, he finished off the first scotch and pulled the second one closer. Looking up, he noticed the stranger was looking at him. He nodded his thanks and brought his shotglass up in a toasting gesture. Much to his dismay, the stranger, who was inappropriately attired in an ice cream suit and Panama straw hat, got up and came over to his booth. Up close, he was a peculiar-looking man with alabaster skin and eyes the color of copper.

"I hope you don't mind my buying you a drink," the stranger said as he slid into the booth across the table from Claude. "I overheard your comments."

"Thank you," Claude replied, not knowing what else to say.

"This has been a hard year for quite a lot of people," the man said. He had taken his hat off and laid it on the table beside his own glass, which contained a bright green liquor, most likely chartreuse. It was an odd choice, but everything about the stranger was eccentric. "My name is Mr. Gabriel."

What's this, Claude thought, an angel for Christmas?

After introducing himself and shaking the cool, dry hand of his new acquaintance, Claude drank half of his scotch. Not used to more than one scotch, the effects of the second began to work their magic.

"I overheard you asking why peace could not be achieved here—on Earth." Gabriel had placed an odd emphasis on the word Earth, but Claude accepted his benefactor's statement without comment, only nodding in agreement. "Well, there is a way."

Claude leaned over the table, deciding to humor this peculiar fellow. "Well, suppose you tell me."

Gabriel looked around to see whether anyone was eavesdropping. His white suit and pale skin were such a contrast to the dark bar that they stood out like a neon light, especially to someone who was in the act of downing the equivalent of three scotches.

"I have the answer right here." Gabriel patted his breast pocket gently.

Even mildly buzzed, Claude was still dubious. Gabriel seemed to be just a well-dressed, possibly wealthy, eccentric. "Come on," Claude scoffed, taking another sip of scotch. "Peace isn't that easy."

"Oh, but it is." Gabriel withdrew a small black object the size of a ring box and flipped it open. In the center was a small red button. "You just press the button and there will be no more wars, no more hunger, no more pain. Everyone will be equal."

Claude had had enough. He finished off his scotch and said, "Well, that's an interesting solution, Gabriel or whatever your name is, and I wish you the best with your device, but I'd better go now."

The stranger reached out and grabbed Claude's sleeve. "Oh, but you don't understand. I want to give this to you. Call it a gift. You can be the one who brings peace to Earth."

Claude just wanted to go home and have some dinner before he became too woozy from the liquor. He started to get up, but Gabriel's grip was strong and Claude didn't want to cause a scene.

"Take this and use it. But beware, there are those who want things to continue the way they have always been." Gabriel glanced over his shoulder toward the front of the bar. "Press the button on Christmas Eve and make a new start in the world."

"Look, I don't want to offend you," Claude replied, "but I find all of this a little hard to believe." He was aware that he was slurring his words. He really had to get out of there.

Gabriel looked up at him with an urgent expression. "What have you got to lose?" He pressed the small black box into Claude's hand. "At least you can believe that peace is possible, even for a little while. And if it works, you'll be a hero."

As he locked eyes with the stranger, Claude began to think that just maybe there was something to this after all. "So who are these people I'm suppose to look out for?"

"There is an organization made up of those who don't want change for the better. They thrive on violence and the status quo. They have been following me, and although I've lost them for the time being, they have ways of finding me. That is why I pass this gift on to you."

Claude nodded again. He had met people like that. Mr. Gabriel stiffened, then hissed, "You see the two who just walked in? The ones dressed in black?"

Puzzled, Claude nodded. Mr. Gabriel had been facing him and could not see the front of the bar, yet he had described the two men perfectly. They were tall and wore similar black trenchcoats and hats. Claude remembered that there was a mirror on the back wall, and decided that Gabriel had probably caught a glimpse of their reflection.

"I will distract them while you slip out the back. Get away from here as fast as you can. And just remember," Gabriel added as he stood up, "don't use the device until Christmas Eve, midnight."

Tomorrow night. Claude nodded his understanding and watched the strange man walk toward the front of the bar. As casually as possible, Claude slid out of his booth, left a tip for Joy, and slipped out the back door. The last he saw of Mr. Gabriel, he was walking out the front and the two men were hurrying after him.

It was drizzling outside—no white Christmas for this town. Claude pulled up his collar and glanced around to make sure no one was waiting to waylay him. He felt the hardness of the black box in his pocket, and he squeezed it until its sharp edges dug into his palm. When he got to the mouth of the alley, he paused and peeked around the corner. Gabriel was nowhere in sight, and neither were the two men in black. Behind him, he heard a hiss. It made him jump, but when he turned around, it was only Joy. "You startled me," he said in a low voice.

"Claude," she replied with a frown, "what's going on? Those men that came in were asking about you." She was standing in the rain without a coat, clutching the drinks tray to her chest and shivering.

He felt his heart leap into his throat. "Did you tell them anything?" He noticed that Joy was looking at him with curiosity and, was that excitement in her eyes?

She shook her head, then made a face. "I didn't, but before I could stop Wally, he'd given 'em your name and address. You'd better not go home tonight."

Claude closed his eyes and groaned, leaning against the slick, wet brick building. "What am I gonna do? I can't afford a motel."

The sound of something metallic jingling made him open his eyes. Joy was holding a set of keys extended to him, and she had a shy look. "I wouldn't normally do this, Claude," she said, blushing. "But I've known you for over ten years. I'm a pretty good judge of character. I don't know what sort of trouble you've got into, but you're welcome to stay the night at my place. On the couch." She gave him the address.

Claude took the keys and thanked her before she went back inside. Joy lived on Vanguard Street on the second floor of a shabby utilitarian apartment building. The elevator was broken, and looked as if it had been broken since the building had opened, and the white tiled stairwell smelled of a mixture of urine and antiseptic. The halls of her floor smelled of cooked cabbage, but when Claude opened the door to Joy's apartment, he could smell freshly baked bread and cinnamon. Joy had warned him that she would be creeping in around two in the morning with her sleepy kid. Her downstairs neighbor, an elderly woman, had been caring for the boy while she was at work.

After turning on the orange glass lamp, a leftover from the early seventies, Claude looked around. Two gifts wrapped in wrinkled but colorful paper sat under a tiny artificial tree perched on top of the old Motorola television set in the corner. Claude wandered into the kitchen to get a soda from the refrigerator and found himself confronted with drawings done by a child's hand. There were pictures of zebras and giraffes and flowers and houses and stick figures that looked like alien beings rather than real people.

Back in the living room, he sat on the avocado-colored couch and took the black box from his pocket and examined it. It puzzled him that he couldn't find a seam or a hinge, and when he tried to open it, it remained locked. Claude frowned and tried to recall how the stranger had

opened it, but he couldn't think of any particularly unusual movements.

After a few minutes, he jammed it back in his coat
pocket and lay down to rest. When he closed his eyes, the
earlier part of the evening came to mind, and he kept running bits of the conversation through his mind. The
scotch still pounded in his head, making it difficult to
think straight, but he did begin to wonder how he had
ever fallen for the stranger's outlandish talk about the
pressing of a button being the solution to the world's
problems.

The smell of eggs, bacon, and toast woke him up.
Claude opened one eye only to see a giant eye. He sat
bolt upright, feeling as if he'd left half his head back on
the pillow. Groaning, he looked down and realized that
Joy's son was staring up at him, a cheap plastic magnifying glass held up to his face. The giant eyeball.

"Mama, I waked the man up." The three-year-old tod-
dled toward the kitchen. Joy peeked around the wall of
the kitchen and grinned. "I see. How are you feeling this
morning, Claude?"

"Like a bunch of ball bearings are rolling around in my
head."

She chuckled, then ducked back into the kitchen to flip
the eggs. "You've never been much of a drinker until last
night."

Claude shuffled into the kitchen and watched Joy drain
the bacon.

"Will you butter the toast before it gets cold?" He did
as she asked, then brought the plate of toast and the juice
glasses over to the small, battered kitchen table in the
dining nook.

Breakfast was a series of mishaps, starting when
Tommy knocked his juice over and ending with toast and
eggs scattered on the drab kitchen floor. Joy seemed to
spend more time trying to get food into her kid than into
herself. Finally, when Tommy had finished and gone back
into the living room to watch cartoons, Joy turned to
Claude and asked, "So who was your friend last night?"

He shook his head. "I've never seen him before."

"He seemed to know you."

"Yeah, well, I'm not sure what to think." He told her
the story and brought out the small black box. Thought-

fully, she took it from him and turned it over in her hands. "World peace at the push of a button? Sounds a little too easy to be true. This is just some kind of practical joke." She tried to pry the box apart several times before giving up and handing it back to him.

"Thanks for the couch and the meal," Claude said, standing up. "And especially the company."

"Anytime," she replied with a smile. For a brief moment, he could see the young carefree girl beneath her weary exterior. As he moved toward the door, she called, "Look, I don't know what you're doing for Christmas Eve, but after we close the bar, you're welcome to celebrate with us this evening." Rolling her eyes, she added, "Wally won't close the Triangle until nine tonight, so it'll be a late celebration."

He paused, hand on the doorknob, and nodded. "I'd like that."

As Claude neared his apartment building, he became uneasy. He looked around, half expecting to see the men from last night waiting for him, but there was no one around. If he didn't have the box, he might have begun to doubt that last night had ever happened. Cautiously making his way up to his apartment, Claude could almost feel that they had been there earlier. Inside his apartment, he hurriedly showered and changed, then stuffed the ham in a small sack and left. Claude spent the rest of the day wandering around, trying to find a gift for Tommy. It would hardly be right for him to go back there tonight empty-handed, especially when a child was waiting for Santa Claus to bring him something nice.

He found a pop-up book of trains for the boy, and just as he was leaving the dime store, he found a necklace made of shells that he thought Joy would like. The day passed quickly when he was thinking of other people, but pretty soon his hand went to his pocket and found the black box. He had made up his mind that if he could get the box open tonight, he would press the button. What did he have to lose?

A little after nine, Claude went up to Joy's apartment. Standing outside her door, Claude inhaled the scent of sage and pumpkin pie which hung heavily in the air. He could hear "Frosty the Snowman" blasting from the

Motorola, and Tommy's childish voice. "Mama! Someone knocked."

Inside, Tommy was in his pajamas already. Joy thanked Claude for the ham and gave him a glass of red wine. Ten minutes later, they had dinner.

"Those men came in to the Triangle today," she said as they cleared the remains of the pie off the table. Claude paused, his heart beginning to pound. Silently, he told himself to calm down. "What did they want?"

She shrugged. "They wanted to know if we had any idea where you might go today. They sounded pretty upset." She walked into the kitchen and dumped the dishes in the hot soapy water. "But you know, there was something about them that gave me the creeps." She turned around to face Claude, her arms crossed. "Do you still have that box?"

He nodded and took it out of his jacket pocket. Joy took a steak knife from a drawer to her left and said, "Let's try to open it."

Together they went into the living room. Tommy was glued to the television as Rudolph danced across the screen, his red nose reminding Claude of the button in the box.

"This is silly," Claude said after five minutes of trying to pry the box open. "Why am I grasping at this foolish notion that pressing a button can save the world?" He tossed the box onto the coffee table. As if jarred by the shock, the box popped open. Joy and Claude stared at it, then at each other. Joy reached out for it, but a knock at the door brought her to her feet.

As she walked to the door and opened it, she said, "I wonder who that can be. I'm not expecting anyone tonight—Claude!"

He stood up and turned around to face the two men in black. Joy had backed toward Claude, then scooted around him to gather Tommy up in her arms.

"Mama," the little boy said as he rubbed his eyes and yawned, "I'm sleepy. Can we have the rest of Christmas tomorrow?"

"You can't just come barging into my house," Joy said with a slight quiver in her voice. "Please leave before I call the police."

Claude had picked up the box and was concealing it in his palm.

"We don't mean to harm anyone," the shorter of the two men said. The brim of his hat was pulled so low that Claude couldn't see his eyes, and he found it unnerving. "We're here to collect the box. Hand it over, please."

Claude shook his head. "I don't have it anymore," he lied. "I threw it away."

The other man stepped toward him in a threatening manner. Claude quickly held the box out, his finger poised over the button. The shorter man grabbed his companion's sleeve and said, "Don't push that button until you hear what we have to say." He paused.

"I'm listening," Claude said.

"The man you met yesterday evening, the one who calls himself Mr. Gabriel, is not of this world," the man began. "Each year, on this date, he comes to Earth and selects someone such as yourself."

"What do you mean by 'such as myself'?" Claude asked.

"Someone who cares about the way the world is, someone who wants an easy answer to peace. He gives him or her the black box and says that it will bring peace to your world." Again, he paused.

"And will it?" Joy asked.

The speaker nodded. "Oh, yes. It will. But so far, we have been lucky enough to find the keeper of the box in time."

"Why do you want to stop me from using it? What's wrong with peace on Earth?" Claude was following the speaker so far, but he sensed that there was more.

"Mr. Meeks, have you ever wondered why Mr. Gabriel, as he calls himself, asks you not to push the button until the next night?"

"Well, he didn't tell me," Claude explained "It was more of a suggestion. He thought it would be really nice if everyone woke up on Christmas Day and the world was better."

The men smiled sadly. "But you see, Mr. Meeks, no one would wake up tomorrow morning. What you hold in your hand is a device so powerful that it would destroy all life on this planet in a matter of seconds. Peace would truly be achieved, but at what cost?"

Claude stared at the harmless-looking box in his palm. "How do I know you're telling me the truth?" he asked. "You're not really from another planet, you're both working for some top secret agency for another government, aren't you?"

The short man shrugged. "I have told you the truth. If you choose not to believe it, then we have failed."

Claude shifted from his right leg to his left. "Aw, this is crazy. This box isn't a bomb, and this button isn't going to bring peace to the world or destroy it. This is all some elaborate joke, isn't it?" He looked over at Joy. "Should I push the button? Should I risk it?"

Joy looked up at him, her eyes wide, a puzzled expression on her face. "I don't know, Claude." She shook her head and brought her free hand up to stroke Tommy's hair as she rocked him from side to side.

He rested his finger lightly on the button, then hesitated as he watched Tommy asleep on Joy's shoulder, his mouth slightly open, his chubby hand gripping his mother's sweater. "What would you do?" he whispered. "Would you risk it to give your son a better life?"

Joy closed her eyes briefly, her cheek resting against her son's curly hair. "I'm not sure I like the alternative if these men are right." Then she opened her eyes and looked straight at Claude. "But you do what you think is right. This is not my decision, Claude, it's yours."

The men had not moved; they stood unnaturally still. Claude caught a glimpse of the taller one's eyes, mostly hidden beneath the rim of his hat. He could have sworn they were glowing. He let out a great sigh, then handed the box to the men. The tall one took it and carefully closed the cover.

"Thank you, Mr. Meeks. You made the right decision."

The shorter one spoke, "You were right about one thing. This was a joke of sorts—Mr. Gabriel's idea of a holiday prank. Some higher life forms have an unfortunate notion of what constitutes humor."

After the men left the apartment, as abruptly as they had entered it, Joy put Tommy to bed, then came back into the living room where Claude stood looking out the window at the city.

Joy came back in. After a long silence, she asked, "Was that your Christmas wish, world peace?"

Claude shook his head. "It would be nice, but my second wish was to find someone to spend Christmas with."

She put her arm around his waist, and they held each other as they looked out the window and up at the stars.

A BREEZE FROM A
DISTANT SHORE

by Peter Crowther

If life can be said to be any one thing, then surely it could be thus defined: a long, sometimes interminable series of arrivals and departures.

   Comings and goings.

   On this brief trip to the limits of human experience, we are concerned with only one of these.

   The leaving.

   If, as all the best ghost stories from our childhood would have us believe, there are occurrences that take place at the very edges of our perceptions—and even more events just waiting to occur—then consider this:

   Always settle your bill while you have the time to do so. Because, afterward, it may be too late.

   Unless you happen to be ... in The Twilight Zone.

Thomas Danby sat in his attic room overlooking the street, feeling older than he had ever felt before ... and older than he might ever feel again.

He had turned into a teenager around the same time that spring had turned into summer, when the skeletal branches of the trees had sprouted green and the sun had shimmered bright across the land.

Any birthday is a special time. But the first day of teenage is another thing altogether, a way-marker on the route from adolescence to adulthood, when the world finally and reluctantly unfolds its pastel petals and exposes the gaudy promise of the future.

But this year the birthday messages had included one he had not bargained for. A card. A card for *his father.*

This card was ominously lacking in good wishes, totally devoid of Gary Larson's wacked-out cartoons. It came in a small brown envelope from FOREST PLAINS GENERAL HOSPITAL, and the message it carried was brief: The tumor was inoperable. It was, the card concluded, only a matter of time.

Hey, but tell your son ... Happy Birthday!

The summer had dragged on and on, baking the ground by the river and alongside the tracks with a special ferocity, turning the pavement around the mall into a hot tar covering that steamed like the fudge sauce on Pop Kleat's sundaes.

Jack Danby had stayed around the house. Doctor's orders.

At first, the big man's resolve had been bigger than the fist-sized growth that pulsed in his stomach. But soon the roles reversed.

Soon Jack's resolve was exposed for what it was: a collection of words and bluster, smart-aleck remarks and hollow bravado, nothing more. No match for a living thing that grew and strengthened during every minute of every day.

And as the optimism faded from Jack's eyes and the doctor's visits grew more regular, Thomas had become increasingly aware that the swelling in his father's stomach had begun to leak a special poison. One they had not bargained for.

And now the dog days of summer had fallen silent, and the trees had turned their leafy covers into burnished golds, reds, and browns, and the sun had started wearing a shimmering rim of orange around its core.

Everything was tired now.

Everything wanted to rest.

And in the Danby household, the rest arrived at last, falling like a dust sheet over everything they knew and held dear.

Jack Danby had breathed his last breath in the world just three days ago ... just sucked in, his face lined with pain, the skin stretched over his head like Egyptian papyrus and the remaining tufts of thin, wispy hair clustered about its top like tumbleweeds ... and stopped. Dead.

Thomas' mother told him that the pain had fallen away like rain off the roof.

Replaying it all in his head, staring out of his window at the steadily darkening landscape of Walton Flats, Thomas Danby let his eyes roam across the symmetrical sprawl of green lawns and garage forecourts, watching the day take its course and the afternoon light lose its glare.

Across the house tops opposite, the fields rolled down to the railroad tracks and then across the valley bottom to the hills that surrounded the town. Everything looked quiet.

Peaceful.

A voice called out. "Tom?" it shouted, and he heard it as though through water or locked inside a dream. Thomas got to his feet wearily and leaned up against the glass so he could see down onto the street beneath. There was a man standing beside a red Camaro, mopping his forehead with a hank of white material. "Tommy? You up there?"

Tommy opened the window and called down, "Hey, Mr. Macready, how's things?"

"Things are just fine with me, boy," came the answer. The man rubbed the handkerchief around his face and squinted up at the attic window. "More's the point, though, how're things with you?"

"I'm okay, Mr. Macready," Thomas said. "We're both okay."

"Your mom?"

"She's fine. You paying a visit?"

Mr. Macready nodded, folding the handkerchief carefully with both hands. "Thought I'd just call round and pay some respects to your pa, Tom. Your mom in?" He thrust the handkerchief into his pants pocket and lifted his belt over his ample stomach.

Thomas shrugged. "I guess."

"I banged on the door a couple times but . . ." His voice trailed off like the hum of a summer fly.

"Hold on and I'll come down and let you in."

Mr. Macready nodded as Thomas turned around from the window. "I 'preciate that," he heard the man say, "I 'preciate that."

Stepping out of his attic room—his study, is what he

liked to call it—Thomas was suddenly aware of the time of day. The staircase was cloaked in darkness, twisting away to his right and dropping steeply to the next landing.

Thomas took a couple of steps and stopped. The house was completely silent. *Awful* silent.

"Mom?"

No answer.

"Mom . . . you down there?"

His parents' bedroom door opened suddenly, and a thin, watery light spilled out onto the landing. "What is it?" Clara Danby asked in a weak voice.

Thomas realized that he had been holding his breath and, when he spoke, the words tumbled out like loose change dropping from a hole in his pants pocket. "Mr. Macready. He's at the door. Downstairs. Says he's come to pay his respects."

The figure of Thomas' mother came into view, pushing a strand of corn-colored hair off her forehead. "Oh, Lord, whatever next!" she said to her feet. She looked up at Thomas. "You tell him I was in?"

Thomas frowned. "I didn't know. He said he wants to come in anyhow."

"I'll go down," she said.

"You want me to—"

"No, just leave us be." She walked along the landing and started down the stairs to the ground floor.

Thomas sat down on the attic stairs and rubbed at a scuff mark on his sneakers. He heard his mother opening the door, heard the *squeeeak* of the screen door and then heard her speak. "Hello, Pat," she said. "You come to see Jack?"

"Clara," said Mr. Macready. "Clara, how *are* you?"

"I'm fine, Pat, just fine. Come on in."

"If I'm imposing, Clara, then—"

"No, you're not imposing at all, Pat. I was just resting is all. Come on in. Jack's in the front room."

The door slammed, and Thomas heard footsteps walking along the hall. The footsteps stopped at the front room door, and Mr. Macready cleared his throat. Thomas imagined that the fat man would be adjusting his suit and necktie as though he were going to see the President on the White House lawn.

Then his mother opened the door.

"There he is," said Mr. Macready, his voice hushed to a whisper. "There he *is*." The footsteps started up again, into the room, and the door closed.

Thomas felt, for one brief moment, the coldness of the grave come seeping out of that room and along the hall . . . up the stairs to the first floor landing and then up the attic stairs, where it spooled and wafted around his legs and feet like strands of sea anemone waving in the water. He lifted his feet and shuffled on his backside, back to his study.

He had come up here in the first place to get as far away from that room as was possible. It spooked him. Having his dead father lying there in his coffin, stretched out in their front room as though he were just having a doze . . . passing the time until dinner was ready and they'd all just sit down and eat. Just the way they had always done before . . .

He shook his head and listened. He could hear muted conversation drifting up through the house, could hear it, the sound of it, but couldn't make out the actual words. Thomas stood up and crept down the stairs quietly, avoiding those that he knew creaked when you stood on them.

He got to the first floor landing and tip-toed along to the stairs. He went down three or four and then sat down again. Now he could hear.

"—look no different, Clara."

"I know."

"I mean *no* different. It's downright amazing what those folks can do. Oh . . . I mean—"

"I know what you mean, Pat, and I thank you. I really do."

"No call for thanks, Clara. I'm just saying the truth is all."

"I know that."

"So, how *are* things?"

"Things?"

"You know, money things? You okay for money, Clara? You don't have no debts or anything I can help out with?"

"It's real nice of you to ask, Pat, but we're okay. Really."

"Really?"

"Really."

"So . . . so Jack left you okay?"

"Jack saw to everything, yes."

"Glad to hear it, glad to hear it."

There was a pause before Mr. Macready spoke again.

"Mind you, it's only what you'd expect from Jack Danby. Yessir, that is some man lying there, Clara."

"I know that."

"Yessir."

Thomas leaned his head on his knees and stared into some dark unfathomable distance.

"How *is* Tom?" The question sounded as though it had followed on naturally from what they were talking about . . . as though they could both see him sitting there on the stairs.

"Tom's fine, he's doing just fine."

"Glad to hear it," said Mr. Macready. "He's a good boy."

"Why, thank you."

"No, I mean it, Clara. A good boy."

Another silence.

When his mother spoke again, Thomas realized she had moved her position in the room. Moving around his father. Maybe they were circling him like a pair of satellites.

"It was bad for Tom, Pat," she said. "Real bad."

"Bad? In what way was it bad, Clara?"

"Oh, I don't know. It's bad losing your father, of course, but this was different. Tommy lost Jack a long time ago. A long time before . . . you know."

There was no response to this.

"He just withdrew . . . pulled himself into himself. You know what I'm saying?"

"I can imagine," Mr. Macready said. "It can't be easy."

"It wasn't. They were hardly talking to each other way before the end. It was like . . . like Jack resented Tommy somehow. Resented his health . . . resented the fact that Tommy was going to be around after he had gone." There was a thud, someone hitting something. Then, "Am I making any sense, Pat?"

Thomas twisted his feet so they were pointing at each

other and tried to stand one foot on the other so that it made one foot without any overlaps, staring at them.

Mr. Macready must have nodded to that because Thomas' mother spoke again without trying to explain what she had meant. "He hasn't cried."

"Tommy? He hasn't—"

"Not a tear. Not a single tear. He just sits up there in his study—he calls it a study, you know, the attic—and stares out of the window. Lord alone knows what he sees out there."

"Has he been down to see . . ." Mr. Macready's voice trailed off.

"No. Not once. I asked him if he wanted to come and see his father—I was standing here, right beside Jack, and Tom was at the door over there—but he wouldn't. He wouldn't come in. Wouldn't set a foot in here. It was like . . . like he had the plague or—"

"Now, Clara . . ."

"Oh, Pat, I don't know. I really don't."

"You want I should have a word with him, you know, talk to—"

"Oh, no. No, Pat. If he does it, it'll have to be in his own good time."

His own good time.

Thomas stood up and crept back up the stairs, back to the safety of his own domain, a place secure against parents and well-meaning friends . . . a place untroubled by death and decay and formaldehyde.

In front of his window eyrie, high, high above the town, his elbows on the ledge, Tom watched the night come. He saw it start on the hills, at first a shadow of the sun itself, setting for the day, but then the tendrils of twilight snaked out and down the slopes and across the fields to the railroad tracks. Then the station and the grain silos up in old Mr. Jorgensson's field, then the far end of Main Street, now bejeweled with tiny streetlamps.

Deep in the bowels of the house something moved and shuddered through the interjoining floors and woodwork. Thomas turned around and suddenly noticed how dark his room had become. He walked across to his table and turned on the lamp, feeling a sharp reassurance as his eyes saw the familiar objects scattered around him. Comic books, an empty glass holding the trapped white ghost of old milk, a plate with a sprinkling of cookie crumbs, pencils, eraser . . .

"Tom?"

His mother's voice.

"Tom, can you come down here?"

He walked to the door and shouted back down the stairs. "What is it, Mom?"

"Mr. Macready's going now, Tom."

Thomas didn't say anything. His heart beat faster as he tried to face going downstairs and facing old, fat Mr. Macready. To face having his hair tousled roughly or his back slapped firmly or being told to *take good care of your mom, now.*

There was a flutter of conversation that Thomas could not make out, but he recognized the tones. His mother's firmness and Mr. Macready's reasoning. Then, "Bye, Tommy," in Mr. Macready's familiar nasal twang. "You take good care of your mom, now, you hear?"

"I will, Mr. Macready," he shouted back. "Bye!"

The front door slammed, and Thomas went back into his room and over to the window. While he had been away, the night had arrived in earnest, stealing what little remained of the light and storing it away for another day.

Down on the street, Mr. Macready opened the door of his Camaro and waved up at the window. Thomas waved back and kept waving until the car had moved off and its taillights twinkled in the distance where Sycamore Drive joined Beech Street. At night, with his head flat against the window, Thomas could see the far-off lights of the cars on the Interstate, traveling to places and from places.

He heard his mother on the stairs to the attic and turned around to see her coming through his door. "Tom, I declare I don't know what's gotten into you, I truly don't."

"What did I do?"

She moved into the room and sat down on the chair beside his table. "You know what, young man. You should have said good-bye to our guest."

"I did," Thomas argued, hearing the petulance in his own voice. "I shouted to him—"

"Yes, you shouted to him. Wouldn't it have been a sight more polite to come down and pass the time of day?"

Thomas shrugged. "I was busy."

"Busy doing what?"

"Things. Just things, Mom."

An uneasy silence fell between them, and Thomas dropped his head forward and looked at his sneakers. Even *they* seemed embarrassed. He felt his mother watching him, then he felt her shake her head and sigh and, lifting his eyes without moving his head, he saw her feet move across the room and back to the stairs. "I'm making us some sandwiches," she called back to him. "I didn't want to cook anything. Big day tomorrow."

Thomas couldn't quite see the connection between the two points, but he let it go. "Great," he said, though the tone of his voice did not match the words themselves.

Big day tomorrow.

That was true. Tomorrow they were burying his father. *Planting him,* Johnny Margulies had said. *Hey, Danby . . . when they planting your old man?* Thomas had shrugged at that one, delivered loudly in the school cafeteria, and wandered the full length of the hall to a table at the far end, where he sat alone and played with his food. He had felt the snickers traveling behind him and stopping just short of his back, where they whispered and chuckled cruelly.

"You sleeping up there again tonight?" Clara Danby shouted.

"Yeah. I guess."

"Your bag still up there?"

Thomas looked around and saw the crumpled sleeping bag sitting over by a pile of comic books. "Yeah."

"You want to come down and get your food?"

He stood up. "On my way."

That night, Thomas left the window open.

He curled up in his sleeping bag and read a Marvel Masterworks hardback collection of old Fantastic Four stories, readily identifying with Johnny Storm. His Uncle Matthew had bought it for him for his eleventh birthday, and Thomas had already read the stories several times. He particularly liked the mole men.

When he had turned out his light, he lay staring at the night outside the window, wondering if there really were such creatures. And, if there were, did they ever burrow up into a cemetery?

Out on the highway a horn sounded sharply and then dopplered away into some distance or other. Was it coming or going? Where was it coming from? Where was it going to?

Questions.

He shuffled around and eventually fell into a troubled sleep in which mole men burrowed into his father's coffin, and when they splintered it open, there was only a big pulsating lump, like a misshapen potato, with his father's eyes staring out of it. *Tommy,* the eyes said, *I'm sorry.*

When he woke up, Thomas wondered why.

He had heard something.

What was it?

He turned over and pulled his right arm from inside the bag. The luminous display on his watch said 2:17. He listened. The house was quiet. So why was he awake?

Then there it was again.

Movement.

Was it his mother? Going to the bathroom, perhaps? He waited to hear the cistern empty and refill, but there was nothing. All was quiet beneath him.

Then, again. Another movement.

Slithering.

The sound of material being trailed.

It lasted for only a few seconds, but he heard it.

Thomas pulled both arms back inside the bag and slid the zipper up until it touched his chin. He shivered and waited.

Nothing.

Outside, a soft wind had risen. He watched it tug at the open window, watched the glass shimmer silently to the window's gentle but insistent movements. Then the wind made a noise, only it didn't come from the open window. It came from the open door that led onto the attic stairs.

The noise was unmistakable.

It was a sigh.

And it was followed by another slither of material.

Thomas knew what it was. It was his father. He had pulled himself out of his wooden box with the mock-gold handles and had dragged his stiff legs out of the room and up the stairs.

Maybe he had already called on his mother.

Thomas' heart was beating like a bongo drum, now.

Maybe he had crawled into her room and up onto her bed while she slept and he—*it!*—had opened his mouth beside her and let the cancer out. Maybe a piece of it was on his mother's pillow right now, skittering toward her, stealthily . . . heading for her open mou—

Thomas pulled down the zipper and threw back the open bag. He stood up and pulled on his jeans. As he fastened the buttons, he felt less vulnerable. He shrugged his way into his sweater and felt another degree better.

The noise had stopped now.

He went to switch on the table lamp and then thought better of it. The light would only expose him to anything that was coming up the stairs. Right now, he had night-sight. That made him and whatever it was even. And if it *was* his father then Thomas had the distinct advantage. *He* had speed.

He was alive.

He walked slowly to the door and edged his head around so that he could see the stairs. They were empty.

Everything below was in darkness.

Thomas had asked his mom repeatedly to leave the light on, but she had said that it was a waste of electricity. And they couldn't afford to waste money any more. *Not now your father is*— She always stopped herself before she said it. The word.

Dead.

Keeping his feet to the edges of the stairs, Thomas crept down. As soon as the first floor landing came into view, he stopped and waited for any sign of movement.

There wasn't any.

He moved forward and down.

The landing was quiet and empty.

Thomas moved along to his parents' bedroom, now his mother's room. The door was partly open. Thomas pushed it and strained his eyes.

It was darker in there than it was on the landing. She always slept with her curtains drawn against the night, and the blackness that sat around her bed seemed impenetrable. He looked quickly behind to make sure nothing was edging its way toward him and then took one step into the room. Then another. Then one more.

He saw the shape of his mother curled on the bed. She was on top of the sheets, still wearing her clothes. Her

face was half into the pillow, and her breathing was halfway to a snore.

Maybe that was what he had heard.

Certainly there was no evidence of any intruder.

Could his father be an intruder in his own house?

Thomas frowned.

Could Jack Danby, dead or alive, be an intruder in his
own wife's bedroom?

A sudden vision flashed in his head. In it, his father
was roughhousing his mother, and she was laughing fit to
burst. Thomas' father was staring at Thomas over her
shoulder, and he was laughing, too.

Thomas shook his head.

The vision cleared, and the sound came again.

This time it was clear. It came from downstairs.

He backed out of his mother's bedroom and pulled the
door closed behind him.

Somehow, Thomas was feeling not so scared any more.
A deep but significant part of himself was telling him the
sound was nothing. But that same part was telling him to
check it out. *Check it out, Tommy . . . check it out all the
way.*

He reached the ground floor and stood for a minute or
so, his head cocked on one side, staring at the closed door
of the front room.

Suddenly he was at the door and turning the handle.

The door slid open silently and, there in the center of
the room, the furniture all pulled back away from it, stood
the casket. The men from the undertaker's had left it on
Thomas' mother's best table, its leaves pulled out full
length to accommodate the entire thing.

And in the casket, Thomas knew, lay his father.

He tried standing on tiptoe so he could make sure his
father was where he should be without Thomas actually
having to go any further into the room. But he couldn't
see that far, and the light was poor anyway.

There was nothing else for it. He moved forward, one
foot at a time, into the room.

Then, there he was beside the casket. But he was still
facing the far wall, just aware that the casket was actually
in front of him and beneath him by virtue of peripheral
vision.

He breathed in deep and held the breath.

Then he looked down.

He was asleep. That's all it was. His father wasn't dead at all, only sleeping. The pain had gone from the lines on his cheeks, their hollows filled by magic, their dark swathes cleared up and skin-colored again.

Thomas leaned forward.

No, he was dead. The skin looked unreal, like a waxwork dummy. It looked as though it were wet, or damp. Thomas lifted a hand and reached into the casket, trailing a finger over that face that he had seen so often and that was now, suddenly, so alien to him.

It felt cold under his touch.

He pulled back his hand and looked back at the door. The last thing he wanted now was for his mother to walk in and see him poking fingers into his—

As he faced the door, the sound came again.

It sounded like waves.

He turned back and stared into the coffin, half expecting to see his father's eyes jerk open.

But everything was as it had been. No difference.

But, still, he had heard it.

He leaned forward so that his face was inches above his father's and listened.

Then he pulled himself to his full height and leaned fully into the casket. As he did so, he rested his right elbow on his father's chest and his own face came down to his father.

That's when it happened.

As he rested on the body it moved upward slightly, like a jackknife, and his father's face came up to Thomas' so that the mouth touched Thomas' cheek.

And at that very instant, the lips trembled and a soft sound escaped from them. It sounded like a balloon letting out air.

The lips against his cheek were dry and yet . . . and yet they were soft. It seemed as though they had been waiting for this instant so that they could open and . . . and kiss him.

For it *was* a kiss.

A kiss.

A single word and yet so much more. A symphony . . . comprising four short letters.

Thomas jerked back and watched as his father's body

settled back gently into the casket, the white satin crumpling beneath his head.

And coming up out of there, drifting lazily out of the casket, was a smell.

It was a scent, nothing more. A scent of stopped clocks and piano dust, of grass stains and sunshine . . . and just the vaguest hint of peppermint.

Thomas felt a huge stone being moved from his heart, and a wave washed up into his chest and up his throat.

His eyes started to sting, and the image of his father shimmered as though he were looking at him through a rain-streaked window.

He left the room without caring about noise.

And he left the door open so that his father might feel a part of the house once more.

A breath, a kiss, an emotion?
Call it what you will.
The scientific answer is both simple and rational.
A pocket of air, a collection of gases released by the application of pressure.
This and nothing more.
Words we make to control and sanitize the magic of life.
Words like "cause" and "effect."
"Action" and "reaction."
But maybe, just maybe, it was something even more elemental.
A freshening foretaste of adventures to come, perhaps, carried to this world of the mundane by the breeze from a far-off distant shore. A beachhead on that vast and wondrous continent that we call . . . The Twilight Zone.

For Rod Serling.

MY WICCAN, WICCAN WAYS

by Brad Linaweaver

They were using her broom to sweep floors. This was the final insult! That broom had seen her through far too much to meet so ignoble an end. It had brought her into this world.

At first she hadn't realized that she was in a new world as the broom had picked up a sudden burst of speed and plummeted down beneath the clouds that were white on top and gray underneath. When she saw desert country spreading out below her black, pointed shoes, she had thought the problem was a simple miscalculation, or maybe too much body fat in the flying spell. Her objective had been London.

The sun glinting off the sand had made a thousand, flashing diamonds that were temporarily blinding, adding to her irritation. Impatiently, she had cast a spell and accomplished more than she intended. The gray clouds turned black and exploded into a torrent of rain. She got the worst of it, of course ... and being drenched did nothing to improve her disposition.

The next thing she knew was that a gust of wind knocked off her hat and sent it spinning away from her clutching hand, a black funnel tossing in the maelstrom, a dark triangle growing smaller and smaller until it landed unceremoniously in a puddle of water. There were a lot of puddles dotting the landscape, alternating with sagebrush to offer some variety to the eye. This dry, flat landscape could not drink the water she had provided. Ungrateful, dead land, it remained impassive to her curses.

The rain stopped. She knew that her anger was foolish, just as she knew she should be paying attention to her

flight instead of craning her head at an impossible angle
to look at her damned hat. That's when she flipped over.

Never, never had she flipped before. She had an undig-
nified view of the horizon upside down, the distant hills
jagged like knives. As she fell through space, she called
out the names of Beelzebub and Belphagor.

Never, never had she been knocked unconscious—not
she, not the Grand Witch of All England. She who was
uppermost in the Queen's nightmares did not usually lose
her dignity by acting like a stupid, common ass. Until
now. These thoughts were still racing through her mind as
she painfully regained consciousness.

A beautiful young girl, not more than thirteen summers, was gazing down at the old, old woman. The clouds
were gone and a perfectly blue sky made a nice contrast
to the young one's light brown locks. The sun had returned in all its fierce glory, and it was slowly roasting
the witch in her heavy black garments so that she envied
the cool white gown of the dark-haired youngster.

"Are you all right?" asked the girl.

The witch spoke many languages, virtually a require-
ment of her trade. Although the girl was speaking English
of some kind, it was an unfamiliar dialect. The Grand
Witch carefully phrased a sentence, but she saw conster-
nation on the young one's face at unfamiliar terms like
"ye" and "thou" and "shew." The witch pressed on. Despite this barrier, it wasn't difficult to coax more sen-
tences out of the attractive child. Then, shading her eyes
against the sun and raising herself on one arm, the woman
in black used her powers to speak in the girl's idiom. It
worked. But even as she felt comprehension flooding
through her withered frame, she also felt strangely exhausted by her efforts.

"Can you tell me where I am?" asked the witch, doing
the best she could to ignore the dizziness that gripped her.

"In Arizona," said the girl, but seeing confusion in the
woman's face amended her statement. "Well, it's
Peaceland now, since the revolution. What used to be
Southern California, Arizona and New Mexico is all
Peaceland. But my mother likes the old names best."

The witch tried concealing her bewilderment and asked
as calmly as she could, "What ... continent is this?"

"Oh," said the girl. "Oh, my. It's America, naturally. This used to be one nation."

It took another moment before the witch got the point, but then it hit her with a bang: "The New World!" She exhaled the words as if she were blowing out a million candles. How the Spanish and the English enjoyed their little games there. But had the child mentioned something about one nation? Inconceivable. Impossible. In what strange universe did she find herself.

She was about to ask another question when the young girl seized the initiative. "By the Goddess, talking to you is as bad as taking one of my herstory tests. But you need to get out of the sun before we do anything else."

Impressed by the young one's presence of mind and self-confidence, the witch allowed herself to be helped to a standing position. She was pleased that she'd suffered no serious sprains or broken bones. A few steps taken in that baking, oven air was all it took for her to realize how thirsty she was. The young girl could be an accomplished mind reader for she pointed at a cart hewn from some mysterious, light-weight wood and said there was water there. The cart was covered by a brightly colored canvas that would look well at any feast or tournament. Under the welcome shade thus afforded, the witch gratefully stood out of the direct rays of the sun and drank water from an earthenware cup.

They didn't speak for at least a minute, the two of them rooted to their safe places in the small pool of shade. The day was so hot that all objects seemed to shimmer, except the two of them in the little, dark circle—a magic circle, of sorts, to keep the blistering demons of heat at bay.

The witch wasn't happy about what she said next but she made the words come out: "What year is this, young one?"

The girl seemed to brighten at the first easy question: "It's the Year 126!" she announced. The lack of recognition on her companion's face mitigated her pleasure. "I mean, since the revolution. That's how the calendar works."

The witch sighed, a most unpleasant sound. "I know nothing of such matters," she said. "Can you tell me what year it is as reckoned by He Whose Name I Cannot Speak?" She spat at the yellow-brown ground and was partly surprised when the spittle did not evaporate in the hot, still air.

"Oh, you mean the Patriarchal Calendar," said the girl, crestfallen. This was becoming as difficult as a test, after all. "I should know that. We had a recent lesson ..." Then she smiled and her eyes flashed, as though the desert had gotten into her after all. "I know the answer! It's easy. Add two thousand years to the new date. We're in the year 2126 A.D., as dated from the Patriarchal Enemy, the Christ!"

At the mere mention of the name, the witch made to cover her ears. "Don't be afraid, young one," said the old one. "Only don't speak that name aloud in my presence. You see, child, I am a witch."

The thirteen-year-old blinked her great, green eyes very slowly, as though failing to understand. "Aren't we all?" she asked.

"Not another one!" exclaimed the mental health coordinator of the sisterhood, first-class. "Someone will have to inform Our Elder Priestess, Blessed Be."

When Tanith, which was the young girl's name, had brought the sorely displaced Grand Witch of England into the Central Community, the two of them were welcomed by a guild song of sharing. The witch was really too tired to fully appreciate the beauty of the harmony or the simple charm of the lyrics. She was tired because she'd had to help the girl pull the cart all the way back to the human settlement. The girl had been in good condition to manage the cart by herself. She'd gone out in the desert in search of plants, gems, and stones that might be used in the craft.

The witch certainly approved of such a reasonably motivated field trip. What she couldn't understand was the absence of any animals to help pull the thing; or failing that, why not use magick? Tanith explained that the first was forbidden as exploitation of animals, and by extension a violation of Mother Earth. As for the second, Tanith put on the gravest expression she could manage and in solemn tones informed the Grand Witch of England that she obviously didn't understand the true nature of witchcraft. The girl was trying so hard to sound adult that the witch couldn't take umbrage with her.

The subject of magick was suddenly a sore point for more reasons than avoiding an argument. Although they had failed to recover her hat, finding the broom was swiftly accomplished. There were no oaths in all of Hell to express the witch's frustration at holding her favorite broom for the first time in centuries and not feeling the least scintilla of energy coursing through the gnarled wooden handle. Whatever spell-sodden bitch from her own time had cursed her to this bizarre world, could the creature have also found the power to strip the Grand Witch of all but the most elementary magick? The idea was more terrifying than a gallon of Holy water.

The only good thing that could be said about a long trek through inhospitable terrain was that it took her mind off more serious matters. She'd managed to keep her cool, more or less, through the discomfort, and the syrupy welcoming committee, and even when the misguided souls had promptly placed her broom in the general storehouse of useful appliances. (Clearly these people had no respect for private property.) But the attitude of this inquisitor across from her, feigning exasperation over a surplus of the genuine article in a world of ersatz witches, well, this was simply too much.

Worst of all, the woman looked just like a certain nun who pestered every self-respecting practitioner of the black arts back home. She had the same square, middle-aged face, the same petrified expression of sour disapproval, the same self-righteous smugness. Tanith had hesitated at the door of this personage's inner sanctum, evidently reluctant to abandon her newfound comrade, and at that moment the witch had felt a genuine fondness for the child. She even promised herself to spare Tanith should she afflict the Central Community with terrors worthy of the Old Testament. (The Devil always said that Holy Writ was His preferred inspiration.)

The middle-aged woman peered over spectacles that would not be out of place in old England and asked in the tone of an order: "Wouldn't you be more comfortable if you took off those black rags and put on a nice gown with earth tones, hmmmm?"

This sudden concern for her wardrobe impressed the witch as lacking sincerity. Besides which, one look at the pale gown with a sunflower design so disgusted the witch that she wanted to throw up. She made no attempt to disguise how she felt about it.

"It's no use pretending," said the matronly mental health coordinator. "You be just as antisocial as you like, but we'll still figure out who you are and how to help you. We've already filed a report with Coven Watch, just in case you really are a foreigner as you claim. Now, are you suffering from amnesia?"

"What's that?" asked the witch.

"Very clever answer," said the woman, making a note on an unilluminated manuscript. "It's a shame you couldn't be more original about your malady. This has become such a cliche, by now. And don't you poor, misguided women realize you're perpetuating one of the most vicious stereotypes of the old Patriarchy? Frankly, I think the Elder Priestess is too lenient. If it were up to me, I'd drop all of you in the nearest well."

The image of sinking in water suddenly gave the witch a solution to the problem that had been bedeviling her. The Grand Witch of Spain had done this to her! The bitch must still be angry over sinking the Armada. With the help of a wizard named Thomas, the Grand Witch of England had done a fine job of protecting England's shores. Her sister witch shouldn't hold a grudge about something like that.

Her reverie was interrupted by the mental health coordinator demanding: "So, what's your name, dearie? I need it for my records."

Holding up one of her bony hands with the abruptness of a salute, the old woman announced: "I am the Grand Witch of All England."

The matronly woman across from her was unimpressed. "You don't even have an accent," she said. "It's a common enough delusion, though. That cursed isle is to blame for much of the patriarchal poison. I'll just list you as unknown."

The Grand Witch would have changed the woman into a toad right then and there and dared anyone to tell the difference, but her powers were not yet restored. Had this demented woman never heard of the Queen of England? The way this lunatic was carrying on, one might think there had been a war between America and England. What arrant nonsense.

"You may not realize how fortunate you are," said the woman. "The Elder Priestess will see you this afternoon instead of a week from now, or a month, or a season! But remember, you can only be cured if you want to be."

Oh, for the power to turn her into a tapeworm or a maggot. Or even just to sew her lips shut! One gets used to magick as one is accustomed to tormenting peasants who forget to pull the forelock. As it was, the witch could do nothing as she was escorted to her next audience. No actual force was used, but the implication was present in the form of two of the most unattractive specimens she had ever seen.

The witch never caught the names of her stolid companions, but the least hint of displeasure on the part of the matron was sufficient to engage the duo's brutal attention. They put her in mind of a matched set of living gargoyles whose diet, she imagined, must consist of human flesh. This pleasant fancy was shortly exploded, however, when the witch was given the even more horrifying news that everyone in the Central Community was a vegetarian.

At least their surroundings were interesting. They were walking up a gently sloping hill. A welcome breeze was making the late afternoon more pleasant than the rest of the day had been. On both sides of them stretched a long line of metallic windmills. The witch assumed these were made from some supernaturally treated steel, as they wouldn't be made of iron, the devil's enemy! To the witch's surprise, her guide muttered something about misbegotten technology instead of praising what must have taken a lot of effort to construct.

At the top of the hill, they saw the temple in which the Elder Priestess held court. The Grand Witch was unimpressed. It was a small structure made of some kind of dried mud. More interesting was the location of the building, dead center in a giant triangle composed of thin, healthy pine trees.

Along the way people came out to see the stranger among them. Something struck the witch as odd about the citizens of the Community but she couldn't put her finger on it. Then as Tanith waved from the crowd—in spite of a disapproving expression from the mental health coordinator—the witch realized that she was yet to see a single male!

Maybe these witches had a magick beyond anything they knew in Merry Olde England!

The Elder Priestess was waiting for them in the open door. She was not what the witch had expected. Instead of a mature woman, lines of care etched around the eyes and the mouth, here was a young woman with a carefree, sun-burned face. She had honey-blonde hair, large eyes, large breasts, a large smile—and a narrow waist, small feet, small and dainty hands, and a small talent for diplomacy.

"Like, how do you like it here?" she asked the Grand Witch of All England. "There's no humidity."

Curiouser and curiouser, thought the witch. "You are the Elder Priestess?" she asked incredulously.

"I sense hostility," replied the young elder, batting her eyelashes. "Let's go inside Our Mother's Temple, you know, and, like, discuss your fate."

Inside it was pleasantly dark and cool. "Native American," said the priestess, gesturing for the witch to sit as she was doing, cross-legged on the ground. The witch declined.

As her eyes adjusted to the dark, the Grand Witch was pleased to note the first evidence that this youthful leader had some idea of witchcraft. Lined up against the wall was a collection of the finest magickal stones and gems she'd ever seen: a lovely chunk of amber, as bright yellow as the priestess's hair; an azure blue lapis lazuli, the perfect size for making accurate prophecies; a dark green malachite and milk-white moonstone; blue turquoise, red agate and, naturally, a Witch's Stone. More than anything else, there was crystal—a galaxy of crystals of all sizes, reflecting the light flickering from the opposite wall.

Turning her head, she beheld hundreds of candles burning and marveled at how a structure so crude as a large adobe hut could have ventilation that worked so well. As there were rocks of every imaginable hue, so too were there candles for every color in the rainbow. There were astral candles, skull candles, image and triple-action and coiled-snake and seven-knob candles. But as to why these specialized weapons in the magickal arsenal should all be burning away at this time of day, the witch could not hazard a guess.

So she asked why. The Elder Priestess had a ready answer: "Hey, it's dark in here."

While the Grand Witch of All England was thinking that one over, her hostess clapped her hands, and two figures emerged from the darkness where the candlelight had not reached. They were men. The witch rubbed her eyes to make sure that she wasn't hallucinating.

The Elder Priestess made the introductions: "I'd like you to meet Chauntecleer, the wizard, and Bob, the genius, or under-genius, or something like that."

The witch felt something very like satisfaction to be in the presence of men again. Chauntecleer reminded her of a monk who had held his own against her early in her career. As they looked at each other in the dim light, it was as if a spark of intelligence leapt the space separating them. His smile carried with it the prospect of an intelligent conversation . . . except for one thing. The Elder Priestess mentioned it in passing: "We've kept a few men around. We couldn't get around it. And like, any man you see is of the most high intelligence. Of course, we can't let them speak . . ."

The witch was horrified all over again. "Have you physically altered them?" she asked.

"Oh, no," said the priestess, pulling playfully at the pipe protruding from Bob's mouth, smoke lazily drifting from the bowl. His toothy smile seemed unaffected by anything she did. "The Goddess doesn't approve of unnatural stuff."

"Yet you've made them mute?"

"For sure."

"How?"

A subtle change came over the young woman, as if a sinister intelligence had just filled a comfortable vacuum. "Don't you know?" she asked.

Of course the Grand Witch knew. Herbs. Potions. Hexes. There were at least a hundred ways to silence your lover. But still the question was: "Why?"

"Because they can't confuse us this way," said the beautiful, young Elder Priestess. She pointed to the door and the two men left with an admirable degree of promptness. "They can't bring us down, you know."

Until this day the Grand Witch thought she'd seen it all. She had new respect for that old motto: live and live and live and live and live . . . and learn. "What were Chauntecleer's last words?" she wanted to know.

"He thought I lacked a sense of humor," the priestess told her.

It went on like that for some time, thrust and parry, a dance of conjecture, the interloper and the authority each searching for weakness—always weakness. The Grand Witch began thinking there was more to this seemingly unfocused child than a first impression would indicate. She learned some immediate history at least. All was not sweetness and light among these self-proclaimed witches.

Before establishing the current system, there had been strife and dissension over hundreds of issues. The windmills had even presented a problem. Those who wished to eschew machines were the problem; the winning side had to persuade their sisters that not all basic technology (a word the witch came to believe synonymous with magick) was a patriarchal plot! Then there had been the fight over the proper Wiccan view on fertility: between those who viewed abortion as in keeping with joy in life and those who thought the Earth Mother did not have sufficient irony to see abortion in that light. Schism begot schism, tracing all the way back to the troubles between Gardenerianism and Alexandrianism. The ultimate offshoot of all these legitimate conflicts, it transpired, were those poor, deluded women who confused the pentagram life symbol with dark Christian myths and mixed up the honoring of the souls of the dead at Hallowmas with the peasant superstition of Halloween. These were the same women who donned the traditional garb of a Halloween witch.

The Elder Priestess finally took a breath. The witch had been thinking over the implications of everything she'd been told and asked: "But if you think I'm a representative case of lunacy, why are you lavishing all this attention on me?"

The younger woman smiled. "Because I'm certain you're authentic," she said. "A real witch. A real, brimstone and demon-worshipping witch."

"But you just got through telling me that I don't exist. I mean, that beings like me don't exist. You don't even admit the existence of my dark lord."

"Yeah, like the devil's a guy. I can get into that. The orthodox deny your world. We just have the boring old Earth Mother and love and peace and vegetables. Blessed

be!" As the Elder Priestess went on and on, the Grand
Witch became even more flabbergasted.

"I'll bet you've made many a cow give sour milk, am
I right?" asked the priestess. The witch nodded. "Well,
that wouldn't get anywhere with us. We don't even use
cow's milk. We say that's exploiting the natural order
again."

The Elder Priestess started pulling her hair. "I had to
get you alone for a while," she said. "Who else can I talk
to about this stuff? It's so boring here. You'd never believe how borrrrrrrrring." She made the last word into one
long moan that had an undeniable sexual component.

The Grand Witch was at a loss as to what should come
next. She was about to tell the priestess that if she wanted
excitement back in the world, she should do something
about increasing the male population when she thought
better of it. Now was the time for caution. Now was the
time to avoid offending the powers that were.

"What do you want of me?" asked the Grand Witch of
the Elder Priestess.

"Simple. Do a trick."

So much for caution. So much for the suggestion, endlessly repeated since she had arrived in this place, from
Tanith to the mental health coordinator, that witchcraft
was about anything but doing tricks.

"I'd like to oblige," said the Grand Witch, and she
spoke from the cold ash heart of deepest sincerity. Oh, the
things she would do to the Central Community if her
powers would only return. "But I cannot perform for your
amusement."

"You will do a trick," said the priestess, "or turn on a
spit." Suddenly the dazzling white smile did not seem as
charming as it had before. "I know you have powers. You
don't think Tanith was in the desert by accident, do you?
I sent her."

"Why?" asked the witch.

"I knew you were coming."

"How?"

"I trust my dreams, you know. It seems like my ances-
tor from long ago bossed the whole gig in Spain. She,
like, sent me a message . . . to take care of you. Blessed
she!"

This, at least, made some kind of sense. Up to this

point the witch felt she had fallen into a pure nightmare where nothing was reasonable. But with her powers at low ebb, or possibly extinguished, what could she do? "I can't perform a trick just now . . ." she began.

"Who are you kidding?" spat the young woman with surprising vehemence, jumping up and stamping her foot. "You were seen to fly. To fly!"

"They took my broom."

"If I get it back for you, will you fly for me?"

This was going nowhere fast. Under normal circumstances she might have tried to bluff her way out of the dilemma; but these were anything but normal circumstances. Despite the impropriety, the witch decided to tell the truth: "Something has happened to my powers. I don't know when, or if, they'll come back."

"Liar!" shrieked the priestess, pulling her hair again. "You're holding out on me."

When all else fails, try logic. "Do you think I'd still be here if I had my magick?" asked the witch.

Unfortunately, the Elder Priestess seemed perfectly impervious to a reasoned approach. "You can't fool me with that bogus routine, babe! We've had you hemmed in with our crystal power since you first arrived. Blessed be."

Now it was the witch's turn to lose control. She laughed long and hard. Even in her weakened state, she could detect the presence of magickal properties in any object. The collection in the temple could be used for powerful spells in the hands of a true adept, but this Wiccan community didn't seem to contain so much as one real sorceress. The Elder Priestess was probably the closest, as witness the dream link with the Grand Witch of Spain (speaking of which, the witch wondered whether any of her sisters still existed in this century). One thing was *for sure:* Not all the crystals on earth could strip a Grand Witch of her powers.

"You remind me of the Church," the witch told her adversary. "You think I have powers beyond your own, and yet you believe a few paltry baubles and trinkets can render me helpless. It is to laugh."

But the Elder Priestess was not laughing. She clapped her hands, and the ugly duo returned. In short order they had the Grand Witch pinioned between them. Somehow

the witch wasn't surprised as force was finally brought to
bear on her pale, emaciated frame.

The last words the Elder Priestess said before they left
the makeshift temple were, "Thanks for giving me a rad
idea. Maybe this will bring you around."

The sun was setting on the worst day of the Grand
Witch's long existence. Off in the distance the clouds
were so low to the ground that they seemed an extension
of a distant mountain range—all blue and white, with a
touch of gold from the disappearing sun. They had tied
her to a stake. Somehow she couldn't appreciate the nos-
talgia of the moment.

Sister Susan and Sister Sarah and Sister Judith and Sister Cynthia and several young lackeys had gathered wood
for the festivities. They all seemed full of malice and un-
seemly glee, with the sole exception of Cynthia. But the
latter's sad expression didn't keep her from doing the
same as everyone else. A crowd of onlookers were being
held back by dozens of women who seemed as muscular
as men, the most horrifying sight the witch had witnessed
yet.

Whatever few men were allowed to live in this world,
none were to be seen at the burning. But the witch was
pleased to see Tanith, off to the side of the crowd, shouting against the proceedings. The Elder Priestess went
over to the girl and used the authority of her position to
bring the brave child into line.

A last appeal to the priestess had accomplished nothing. The basic truth that witches and warlocks were no
longer human beings seemed lost on everyone here. Ser-
vants of the dark forces were either born that way or
crossed over (to use an unfortunate expression). For instance, the Elder Priestess could make a flying potion
with the correct proportion of baby fat or be given a fully
powered broom, and it would avail her naught. Without
witchery in her blood, she wouldn't get an inch off the
ground.

But what did the Grand Witch of All England expect
from people so careless of their males? She was still reel-
ing over the idea that some of these women believed in
aborting perfectly good human stock before it was born
and *useful*. Exposure to this sort of waste could make her

sympathetic to the puffings of some old blowhard of a bishop! Waste not, want not.

What a bother that her powers had not yet returned. Time was running out. Clearly this was the work of the Grand Witch of Spain. But there would come a reckoning. Already a plan was beginning to form.

The women gathered the wood while another, Sister Morgan, kept time by beating a small drum with a slow and steady beat. Suddenly another woman ran up shouting, "Stop! You can't use that wood."

"Oh, no, it's Sister Lind Seed," muttered Cynthia.

The agitated young woman went on: "That's wood from a Joshua tree. It's on the protected list."

This was, as someone once said, the last straw. The final absurdity struck home as the sisters began gathering up the wood and looking for an acceptable substitute. The Elder Priestess couldn't legitimately oppose enforcing an official rule of her domain, but the Grand Witch could see frustration crawl over the young authority's face.

Anger had been the missing ingredient. Blood burning hotter than any fire, the Grand Witch felt her power surging back. She appreciated the irony that the plan she had just formulated was too good to change now. After all, her real opponent waited for her somewhere in the mists of time, and she intended to use strategy, as she had when she sank the Armada.

"Oh, lassie!" the witch called out, capturing the full attention of the Elder Priestess. The young woman's eager smile spoke volumes. She obviously expected her reward in ill-gotten magick. She started toward the old woman tied to the stake.

"I sense a decrease in negative vibrations," said the priestess to her admiring retinue. "The stranger has seen the error of her ways."

The Grand Witch of All England waited until the priestess was only a few feet away. Then she said, "You can tell the sisters they don't have to forage for any more wood. I believe this is the result you want."

The Grand Witch set herself on fire, to the astonishment of the priestess and the entertainment of the onlookers. The Elder Priestess was standing near enough that her arch little eyebrows were singed, and another layer of red was added to her sunburn. The Grand Witch enjoyed the sight as everything was eaten up by red and yellow flame, and she listened to Morgan's drum fading away like a slowly dying heartbeat.

The plan she had developed, a *master* plan one might say, was to go straight to the head office in Hell. The Grand Witch of All England had enough seniority for that. There she would bask in the masculinity of Satan Himself and persuade Him to help her alter history so that no timeline such as this one would ever exist. That would be an approach her enemy would never expect; and if all went well, the Grand Witch of Spain might even undergo the sort of severe punishment at which her countrymen excelled.

The target of the New Inquisition would not be witchcraft in general but the Wiccan movement in particular. A more worthwhile cause seemed inconceivable to the Grand Witch as she plummeted down and down to the warm embrace of a domain that cared.

DARK SECRETS
by Edward E. Kramer

"Chicken!"

"Am not!" Patrick retorted, aware that the level of conversation had sunk to kindergarten levels.

"It's just a ridge—you ain't gonna fall or anything. We're almost there."

"We were *almost there* an hour ago." Patrick paused to check his watch again. "That means it'll take us at least three more hours to get out, and it's almost midnight now."

"Past your bedtime, Mamma's boy?" Stuart quipped. "I told you it'd be a mistake to take your cousin along—but *you* wouldn't listen."

"Look, Stu, the ground rules were either he went or I couldn't go." Turning back to Patrick, he said, "Ignore him. If ya don't think you can make it, wait here. We'll go on ahead and catch up with you on the way back. Okay?"

Troy hadn't wanted to take Patrick either. Their camping trip was planned weeks in advance, and a thirteen-year-old cousin was not part of the package. Over the past year, Troy and Stuart had camped out over a dozen times at Fort Ridge Park, venturing further and further into a hidden cavern entrance they had found while scouting the area. They had explored the cave so often that they considered it their secret clubhouse, safe as a second home. Troy and Stuart swore to each other that they'd never share the knowledge of their excursions with anyone—especially parents. Cousins, Troy considered, ranked a close second.

Patrick surveyed the ridge again. His flashlight was getting dim as it was. The beam caught a five-inch wide ledge circling a large rock formation. Beyond the ledge, a stream trickled some fifty feet below—so his cousin said. Patrick couldn't even see the streambed with his light, but he could hear its gentle rushing against the rocks beneath. Troy told him that he was sure the cave led to a waterfall that fed the stream. It was the goal of this trip to finally reach the falls.

When Patrick's mother first told him that he'd be staying the weekend with his Aunt Beth, he was angry and upset. The last time he'd spent the night, Troy invited several of his friends over to play Secret Agent. Patrick pretended to be a spy, was promptly "taken into custody," and spent the remainder of the evening tied to Troy's bed "under interrogation." He remembered being blindfolded and beaten. Every time he'd started to cry, the boys had chided, "Stop being such a baby, it's just part of the game." That was three years ago, about the time Patrick developed an intense fear of darkness. He had never made the connection.

His mother explained, "Your Uncle Frank is back in the hospital again, and I promised I'd go visit him. Aunt Beth promised me it wouldn't be so boring for you this time."

He never told anyone.

"She tells me that Troy's going camping in the mountains with a friend this weekend, and you can join them." She paused for his reaction, then continued without receiving one. "You know he got his license last year. Beth says he's a really good driver."

Patrick rationalized to himself. Camping would be a new experience. His mother wasn't the outdoorsy type, and his father wasn't around enough to even remember his birthday, let alone be present for any father-son type activities. On weekends, Patrick could go off to the movies or the skating rink with friends, but getting up to the mountains would be a treat.

She caught the glimmer of his smile, then brightened up. "Good boy. I'll call your Aunt Beth and tell her you're coming. I'm sure Troy will be thrilled."

When Patrick and his mother arrived, Troy and a friend were packing for the trip. Troy waved at the car, then continued to stuff a beat-up old Volkswagen. Patrick almost didn't recognize him. When he was last over, Troy had hovered just over five feet tall with pale white skin and a short preppy haircut with clothes to match—a description that could easily have been used for himself, thought Patrick.

"It's been such a long time, Fran," called Beth, approaching the car. "My, my, how Patrick has grown."

He grabbed his overnight bag and ran over to the boys, a safe distance from one of Aunt Beth's inevitable sloppy kisses.

"Hey, Troy," Patrick called, out of breath. "Thanks for inviting me."

Troy glanced over to Stuart with a smirk. "Yeah, right . . . whatever." He pointed to the back of the open car. "Throw your shit in and let's go."

"Do you have an extra sleeping bag?" Patrick asked. "I couldn't find one to borrow."

"Don't worry about it; where we're going, you won't need one," Stuart piped with a sickly grin, as he coiled a hundred or so feet of thick rope.

"Sorry, he's just being an asshole," said Troy. "You remember Stu, don't you?"

Stuart's grin turned into a wide smile as he held out the coiled rope toward Patrick with the delicacy of an oriental vase.

"Why don't *you* pack it into the Bug?" Stuart offered. "You'll be very used to the rope by the end of the weekend."

Patrick felt his heart skip a beat. He suddenly recognized Stuart as one of the kids who had bound him—it was Stuart who'd covered his mouth as he had tried to scream.

Troy stepped over and grabbed the rope from Stuart. "He's kidding, Patrick," he said, knowing that he wasn't. "We're going to be doing some spelunking over the weekend. I'll tell ya about it in the car."

Patrick surveyed the situation. Both Troy and Stuart had grown almost a foot since he last saw them. And, well, they'd matured a whole bunch. He knew he wouldn't have a chance if they decided to get him. Patrick dug into his pocket and clenched his fist around a small pen knife he had brought, as if a reasonable answer

to the threat. He could stay the weekend at home with
Aunt Beth . . . No, camping it was. He'd take his chances.

Spelunking, as Troy fondly called it, was something
Patrick had never even considered . . . like skydiving or
bungee jumping. Well, he'd actually considered bungee
jumping once, but only for a fleeting moment. Patrick
wasn't sure at first that he wanted to try, but the alternative of sitting at the campsite alone at night while they
explored held little allure. Troy explained their pact—the
cave's location and any knowledge of their exploration
were never to be repeated. Period. Patrick saw no reason
to disagree; he could keep a secret.

They pulled into the park and found a suitable site.
Troy set up camp while Stuart gathered the equipment for
the excursion. Patrick imagined the complexity of gear
they would need; he remembered watching a program on
television about the care and preparation needed in packing a chute for skydiving.

"Grab a flashlight and a helmet and let's go!" Troy
called out. "Stu, you grab the rope."

Two large flashlights were snatched up by the veterans,
leaving a small Radio Shack two-battery special for Patrick.

"Hey, he took my backup light," Stuart complained.

"Pipe down," responded Troy, irritated at Stuart's con-
tinual bickering. "He needs a light, doesn't he?"

"Oh, fuck it. He can use my light, but I'm taking the
extra set of batteries." Stuart stuck six new D-cells into
the backpack that held their rope and headed to the entrance. Troy and Patrick followed.

"Step over this barbed wire here," Troy cautioned,
while pinning it to the ground with his boot.

"I thought we were in a state park. Why the barbed
wire?" Patrick asked.

Stuart replied, "Cause we're going somewhere they
don't want us to, stupid—but, hey, that's half the fun.
Give me a hand with the grate."

Troy and Stuart lifted a heavy iron grate off a small
rock pile. Patrick could see how the grate was once
welded in place. Troy had explained how they had spent
two weekends breaking the grate from its frame. Beneath
the grate was a two-foot diameter hole. As the three

crawled through, light rain glanced off the iron grating in an irregular pulse that only Patrick seemed to notice.

Crawling around in the cavern was cool at first, but as they got deeper and deeper in, the nocturnal terrain grew more challenging. Troy stopped to point out interesting rock formations and sleeping bats along the way; Stuart grew more annoyed each time the pace slowed.

Patrick felt they were under-prepared for such an excursion, but he did not share that thought with Troy or Stuart. He'd had to plead with them to let him go in the first place and then swear their trip to total secrecy. Stuart had even suggested they tie him up by the campfire to keep him occupied until their return. Patrick didn't want to screw things up even further by suggesting that what they were doing was downright dangerous.

"We're wasting time, Troy. I'm already on my second set, and your light's getting dim." With handline in place, Stuart started around the ridge.

"Patrick, why don't you crawl up the side of this rock and wait in the alcove. We'll be back after a while. Really." Looking at the hollow beam from his cousin's light, he added, "Once you get settled, you'd best turn that off or you ain't gonna have enough light to make it out."

"How much light can you get out of a set of batteries?" asked Patrick with clear concern in his voice.

"About eight hours—but we used these lights on our last trip and haven't changed batteries yet. Except Stu—"

A loud cry pierced Troy's concentration. The sound of falling rocks followed almost in synchrony. Then silence. Patrick jerked his head in the direction of the ridge, his mouth too numb to respond. His flashlight beam trembled.

"Very funny, Stuart Alice," Troy called out toward the ridge with little distress. No response.

Patrick knew he was really trying to be serious when he used Stuart's middle name, Alister. It was a habit he learned from his mother; he could almost hear Aunt Beth shout "Terrence Carter."

"Well, get your ass over here already—I've already crossed the ridge," echoed Stuart's voice as he spoke. "Hey, how did that sound?"

"Didn't fool me for a second," Troy called back. Looking toward Patrick, he added, "but I think my cousin pissed in his pants."

"T-Troy," Patrick stammered, in a voice too low for Stuart to hear, "please don't go." He reached out for Troy's hand, half-expecting him to lay down his pack and sit alongside him until their trip back out—as the big brother he never had would have done.

Troy turned and eased toward the ridge without noticing Patrick's still-outstretched hand. "Be back in a bit. Remember . . . save your light."

Patrick's hand fell to his side as Troy disappeared around the rock formation. He focused the flashlight on his watch: 12:13 A.M. He could still hear Troy and Stuart calling back and forth to each other. He wished he had the courage to join them. Patrick darted his light beam back at the ridge again. The handline was still in place. He could cross and catch up with them in no time.

Mud parted with a distinctive "pluck" as Patrick lifted each foot from the cave floor. He'd been standing in the same place for almost twenty minutes, unconscious that his sneakers had sunk completely into the mud. Mom is going to kill me when she sees them, he thought. She just bought them last week.

He cautiously crept over to the ridge. The stream seemed a great deal more active than before, its gentle rushing replaced by a rhythmic pounding. Patrick stared at the ledge and gently shook his head. He couldn't go across on hands and knees; he would have to stand. Balancing to a crouch, his mud-soaked sneakers caught his view; both Troy and Stuart wore army boots. He could never make it.

Crawling back to the alcove, he noticed the mud was getting thinner. About an inch of standing water had collected since they'd arrived. He really hadn't thought about the rain, since he was in a cave. Troy had told him that many caves, like this one, were formed by rushing water over time. That's why many still had streams and waterfalls in them. Patrick's mind raced again. What if we get flooded and trapped in here? I *can't* die; I just turned thirteen.

He climbed into the rocky niche Troy had suggested and drew his knees up close to his chest. It was all he could do to minimize his trembling. The flashlight beam focused on the rock six inches in front of him. He *could* turn it off. I'm not going anywhere right now, I don't need the light, Patrick rationalized to himself.

He concentrated on the beam one last time. It was a great deal dimmer than when he started. He needed to conserve the batteries. Nervously, his finger found the switch. All I have to do is *press* the button. There's no one here to hurt me.

It was Patrick's greatest fear—darkness. For the last three years, he hadn't been able to sleep without a night light. That one limitation prevented him from staying over at friends' houses, because he could not be sure that they, too, had night lights in their rooms; he certainly could not bring one along. Patrick could not even come up with a single excuse why he needed one. He would never let any of his friends know of his fear.

Pressure built on the small, round plastic button. He closed his eyes tightly. With a "click," the light was gone. Flashes of color still reflected off his closed eyelids. Cautiously, he opened one eye, then the other. Darkness. Blacker than he ever imagined. He closed his eyes again.

You'll be okay. There's no one here but you. There's nothing to worry about. Troy and Stuart will be back soon . . .

Keep it up, it's working.

. . . unless they find another exit and leave you to rot. You know they hate your guts, and they're not coming back for you.

No! Stop it!

Patrick felt something glance off his shoulder—not a rock, something alive. His eyes snapped open: darkness. Reflexes heightened, he instinctively turned and struck at the creature. Swiping the air in front of him without restraint, the flashlight smashed into the side of the alcove. Patrick felt the plastic grip crack as the batteries sprung across the cave floor. He dropped the flashlight and dug for his knife. Flipping one of the four blades open, he held the knife rigidly in his outstretched fist. Don't show any fear, he thought.

"Take one step closer and I'll kill you!" Patrick yelled, his voice quivering.

Silence. Dead silence. Then fluttering. It must be a bat,

a goddamned bat. He wasn't really afraid of bats, just darkness. Now he had both.

Patrick was angry and confused: angry with himself for reacting the way he did, knowing that if it happened again, he would probably respond identically; confused about what to do next. He felt trapped, and he was scared.

The cord bound his wrists and ankles, slicing into him as he struggled to break free; a large bandanna was tied tightly over his eyes. Aunt Beth and Uncle Fred were out for the evening; he knew there was no one there to stop the game. Two at a time, the punches began. They demanded a confession of make-believe information he never knew. Through his cries, Patrick made up secret after secret, but they said all of his admissions were lies. The kids laughed and laughed as he writhed in pain.

Patrick knew it was only his imagination, but the trickles of blood felt so real that he couldn't be sure. Tears began to well up in his eyes. Don't cry, he told himself. It won't help the situation any.

What he wanted was to crawl into his mother's lap and rock back and forth with her until he fell asleep. He remembered the last time: He was eight.

Dad returned home after being on the road a whole month. He was drunk as usual, and in a vicious mood. He just came in, slammed the front door shut, and propped himself on the sofa in front of the game. He didn't even bother to say hello to me or Mom. I offered to unpack the car for him, but he ignored me.

She went over to comfort him, but he pushed her away. Mom tried again to talk to him. I'll never forget his response: "The only reason why I have to put myself through this shit week in and week out is because your son is too much of a pussy to stay home by himself after school and let you work. I wish the little son-of-a-bitch had never been born."

For that moment, Patrick had wished it too.

She slapped his dad across the face, knocking his glasses off at a right angle. One lens splintered on the hardwood floor. As she turned away, he grabbed her by the neck and spun her back around, her face smashing into his forearm. Patrick screamed and ran to her aid.

He watched as his mother slowly sank to the kitchen floor, blood flowing from both nostrils. Pounding his fists into his father's chest, Patrick screamed, "I hate you! I hate you! I hate you!"

He'd looked at Patrick and laughed. With a shove, the boy was propelled backward, falling head first next to his mother. "Don't you two look cute?" he smirked. "It's enough to make a grown man sick."

Patrick crawled into her lap and began to wipe the blood off her face. He was bleeding, too; his forehead would need stitches. She put her arms around him and clung as though there were nothing else to live for.

"I've had enough of this shit. I'm leaving and I ain't coming back." Leaving the front door ajar, he stormed back into his car and drove off.

The two of them rocked back and forth for what may have been hours. Patrick knew everything would be all right. In the morning, she would take him to the emergency room to get sutured. He would tell them he fell off the top bunk bed during the night. Patrick knew he didn't even *have* bunk beds, but that didn't matter. His mother told him to keep what had happened a secret.

Concentrate, he told himself. You have to get the flashlight working again—otherwise, you might just as well give it up. He closed his pen knife and burrowed it deep into his pocket.

Feeling around the mud where he sat, Patrick tried to relocate the flashlight parts. His fingers sifted through mud and small rocks. Nothing within reach. In complete darkness, he was too afraid to move from the alcove. He wished he hadn't given up smoking; then he'd have a lighter on him, or at least a pack of matches.

How long had it been since Troy had left? Fifteen minutes? An hour? He wished he could tell. He stared down at his watch but saw nothing. The Timex *had* a back light on it, but it didn't work. When he went to change the batteries in it last year, he could find only one replacement cell at the local drug store. He had left one of the dead cells in the slot that powered the light and hadn't thought about it since.

Wait. Maybe I can open the watch up with my knife and swap the batteries. That would work!

He remembered how difficult, and dangerous, it was to pry open the back of his watch with a knife. He had sliced open his thumb the last time he tried—and that was in broad daylight. This would be much more difficult.

Patrick remembered Ruth Ann. The best math tutor in junior high, she spent an hour or more each week to help him catch up in pre-algebra. Not only was she the best, Ruth Ann was totally blind. Not just legally blind, like his grandma, but completely blind—from birth.

Ruth Ann, he thought, would know just how to handle this situation. For one, she *wouldn't* be afraid of the dark. She probably could fix anything in the dark, too. I guess. But she's not here now ...

Patrick reached back into his pocket and pulled out his knife. Checking each of the four blades, he chose to keep the short, blunt one open. He unstrapped the watch from his wrist and carefully laid it face down across his knee. His trembling had stopped; he had a plan.

With a jeweler's precision, he circled the rim with his index finger. Locating a small indenture in the casing, he firmly placed the blade point in, and twisted. The blade slipped forward, stabbing into his palm. Intense pain shot through his hand and arm, but Patrick locked out his emotions—it would not hurt.

He pulled the knife out and wiggled each finger to confirm a response; the puncture was not deep and did not bleed a lot. Resettling the watch and blade, he tried again. The metal cover made a familiar "snap," like that upon opening a can of pop. He placed the knife at his side and cautiously lifted off the cover.

Working in small concentric circles, Patrick's index finger probed inside the watch. Resting his nail across both batteries, he felt a small metal plate that he had forgotten about. The plate held the cells in place, but as Patrick recalled, it was also necessary to complete the circuit.

A tiny retaining screw fastened with a precision screwdriver locked the plate in place. A miniature screwdriver that Dad had used to tighten his eyeglasses worked just fine. Patrick pondered, what could I use in its place *now?*

He picked up the knife and closed the short, blunt blade. Inspecting each of the other blades by touch, he kept the longest and most slender extended. Using his nail as a guide, Patrick maneuvered the tip of the blade to the center of the screw head. He gently turned the handle of the knife, but the screw failed to follow.

Maybe the tip was too sharp, he thought. Patrick searched the alcove walls for a flat surface. Finding a vertical slab, he drew the tip back and forth across the surface. Confident of his technique, he tried again.

The blade tip met the surface of the screw, but it was too blunt to fit. In frustration, he wedged the blade beneath the plate to pry it from the screw. As he twisted the knife, the thin plate snapped in half. Realizing his failure, Patrick released the watch and knife from his grip. He drew his knees up to his chest and began to rock, wishing his mother were there to comfort him.

Patrick listened for a sign of his fellow explorers, but the sound of rushing water filled his ears. Nothing could be heard over the stream's turbulence. He felt a drop of water fall from overhead, then another. Patrick looked up, instinctively, but darkness still prevailed. Sliding his hand across the top of the alcove revealed a growing reservoir of droplets. One thought raced through his head: The cave's flooding; I've got to warn the others.

Frantically stepping from the alcove, he landed calf-deep in a swiftly flowing stream of cold water. The recent rise in the water level echoed his distress. He could feel a current tugging at his feet. In a louder voice than he thought possible, Patrick screamed, "Troy! Stuart! The cave is flooding! Get back here now!"

Patrick spun around, waving his arms wildly. The swift circulation of air felt good.

"Can't you hear me? This isn't a joke; I really mean it!"

He spun again, only faster, his voice cracking through the tears.

"Listen to me, dammit! We're all going to die!"

Losing all sense of orientation, Patrick continued to spin. Kicking and splashing as he turned, his cries were replaced by laughter—growing louder than even his screams.

Dizzy and light-headed, Patrick lost his balance and collapsed sideways to the cave floor. Bracing for impact, he stuck one hand out to hit bottom; through two feet of water, his fingers sank into mud. Patrick hit the water face first—the shock squelched his laughter.

The current was stronger than he had imagined. He could feel himself being pulled. Patrick tried to get up, but he was still too disoriented; he felt lucky to keep his head above water. Grasping for anything to stop movement, he had only collected two fists full of mud. The rushing sound grew closer.

It all made sense now, he realized. The raging stream he now heard was not the same one he had heard when he first approached the ridge. The maelstrom about him was a stream of water—a result of the flood—cascading over the ridge and crashing fifty feet below.

He tried again to stand but toppled over. It was no use. There was nothing left to stop him. He reached out for the cave wall, and as he felt his feet cross over the ridge, his fingers caught onto a rope—it was the handline Troy and Stuart had mounted to cross the ridge.

For a fleeting moment Patrick thought of letting go of the rope, but his concern shifted to the others. If they were in trouble, he was the only one left to help.

Patrick pulled himself back to the ridge and clung tightly to the handline. His entire body was soaked; he began to shiver uncontrollably. Troy had warned him not to get his chest or back wet; he said it could cause something called "hypothermia." The next stage was called "shock."

"It's time to go, Patrick."

Patrick jerked his head toward Troy's voice. "Where are you Troy? I-I'm scared ..."

"I'm right beside you. Move off the ridge to your left, then wait. Follow my voice and I'll lead you out."

Patrick did as he was told, his feet sinking deep enough into the mud to work against the current. The water had risen to well past knee-level.

"Now, follow me. I won't go too fast."

A renewed panic struck Patrick. He still couldn't see. Could he be blind?

"A-Are you using a flashlight?" Patrick stammered.

"We don't need one right now. I told you I know the cave like the back of my hand."

Patrick wanted to say that without a flashlight, Troy couldn't possibly see the back of his hand, but thought he'd best not. He followed without further comment. Climbing and crawling at Troy's command, they had reached a point in the cave where the remainder of their retreat would be on drier ground. With his shivering under control, they had made good time.

By the time they had reached the grate, the rain had stopped. Illuminated by moonlight, the iron frame glowed like a silver beacon beckoning them. Patrick turned to thank Troy again, but he had already vanished back into the cave's depths. He had told Patrick that once they reached the entrance, he would go back to wait with Stuart.

Patrick crawled through the opening and made his way to the campsite. The darkness of night was the most welcome source of illumination he could wish for. Patrick unzipped the tent, and crawled into a dry sleeping bag. He thought to wait up for Troy's and Stuart's return, but exhaustion overcame him—and he slept.

"Son, are you all right?"

Troy opened his eyes. It was daylight. The green figure over him drifted into focus.

"He's coming to. I think he's okay."

As he sat up in the tent, red and white pulses of light reflected off its translucent gray material. The figure's uniform identified him as a ranger.

"Son, how many of you kids were camping here last night?"

"It was me, Troy, and Stuart. Have you seen them?" Concern built in his voice.

The ranger pondered. "Are you sure there were only three of you?"

Patrick nodded.

The ranger ducked out of the tent.

"Roger," the man responded to the static of a radio. "I think we got all three accounted for now."

Patrick pulled himself from the sleeping bag. His concern grew to alarm. As he crawled from the tent, he could see the damage that had gone unnoticed in the night. Many large trees had fallen over; their camping supplies were scattered beyond his vision. He was glad that Troy had thought to stake the tent down well.

"Is Troy okay?" he called after the ranger.

The man turned to wait for him.

"I'm sorry, son," the man said quietly. Patrick felt all

the muscles in his body give way at once. He clung to the ranger for support and cried.

Sitting in the jeep, the ranger told Patrick that they had been called around midnight by Troy's mother, soon after the tornado warning was announced. The rangers had located their car, but the campsite was vacant. When the search began, they found the locked grate to Ridge Cavern open, so they called the cave rescue team.

"The rescue team entered the upper regions of the cavern and tracked three sets of footprints going in," explained the ranger. "When they got within a few hundred feet of the first chasm, they lost 'em due to the flooding."

"I waited for Troy and Stuart in a small alcove by the ledge. My watch and flashlight are still back there somewhere . . ."

The ranger continued, "Diving through the flooded regions of the cave, the rescue team found two bodies trapped at the cave's deepest point. They had drowned in a chamber submerged beneath a great waterfall."

Patrick's head lowered to his chest.

"It's a good thing you brought a second light," the ranger added in a more cheerful tone.

"I didn't," Patrick admitted, turning toward the ranger. "Troy led me out."

"You must be mistaken, son," the ranger replied. "There was only *one* set of footprints leading back from the ledge."

"NO!" Patrick insisted, "Troy led me out. I know he did!"

"Okay, son, okay," the ranger consoled. "We'll talk about it later. Why don't you rest now while we wait for your mother to get here."

Patrick said no more. He didn't dare add that Troy had led him out *without* a flashlight. That would be *his* secret.

"Much of what happened that evening is still fuzzy."

The camp fire glowed as Patrick spoke. The two boys had listened intently to the story.

"It was three years ago tonight, and I'll never forget it as long as I live." He paused. "Other than you, no one knows the secret of what really happened."

"We won't tell anybody, I promise," said one boy.

"We can keep a secret," agreed the other.

Patrick smiled as he stood. "Good. I *knew* you could. C'mon, it's getting late."

He led the boys to the entrance of the cave. They had already removed the grate by early that afternoon.

"It's just *dark* in there," Patrick said confidently, leading the way in. "There's nothing to fear."

Patrick checked his watch: 9:02 P.M. They'd have to hurry, he thought. It had already begun to drizzle.

REALITY

by Steve Antczak

Rusted metal rods interconnected to form a chaotic framework around a space big enough to walk through, following a twisting pathway that curved in on itself, spiraled, zigzaged, wobbled through the industrial behemoth called *Reality*. Throughout, along the path, were placed knobs, levers, switches, cranks, chains, and wheels. Turn a knob or a wheel, throw a switch, pull a lever or a chain ... the sculptor had intended the piece to be interactive. A twist on a crank, and part of *Reality* shifted, changed, made the sculpture different.

The plaque that stood at the "entrance" said: *Reality is Art. This piece represents reality. Like reality, you can walk through it, and like reality, you can affect it. But be careful: Once you alter something, you may never be able to put it back the way it was before.* It was the centerpiece of Random, Oregon's, town square. Random had a population of around 10,000, not much bigger than in the early part of the century when *Reality* was built. Located in the midst of an old growth forest, surrounded by the wilds of the northwest, Random was as isolated as it could be. Highway 26 passed within 15 miles of Random at its closest point. Stories about Big Foot, man-eating grizzlies, ghosts, Aryan Nation encampments, and the like abounded, but in a quiet, accepted sort of way. The folks of Random weren't trailer park hicks, but neither were they a community of Mensa.

However, it was no longer legal to walk in and turn any of the knobs or pull any of the levers. That didn't stop someone like Osgood Kramer from casting sidelong glances of desire toward it whenever he passed by, to and from lunch over at Pete's Grill, which was across the street. Sometimes Osgood would sit there and let his coffee get cold while he stared at it. Even at Home Depot, where Osgood did customer service in the complaints department, he'd daydream about walking into *Reality* and pulling a particular lever he'd already spotted and *knew* without a shadow of doubt would change what he'd decided needed changing. Once the deed was done, he didn't worry about whether or not he'd get arrested or anything because things would be *different,* and that was the whole point.

One morning, when Osgood's coffee at Pete's had become lukewarm, the town sheriff, Jake Sky, sat in the same booth, across the table from him.

"Mind if I join you?" the sheriff asked, but the question was more or less rhetorical since he'd already effectively joined him.

But Osgood nodded anyway and said, "Sure, have a seat." Jake grinned at him like a wolf facing down a moose. The sheriff was a big Cree Indian, known for his joviality and ready chatter. He waved at Bea, the waitress. She didn't bother to walk over but yelled out to ask if he wanted his usual, and he gave her the thumbs up and looked at Osgood, rolling his eyes.

Osgood knew it was an act, though. He knew why the sheriff was lavishing this attention on him. But that didn't matter. Nothing mattered, or none of it *would* matter once things changed.

"What's up?" Jake asked, amiably enough.

"Not much," Osgood said, which was usually true. Nothing much in his life was ever what he would term "up." Nothing bad, just nothing great. Maintaining status quo was what Osgood had been best at ever since he could remember. Status quo was like a drug for him, a syringe filled with mind-numbing heroin he injected into the pulse of his existence. It kept him warm, safe, and sound of mind and body, or so he fooled himself.

"Anything on your mind?" Jake asked. "Anything you want to talk about?"

"Not really," Osgood answered. Playing the game, but this wasn't a game, it wasn't a joke, it wasn't a scene in the school play. It was *Reality.*

"Sure?" the sheriff persisted. "You've been looking rather . . . contemplative, lately."

Osgood concentrated on the patterns in the linoleum table top, imagining it as the speckled surface of some gigantic eggshell. "Yeah," was all he managed to say, which wasn't what he'd wanted to say. You have to say *something,* though, when the town sheriff expects you to.

"You know," Jake was saying, "I oftentimes wonder . . . what life would be like if the white man had never made it to America. What if he'd never taken blacks as slaves, or forced Chinese immigrants to build his railroad across the red man's land? Sometimes I think these things when I look out the window of my squad car and see that big ol' sculpture towering over the town square."

Osgood regarded the big Indian with some caution. Jake Sky was talking along a thin blue line, saying things most locals wouldn't say to their best friends. He felt that maybe Jake expected him to say something *now,* while Jake paused to let Bea set his food on the table. Ham and cheese on rye with hot mustard, Polish Dill on the side.

"But you know what?" Sky continued. "I wouldn't do anything to change the past, not one thing. Because how do I know it would actually make things better? How do I know Native Americans wouldn't have wiped each other out, or wouldn't have been conquered by someone else? I don't, I *can't.* And besides, some of my best friends are white, and black." He paused to eat part of his sandwich, then said, "Haven't met any Chinese yet."

Now Osgood realized he *had* to say something if he intended to keep the sheriff at bay. "I wouldn't change anything that major, even if I could."

"What about something small?" the sheriff asked. "Something that wouldn't affect anything else."

Osgood shrugged. "I can't think of anything offhand. Besides, I have enough trouble changing the *now.* You know me."

"That's the problem," Jake said, "I *don't* know you. Not really."

Enough of this, Osgood thought. It was all but right there on the table between them, next to Jake's sandwich. He decided to put it there.

"Okay, Sheriff," he said. "You're afraid I'll mess with *Reality,* right? You're afraid I'll walk in there and pull some lever and suddenly the Sun'll be green or something." That got the attention of a few eavesdroppers, each of whom reacted with a cough or a start. One even dropped a fork. Jake Sky ignored everyone but Osgood.

"This isn't something I normally discuss in a public place," Jake said, his voice lower than before. "But since you've already, ah, broached the subject, let me say this: Remember Sarah Cole. Remember Jack Kennesaw. Then, last of all, remember Haver Compton. Think about them, then do what you're best at doing. Keep on keepin' on. Make no waves. Don't rock the boat. Understand?"

Osgood nodded, quelling the urge to make a remark about extensive cliche usage. He got up to leave, throwing down money for the coffee he hadn't even drunk.

It was cold now, anyway.

Sarah Cole. Osgood was convinced there had never been a Sarah Cole, not in this reality, not in *any* reality. Supposedly Jake Sky and several others had seen her walk into *Reality,* and before anyone could stop her, she had flipped a switch. A metal rod turned, a section of the sculpture swung to hang lower than before, and Sarah Cole disappeared. Whatever effect she'd had on the past had wiped out her existence.

Jake and two of his buddies had been hiding deep in the bowels of *Reality* to smoke hash and drink cheap beer. This was back during their senior year at Random High. One of them had climbed up to sit atop a massive gear, his legs hanging down from between the teeth. When the sculpture changed, that gear moved. Jake's old high school pal was now one of Random's few panhandlers. They called him Legless. He never rolled his rickety, twenty-year-old wheelchair far from the square, where he spent his days staring at the industrial monster that had bitten his legs off with iron fangs. Every now and then Jake bought him a cup of coffee or a hamburger, for old times.

Jake and his friends swore on the graves of every one of their ancestors that this Sarah Cole person had done it, had altered *Reality* and then disappeared. Their reputations were better than good. Jake was a star linebacker on the football team, Legless was a wide receiver, the other was the president of the senior class. Local heroes each of them, which made it real easy to believe their story. No one remembered Sarah Cole, and speculation arose about the connection *Reality* had to reality.

There was already a bit of superstition surrounding the sculpture anyway. Even before its completion, a group of churchgoing citizens protested its construction, claiming the artist had to be inspired by Satan to even imagine such an evil looking contrivance, never mind actually build one big enough to loom over downtown like a mechanical sentinel. In a freak accident, the crane being used to build *Reality* malfunctioned and dropped several hundred pounds of scrap metal on the protestors. It had been unmanned at the time.

That was when folks started remembering Sarah Cole. They'd seen her at the prom, seen her shopping with her Mom, who, by the way, also no longer existed. Perhaps Sarah wiped out her entire bloodline! Like a virus, the memory of Sarah Cole spread from person to person, household to household. Some reasoned that those who lived in the immediate area around the sculpture were less likely to totally forget what had gone before things Changed with a capital *C*. Why? Who worried about why? This was some bizarre link between the universe and art, two things people accepted as without reason, without design.

Through dreams, through creative interpretations of some fuzzy memories, people rebuilt Sarah Cole. They rebuilt her life, her family, reconstructed memories to include her ghostly presence in the background, a peripheral attendance to their different pasts.

Rebuilt, or built from scratch. Osgood had gotten caught up in it, too, even though he knew in the back of his mind that something was wrong.

There was always a handy blank spot in someone's Polaroid from a Fourth of July parade or birthday party, empty space that invariably wound up being filled by Sarah. Osgood had a picture of him sitting in the driver's seat of his then brand new sky blue '68 Ford Mustang. He looked too happy for someone with *just* a new car. As if the most beautiful girl in town were sitting there beside him in it, and they were about to go on their first date.

Sarah Cole. It was almost too embarrassing to even

think about now, but he had to. No sooner had he jumped on that bandwagon than he distinctly remembered that first drive in the old 'stang. Cruising the winding roads around town, enjoying the sensation of a 350 vibrating all around him, humming the sacred hymn of a boy and his car with miles of pavement unfurling before them. Absolute freedom, a true release of the spirit to go wherever and whenever he wanted. Just get in his car and *go*.

That was the grin on his face in the picture, as he sat for the first time behind the wheel of a bigger world. *That* was the reality he remembered, the reality that had been, was, and always would be. When he realized this, it was as if he'd been awakened from a dream, snapped out of deep hypnosis, or freed from a hex.

The town of Random was under the same spell, enchanted by a ton of scrap metal bolted and welded together into a crude representation of existence. Osgood knew he had to be the one to break the spell.

Once he had himself freed of the delusion, Osgood found it easy to see contradictions about Sarah, the most obvious of which he was surprised no one else had noticed. There were at least nine different men who claimed to have been the one to "deflower" Sarah Cole. The locales ranged from the backseat of a car (five of those) to a park bench. One claimed it had happened inside *Reality* itself.

A blanket of self-deception had settled over everyone, a nightfall of delusion, a shared sham. It was a town-wide dementia, which Osgood understood only he had escaped.

People believed in *Reality*.

Jack Kennesaw. Had it not been for Jack Kennesaw, there would still be *two* moons, two lunar orbs keeping us company, keeping each other company in their otherwise lonely trajectories around the Earth. But no, because Mr. Kennesaw stepped into the sculpture and interacted with it, touched something, turned something, that second moon ceased to exist forever . . . backwards and forwards in time. Had never been, would never be. Wasn't, and that was that.

Except, again, for some who dreamed.

Folks seemed perfectly happy to gaze up at ol' Luna and point at the Man in the Moon and proudly remember that July 20th, 1969, when a man, an American, set foot on it for the first time. There weren't many lights to crowd out the night sky in Random, and a wide-eyed kid with a telescope could pick out the luminaries of the northern sky with ease. Kindergarten classes drew crayon pictures of the constellations; everyone knew the names of all the visible stars.

Jack Kennesaw had been around for years and was as basic as a Crayola crayon could have made him. All broad strokes, no subtleties. According to him, he'd been bilked out of triple-dipping into the government retirement fund as an ex-Marine, an ex-letter carrier, and a former Park Services ranger. Dismissed from the Park Service without benefits for accepting a bribe by undercover Drug Enforcement agents to look the other way while they grew marijuana on the National Forest land in his charge. Now he took every chance he could to hit back at the government.

Kennesaw had been a Commie-hating patriot of the McCarthy era, a blacklist keeper of weirdos and freaks he knew had to be Stalin's vanguard in America. He took credit for wiping out Uncle Sam's most embarrassing failure in the face of the Red Horde, using *Reality* to perform his patriotic duty by eliminating that other moon from existence. He claimed the U.S. had allowed the Soviets to put a man on that moon in the early '60s, before Armstrong's *Eagle* had landed on Luna, in another reality. He may have actually believed it himself. After Sarah Cole, Randomites were ready to swallow anything, and they ate Kennesaw's story for dinner. Jack Kennesaw had used *Reality* to put the U.S. ahead in the space race! Sure, why not?

Then there was the case of Haver Compton.

His wife had left him, and he was known as a quiet, chronically depressed drunk who spent his time on the porch, sipping malt liquor while staring at their wedding portrait.

His suicide, disemboweling himself with a steak knife, was the culmination of a week-long frenzy of madness brought on by some of the wildest speculation about what the manipulation of *Reality* had done. One day someone noticed it had been tampered with, had been changed. No one saw who had actually gone in there to yank on whatever chain or pull whatever lever, but there was something *different* about it. And while everybody could agree on that point, none of them could agree as to *what* was different about the sculpture.

Osgood remembered hearing them, standing around it all that Monday morning, trying to figure it out.

"That part there's higher than before."

"No, it's lower."

"It's that section there on the side, it's moved in a bit."

"No, it's moved *out* more."

"That bit up top's shifted to the left."

"To the right!"

"Higher."

"Lower."

"In."

"Out!"

"Left!"

"RIGHT!!"

And on and and on and on. They were still at it when Osgood walked across the square to take his usual lunch at Pete's, only the argument had intensified into a screaming mob. He remembered looking at *Reality* that morning going to work, and it looked exactly the same as the day before, but he didn't say anything. They probably would have lynched him, because by God they were all absolutely, positively, one hundred percent certain it had changed. "Higher!" "Lower!" "In!" "Out!" "Left!" "Right!" At least they had it narrowed down.

Eventually someone realized that if *Reality* had been altered at all, then so too had reality. The mob paused, ceased being a mob for a moment and became just a lot of folks standing around, and then it became a riot. The fighting only broke out because people were in each other's way as they tried to run home to check those old photographs again or to catch a nap so as to dream about what might have been. It was at that moment that Osgood first conceived of the notion that there had to be a way to put *Reality* back the way it had been originally.

Among the speculated lost realities that arose then, there was one that, at first, seemed way too outrageous for anyone to take seriously. In fact, Osgood was sure that it had been put forth more as a joke by the skeptical few, maybe a half dozen people, of Random who regarded the whole business with disdain. Their opinion of

Reality was that the materials it was built out of would have been put to better use at the recycling plant. Their status as art critics notwithstanding, among them they probably had enough imagination to come up with the concept of the Thirdmate.

It went like this:

Humans had originally consisted of *three* sexes. Male, Female, and the so-called Thirdmate. Men and women could not procreate without the Thirdmate. The man provided the semen to the Third, then the Third impregnated the woman with it. Men and women were never meant to interact sexually! That could explain a lot, some folks reasoned.

Osgood watched as the idea caught on, managing to keep his own head above water while everyone else drowned in this newest flood of madness. Why had the Thirdmates been wiped from existence? Who had done it?

Then the anonymous confession appeared, words made up of letters cut from the newspaper, which was found Scotch-taped to the window of the mayor's car, saying, "Our Thirdmate cheated on us so we got rid of *all* of them!" That was it.

People started dreaming of their Thirdmates. Husbands and wives who suddenly realized they didn't "belong" together suddenly found an excuse to file for divorce. The sheriff and his deputies had their hands full with hundreds of nightly domestic situations. Some spouses had affairs with those they were sure had been their Thirdmates in the other reality, which led to even more problems. Luckily there were no fatalities, although there were a fair number of close calls as jealous husbands and wives turned everyday household appliances into weapons. There were plenty of serious injuries pouring into the emergency rooms at Random General and Baptist hospitals.

Until Haver Compton.

When he performed his unceremonious *hara-kiri*, there was no *kaishaku* there to cut his head off for him. He died from loss of blood and guts.

Poor Haver Compton. Poor, lonely, fever-dreaming Haver. It so happened that around this time Haver was sick and running a temperature of 104. There was no one around to care for him as his wife had done when they were together. He stared at their wedding picture and wished she were there with him, to ease his suffering with kind words and a cool hand on his forehead. Decked out in his tux, Haver looked smart and full of promise in that picture. His new wife, Melanie, looked rapturous in white. But there was this space between them, a space big enough for a third person.

Thirdmate.

Maybe it was more than Haver could take, to realize then that in another reality, even after his Melanie had left him, he might not be alone. But in *this* reality, because someone had messed with *Reality*, he was alone and miserable. He decided he didn't want to live in this reality.

The town was stunned. Jake Sky, newly elected sheriff a few weeks before, put the town under martial law until things calmed down. He made it illegal to even enter *Reality* and posted TRESPASSERS WILL BE SHOT signs around the industrial monster.

Osgood, who had been going back and forth about whether or not to try to *do* something about all this, finally decided. It had to stop, no matter what.

ARTIST TO MAKE SCULPTURE OUT OF SCRAP METAL was the headline of the morning edition of the Random Times on July 19th, 1911. There was a picture of the artist, Jay Elroy, who disappeared as soon as *Reality* was finished and never resurfaced *anywhere* as far as anyone knew. He'd been heading onward to Portland, where he'd hoped to start an art movement there, emulating what Alexander Calder had been doing for a year. Massive industrial sculptures were a purely American form that Elroy was positive would forever alter the face of the art world and probably have a profound effect on society as a whole. Like every other art movement before and since.

In the two-column interview with him, Elroy predicted that at the very least industrial sculptors, utilizing scrap metal and mechanical means, would spell doom for stone and clay. While he lamented the inevitable demise of marble, he felt sure that eventually scrap metal sculptors would someday be able to achieve a similar, and probably superior, effect as they perfected their craft. He stayed in

Random for six months while he built *Reality,* the flagship of what he envisioned as a series of sculptures that would ultimately be the centerpiece of every town in America. That was his contribution to the Movement, which he hoped to ignite in Portland with the spark of his own pure devotion.

Osgood figured Elroy probably didn't manage too well in Portland, which wasn't exactly an artistic Mecca at that time, and wound up spending his life slaving in a factory, the ultimate industrial work of art. Maybe he was happy. Not that it mattered.

Osgood had acquired several grainy photographs of *Reality* right after it was finished, before anyone had a chance to "interact" with it. He was almost certain he knew what it had looked like originally, despite the poor quality of the pictures. He studied *Reality* from his usual booth in Pete's everyday at lunch, until he started to see a pattern, and he could trace the changes the sculpture had gone through over the years to arrive in its current form. That was how he discovered the lever, right near the entrance, that he knew if pulled would revert *Reality* back to its original form and would show once and for all to everyone, including that stubborn Indian sheriff, that it had no effect on *real* reality.

All he had to do was get to it.

Sky would be watching *Reality* like a mother watching a child. He was thoroughly convinced of the sculpture's power, utterly brainwashed by the hysteria it inspired. When the call to dismantle the thing had risen, Sky sided with those who feared it might be like dismantling the universe. No one knew what would happen, so it was better to just leave it be.

Some folks were even convinced that Jay Elroy had actually been an emissary of God, testing the Faith of the good people of Random by placing *Reality* in their hands to preserve for Him. It was becoming an underground religion.

The big question, as far as Osgood could see, was this: Would Jake Sky shoot him if he simply walked into *Reality* and pulled that lever? Was the sheriff *that* far gone?

He drank his first cup of coffee while it was still hot and wound up burning his tongue. When he requested a refill, he also asked for a glass of ice water. He was sucking on a piece of ice now, running it over his sore tongue, and waiting. Breakfast and lunch smells filled Pete's Grill. Bacon, hamburgers on the grill, cinnamon rolls, chicken soup . . . Osgood took it all in, savoring it. His heart beat rapidly, his palms were sweating. He wasn't sure he'd live through the day.

He almost tried it on his way over but lost his nerve when he imagined Jake's, or his deputies', guns trained on him as he walked, ready to shoot him down in the street if he even so much as glanced in the direction of *Reality*. So he didn't. He didn't even look. He decided to go ahead and eat his usual lunch at Pete's and work up the nerve while he ate to do what needed to be done. Besides, if he *was* going to get shot, he didn't want to die on an empty stomach.

The door to Pete's opened, and Jake Sky entered. He nodded greetings to several other patrons, nodded to the cook and to Bea, and walked right up to Osgood's table. This time he didn't bother to ask if Osgood minded; he just sat.

"How do you know?" Osgood asked suddenly, surprising himself as much as confusing the sheriff for a moment.

"Excuse me?" Jake frowned. "How do I know *what?*"

"How do you know anything'll happen if I . . . if *someone* changes *Reality*."

Sky leaned back in his seat, the padded bench creaking under his 260 pounds. He absentmindedly reached up to twirl one of his black braids. Maybe not so absentmindedly. Maybe he was reminding Osgood that he was an American Indian and therefore more in tune with Nature and Reality, or something like that.

"I don't," he said. "Nor do I know *nothing* will happen. I mean, what if it *does* change reality, Osgood? What if it were possible for someone to, say, erase my people's existence from reality, make it so Native Americans never were? I wouldn't like that very much."

"How do you know you wouldn't just suddenly become white, or black? Or Chinese?" It was purely a hypothetical question, but a tic started in Jake's neck. Stepping across the line of racism, Osgood realized, was a tricky business.

"My people would no longer exist," Jake said in a con-troled tone. "I still wouldn't like that."

"Come on, Sheriff," Osgood said, leaning forward in his seat a little, trying to appeal to the Indian's common sense, to the intelligence behind the fear of the unknown. "Think about it. Based on evidence that is far too easy to disprove, that is sometimes so obviously self-contradictory I could cry ... you're willing to even con-sider the possibility that altering that piece of scrap metal out there could alter the fabric of reality. Change history, change *now.* I mean, *come on!*"

"Can you prove that it doesn't?"

Osgood and Jake Sky stared at each other for a while. Jake's eyes were impassive; the Indian could probably stare down a grizzly. If Osgood didn't look away, he'd lose his nerve for sure, so he turned to regard *Real-ity.*

"Yes," he said, the word almost sticking in his throat like bile. He pointed toward the sculpture. "See that big lever right at the entrance there? If that lever is pulled, *Reality* will return to its original form." Sky was looking, and Osgood knew he'd see it. That was one of the weird aspects of *Reality,* which Osgood couldn't figure out: that one could see a pattern within it, see a change that corre-sponded somehow with an idea about the real world out-side, an imaginary connection to be sure, but still ... Pull that lever, that part of the sculpture would dip and that part would spin around and that other piece would slide over, and the next thing you know it's back to the way it was when Jay Elroy first built it. Perhaps he disappeared into obscurity because *Reality* had been his one wad, shot prematurely in a town no one ever visited, his single vi-sion wasted on people who would never understand *Real-ity's* connection with reality.

"Maybe," Sheriff Sky finally said, after staring at that one spot long and hard.

Maybe.

But Osgood wasn't there.

Sky looked frantically around, only to see the portly, middle-aged Home Depot clerk deftly dodge one of the deputies outside, pushing him backwards over a curb. The others Sky had placed around the sculpture were too far away to catch Osgood before he made it to that lever. He tramped through a flower bed bordering the square and headed straight for *Reality*. Jake rushed out of Pete's, almost subconsciously pulling his service .38 from its holster.

"Stop!" Jake yelled. Osgood did, maybe ten feet from that lever, and turned to face him. Jake kept a bead on him with the gun and slowly advanced on him. His deputies had explicit orders not to draw their weapons. If anyone was going to shoot Osgood Kramer, it would be the sheriff.

With his arms outspread, Osgood said, "What are you going to do, Jake, kill me?"

"If I have to," Jake said.

Osgood started backing toward *Reality*. The fear that had built inside him all morning was gone. The air outside was cool, energizing, and he breathed it in as though he'd never noticed it before. Maybe he hadn't. Everything around him appeared with a sharp clarity he remembered seeing only as a child. It was all more real to him at that moment than it had been for the last twenty-five years. He smiled and saw Jake frown in response.

"You don't have to shoot me," Osgood said, and he lowered his arms. "You know I'm right, Jake Sky." With that he turned and began walking toward the lever, taking his time because he knew there was no way either Jake or any of his deputies would be able to reach him before he got to it. Unless Jake shot him.

"Stop!" Jake yelled again, but this time he was ignored.

Osgood kept walking until he was at the entrance to the sculpture. It towered over him, an industrial Sphinx spouting riddles. They all had the same answer, he realized as he grabbed hold of the lever, then looked at Jake.

The sheriff still had the gun pointed at him, still stood with his feet spread apart, his knees slightly bent, like he'd seen in the movies. *Draw.*

Osgood grunted with the effort it took to pull the lever down, straining against rust and inertia; then it moved, imperceptibly at first, but it moved. His muscles burned, his face was on fire, his breath came out in explosive bursts, but inch by creaking inch, the lever gave.

Then *Reality* changed. A chorus of groaning metal was

wrenched from within as it moved, as joints and axles that hadn't been used for years suddenly came into play. *Reality's* shape altered subtly at first, then dramatically as entire sections slid forth or disappeared within the mass. Osgood ran from beneath it, stumbled in the grass to where Jake stood, his gun lowered now, and watched the transformation. They both watched. It was difficult to pinpoint any single aspect of the sculpture that changed; there was just a perception of differences here and there, but nothing obvious.

It seemed to last forever, seemed to get louder and louder until Jake fell to his knees beside Osgood, both hands over his ears, .38 dropped and forgotten in the grass. All around the square, the deputies, the lunch clientele in Pete's, the businessmen and women, the bums, they all fell to the ground clutching their heads as the cacophony battered their senses.

Then it stopped.

A faint echo of it could still be heard in the high country around Random, but *Reality* was quiet. Sky was the first one to his feet. He retrieved his gun, then roughly helped Osgood stand. They both looked around, at the town surrounding them, and beyond that the world, the universe. Osgood turned to regard Jake with a grin, triumphant yet sober in the face of this new cosmic truth.

"Well?" he asked.

The sheriff shrugged. "We'll see." Then he turned and walked away, back toward Pete's Grill.

A woman, attractive despite the encroaching of middle age around her eyes, walked onto the square and stood beside Osgood. He nodded hello to her, then kept looking at her because she seemed somehow familiar, although he was sure he'd never seen her before.

"It's ugly," she said, nodding towards *Reality.*

"Oh, I don't think so," Osgood said.

Then the woman looked at Osgood. "You should learn to just leave things alone, you know." Without waiting for a reply she started walking toward *Reality.*

"Sarah!" a voice yelled, and Osgood turned to see Jake Sky running towards them. "Sarah, don't!" He didn't catch her. She stepped into the sculpture, walked right up to a certain switch and flipped it without hesitation.

Metal shifted with a baleful moan, and *Reality* changed . . . .

MARTICORA

by Brian McNaughton

The instant the driver disappeared into the rest room, Phil Howard made a dash for the garishly repainted schoolbus.

"Hey!" He ignored that cry from the kid pumping gas. "Hey, you from the bus! Some guy's messing in it."

Frozen child-faces locked startled eyes on Phil as he plunged down the aisle. Could he still recognize her? They all wore the same red and gold gowns.

"Daddy!"

If she had kept quiet, he might have missed her. He had been concentrating on those who looked eight, and she was very big for her age. Maybe she had a thyroid problem; her eyes bulged more than he remembered. Doctors were part of the real world rejected by the Waywarders. He angrily dismissed the thought of abnormality. He was a big man, and she was his daughter.

"Come on, Suzy." He had gripped her arm more firmly than necessary, for she seemed willing. "We're going home."

"He's got Marticora!" the children shrieked out the bus windows. "Marticora!"

The attendant stood in a puddle of gas that the forgotten nozzle kept spreading as he gawked, but he was the one who asked: "What do you think you're doing?"

The driver looked even more foolish, with his red and gold skirts hiked up, his sandals slapping the tarmac as he raced to cut them off. Phil might have laughed if the man had been a little older, smaller and slower.

He slung Suzy over his shoulder. *Willing* was the wrong word. *Pliable,* more likely, twisted into complaisance. Grief for the lost years blurred his sight.

Her weight threatened to buckle his knees, but he forced himself to stagger faster. He dumped her in the car, slammed the door and turned to catch a punch in the belly.

"Love your enemies," he gasped, retreating from the bus driver. "Don't they teach you that?"

"No." A clumsy blow clipped Phil's ear.

His right fist felt massive with anger and loss, as if it could fell the other like a sledgehammer. A cold voice assured him that it could not. A fight would only delay him, to their advantage. He sprinted for the left-hand door.

He screamed at his own stupidity when the other sprang for Suzy's door, but she voted for escape by depressing her lock-button. His heart swelled. She was still his little girl.

"What's your name, sweetie?"

"Marticora."

"That's a mouthful," the weathered redhead said. She was curious, either because of Suzy's getup or because customers were a novelty in her fly-blown cafe. "You don't look Mexican."

"That's a game," Phil said. "Her name's Suzy. Susan."

"That's right." Suzy smiled shyly. "I forgot."

"You don't like your burger?" the woman asked.

"It's okay." Her large, pale fingers had torn it into neat bits, which she had shuffled, drowned in ketchup and forgotten.

"I think the dog's making her nervous."

Whining and grumbling and casting furtively hostile looks, the collie would have made anyone nervous, but the woman ignored the hint to put the damned thing outside.

"Sheena wouldn't hurt nobody. Want to see her pups?"

"Oh, yes!" Suzy's doughy face lit with enthusiasm. For the first time he caught a glimpse of the happy child he remembered. She turned to him. "Can I?"

"Sure, honey."

"They're out—*Sheena!*" The proprietress turned from the screen door to fend off the dog as it rushed up with fangs bared. Unperturbed, Suzy slipped out. "God damn it, Sheena, you lay down! You hear me?" She called:

"Out by the back door, Suzy." She threw Phil a sheepish smile. "She's touchy about her pups."

"Aren't we all."

"The puppies are Leos. What's your little girl's sign?"

Alice would have seen nothing perniciously silly in that question. She had believed: astrology, tarot, witchcraft, and from witchcraft to the Waywarders—not wayward persons, as they surely were, but guardians of an imaginary way to some other dimension. After Suzy's birth, Alice grew fanatical.

In a rational world, his wife's kinks would have been ironed out in a mental hospital, and she never could have absconded to the cult's retreat with their daughter. Nor could she have denied him his court-ordered visiting rights by fleeing across country to hide Suzy in another commune, where he had just tracked her down after two years. But this world, as Phil had learned at great expense of cash and spirit, was not rational.

Suzy would escape the trap that still held her mother. While her little friends skipped off to Sunday School to have their minds bulldozed and paved for the conveyance of any and all chimeras, she would be reading Lucretius and Gibbon. If she insisted on fairy tales, she would get Voltaire and Swift. And anyone who mentioned gods, devils, UFOs or ESP within her earshot would find himself capable of levitation: through the nearest door, at the end of her father's foot.

The redhead stared at him. His bitter laugh had offended her. At times he could admit that resentment had made him the flipside of Alice's broken record.

Before he could apologize, she dashed into the kitchen, where the dog had begun barking furiously at the back door.

As he stood to count bills from his wallet, a shimmer in the grimy window caught his eye. Down the long desert road, a harlequin blob contracted and elongated in the heat-haze. The bus was on their trail. He told himself wryly that their pursuers must be psychic.

"Suzy!" he shouted as he ran to the car. He blasted the horn. "Come here, quick!"

She whipped around the corner of the cafe more gracefully than he would have thought likely. Hearing a fearful din erupt behind her, he expected the odious dog to appear on her heels. He flung the door wide and jerked her in. The rear end slewed in a spray of gravel as the woman came screaming after them, her red face now a match for her hair. He had no time to explain that the money was on the counter. The bus was pulling in.

The driver had somewhere exchanged his load of children for adults. In the rearview mirror, Phil saw Alice alight from the bus, her elegant posture transforming her foolish outfit into the robe of an enchantress. He felt suddenly hollow. He had forgotten how much he once loved her.

Gazing back, Suzy said, "Mama," with cool detachment.

He stole another look. It was a fleeting glimpse through dust, but the cultists seemed to be comforting the woman from the cafe. Was she one of them, and had this been a trap?

He forced himself to say, "Will you miss . . . ?"

The last word could not be forced, but she said, "No. You won't tie me up at night, will you?"

"Of course not! Did they do that?"

"They said I was bad."

"You have to forget everything they ever taught you."

"Okay." She giggled and plucked at her sleeve. "What do you call this color?"

It took him a moment to understand her joke, but he didn't laugh. His child had become a person in his absence, a stranger with her own sense of humor. It shocked him.

"Marticora," he pronounced thoughtfully when they were on the plane. "Is that Spanish?"

In the pinafore and braids he had thought right for her age, she looked even bigger and more ungainly. The flight attendants showed reserve, as if she were his bizarrely costumed mistress.

"No. What's that place? Not Asia. *Persia*. It's a name from Persia."

She didn't look much like a Suzy. Maybe she should keep the name if she liked it. "What does it mean?"

"It's like a manticore."

That she should know such an odd word pleased him, but his pleasure faded. She knew it only because the Waywarders believed such nonsense. His daughter would not bear the name of a mythical monster. He fell silent, and she resumed her rapt contemplation of their world's wooly floor.

Too keyed up to sleep, but apparently content in his apartment, Suzy watched television in the bedroom he had lovingly prepared for her. In the living room, he watched the telephone. On the thirty-third ring, he picked it up.

"There's nothing you can say—"

Alice interrupted: "Phil, it's not your daughter."

"Not even that. Damn you, I know my own child!"

They had said these things before. Their conversation could have been conducted just as well by a pair of answering machines. "If you want to see her—without your coreligionists—you can. But I—"

"It's—"

"*It?* God damn it, Alice, stop referring to our—"

"*It*, Phil, and it's dangerous. You don't know. Evil."

"Is that why you tied her up at night, you crazy bitch?"

The facing window reflected movement in the dim hallway behind his chair. Backlit by shifting cathode beams, Suzy's form was gross and indistinct, but he glimpsed the ball that she repeatedly tossed and caught. With everything from a child-sized Raggedy Ann to the latest video games to divert her, she had dug out one of his tennis balls, an oddly soiled one, to play with.

Alice yammered on. He tried to bore her into hanging up by reciting a favorite maxim: "Ignorance is the only evil."

The sudden hiss of the radiator startled him. The ball landed in his lap. He checked a shameful impulse to vent his anger by yelling at Suzy.

"Is it midnight in New York yet, Phil? Phil?"

It struck him that the radiator would not hiss like that in August; nor would a tennis ball, even though its fuzz might somehow become matted with blood, have ears like a puppy.

Suzy hugged him so tightly that he dropped the phone, so tightly that he couldn't cry out. Or even breathe.

The phone tinnily repeated, "Phil?"

THE SHACKLES OF BURIED SINS

by Lois Tilton

A sudden chilling gust flung broad, dry-brown leaves against his horse's fetlocks, and the animal shied. He fought it still, then shivered, pulling his coat up around his neck.

Tall, patchy-barked sycamores surrounded the house at the top of the hill. A dark, red-brick house, a tight, narrow front, narrow windows. Narrow and stiff. *Like a Yankee preacher in a tight, high collar.* So he pictured in his mind the man who owned it, the Reverend Theophilus Wheatley.

Damned abolitionist!

Tobacco-streaked spit hit the leaves with a sharp, dry crack. Hard to blame the blacks, almost, running off, not with the damned abolitionists everywhere, stirring them up. He'd seen an abolitionist horsewhipped once, run out of town, down in Bolivar County. *Whipping's almost too good for them, even if they are preachers.*

Well, preacher or no, the horseman thought, he had the law on his side. The law and a little more, but you needed that, alone up here in Yankeeland. Carefully, he checked the loaded pistol at his side, a single-action Colt Dragoon revolver. And shackles ready in his saddlebag, good stout iron. *Not taking any chances, not this time.*

The runaways were here, his informant was sure of it. The man had charged him ten dollars, plus another ten if it paid out. But worth it. *Can't let them get away again. Got to get back home. Sallie waiting for me. Going to have the baby by Christmas. Got to be back before then.*

The horse side-stepped beneath him, snorting white steam from its nostrils. *Cold. Winter coming soon.* He shivered again, hating this cold, hard northland, wanting to be home. With a raw, red hand, he pulled out a leather wallet from his inside coat pocket. *Got to buy gloves, it's getting that cold.* He had the warrant ready, and the power of attorney from Mister Abbott. He unfolded one of the circulars, the words he already knew by heart:

RUNAWAY COUPLE

Runaway from my plantation, in Bolivar County, Mississippi, the first of September, 1858, a NEGRO COUPLE.

Man NATHAN, aged twenty-eight years, near six feet tall, well set-up, medium color, good teeth; burn mark in the shape of an S on right forearm.

Wench DELLA, aged nineteen years, four feet, ten inches tall, buxom, copper color, green eyes; marked with the whip about the shoulders; seamstress; insolent disposition.

They will likely be traveling together on a forged pass as man and wife. The man has been used to hiring himself out as a farrier or blacksmith. They may be headed to Fayette County, Tennessee, where the wench has got children.

Contact Jonathon Abbot, Esq.

Garland, Mississippi

He folded the paper carefully and put it back into his wallet, into his coat. Three hundred dollars if he brought the pair of them back, plus his expenses. The pair were worth ten times that, though, on the block. Mister Abbot would likely sell the man down to New Orleans, but he wanted to keep the wench for a breeder, once she had the meanness whipped out of her.

The horseman rubbed his chin, worried, weary. Too much time lost, tracking the runaways to Tennessee, only to find the wench's suckers already gone, sold to a trader that spring. From there, the trail had led up the river into Illinois and now here, to this abolitionist's house, just a couple of days' ride from Chicago. *Couple of niggers couldn't make it all this way from Mississippi without the abolitionists hiding them.* He knew that if Mister Abbott's

two runaways managed to get onto a steamer to Canada,
they were lost for good, and the money with them. He'd
followed them too far for too long to let that happen.
*Three hundred dollars. Enough to live on for a year, me
and Sallie. And the baby coming. Can't afford to lose so
much.*

He breathed on his hands, then kicked the horse into a
trot up the gravel drive, the dry leaves crackling under its
hooves.

*This has got to be the place. I got to find them here.
Could be my last chance.*

*

Caroline Harris raised herself up on her toes to kiss
Mike good-bye. She watched as he backed the Porsche
out of the driveway. The commuter train could get him
into Chicago in half the time it took on the expressway,
but he actually seemed to like the driving.

She supposed it was one of those man things.

Mike had resisted the move to the suburbs at first, but
Caroline's family had lived in this area for four generations, until her grandfather had moved to California after
World War II. "I don't want us to live in some highrise
condo," she'd insisted when Mike took the transfer to
Chicago. "I want a real home, with a big yard, where we
can have kids someday. And it's not just all white people,
either. I bet I've got relatives still living around Sycamore
Hills."

She carried the argument when she got the teaching
job—history and civics—at Sycamore Hills High School.
It was when she was driving back from a meeting with
the principal that she saw the house for sale, just outside
of town.

"The old lady who lived there just died," she told Mike
the minute he got back from work that day. "Listen:

"The historic Wheatley house on 1½ wooded acres.
Brick construction predates the Civil War. 9 spacious
rooms, parlor, dining parlor, four bedrooms, library.
Many original features."

"How much?"

"Only $250,000."

He made choking sounds. "Shit, Carrie, I mean, I know
you want a house, but a place that old! I bet it's crawling

with termites, or dry rot, or something. For that much we could buy a new place—"

"I don't *want* a new place, Mike, out in some development where they don't even have trees! Look, I stopped at the real estate office and talked to the listing agent. She said the house hasn't been remodeled, but the structure is still sound. The lot has less than a hundred feet frontage, so it can't be subdivided, and there's a water tower and pumping station next door, otherwise it would be worth a lot more than they're asking. And it's close to the school. We won't find another chance like this, Mike!"

He had already seen enough of real estate prices in the far western suburbs of Chicago to know that the Wheatley house really was a bargain, and it wasn't long before they had signed the papers, assumed the mortgage, and were moved in.

Now Caroline, alone in the large, square kitchen, took a sip of her coffee, staring down at the floor where she had already ripped up half of the ancient linoleum. She wanted to get as much of the remodeling as possible done this summer, before school started.

The coffee was already cold. There was so much work, but it was a temptation to think of pouring a fresh mug and taking it to sit out in the back yard. The lilac blooms were just past their prime now but still fragrant—and the grass was studded with yellow dandelions, another job they had to get around to. It was such a shame the way a house like this had been let go for so many years, even though the neglect was the only reason they'd been able to afford it.

It was almost as if she'd been meant to have the place, the real estate agent had remarked at the closing. "A teacher, someone who can appreciate the historical value."

Only a week ago Caroline had attended a meeting of the local Historical Society. Except for one other woman, everyone there was white, but people were friendly, especially when they learned that they had just bought the Wheatley house. The group's president had suggested she might want to check out the library at Wesleyan College to read up on the house's history.

"Doctor Pettit," she called out to an elderly gentleman in a dark suit, "this is Mrs. Harris. She's going to be teaching history at Sycamore Hills High School this fall, and she and her husband have just moved into the Wheatley house!"

A dry-skinned, fragile white hand took Caroline's. "So you're the young lady," said the Reverend Doctor Pettit.

Caroline was bemused. The last time anyone had called her a "young lady" had been her mother, when she was about sixteen and running after boys. *Now you look here, young lady!*

"Yes," she said, "I'm very interested in learning all I can about the house's history."

Doctor Pettit nodded. "The College library was named after Reverend Wheatley, you know—the Wheatley Library. It's really a nice collection. We have all of Reverend Wheatley's papers, of course. I was College chaplain until I retired about a dozen years ago. Now I'm sort of unofficial curator of the collection. We have most of the issues of Lovejoy's *Observer,* some of Beecher's papers . . . Are you interested in the abolitionists, Mrs. Harris?"

"Well, yes, I suppose I am. My family came from this area, you see. My grandfather always told us that *his* grandfather came up North on the Underground Railroad. His name was Joseph Cobb."

"Cobb. Yes, let me see. I think I remember some Cobbs."

"I hope I can find some cousins still living in the neighborhood."

"Well, you're quite welcome to use our collection any time you'd like. I know we have pictures of your house."

"Photographs?"

"Oh, my, yes. I think we even have a picture of your house in the official history of the College. They called it the President's House, you know, even after Reverend Wheatley retired. So, you see, you really should stop in and see our collection. I'm there every Tuesday and Friday morning."

Now, in the kitchen, Caroline glanced up at the calendar she'd hung next to the ancient white refrigerator. It was Tuesday. She sighed, glancing again at the scabrous-looking floor. It wouldn't hurt anything to take a morning off, not just this once.

A half hour later she had changed and was pulling her

Volvo out of the driveway. Wesleyan College had been out in the country when both house and college were first built, but the town had grown up around them. Most of the older homes in the area had originally been farmhouses.

Caroline parked her car in the small visitors' lot and asked directions to the Wheatley Library. It was one of the original buildings, although the college had added a wing around the turn of the century. The collection of abolitionists' papers was housed in a striking old wood-paneled room, all dark walnut and bookcases.

Doctor Pettit recognized her at once, and she was almost embarrassed to find that he had already assembled some of the information he thought she might want to see, material related to Theophilus Wheatley and the Underground Railroad activities in the area before the Civil War.

There was an old, sepia-toned lithograph of the house. The black, wrought-iron fence hadn't been there originally, and none of the trees looked the same, but the basic exterior of the house itself didn't seem to have been altered since the day it was built.

"Was it in the Wheatley family for a long time?" she asked.

"Mrs. McClintock—the old lady who just died—was the widow of Reverend Wheatley's great-grandson. I'm a Wheatley descendant myself, you know."

"No, I didn't."

He nodded. "Theophilus Wheatley built the house in 1851, when he came here to take up the presidency of the Seminary—it was the Seminary then, you know. He was already an outstanding figure in the abolitionist movement. But there's a mystery about him, you know. Just seven years later, he retired, quite suddenly. Not just from the presidency but from all public life. He gave no reason." The old man sighed. "He lived there for thirty years, almost a recluse, until he died. His grandson, Archibald McClintock, inherited it after him, and his son's widow lived alone there for nearly thirty years.

"But times change, I know. People don't stay in one place. I don't suppose you and your husband will want to live there for sixty years."

"It really depends on my husband's job. If he's trans-
ferred again. But my family came from this area."

"Ah, yes, you did say so, didn't you? Cobb, wasn't it?
I have the name Cobb in some old records here. Let me
see. The Seminary was quite influential in the Underground Railroad days, you know, and slave-catchers
didn't get too much cooperation from the local authori-
ties. The Seminary ran a school for the children of the escaped slaves. Yes, here it is: the records of the pupils and
their families."

He stood aside to let her read through the old ledger.
The paper was a dark yellow-brown and obviously very
brittle, with names and dates inscribed in thin strokes of
India ink. She made out the names on the page he'd
showed her: *Joseph Cobb, junior, aged ten. Wheatley
Cobb, aged nine. Sarah Cobb, aged seven.*

"I can't believe it!" Caroline breathed. "My great-great
grandfather was Joseph Cobb! He took the name when he
came out of slavery. Like Joseph came out of slavery in
Egypt, he said. But he had a son named Wheatley?" She
stared again at the page, this visible link to her own past.

*

*Winter coming. Got to get back home. Sallie, waiting
for me. Going to have the baby.*
Got to find them niggers. They got to be here.
So dark now. Can't see. Got to find them.
It's cold here. So cold.

*

Caroline could hardly wait to tell Mike, as soon as he
got home.

"You mean you found your family? Living here?"

"No, my ancestors! Records of them! Do you realize
what this means? My own great-great-grandparents might
have come right here to this very house when they escaped from slavery! I'm sure this Joseph Cobb Jr. in the
records is my own great-great-grandfather! And he had a
brother named Wheatley! You see? This house was a station on the Underground Railroad. Joseph Cobb settled
just a few miles away, just before the Civil War! It all
fits!"

She bounced slightly on her heels as she looked around
the kitchen, imagining her own ancestors sitting at a table

in this very room, hungry and tired after their long flight from the South, finally safe, finally free.

"Tomorrow, I'm going to go check the County records and see what I can find out. Or maybe my father knows. I think I'll call him tonight!"

"Look, Caroline, I'm glad you're finding out about your ancestors and all that, but you're not going to forget about everything else, are you?" He looked pointedly down at the floor with its stubborn fragments of old linoleum, reminding her whose idea it was to buy this old house in the first place.

"Anyway, what's for dinner?"

*

The next day Caroline went to check the County records of births and deaths, where she found, to her disappointment, that Wheatley Cobb had died in 1876, at thirteen years old. Joseph Junior had had four children, and one daughter married a man named Marcus Richardson.

Her father, when she talked to him that night, remembered the Richardsons as being his cousins, and Caroline looked up the name in the phone book. Nervously, she called asking for Marcus Richardson and explained to his wife, who answered the phone, who she was and why she'd like to meet them. Vivian Richardson confirmed that her husband's grandfather had been Marcus Richardson, a descendant of Joseph Cobb. She was delighted to hear that Caroline had moved here, and, yes, she knew the other cousins, and Caroline and Mike were just going to have to come over this weekend to meet everybody.

By Friday Caroline had gotten up all the rest of the linoleum and had a contractor come to give her an estimate on the kitchen remodeling. The contractor was a youngish white man named Tom Michalek, and for over an hour they stood in the kitchen drinking coffee and discussing the fine details of house restoration. Did Caroline realize that the woodwork was walnut, even the floors, underneath that linoleum? "A lot of people, you know, go tearing out walls and floors without really seeing what they're destroying. So many of these features are irreplaceable."

"Oh, I want to preserve whatever we can. I think it's

like archeology, almost, digging down to discover the original house."

"You an archeologist, are you?"

"No, a history teacher. But I've been on some digs, summers when I was in college. Indian campsites, that kind of thing. Once, we found a grave."

He told her he should be back with an estimate on Monday. Afterward, Caroline sat in the kitchen, thinking about the history of the house. If it had really sheltered fugitive slaves, somewhere there should be evidence: false walls or a trap door leading to a secret room. She wanted to see the place where her ancestors might have hidden. It would almost be like touching hands with them after almost a century and a half.

Then there was the matter of Theophilus Wheatley's life. He was universally supposed to be involved in the Underground Railway, yet there was no concrete evidence linking him to the shadow organization. And the mystery of his abrupt and complete retirement from public life. She might actually end up making a significant discovery.

Whether Mike would share her enthusiasm was a different matter. As far as he was concerned, it was one thing to restore the house and make it a comfortable place to live, another to start tearing it up looking for buried secrets.

Caroline already knew there were no old trunks or diaries up in the attic. But what about the basement? Basements and cellars had been common hiding places for fugitive slaves.

Just in case, she dug out a flashlight from a kitchen drawer. The basement door was just off the back porch of the house, next to the pantry that she'd designated as a laundry room when the remodeling was done. Caroline shivered when she opened it. It was chilly down there, especially after sitting in the sunwarmed kitchen, but now that she'd made up her mind to do this, she wasn't going to be put off by a little draft.

The basement was like a cave, the air musty, cool and dry. Here, more than anywhere else, the house's extreme age was visible. The foundation walls were stone: glacier-tumbled boulders cemented into place with a coarse mortar—irregular shapes, various colors of buff and gray in the matrix. Above it, the structure of the house rested on huge, rough-hewn beams, fully a foot square, still solid and sound after a century and a half.

Having grown up in California, Caroline was not much used to basements. Of course, she'd been down here a dozen times already, both before they'd moved in and since, checking the furnace, the hot-water heater, the maze of pipes and BX cable that made the house somehow seem like a living organism. But now she felt a knot of tension in the pit of her stomach as she stood at the bottom of the stairs, noting the marks on the concrete floor where some ancient huge furnace had once stood, the remains of a coal bin below one of the windows.

Slowly, she moved around the perimeter, using the flashlight to examine any cracks or unevenness in the wall or floor. It wasn't a full basement, only an area about twenty feet square at the back of the house, beneath the kitchen. She glanced curiously at the east wall, where the stairs came down. What was beneath the pantry, then? Behind it?

She stepped up to the wall and shone her flashlight into the south-east corner behind the stairs. There, the mortar around one boulder looked different, lighter in color. Kneeling down, she discovered that the shifting of the house over the years must have cracked the thin layer of cement.

Could this be the entrance to a secret room? She put her weight on the boulder, and it shifted slightly. She jumped backward, startled, her heart pounding. There was a rush of cool air past her face, the scent of dust and old secrets.

Now the boulder was visibly out of place in the wall, tabs of old mortar clinging to it. She worked her hand into the crack at the top and grasped the mortar like a handle. The stone rocked slightly. She wondered how much it must weigh. Maybe it might roll back and crush her fingers. What she needed was a lever. Like a crowbar. She thought she remembered one on the old tool bench.

Bringing it back to the wall, she inserted the claw end of the iron bar into the gap and strained to move the rock again. There was a grating of stone, then suddenly the crowbar flew out of her hand as the boulder rolled forward, hitting the concrete floor with a deafening crash.

Caroline was shaking. Oh, God, had she cracked the

floor? How was she ever going to get the stone back into the wall?

She shivered again in the draft coming from behind the wall, and curiosity started to overcome her momentary panic. Why was it so cold? What was back there?

She picked up the flashlight and shone it into the hole where the stone had been. There was a space behind it, a space as large as a room. This must be it! The hiding place! Eagerly getting down to her hands and knees, she squeezed her way through.

It was a room, maybe eight feet by twelve. Dirt-floored. She moved the flashlight around the room, revealing the shelves of rough wood on three walls, like a root cellar. Then she saw the thick planking stairs and the obvious signs where an outside door had been sealed off, leaving a solid foundation wall.

Her heart raced with the excitement of discovery. She could think of only one reason to seal the cellar off this way—if this really had been a station on the illegal Underground Railway. How old was this section of the foundation? She went over to the stairs and shone her flashlight on the wall above them. It was the same stone and mortar construction. Then, curious, she knelt down. The dirt underneath the stairs was loose, not worn hard like it was everywhere else. Using the flashlight, she probed, then started as it struck—wood?

She scraped more dirt away. Yes, wood! Some kind of trap door set into the floor underneath the cellar stairs!

Using a broken piece of an old shelf, she cleared the rest of the dirt away, exposing the door, a square of planks roughly nailed together—square-shanked nails, she noted. Old ones. She found the handhold and started to lift. The thick old planking was heavy. Caroline had to strain with every muscle fiber she possessed to shift it even as much as an inch. Rusty hinges grated in protest.

Cold air from below rushed up at her, making her shiver. Was it an old well down there?

She needed a lever again. The crowbar. She reached through the hole in the wall to retrieve it, inserted it under the edge of the trap and heaved. The door rose, and she lifted it up, then knelt to look down inside the hole under the stairs.

It was a tunnel, not a well. The shaft dropped down

about five feet to the bottom of the foundation, then angled underneath. An escape tunnel!

Now there was no doubt. This was what she'd been searching for, the concrete link between Theophilus Wheatley and the Underground Railway! Her first impulse was to climb down there and see where it went, but she hesitated. Crawling into an unexplored tunnel alone was dangerous. What if it collapsed on top of her? She shivered again, imagining herself trapped underneath tons of dirt and rock. How long might it be before Mike figured out where she was?

She bit her lower lip, recalling that Mike would be coming home from work. What would he say about her crawling through here? She wasn't sure why, exactly, but she didn't think she wanted to tell him about it. Maybe because they were her ancestors, not his, he was just slightly impatient lately with her "obsession" with the house's history. He wanted it remodeled to live in, not torn apart. Guiltily, she wondered if she'd damaged the foundation by shifting that boulder, and how she was ever going to get it back into the wall.

She backed with some reluctance through the hole out into the main basement and tried to wrestle the stone into place, but she couldn't even shift it an inch. It was too late now to explore the tunnel, and tomorrow was the weekend. She was going to have to wait.

*

She's here! Know she's here. Knew it all along. Right here in this house.

Damned abolitionist! I remember now. Almost had her. Almost . . .

It hurt. My head . . .

Oh, Sallie!

Got to get back home. Three hundred dollars. Winter coming. The baby . . .

*

On Sunday they went to dinner at the Richardsons'. There were over two dozen relatives, kids and all, gathered around the gas grill in the back yard. Caroline found herself being hugged and pulled into the center of attention. She'd wondered at first how Mike would take all these relatives, but there he was next to the barbecue grill with a beer in his hand, talking amiably with Marcus Richardson.

Everyone had something to say about just how everyone was related to everyone else. One woman turned out to be a first cousin of Charles Cobb, her grandfather, and Caroline had to promise that she would invite her father out from California to meet all of them as soon as the house was fit for company.

"We're home," she thought, for the first time, really, since they'd moved out here. It was a good feeling.

*

The contractor had been supposed to come Monday, but he called and told her there was an emergency on another job. Caroline was almost glad. Now there was no excuse not to go down to the tunnel again. Theophilus Wheatley and the Underground Railway. History just a few feet beneath her, in her own house.

Remembering the chill and the dark, she put on a sweatshirt and conducted a quick, futile search for fresh flashlight batteries, dismissing the danger of the tunnel caving in. If you're afraid—here, now—she told herself firmly, how had *they* felt, a hundred and fifty years ago? After weeks, maybe months on the run, slave-catchers after them with guns, dogs, chains. They didn't have a choice.

Finally, to quiet her misgivings, she scribbled a note to Mike and left it on the kitchen table. Just in case. He could come and dig out her lifeless body.

She checked one more time to make sure the trap door was propped open securely, then dropped down into the hole and started to crawl on her hands and knees through the opening under the wall. She grazed her head against the rock and felt her heart speed up in panic, suddenly imagining that she might have brought the whole foundation crashing down on her head.

Recovering herself, she crawled on through. She kept trying to put herself in the place of the fugitives, so long ago. Without even a flashlight to show the way.

Crawling awkwardly with the light in her hand, she moved slowly forward through the tunnel's narrow length. Her small size was an advantage down here. A man as big as Mike might have to wriggle through on his belly, if he didn't get stuck.

It was impossible to tell how far she'd gone. Fifty feet? A hundred? Too late, she started to wonder about the ventilation. But, no, that cold draft had to mean air was coming through from somewhere.

Then the beam of light picked out an open space ahead. After a few more yards, Caroline found herself in what seemed to be a natural cave, large enough that she could stand upright. A half-dozen people could have hidden in here! At the opposite end, the cave narrowed, but the exit, if there had been one, was choked with dirt.

She looked around, grinning with excited relief. People *had* been here! The ground was littered. She knelt again, finding chicken bones, a broken Mason jar that looked like Civil War period, some scraps of disintegrating cloth. The jar seemed to be the most datable object. She wished now that she had brought a backpack with her, maybe a shovel. What else was buried under the dirt floor of the cave?

She swept the flashlight beam across the space, and from the narrow end of the cave, where the roof lowered, it seemed to reflect back. Caroline went closer, looked down. There was a thin slab of limestone, and something about the size and shape of it—she knelt and brushed dirt from the surface, uncovering the letter R carved into the stone. Curious, she cleared away more dirt; then, abruptly, she sat back.

R I P

It was a gravestone!

She fought down her horror. There was no reason to be afraid. She'd seen gravesites before, even helped excavate one. Remember? She imagined that an escaped slave might have been buried in this place, dying so very close to freedom, only a few days journey away, but still infinitely too far. Perhaps the secrecy had been necessary in those days of the Fugitive Slave Act, not to reveal the hiding place.

She started to clear the rest of the stone. It was about six feet long and just over two feet wide, a roughly rectangular slab laid in the earth. But no date, no name or any other inscription on the slab, just the crudely carved letters and the shape of a cross scratched into the stone below them.

Caroline stared speculatively down at the grave. No, that would be going too far!

But would it, really? After all, she couldn't just leave it down here, could she? And she couldn't call the police. It wasn't as though this could be a recent grave, that old Mrs. McClintock might have been some kind of serial killer, burying her victims down here. From all the signs, this cave had been sealed off for over a hundred years.

Caroline worked her finger underneath the slab, wishing she'd thought to bring the crowbar from the basement. There was no way she could lift it, but she strained to pull it aside. There was a grating of stone and a rush of frigid air that sent her tumbling backwards, tripping over the flashlight. In the sudden darkness she felt frigid hands clutching her, a cold heavy weight around her wrists, like iron shackles. She screamed, tearing herself free and groping frantically on the floor of the cave for the flashlight.

It was underneath her. Caroline knelt on the ground hugging it to her chest, shaking violently and gasping for breath. It was almost as if something had been trying to pull her into the grave!

*

Almost had her!

Almost had her that time! Get the shackles on her, good stout iron. Take her back. Get both of them. Take them back home. Three hundred dollars. For Sallie and the baby.

Sallie waiting. All alone back home. Never wanted me to go, not so far, not with the baby coming. How she cried the day I rode off.

Promised I'd be back, back home before winter, before her time. Told her, it's three hundred dollars. Enough to see us through till spring.

Got to get home soon. Winter coming. Getting so cold.

*

Caroline forced a laugh at her wild imagination. It was dark down here, and she was nervous, that's all. It made her imagine . . . things. There were human remains under the stone, probably nothing but a heap of old bones. Nothing she hadn't seen before, nothing to get all worked up about.

Carefully propping the flashlight at an angle to shine

into the grave, she bent back down to the slab and braced herself with her legs to move it aside. Inch by inch it shifted, exposing a human skeleton.

The grave had been shallow, the slab laid directly over the body. Caroline studied the remains with fascination, her momentary fright nearly forgotten. The bones were well preserved, the skeleton intact except for the skull, where part of the forehead and upper orbit of the right eye had been shattered.

She lifted the skull free to search under it for the missing fragments, but turning it around she noticed a smaller hole in the back of the head. She frowned, wishing she knew more about forensics, but the smaller hole looked a lot like a bullet's entrance wound: a shot at close range, the bullet entering the back of the skull and exiting just above the right eye, splattering the cave with bloody pulverized brain tissue and bone splinters. It was such a sudden, vivid image! An execution-style killing, a shot in the back of the head. Or should she be calling it a murder? That would explain why the cave's entrance had been filled in, the cellar sealed off. But it must have been over a hundred years ago!

Wanting to be certain, she shone the flashlight down into the grave again, and there, half-hidden under the slab, she saw the saddlebags at the skeleton's feet. Stretching to reach under the stone, she got hold of a strap and pulled the bags out. They were heavy! She opened one flap, then her hand pulled back. There were chains in the bag, links of heavy rusted iron. With horror, she recognized what they were—slave shackles! The clank of iron echoed in the cave as she let them fall to the ground, reacting violently to the chill touch of the metal.

Her skin prickled as the aura of slavery filled the underground chamber, and she *knew* the terror of the pursuit, the constant danger, the knowledge that a man was after her, determined to lock *these* onto her wrists. She could still almost feel the cold weight of the iron.

For a moment, the impulse to run was almost overwhelming. Then she noticed there was something else in the grave that had been underneath the saddlebags. Still shaking, she reached in and pulled out a kind of large leather wallet, with a flap that folded down to protect the contents. Carefully, she lifted the flap, then inhaled sharply. There were papers inside!

She leaned back on her heels, gently holding the valuable documents against her chest. The answer had to be in here. But the papers would be fragile, and she couldn't read them properly by flashlight, anyway. She closed the saddlebags again, hiding the chains away, and hung the strap around her neck, tucked the wallet with its precious papers inside her sweatshirt. Then she started back through the tunnel, trying to ignore the sense that there was something behind her, reaching out for her through the darkness, trying to drag her back.

She emerged at last, rushing up the basement stairs into the warmth and light of a bright spring day. She blinked in the sunshine coming in through the windows, feeling like Lazarus just climbing out of his tomb. Alive. Free.

Trembling with exhaustion, she dropped the saddlebags and wallet down on the kitchen table. There was her note to Mike. She crumpled it with a sense of relief.

The first thing she looked at was the leather wallet. Its flap was stamped with initials: HDC.

She lifted it up slowly. The leather was stiff and cracked, with a few patches of mold where it had lain on the ground, but the wallet had served to protect the papers inside. Carefully, she drew them out, wincing whenever a brittle edge broke off. The papers were folded together, the outside sheet stained dark brown and illegible from either age or contact with the leather. She started to unfold it, but it broke along the crease line with a faint but audible snap.

Caroline hesitated. Maybe she should call Doctor Pettit or someone for help. But the next sheet seemed to be in better condition, torn only a little at the edge of the crease where it was folded. With utmost care, she spread it open and began to read.

The details fascinated and horrified all at once. *Runaway couple.* Not man and wife. Slaves weren't allowed to marry, to be joined together by God so that no man might put them asunder. Slave families had been put asunder every day.

It was the small details that were worst, the matter-of-fact statements. *A burn mark in the shape of an S.* An accident at the forge? Or a brand? What would an "S" stand for?

Marked with the whip about the shoulders. The slave woman had been flogged hard enough that it had left scars. What for? Her insolent disposition? Running away to find the children they'd sold away from her?

Nathan and Della. Not her ancestors' names. Except that escaped slaves often changed their names, to avoid recapture or just to make a fresh start in life. Joseph Cobb—Joseph, who had been delivered out of slavery in Egypt. His wife's name—Caroline's great-great-great-grandmother—had been lost. It could have been Della, she told herself.

The saddlebags lay across the table, heavy with the weight of iron shackles. The slave-owner's name had been Jonathon Abbott. Caroline frowned, looked again at the initials on the wallet—HDC. If those were the initials of the man in the grave, he was probably a professional slave-catcher, tracking the two runaways all the way from Mississippi to northern Illinois for the sake of the bounty money.

Tracking them right to this house. And then? What had happened here, down in that cellar, almost a hundred and fifty years ago?

She could almost see it: the two fugitives, Nathan and Della, hiding down in the cave, holding each other there in the darkness, hardly daring to breathe aloud. The slave-catcher on their trail, chains in his saddlebags, ready to claim them and drag them back South to bondage. The abolitionist preacher, Theophilus Wheatley, leading them down to the tunnel beneath his cellar.

But what had happened next? Was it the slave-catcher dead down there? Caroline recalled the skull, the entrance wound in the back of the head. Shot from the back. But whose hand had held the gun? Who had laid his body under that slab?

And how long had the Wheatleys kept the secret buried? Doctor Pettit—he was a Wheatley descendant. Did he know about this?

Shaken, Caroline turned back to the papers and unfolded the next one, but it was just another circular, a copy of the first. The wallet held a dozen of them, folded together. Then, almost illegible, a power of attorney,

made out by Jonathon Abbott to Hosiah Caldwell.
HDC—Hosiah D. Caldwell. It had to be.

Hosiah Caldwell, murdered far from his home, shot in
the back of the head and buried in a nameless grave.

Caroline shook her head in vehement denial. No, not
murdered. It was self-defense. They had no choice. For a
moment, down in that cave, she had almost *felt* the
weight of those chains around her wrists. She knew she
would have done anything, *anything*, to keep from going
back.

But now the saddlebags lay on her kitchen table in the
sunlight, heavy with iron and cold secrets. What should
she do? Who could she tell? The police? Mike? Why did
she feel, somehow, that she was involved in a crime,
guilty as an accessory a hundred and fifty years afterward?

Finally, not knowing what else to do, she put the
leather wallet into a desk drawer and hid the saddlebags
away on the back of a shelf in the basement.

*

It hurts! My head, it hurts.
So cold here.
Got to get home.

*

Mike couldn't help notice that there was something
wrong. "You've hardly touched your food," he said at
dinner. "Are you sure you feel all right?"

"I'm just tired, that's all. A hard day in the house restoration business," she said, grinning weakly. In fact, her
hands and knees were sore, and her back was aching and
stiff from the effort of moving the heavy stone.

Mike looked around the kitchen where they were eating, a slightly puzzled look on his face, trying to figure
out what she could have been doing all day. Then he
pushed his chair back. "Why don't you go out in the yard
and I'll make us both some coffee."

They sat in the lawn chairs, mugs of coffee on a small
glass-topped table between them, while the fading lilacs
glowed in the last hour of late spring sunshine. A cardinal
sang out a territorial challenge from the branch of an ancient sycamore at the side of the house. Caroline could
see the contentment on Mike's face as he glanced over
their property, the green acre of lawn he had mowed just

two days ago, the fragrant, gnarled old bushes. He was coming to like it here, she realized with a pang.

But staring across the lawn, she could only think that somewhere out there, under the grass, was the cave and its dark secret. Estimating the distance she'd crawled underground, she thought it must be below that overgrown stand of trees back where the property took a sharp slope down into a gully. She recalled the tree roots penetrating the roof of the cave.

The memory made her shiver again, and she drew her arms up around herself. Mike frowned in concern. "You know," he said, "maybe this weekend I can give you a hand, ripping up the floors or the walls or whatever you're doing. And I was thinking, you know, we might put in some kind of terrace back here. We could buy some of that wrought-iron furniture." He put his hand on her knee. "Remember when we took that trip to New Orleans, the gardens in all those old houses?"

Caroline forced herself to respond cheerfully, but her smile was hollow. She refused his offer to do the dishes while she stayed out here to rest. The familiar mindless task of cleaning up the kitchen helped take her mind off other things.

It was hard, that night, falling asleep. Despite the heat in the bedroom, the tunnel she was crawling through was dark and cold, and it led endlessly down, deep into the earth. The crawling was hard and slow. The earth pressed down on her, heavier with every step. It weighed her down, but the slave-catcher was right behind her, shackles clashing. A cold, bony hand closed around her ankles, and she could hear his voice, like the rattle of dry leaves.

Got you now. Got you now, girl. Won't let you get away, not this time.

Damned abolitionist!

Gonna take you back to Mister Abbot. Take you back . . .

She couldn't move, she could only cry as the iron clamped around her arms, heavy and cold, heavy and cold.

She sat bolt upright, gasping aloud.

The room blazed with light. Hands grabbed her shoulders, and she saw Mike, holding her. "Carrie, what's the *matter?* You're *shaking!*"

"Nothing," she managed to say despite the convulsive chattering of her teeth. "Just a . . . bad dream."

"You were so cold! Like ice!" Suddenly he shivered himself, as if something had touched him, a hand from the grave.

Caroline reached for her robe, belted it tight despite the lingering heat in their upstairs, unairconditioned bedroom. "I think I'll go down to the kitchen and get myself some warm milk."

He followed her, and she put two mugs of milk into the microwave, watching the clock tick off the seconds. They sat at the table together, silent and uncomfortable. Mike looked confused and a little hurt at her distance. Finally he said, "Funny, I was having a dream, too. Do you remember what yours was about?"

Caroline shook her head, not looking in the direction of the closed basement door. How could she tell him that she'd dug up a man's grave? Released a restless, malevolent spirit into their new home? If he knew . . .

"Well, I'm going back to bed." It was an invitation, but she said, "You go on. I don't think I could sleep just yet. You've got to get up early in the morning."

Alone in the kitchen, she rubbed her wrists, one at a time. The weight of the iron—she could still feel it. And the ringing echoes of the gunshot in her ears, and the red, red explosion.

Damned abolitionist!

It hurts!

She didn't believe in this kind of thing. Didn't want to believe. It was a dream, that's all.

But if she didn't believe, why was she afraid to look at the basement door?

*

Close to them now. Both of them. I know they're here. In this house. Know it. So close.

Get the shackles on them, irons on them. Take them back. They won't get away this time.

Three hundred dollars. Got to get that money. Don't know how else we'll get through the winter. For Sallie. For the baby.

Damned abolitionist! I was so close. So close. Can't let them get away again. Not again.

So close.

*

Caroline had lain awake while the storm gathered and broke, finally falling asleep when the sun rose around five o'clock the next morning. She woke a few hours later to find sun pouring in through the open bedroom window. Mike had already gone to work, letting her sleep half the morning through.

He'd even made a fresh pot of coffee before he left. She poured a cup and sat down at the table.

She couldn't let this go on. She'd hoped that in the fresh light of day everything would be clear, but whether or not her dreams had meant anything else, there was still the brutal fact that the remains of Hosiah Caldwell—if that's who he'd been—were still buried in the cave at the end of the tunnel. She couldn't just leave them there. Haunting her. Haunting even Mike, if he'd shared her dream.

She had been afraid to ask just what Mike had dreamed.

She twisted her fingers around the coffee cup. Why did she feel such *guilt?* She hadn't been the one to pull the trigger. It was . . .

It had been Theophilus Wheatley. She knew it, as clearly as if she'd seen him put the gun to the back of the slave-catcher's head and pull the trigger, as if her ears still rang with the report of the shot and the acrid gunpowder smoke still lingered in her nostrils. More than just a dream.

Theophilus Wheatley. A chill, dry voice whispered and whispered in her head: *Damned abolitionist! Abolitionist preacher!*

What had it done to Reverend Wheatley, to shoot a man that way? Despite the justification, to save the slaves he was hiding, to keep them from being dragged away in chains, it was God's law: Thou Shalt Not Kill.

The date on the papers in the saddlebags was 1858. It had been 1858 when the Reverend Wheatley had abruptly resigned the presidency of Wesleyan Seminary and gone into retirement, shut himself away from the world.

A mystery, Doctor Pettit had said.

But not to Caroline. Not any longer.

She dropped her head into her hands. She couldn't

cope with this by herself. She needed help. Fortunately, it
was one of Doctor Pettit's days to be in the Library.

"Doctor Pettit? This is Caroline Harris. I'm sorry to
bother you, but I've come across something here at my
house, something . . . disturbing. I've got to tell someone
about it, but I'm not sure who. You're the only person I
can think of. It concerns Reverend Wheatley and the Underground Railroad, but it isn't something I can talk about
over the phone. Do you think you could come here and
see for yourself?"

While she was waiting for him, Caroline brought up
the heavy saddlebags from the basement and laid them
down on the kitchen table. She realized that she hadn't
looked through the second bag, only the one with the
shackles. She unbuckled the flap. The first thing she saw
was a gun, a Civil War era revolver. The steel barrel was
only lightly corroded, compared to the rusted iron shackles. Was it the murder weapon? she wondered.

But the rest of the contents were more prosaic: underwear, a woolen shirt, two pairs of socks, a straight razor
in its sheath. A small cloth packet holding needles,
thread, and a few pins—a housewife, it was called. The
socks were darned, with small, expert stitches. Caroline
thought involuntarily of a woman, bending over a darning
egg, working in the dim, flickering light of a lamp. Darning his socks, folding his clean underwear. Packing his
clothes for a journey.

Waiting for his return.

Now the small heap of possessions lay on her table,
next to the shackles and the gun. Such ordinary, human
things to belong to a man who hunted down other human
beings for money. Hosiah Caldwell—what kind of man
had he been? Had he really deserved to die the way he
had, shot in the back?

The doorbell rang.

"Oh, Doctor Pettit, I'm so glad you could come! I
didn't know who else I could tell about this."

She recalled her manners. "I'm sorry. Would you like
some coffee?"

"Yes, please."

Taking his cup, he asked her, "Now, what is it that's so
disturbing, Mrs. Harris?"

In answer, she showed him the saddlebags and the

wallet. As his fingers carefully unfolded the papers she explained how she had discovered the tunnel in the basement and followed it to find the cave, how she had uncovered the crude gravestone.

"Maybe I shouldn't have moved it," she admitted, "but I wasn't really sure there was a body there, or who it might belong to, or ... anything really. But it was a man's skeleton, and these things were in there with it. They prove he was a slave-catcher, I think. And, I'm no expert, but from what I could tell from the skull, he'd been shot in the back of the head."

Doctor Pettit was silent for a moment, reading one of the handbills from the wallet. Then he whispered, "Eighteen fifty-eight. Now I understand. How long he must have lived with this pain, saying nothing!"

"It was a Christian burial," Caroline said slowly. "There was a cross cut into the stone. And the letters RIP. Only ..."

She paused, embarrassed, but he urged her to go on. "I don't ... I've never believed in this kind of thing. But when I was down there, I had the most intense feeling—I can't describe it, as though I were there when it was all happening. I felt ... I thought I felt something touch me, something cold. And then last night, I had these dreams. Terrible dreams, so *real*.

"Do you think I'm crazy, Doctor Pettit?"

He shook his head slowly. "I think you'd better show me this grave, Mrs. Harris."

Caroline led him down the basement to the boulder she'd dislodged from the wall. "I could see that it wasn't set into place," she explained, "and when I shifted it just a little, it rolled out."

"I see. And behind here?"

Caroline went through and gave him a hand to help him follow. Fortunately, Doctor Pettit wasn't much larger than she was. "Here," she said, shining the flashlight onto the hidden trap door. He stood beside her, looking down into the pit, then said, "I suppose we have to crawl through there."

Caroline stared at the fragile old man, realizing suddenly that he couldn't go climbing down in that place, not at his age. What had she been thinking of? "Doctor Pettit, you can't be thinking of going down there! It's much too dangerous!"

"Mrs. Harris," he said firmly. "I know you own this house. But, in a way, I have a claim on it, too. I'm descended from the man who built it. He was a man of God. To bury a man like that, in unconsecrated ground, where he couldn't rest. No wonder he shut himself away!

"And if what you say is true, this is my duty, as a minister of God."

Caroline stood silent, unable to argue while he took a small book from an inside pocket of his jacket, a Bible, and held it a moment as if to draw strength from it. "All right," she said finally, reluctantly. She slid down into the hole and helped him down after her.

"We have to crawl," she explained apologetically, and he nodded, looking pale in the dim beam of the flashlight. She hoped he wasn't afraid of enclosed places or the dark, in case the batteries gave out. (Damn, *why* hadn't she bought fresh ones at the store?)

She crawled slowly, hearing the wheeze of his breathing behind her. "Are you all right? Do you want to rest?" she called back to him every few yards, but he always answered, "Yes, I'm fine, go on."

Despite their slow progress, the distance through the tunnel seemed less endless this time. Caroline estimated it was really only a hundred feet to the opening of the cave.

As she stood to help Doctor Pettit to his feet, a chill ran through her. The old man tensed. "Did you feel it?" she asked him, whispering.

He nodded. "An uneasy soul. You did the right thing to bring me here. Can I have the flashlight, please?"

He knelt beside the stone slab, tracing the letters that were carved there, and the cross. His fingers were trembling, and she could see his lips moving silently. He looked up at her finally. "Those letters: 'Rest in Peace.' Theophilus Wheatley was a man of God," he whispered. "He would never have laid a man to his rest without God's blessing. Not even a man such as this." He had taken out his Bible again, was clutching it tightly against his chest.

"I can't believe that—"

Doctor Pettit suddenly gasped as if his breath had been

cut off. He swayed, clutching at his chest, and the flashlight fell to the ground.

The air was suddenly frigid.

*

Damned abolitionist! Damned abolitionist preacher! Damn you!

*

Caroline cried out and grabbed Doctor Pettit as he fell. His breath rasped as he fought for air. It must be a heart attack. Or a stroke, maybe, but what could she do? Get him out of this place! Desperately, she got her arms under his shoulders and started to drag him back through the tunnel. Inch by inch she pulled him, crawling backward, sobbing, begging him to hold on, not to die. "I'm getting you out of here. Just a few more minutes, and we'll be out! I'll call the ambulance! Please!"

She was crawling through the dark. The flashlight was still back in the cave. Its dim glow receded slowly as she struggled to drag the stricken man to safety. He was an awkward burden. She slipped, fell back with his weight on top of her, pulled herself back up, pulled him with her, hit her head against the roof of the tunnel, pulled him again, another step, and another.

The dark grew absolute. Doctor Pettit's head lolled loosely against her chest. She pulled him backwards, sobbing. The tunnel was endless. The dark enveloped her, heavy and chill. It clutched at her, trying to drag her back, to drag her down into the dark. The cold weight of shackles made it hard to move, the chains tripped her.

Not this time! Not going to get away, not this time!

"Damn you!" she screamed aloud. "Leave me alone!" She kept crawling, dragging her burden. The cold presence was still there, clinging to her, but she refused to let it pull her back. It couldn't have her, not her or Doctor Pettit, either. She was going to get them both out of here.

She crawled backward. Another inch. Another. And then she was beneath the foundation of the house and pulling her burden through the hole into the cellar.

After the passage through the tunnel's black heart, the light that drifted in from the basement was enough to allow her to make out Doctor Pettit's limp form, and for the first time she realized he was no longer breathing.

She sank down to her knees, his inert weight falling

across her, and sobbed helplessly. This was her fault! Her fault, letting such an old man crawl down there into that place!

Eventually she realized she had to get him upstairs. Even as light as Doctor Pettit had been, Caroline couldn't lift his lifeless body up out of the hole. At last she climbed out herself and found a rope in the basement. With her fingers numb and trembling, she secured it under his shoulders, climbed out again, and pulled the body, inch by inch again, up from the pit.

Then the stairs, one by one, her arms around him again the way she had held him in the tunnel, his head fallen forward, legs dragging limply behind, the sound of his shoes striking the steps, the sound of her sobs.

Somehow she managed to call 911. The paramedics came in a rush of flashing lights and sirens, bursting into the house with their equipment. They found her sitting on the floor beside the phone and one of them lifted her into a chair while his partner bent down over Doctor Pettit on the floor of the pantry. He looked up and shook his head.

"What happened?" they asked her, very quietly, very gently.

She looked up at them, blinked. "I . . . we . . ." She took a breath. "Doctor Pettit . . . was helping me research the background of this house. My husband and I . . . just moved in. It was an Underground Railroad station before the Civil War, and . . ."

She was babbling, talking too much, not making sense. She took another breath and went on, choosing every word very carefully. She couldn't make them suspicious, make them want to call the police. She had to force herself not to look at the kitchen table, where the contents of the saddlebags were in plain sight. Oh, God, had they seen the gun?

"There was . . . a kind of crawl space down in the basement. It was dirty, and there wasn't much air. I never should have let him go in there, he was too old for that kind of thing, crawling around like that. I should have known, but he insisted . . ."

She was starting to cry again, and the paramedic patted her arm to stop her. "There, that's all right. Do you want something to help you relax? This kind of thing is always a shock." He turned to where his partner was setting up a stretcher. "We've got to be going now, Mrs. Harris. Will you be all right here? Is there someone who can stay with you?"

"My husband," she said quickly. "I called him . . . after I called 911. He should be home . . . soon."

The paramedic nodded. "That's good," he said. He helped his partner lay Doctor Pettit on the stretcher and cover him up.

Tears started again in her eyes. That good old man. She stood at the front door and watched the ambulance take him away.

She was alone now. Oh, she wished it were true that Mike was on his way home. She wanted him, wanted his strong arms around to hold her so she could cry. But there was something she had to do, first. Doctor Pettit had said it was his duty, as a minister of God. But it was Caroline's duty now. She couldn't ask anyone else.

The flashlight was still down in the cave, but Caroline didn't need it any more to find her way back. With the heavy saddlebags around her neck, she crawled on raw and aching hands and knees through the dark. Chill hands clutched at her, she could feel the weight of iron shackles on her wrists and ankles, but they couldn't stop her. Hosiah Caldwell couldn't hurt her. Doctor Pettit had been an old man with a weak heart, exhausted from crawling the length of the tunnel. Caroline Harris was strong, she was alive, and he wasn't going to take her back, not now, not ever again.

The flashlight was on the floor of the cave where Doctor Pettit had dropped it, the beam flickering. His Bible lay a few feet away.

Caroline stepped up to the open grave and carefully placed the saddlebags and wallet back where she'd found them. Then, bending down to the stone slab that had covered the pit, she began to push it back into place.

The batteries were failing by the time the grave was sealed again, but she needed no light for the last thing she had to do. Standing over his unmarked resting place, she could almost feel sorry for Hosiah Caldwell, buried here alone in the dark. Had someone missed him? Had there been someone to grieve when he never came back home from the north?

She didn't doubt that Reverend Wheatley had said the

words, just as he'd carved the letters and cross in the stone. She only knew it hadn't been enough to let the unquiet spirit rest.

Holding Doctor Pettit's Bible, Caroline began to recite from the burial service, as well as she could remember:

"Unto Almighty God we commend the soul of our brother departed, and we commit his body to the ground. Earth to earth, ashes to ashes, dust to dust. The Lord bless him and keep him, the Lord make His face to shine upon him and be gracious unto him, the Lord lift up His countenance upon him and give him peace."

The flashlight flickered one last time and went out. In the darkness, Caroline held her breath for a moment, but the cold weight of the shackles was gone.

She exhaled, then whispered, "Rest in Peace."

Whose peace had Theophilus Wheatley sought, she wondered, when he carved those letters on the stone: the murdered man's or his own?

She turned to crawl back out of the darkness for the last time, but as she did a faint breath of air seemed to sigh up out of the grave, and she thought she could hear a whispered voice:

Cold. So cold.

SORCERER'S MATE

by M. E. Beckett

When Homer ate Franny's grandfather, he gave little thought to any possible consequences of his action. It began as a party trick, and he ate only a little of the old fellow anyway.

Tasted just like any other ashes, he said, as he gnawed on a bone to emphasize his disregard for the customs of Man and the Word of Gods unknown.

Franny didn't mind. She'd never liked that grandfather anyway.

It was the second party trick that turned Homer's life into a swirling nonsense from which he would never really recover. The earwig bit him before he managed to eat it alive. And the earwig was the fulcrum, and the entry of the earwig into the Homer-Grandpa dyad triggered a response untouched in the breast of Gaia since the days of the great Sorcerers.

Many of the Sorcerers were killed in the mass slaughter that led to the fall of Atlantis and that sundered Cretaceous from Tertiary at the K-T boundary and did in the dinosaurs for ever and all. (Don't tell me about the Time being out of joint—I know that. How do you think it got that way?)

And many of the Sorcerers, who were partly human and became more so over the next millennia, did not die but withered as fruit left upon trees in the autumn or windfalls left to their own devices, cut off from the motherlode of nourishment that is the Tree.

And one of the Sorcerers did neither.

Grandpa had been one of the middle sort of Sorcerer. He had withered many years in the shadow of the Great

Days, lingering just because he liked women and the production of children upon their bodies, or rather the play that leads thereto. From one continent to another he moved, and it is moot whether he came to resemble Humanity, or Humanity him, for his offspring were far more than Legion. Families, tribes, yea nations of progeny did he produce during the long, dark lingering of his soul upon this Earth, and he knew not which of the children of Woman might also be a child of Grandpa.

He had a lot of fun doing it, too.

But he never kept track; never watched over the young he engendered nor the young they bore with others or with each other. And by and by, Grandpa became a large part of the gene pool of Mankind.

And Mankind flourished.

The first of the ladies upon whom Grandpa bestowed the blessing of offspring and a bit of love was a small lady. Pithecanthropus her name was, and it suited her. She lived very long ago indeed, and she bore him only one child, and that child was feared and hated by the tribes of Pithecanthropus, for it was different. It was like Grandpa, and slowly Pithecanthropus began to change—and died out at the hands of unfeeling Evolution.

Again and again, Grandpa strove, and again and again the result was either deadly or simply increased intelligence in a dying race that might now know of its end rather than coming upon it in the ordinary way of animals—unaware and unafraid.

And so the tribes of near-Man began to know and to fear Death, for Death walked among them and made children in their laughing women and made them cry and love and hate before their kind disappeared forever.

And one of them did not.

In the savannahs of mid-Northern Africa, Grandpa was particularly active one era when his despair in his lonely state turned to horniness in his rather one-track mind. Furrow after furrow did he plough, and the offspring of the little hominids of the forest-edges and the plains came to be, and some of them killed their mothers in the doing of it, since Grandpa was large and they were small and delicate.

But some of them lived. And some of them managed to breed with others of their kind, avoiding Grandpa somehow, and so they didn't die out entirely but became an animal for whom birth is often a particularly painful and unpleasant phenomenon.

The families and the tribes grew slowly in numbers and in intelligence, fed constantly from the abundant scrotum of Grandpa, who at that time felt an inexhaustible store of Genesis within him, and who wanted to be revered, now, as well as laid.

And revered he was. First Pan under many names, then other gods, Grandpa continued to propagate and plunder at the same time, producing in the female of the species he was helping to create a wiliness in dealing with mates and the saying, "It's a wise man who knows his own father," which is the earliest and most all-encompassing of trite sayings or religious tenets.

But Grandpa, remember, was not alone.

For there was another, the One Sorcerer who was different and who neither withered nor died; nor did his nature change in any significant way. And this was Zelimann, the One Zelimann, who thought of Grandpa and a few other withered ones too shy or too weak to procreate as the chaff of his own race and the bane of the one into which Grandpa was busy burying his genes.

Like the others of the time of the Great Ones, Zelimann was a polymorph. He was powerful, also, for it was by his own desire that he did not crumble with the rest of his kind in the cataclysm that dropped the giant Saurians into that mire of history and propelled a tiny warm creature into prominence that might end in the end of the planet itself.

In his own form, Zelimann was frightening. He would have stood fifteen feet tall had feet yet been invented, and he would have massed four hundred kilograms had they been. He would have been ugly, too. (Not human ugly, *noumenally* ugly. Ugliness personified.) But he didn't mind that. What he did mind was that there appeared upon the Earth race after race that seemed *almost* ready. Almost ready to become Sorcerers in their own right. Almost ready to follow Grandpa into greatness, for Grandpa, in between ruttings, had discovered a fondness for the hominids with whom he made more little hominids and liked as well as lusted after them.

Zelimann the Sorcerer, of the true blood and unwithered, hated that.

He was an avowed racist and speciesist and would have been proud to announce it if there had been anyone bright enough to hear—other than Grandpa, who already knew.

The withering of Grandpa was a sometime thing and did not affect all of his faculties or characteristics at once. Sometimes he would lift his now-shaggy head to the skies, and *scry* the stars, and look once again upon the planet of his own origin. He would cry a little in those times, and the little people of his family would look on in awe and try crying too. They became good at it. The Sorcerers gave them reason to become good at it.

Zelimann determined early that Grandpa, whom he called *Worm,* and *Mammal-Lover* (which was a mistake— Grandpa liked that one; it made him feel grandpaternal) and sometimes by his own name, which is a secret name in the tribes of Man.

Killing a Sorcerer (might as well call them that—it's as close a word as there is if we do not call them God) is not an easy thing to do. It happens quickly or not at all, since all Sorcerers have instant reflexes and very good psychokinetic defenses. Grandpa was withering, but he was by no means dead, and he simply fended off the first five or six hundred attacks, usually with a great shout of pleasure, for Zelimann would try to catch him in an unguarded moment, which was often with his penis buried in some sad or lonely or beautiful and often ecstatic woman or other. But Grandpa would simply shout his reply wordlessly to the treetops or to the sky or into the startled woman's ear, and she would smile (after the invention of smiling civilized the snarl) at her ability to make the great being happy. (And sometimes shout right back at him, after that was invented.)

And Zelimann would stump away, defeated and unlaid and frustrated in many ways.

He began after a time to think that the only way he'd ever catch Grandpa (whom he called *Talleus,* as had great-Grandma) would be to go back to a time when Grandpa was not yet alert to the dangers of assassination, and that meant back very far indeed, beyond the Cretaceous boundary, to the Time of the Great Ones themselves. He was a very vicious as well as a very intelligent and frustrated Sorcerer.

Time flowed as the juices of the withering being himself, and soon Grandpa became legend under names as varied as the names of the gods of the history of man. (Which, if you think about it, is not at all surprising.)

And the genes bore fruit, and the Twentieth Century arrived with a terrible rush and noise and belching of smoke and disruption of the other flows of the world. It is in the nature of a withering Sorcerer to be a little monomaniacal, and Grandpa was determined that his Race, for he now thought of himself as one of the new ones, would rule as had the Sorcerers in their Time, if he had to pleasure every woman on the now-overpopulated planet to do it.

(He damn near did, too.)

And the computer revolution followed the industrial one, and the information age was born, and Zelimann became desperate.

He had hidden himself well, deep in the side of a mountain in Peru, but not deep enough to be missed any longer by the children of the Sorcerer. What they lacked in innate ability they more than made up for in inventiveness and intelligence, and their orbiting instruments soon detected the abode of the brooding Old Sorcerer.

A gravitational anomaly, they called it. And it was that, too. But mostly it was the home of the Sorcerer Zelimann, and he really resented their prying Eyes in the Sky.

He thought they were making fun of him, too. The lines and markings that indicated his comings and goings were called "phoney" and "natural phenomena" (well, that one was all right with him), and then, once picked up on satellite cameras, "man-made." And that enraged the already surly Sorcerer. They were not man-made but Sorcerer-made. He hated the cute little offspring of his enemy, and he hated more that they aspired now to Godhood, or worse, Sorcererhood.

And then Homer ate Grandpa.

Grandpa had withered over the millennia to the point where there was not much more of him left than was required to activate his apparatus of propagation and to erect the defenses that kept Zelimann from finally doing him in. "A shadow of his former self," he had written once in a fit of both pique and witty intrusion upon the literature of Humanity. And he was that. And less.

So he decided to die. Not as the victim of Zelimann, not as the victim of the fate that had befallen his own race, but just to die quietly, in such a way that Zelimann would not know of it until long after the new race was strong enough and wise enough to defeat a Sorcerer on its own.

With the invention of nuclear weapons, he heaved a sigh of relief and prepared for himself a final resting place. A monument, it would be, but one that would be undetected by the Sorcerer Zelimann and by the wily creatures he called his own.

He dug himself a burrow as had Zelimann, for the Sorcerers were originally an underground species, and moved into it such of his human belongings as he thought he might need while he waited to die; and then he caused a great-(x 10^{67})-Grandson (also his nephew) to choose that site for the construction of a huge rocket-launching facility, thus assuring himself of a solid final resting place, and of a secure one. The new species guarded its toys well.

And then he made a mistake. It was not the first mistake of his life (that one had been the cause of the demise of the Age of Sorcerers in the first place), but it was by far the biggest. And Zelimann struck from far in the past where he had been working to destroy Grandpa before any of this could happen.

Zelimann sent a tiny probe into the future where Grandpa lived and made it into a tiny likeness of himself and then moved all of what mattered of his *self* into the probe, in order to better appreciate his triumph; and when Grandpa died, which he did just a little prematurely, he laughed and paused to look at the subject-race that he could now have for the taking or destroy for the re-building of the species Sorcerer.

And he took to following the corpse of Grandpa about and seeing where the new species took their gods and what they did with them when they died.

He was a bit disappointed, because all that Franny did with Grandpa was to burn his body as quickly as she could, in order to get on with the business of doing unto Homer as Grandpa had done unto Grandma (and others).

Zelimann readied his (science indistinguishable from magic) and prepared to obliterate the tiny creatures whom his enemy had caused to displace and supplant the Great Ones in the midst of the Earth, and then he made one more foray into the world, to laugh at Grandpa and to spit goodbye at the species Man.

And he rose and crawled up to look with gloating passion one last time upon the charred bones of his forever enemy.

He managed only one feeble but painful bite before Homer, carrying the dare further than even he had thought he might, picked him up and ate him alive.

The word is that Homer has become a bit of a magician and a ladies' man to boot. Franny seems not to mind.

DADDY'S GIRL
by Kimberly Rufer-Bach

My best friend, Janet Zimmer, grabbed my arm as I slammed my locker door. Her expression was strange: as excited and thrilled as a smile, but her lips weren't turned up. "Kellie, did you hear what happened to Becka's father?" As usual, she didn't wait for a response. "His car went off a bridge, and he's dead."

Dead. The word seemed to echo in my head. "Where'd you hear that?"

"My mom saw it on the news."

It was so strange . . . your father dies and he gets on the news. I wondered if they only did that if it was an accident.

"Kellie? You okay?" She was staring at me.

"Yeah. Sure."

"Hey, I wonder if she'll be in class."

"Huh?"

"I said, I wonder if she'll be in class. You deaf or something?" She tucked her hair behind her ear. Janet was very neat; mothers encouraged their daughters to be friends with Janet, who reminded them of the little girls in ads in women's magazines.

We went into the classroom, and I opened up the hinged top of my desk and crammed my books into the mess of papers. Mrs. Krysinsky stood by her desk and twisted her string of pink plastic beads as she spoke quietly to Mr. Loftgren, the school psychologist. He sat at her desk when the bell rang. Becka's seat was empty. Mrs. Krysinsky read the attendance list. She didn't say Becka's name. Janet kicked my leg.

After attendance Mr. Loftgren walked to the front of

the room. There were faint faded inkstains on his shirt pocket and a tiny bit of white-something at the corner of his mouth. He eagerly wrote his name on the board, dropped the chalk, and picked it back up.

"Children, I have some unhappy news for you today. One of your classmates, Rebecca Thompson, is absent today because her father died over the weekend."

The room was quiet except for the creak of many chairs as everyone leaned forward to hear what had happened. I glanced over at Janet. Her face was serious.

Mr. Loftgren had the air of a man who was about to pull a rabbit from a hat. "How many of you know someone who has died . . . or had a pet that died? Raise your hand." He half-raised his own, as if to show "this is how to raise your hand." A few hands went up.

A fly landed on the chalkboard behind Mr. Loftgren. I watched it crawl over the letter "G," the letter "R," and pass between a word and the exclamation point modifying it. With a casual backhand, Mr. Loftgren smashed the fly. It dropped onto the eraser ledge. Mr. Loftgren wiped his hand on his baggy pant leg.

"Death," he said, "is kind of like dropping a glass on the floor. It breaks. You can clean up the glass, but you can't put it back together."

What? Everyone else was shifting in their seats, too. I heard a muffled giggle come from the direction of Frank Butcher, the class jerk.

"What I mean to say, children, is that you can't go back and change the way things happened. It's just an accident, but it's permanent. A dead person, like Rebecca's father, is never going to wake up or come back."

It seemed wrong to me. Your father couldn't just disappear.

Mr. Loftgren said we should be especially nice to Becka when she returned to school and added, "And children, my office door is always open if you have any questions about any of this, or if you want to talk about any other problems . . . anything at all." He smiled proudly and paused for a minute. Then he left, and it was a day like any other, except for the jokes about Mr. Loftgren, the gossip, Becka's empty seat, and my own fascination: *Becka's father is dead!*

* * *

Becka missed a few days of school, and when she returned she was pale and quiet. It was scary to see someone my own age look so old. Everyone avoided her. They said, "Sorry about your dad," or nothing at all and got away from her as quickly as possible, as if she had a disease. I spied from behind my reader. With each one who scurried away from her, Becka's shoulders slumped more and more. I could tell she was trying hard not to cry.

At lunch time, she was alone at a table. While Janet and I were standing in line, I said, "Hey, we should go sit by her." She looked at me as if I were nuts, with her mouth hanging open purposely. "Come on. Her *dad* just died."

Janet closed her mouth abruptly. "Okay." She didn't even complain that lunch was fish sticks again.

I set my lunch tray down across from Becka's. "Becka?" I asked quietly.

"Yeah?" She squinted up at me as if there were a bright light behind me. Her eyes looked even bluer than usual because of all the bloodshot veins.

"Can we sit by you?"

"Yeah." She seemed relieved as she turned back to her food, as if she were glad I hadn't asked any more of her.

Janet set down her tray next to mine. "I'm sorry about your dad."

Becka looked up at her, and her hand closed on her fork in a fist. Janet looked away and hurriedly bit a fish stick.

I didn't know what else to say, so I ate quietly. I surreptitiously watched Becka: every rub of her nose, every bite she ate. Is this how you ate after your dad died? Is this how I would look? Her plaid jumper was rumpled—would my clothes be rumpled, too, if my dad died? Would my ponytail be off-center on the back of my head? Wouldn't my mom care enough about me anymore to get it straight before she sent me back to school the first time after Daddy died?

Becka caught me looking at her. She locked her eyes with mine. There was something in them I had never seen before: a shadow, something extra. "Are you thinking about my daddy?" she asked.

I blushed. "Uh ... yeah. Kids have been talking about

it." I glanced at Janet, who seemed to focus her entire being on her creamed corn.

Becka said, "He's not really dead, you know."

"He's not?" Janet blurted around a mouthful of corn.

"No. He just went away for a little while. He'll be back."

Janet said, "Oh. But Mr. Loftgren said—"

"What you heard was true." She sighed. "But he's going to come back. Daddy promised me he'd never go away from me. He went on trips, and he always came back. He'll come back."

I managed a faint "oh." Janet looked at me and bit her lower lip.

Becka smiled; it was incongruous on her stricken face. "Want to come over and play after school?"

"I have to ask my mom," I said. "You live kind of far."

"Yeah. I have to ask my mom, too," Janet said.

Becka nodded knowingly.

After we finished our lunches, Becka had an appointment with Mr. Loftgren. Out on the playground Janet asked, "Are you really gonna go to her house?"

I stopped digging in the sand with a stick. "Aren't you?"

She grimaced and rolled her eyes. "It's too creepy. I mean, is she talking about ghosts, or what? I think Becka's . . ." She whirled her finger beside her ear.

"Her *dad* just died. What's wrong with you? What're you gonna do if my dad dies? Are you gonna stop being my friend? It's not like a dead dad is catching or anything." I kicked sand at her.

Janet held her hands up to block the sand. "Of course I'd still be your friend. But I wasn't friends with Becka ever, anyway." She carefully brushed the sand from her pink dress.

"Yeah, and now nobody is." I attacked the sand with the stick.

Janet watched me silently for a minute. Then she said, "I thought your dad was getting better."

I didn't look up or stop digging. "He went back in the hospital Friday night."

Janet patted my arm awkwardly. "He'll be okay. They said so. And if . . . something did happen, I'd still be your friend."

"Yeah. Okay." Janet really was my best friend. "Come on, you can help me dig this canal if we can find you a good stick.

Of course, my mother didn't care if I went to Becka's house to play. She said, "Fine, honey," and shook a tranquilizer from the bottle. Remembering my mother at that time, that bottle is as much a part of the image as the gold locket with Dad's picture, or her pastel floral dresses, or her tired eyes. "I'll pick you up around four, and we'll go see Daddy." The smile she offered was strained and sweet.

Becka's house was smaller than ours, but the yard was bigger. Becka gestured grandly at the swingset in the side yard and proclaimed that her dad had put it together for her. I wanted to play on the swings, but Becka said we should have a snack first.

"Shh—we have to be quiet," she whispered as she tiptoed into the kitchen.

"Why?" I whispered back.

"Mom's lying down. It seems like she can only sleep during the day now."

I looked around while Becka took the milk from the refrigerator and the cookies from the bear-shaped jar. There was a stack of dirty dishes in the sink, and the garbage can was smelly and full. She turned to me and squinted. "It seems like she has bad dreams. She looks tired even after she just got out of bed."

Just like you, I thought. *At least your ponytail is straight today.* Her pants and blouse were still wrinkled.

Becka led the way to the den and sat down in a red leather recliner with a small table next to it. She set the cookies and milk on the table, between the marble ashtray and the lamp with a duck decoy for a base. I pulled up a rocker.

"This is my dad's chair." She slapped the arm of the recliner. "And look here . . ." She pulled a small box from behind the lamp and took a pipe from it. "This is his, too." She put the pipe in her mouth.

"Are you sure you should . . . uh . . ."

"Sure. Daddy lets me do this all the time."

Becka had been referring to her dad in the present tense all afternoon. *Well, maybe that's the best way to do it when your dad is dead—to just pretend that he's gone away on a trip and will be back soon.*

"You know," Becka said, "my dad always said that if I was a boy they would of named me Tom, after him."

"Oh."

"That's right. Want to see a picture?"

"Okay."

She got up and took a picture from the shelf behind her. I took it from her gingerly; there was something creepy about it . . . about all of this. It felt as if the ghost of Becka's father was going to jump from behind his chair any minute, mad because we were disturbing his things. I glanced nervously at a closet door that was ajar.

The picture showed Becka and her father at the beach. They held each other tightly and grinned at the camera. Becka's father was just . . . well, he looked like anybody's dad. He was missing some of his hair, and he wore a green shirt and glasses, which made his dark eyes seem distant. "Uh, nice picture," I mumbled.

Becka took the picture back and put it on the shelf. "After we eat, do you want to go and play Barbies?"

She looked a lot better, and here, at last, was a situation I knew how to deal with. "Okay."

We ate the cookies and milk and talked about school. The conversation was amazingly normal. Then Becka took me to her room and got the Barbies from under her pink canopy bed.

She had one Barbie and one Ken. "You can take Barbie," she said.

"Hey, thanks."

It was good to know you could still play Barbies when your dad was dead.

During the fourth grade I learned to write in cursive. For Halloween I wore a surgical gown we got at the hospital when we were visiting Dad, and I was "The Mad Doctor." Thanksgiving dinner was in plastic trays at the hospital, in Dad's room, with the television on. Dad didn't eat; he said the tube in his arm fed him just fine. Janet won the spelling bee again. Mom seemed to always have that bottle in her hand, and sometimes there were no clean clothes to wear to school. I had a lot of frozen pizza for dinner.

Every other Christmas I could remember Dad and I had snuck out to the fireplace before Mom got up, to take everything from her stocking and fill it with rocks. That year Mom and I went to the hospital at regular visitor's hours. Dad was awake but in bed with the blankets pulled up under his arms. I handed him my present, which I had wrapped in paper with Rudolf on it, because that was the best, with a red bow, which was the best color for bows. I hadn't even let Mom see it at all: It was my surprise. Dad smiled, and I was so happy because he hardly smiled any more. Mom looked better than she had in a while, too. She'd even put on makeup.

Dad shook the present, but he couldn't guess what it was. He opened it carefully, without ripping the paper, like always. I expected him to say something, to smile, to try them on; but he only stared down at the blue slippers.

"Don't you like them, Daddy?"

He looked up at me very suddenly. His jaw was clenched, and his eyes were wide and watery. I almost took a step back. Then his face changed expression and smoothed out, but his smile was like someone else's. "My favorite color, honey. Thank you." He held his arms out, and I leaned over for a hug.

Mom was smiling too much. "I'd like to talk to your father alone for a minute, Kellie." I went out into the hall. Even with the door closed, I could hear the strangled shriek that began my father's crying. It was like the sound of the world splitting open.

Since I was a kid, my mother didn't usually tell me very much about what was going on. She drove me home and heated up a can of chili for lunch. The mascara that had looked so pretty had gone into the crinkles around her eyes. Without looking at me, she explained that Dad didn't have legs any more. Then she dug through her purse for her pills.

By the end of the school year, Becka had become the official scapegoat of the third grade. On a typical morning, Frank Butcher spotted Becka getting off the schoolbus. "Look out! Here comes Becka!" he warned. Everyone, except Janet and I, ran wildly across the playground, kicking up sand. "Don't let her touch you! Cooties!" Frank yelled.

"Ghost cooties!" someone added.

Becka squinted across the playground at her tormenters, frowning miserably.

Frank squinted back. Then he mussed his reddish hair and pulled out his shirttail. "My dead father—he speaks to me from the great beyond," he intoned. Kirk Spasky began mussing his own hair. He always did what Frank did.

"Just shows what they know," Becka said, quietly and bitterly. "He will so come back."

Frank yelled, "You guys are gonna get cooties, too!" There was menace in his voice.

Kirk added, "Yeah, ghost cooties."

Janet only met my eyes for a second. "I'll see you later." She raced across the playground to get the "cootie protection handshake."

"You gonna go with them, too?" Becka asked.

I couldn't meet her dark-ringed eyes as I said, "nah" because what I really wanted to do was to get away from her as soon as possible. She had gotten a lot creepier.

Becka said, "You know, if you hang out with me, no one will like you anymore."

I looked at her—really looked at her—for the first time in a long while. Her hair, as usual, was messed up. Her face seemed gray and hollow, and there was a wild look in her squinting, blue eyes.

"You know, Becka, not to be mean or anything, but . . ."

She scrunched up her eyes more than usual.

"Well, maybe if you took care of yourself . . . I don't know . . ." I noticed the mismatched skirt and blouse which were at the same time too short and too baggy on her gawky frame. "Maybe if you wore better clothes or something. If . . . you . . . stopped talking about your dad all the time. It gives people the creeps."

"Everybody else talks about their dad."

"Yeah, but, Becka, your dad . . . he's . . ."

Her eyes widened. "I thought you understood."

"I guess not."

She shook her head and walked away.

Janet rushed up to give me the elaborate "cootie protection handshake." "Eeew, Becka cooties!" she squealed.

"Yeah, ghost cooties. Better give me the handshake twice."

I felt better than I had in months. The whole Becka situation had been between Janet and me. Except for the fact that my dad was still in the hospital, the schoolyear ended on a pretty high note.

That summer, Dad became so ill that I wasn't even allowed to visit him at the hospital. I still didn't know what was wrong with him. Mom wouldn't talk about it, and she didn't do anything but go to the hospital, watch TV, and sleep. She slept during the day. Whenever I tried to talk to her, she told me to go out and play.

It seemed my entire life was falling apart. I had become used to my father being in the hosptial, he'd been sick so long, but now I couldn't even visit and tell him how my day had been. My mother didn't listen to my stories, but she repeated at intervals, "That's nice, hon." Meals didn't come on time, if at all. There was rarely anything in the clean laundry pile—and the stack of dirty laundry had become so huge that I suspected the two heaps had commingled. The only constant in my days was the television schedule.

To distract myself from my horrible, unavoidable imaginings about what was happening to my father, and to add a sense of normalcy to my life, I began to clean the house. I learned how to run the vacuum and the washer and dryer. I made meals and tried to make my mother eat with me at regular mealtimes if she was awake. I scheduled everything . . . became an absolute perfectionist, which is a terrible goal for a child because you're bound to fail. Every time dinner turned out poorly or something shrunk in the dryer, I berated myself angrily and cried. My mother never even noticed. I had hoped that somehow my efforts would please her and rouse her from her perpetual daze, but she slept and stared and slept some more. One day I hid her pills, but she hit me and I told her where they were.

My grandparents arrived in their sleek black car and said I was going to "vacation" at their house for two weeks, and wasn't it going to be fun? Just like that, ripped away from my careful schedule and clean house, away from even hoping to see Daddy for two whole weeks!

Two weeks at Grammer and Gramper's house: television, bland food, cigarette smoke, boring stories, and introductions to more elderly people—all of them seemed to smoke, leaving ashes and butts everywhere. I surreptitiously cleaned up after these vistors, but whenever my grandmother caught me, she told me to "run along and play." With what toys? There were no other kids in the neighborhood. There was nothing to do but to stare at the television and try to nod in the right places as I heard the same stories I always heard about relatives I had never met. I thought of my dad, and wondered if he thought of me. *No matter how sick he is, I bet he's thinking about me. Daddy would never forget me.*

When I went back home, a week before school started, they told me my dad was dead—already buried. They said they had "spared" me. I locked myself in my room and cried. I didn't come out to clean, or do laundry, or anything else. I think I did nothing but cry for three days. *Gone forever.* How could my Daddy be gone forever? Not for my whole life . . .

On the first day of fifth grade I stood in front of the mirror and held another mirror behind my head to be sure my ponytail was straight. Then I double-checked my skirt for wrinkles and creases. I looked back in the mirror: I still looked crummy. I looked as bad as Becka had. *But isn't that how it's supposed to be when your dad is dead?* I commanded myself not to think about it anymore. If I cried again, my eyes would be bloodshot.

I wonder if Mr. Loftgren will make the same speech.

Everyone at school had already heard. Lots of people said, "Sorry about your dad," and then just looked at me mutely until they could find an excuse to get away. When Mrs. Murchison wrote in the names on the seating chart, the only empty seat was next to me.

At recess, Janet said, "They just don't understand how it is."

"I guess." *They didn't understand Becka, either.*

"You wanna play in the sand?" I shook my head. "You wanna climb on the monkey bars?"

"No."

Janet sat on the sand beside me, tracing figures with her painted fingernail as I told her how my father had taught me to make and fly a kite, and it didn't fly, so he went out and bought one minutes before the store closed, and we flew it in the dark. I explained about the way he'd stumble around blindly in his underwear in the morning, unwilling to open his eyes until he'd reached coffee. I described his gray flannel jacket—his very favorite, and the time he bought me the exact dollhouse I wanted for Christmas even though my mom said we couldn't afford it, and she got mad at him.

During all this, Janet didn't say a thing. She just squirmed nervously and doodled in the sand. At lunch recess she wasn't at the usual place: She was off with Frank Butcher.

The next day the empty seat next to me was filled: Becka. She looked terrible. The first specific thing I noticed was that she wore a pair of thick glasses with black plastic frames—and she wasn't squinting anymore. Then I noticed that her hair was thin and dull and that the rings around her eyes were even darker than they'd been in the spring. As usual, her clothes were mismatched. As I sat down, she said, "Sorry about your dad."

Automatically, I said, "Thanks. Where were you yesterday?"

"At the doctor."

"What's wrong with you?"

"My hair's falling out, and I keep growing." She stood up.

"Jeez, Becka, you're taller than anyone in the whole school."

She sat down and said, with a note of pride, "They think maybe it's my pituitary, or hormones." She pushed her glasses back up her nose.

"What's that?"

"I don't know. But it's pretty important."

Frank, who was a row up from us, asked, "How do you make a hormone?" He laughed. "Don't pay her!" Kirk Spasky let out a high-pitched cackle.

Becka glared at them, and she was so scary-looking that they stopped laughing. "Four-eyes freak!" Frank blurted.

All of the iron went out of Becka ... she was a girl again, and not a ghost-monster. Frank smiled and began bartering Polack jokes with Kirk.

At recess, when Janet came to meet me by the bench, Frank yelled, "She's got ghost cooties, too!" Janet changed her course, eyes downcast, and went to play with everyone else. They gave her the "handshake."

I found Becka sitting against a tree and sat down beside her. "I can't believe my dad is gone," I said. I held my hands out and stared down at them. "I mean, he was sick for so long, but now he's dead, and I ... I mean, he can't get better, or come home, or even ... I can't even visit him now!" I started to cry. "He ... I mean, even if he was there, in the hospital, asleep all the time ... I could *see* him. And my mom is so messed up, and—" I snuffled liquidly. "He used to always help me blow out the candles on my birthday cake, and my birthday is in a month, and he won't be there!" I gave up trying to wipe my tears away.

Becka just watched me through her glasses, blue eyes bloodshot, as they'd been since her dad had died. I wondered if that was because she still cried every day after all this time. Was I doomed to do the same?

"Becka, you still think your dad is coming back?"

"Of course." She wrinkled her nose to resettle her glasses. "You want your dad back, too?"

"He's *dead*."

"So's my dad. But he's coming back."

"Yeah, right." My crying was slowing to a stop. "How do you make him do that?"

She stretched lazily, pleased with her role as keeper of wisdom. "You got to hold his place for him until he can come back, that's all."

"Huh?"

"Like, does he have a favorite chair?"

"No. But he always sat on the same end of the couch, and he kept his cigarettes and ashtray there until he quit smoking. Then he switched to gum."

Becka nodded sagely. "Okay, what you have to do is sit

in his spot every day. You have to drink from his coffee
cup and chew his brand of gum. Save his place. Then everything will be the same for him when he comes back."

"You sure about this?"

"Yep." She pointed to a small, heart-shaped birthmark
on her chin. "My dad always says he put that there when
I was born, to show how much he loves me. He always
kisses me right on it when he comes back from trips and
says I'm Daddy's Girl. Real soon, he's gonna get back,
and he's gonna kiss it, just like always. I made sure everything will be the same."

I looked at her worn face. At least *she* believed it could
work.

After school, my mom was asleep. So I was quiet when
I took my dad's coffee mug from the shelf. I blew the
dust from it, poured in some Hi-C, and went to Dad's
place on the couch. The gum wasn't there anymore; I resolved to buy some. Then I picked up the remote control
and put on Dad's favorite channel for news. The news
wasn't on yet, but there was a talk show on, so I watched
it. Then I remembered something. I took my dad's favorite gray flannel jacket from the hall closet and put it on.
Everything had to be the same.

Just as I finished the Hi-C, my mother came in. She
looked at me as if she'd seen a ghost and put a hand over
her mouth. Then she went into the kitchen. I could hear
her crying.

I only did this one more night before my mother made
an appointment for me with Mr. Loftgren. I took extra-
special care to make sure I looked neat and clean the day
of the appointment. It was scheduled during math, which
bothered me a lot. I had become just as careful about
schoolwork as keeping the house clean, and missing a
class was a bad thing . . . any sort of disorganization was
bad.

Mr. Loftgren studied me as I came into his cluttered office. I felt like a bug under a magnifying glass. He did everything as if he was doing something else—something
greater.

"I'm glad you could come, Kellie. Sit anywhere." He
watched as I sat in the chair next to his and seemed to

mentally catalog it. "I understand your father died recently. I'm very sorry, Kellie. I know this must be a hard time for you." I shrugged. It seemed best not to say too much, or it might invite questions. "Your mother tells me ..." he began, as he pulled a paper from the file on his desk, "that you've been acting, well, a little strangely, Kellie. Is there anything you'd like to share with me?"

Share? With you?

"Now, I don't want to push you, Kellie, but the behavior your mother described to me was ... Well, Kellie, you know your father is never coming back?"

I looked up at him sharply.

"Dressing up in your father's clothes like that ... it's upsetting your mother, Kellie. She's worried about you."

"It's nothing," I muttered.

"Um-hum." He made a note.

"I won't do it anymore."

"It's not that it's wrong," he said quickly. "In the world of emotions, nothing is wrong. But maybe there are better things you can do."

"Like what?"

"You can keep his memory alive. You know, remember the good times with him. You'll always have those. For instance, Kellie, can you remember a happy time you had with your father? A holiday, perhaps?"

Christmas. The smelly hospital room. Mom dressed up so nice and Dad in the bed. And the look on his face as he unwrapped the slippers. The world-splitting scream.

"You see, you'll always have that, Kellie." He offered a wide smile.

I began to cry. *You made me cry!* I was going to be like Becka! I resolved never to "share" with Mr. Loftgren again. Telling me Daddy was gone forever ... making me cry ...

"That's it Kellie. Tears are good. They help wash away the pain."

Wash away the pain? If I washed away the pain of Daddy being gone, the memories might wash away, too! Daddy would be gone forever! I snuffed back my tears.

"There. Feel better now?" He patted my hand, precisely, three times.

"Oh, yes," I said. *Just let me go to math!*

"I'm glad I could help, Kellie." He made a note and

glanced at his watch. "Feel free to come see me anytime.
My door is always open."

I escaped to math, passing the bench in the hall where
another kid waited, Mr. Loftgren's next sacrifice to the
science of psychology.

In February, on days when the snow turned to miserable sleet, most of us usually stayed in the cafeteria during
recess. Janet was beating me at jacks on the tile floor.
"Don't go near her," she warned. "She'll give you cooties."

I looked at her tiredly. Having Janet as a friend, no
matter how good it was for my "stable and normal" image, was becoming hard. She was also trying to be perfect
all the time, to follow a normalizing schedule and rules,
but her idea of perfection was winning the simultaneous
affections of every kid in the school. Especially Frank,
since he was so popular.

"If Frank finds out you're talking to Becka and then
that you're talking to me, he'll say *I* have cooties!" she
said.

"So what?"

"So what? So *what?*"

"Yeah. So what?"

She dropped the jacks with a clatter. "So Frank won't
be friends with me anymore."

"Big deal. Frank's a creep. I wouldn't hang out with
him if you paid me. The only thing about Frank is that
he's got a big mouth. He'd pick on anyone if he thought
it would get him friends." She looked at me but didn't say
anything. "It's not like I talk to Becka a lot, or anything,
anyway. I mean, she's always sick or at the doctor, anyway. I only just say 'hi' to her."

Janet smiled. "Then it wouldn't really matter much if
you didn't talk to her at all, right? You don't really like
her, or anything." She happily bounced the ball and
scooped up jacks. It seemed she thought the problem was
solved.

But it wasn't that simple, and I didn't know how to explain it to her. I just looked down at the floor, watching
her pick up jacks. After that day on the playground, telling Becka about my dad ... I didn't talk about my dad
with anyone else. No one else understood.

"Janet," I said, "I'm still going to talk to Becka."

She missed the red rubber ball, and it bounced under a table. She didn't even watch it go. Someone chased it down . . . it was Janet's, after all, and she was popular. "Don't talk to her anymore, Kellie. Otherwise I won't be able to be your friend anymore."

"We've been best friends since first grade!" I pleaded.

She looked away. "Yeah, but you aren't my only friend. What if no one else wants to be my friend?"

"You can't be everybody's friend."

"Can so." She picked up a jack and rolled it around in her hand, nervously.

"What about Becka? You're not her friend."

"She doesn't count."

I paused for a second. "What about me?"

She looked up at me sorrowfully, but she didn't say anything.

"Well, good-bye, then. Been nice knowing you." I stood up and walked outside, into the gray sleet. I pulled my coat over my head.

Becka was on the playground, standing under the slide and watching the sleet. Her back was to me—she was so tall! I always forgot how tall she was. She had to bend a little to keep her head from touching the underside of the slide. She was as tall as a grownup.

"Hi, Becka." I stepped under the slide. She turned around. Her hair was slicked back with melted sleet, and I could see how far her hairline had receded. Her eyes were sunken and distant behind her glasses—blue life at the bottom of pits.

She smiled, and deep lines creased at the corners of her mouth and eyes. "Hi," she said, her voice low and strange, as it had been since the middle of the year.

"How're you doing?"

"How come you're not with Janet?"

I knew it would be cruel to tell her, so I shrugged. "She's a jerk anyway . . . her and Frank."

Caught in the middle again . . . I was getting pretty tired of the whole thing. "Hey, don't go picking on my friend," I said dutifully.

The ghost-look came over her face, full of menace. "Oh. Is that what she is?"

"You shut up."

A wicked, tired smile came to her. It was despairing and gloating at the same time. "You gotta stay friends with Janet, or else who's gonna give you the cootie protection handshake?"

"You just shut up!"

"It's true, isn't it?" She pushed her water-spotted glasses up her nose.

She was so ugly! So crazy and ugly—there were even hairs, long and curling, growing from her chin. I kept trying to be nice to her, and now *this!*

"Why aren't you off with Janet, huh? You don't believe me. You don't believe. You didn't even try to get *your* dad back."

I shrieked and pushed her as hard as I could. She fell on her butt with a splash. I stood over her and yelled. "You're a freak! You're a freak, just like they say! And you're crazy! Your dad is dead, Becka, and he's never going to come back!" I stood in the gray drizzle and watched Becka begin to cry. I was crying, too. I turned my back on her and wandered to a bench to sit in the cold slush and marvel at this new reality: *Never coming back. Nothing can change it. Not even Becka, with all her freakishness and belief.*

Becka was rarely in school after that. I didn't pick on her, but I didn't talk to her, either. Janet was off with Frank all the time—she took the toady spot from Kirk Spasky, and her grades began to go down. I hung out with Debby Petty and Fran Chong, who were both normal and average. My mother weaned herself from the pills and began to do laundry and cook once more. Life, it seemed, was losing those sickening hills and valleys and becoming routine once more.

A couple of weeks before the school year ended, Mrs. Murchison said we were all going to write a get-well letter to our sick classmate. It took me a moment to realize she was talking about Becka. She had been out of school so much that when she had stopped attending, I hadn't even noticed.

We wrote what Mrs. Mruchison put on the board, "in cursive, class!" I signed the letter with the most-recently-practiced variation of my signature, and that was it. I was sure I'd get an A for neatness—I always did. But I felt naggingly guilty, as I had a long time ago, when I had heard about Becka's dad dying. Everyone avoided her, and all I could think then was: *Her dad's dead, and all of her friends have left her!* What if Becka was dying? She had certainly looked like she was going to.

After school, without even calling my mom for permission, I stayed on the bus until it got to the stop by Becka's house. Even though the thought of going into that house again was scary, I was driven on by the guilt from yelling at Becka back in February.

I went up the steps and rang the doorbell. It chimed inside the house. I wondered how close or how far I should stand from the door, and I carefully struck a nonchalant pose. Just as I reached to try the bell again, the door swung open. In the doorway stood a man who was missing some of his hair, and he wore a green shirt and glasses that made his blue eyes seem distant. *Becka's father: a ghost!* I took a step back.

But his eyes were the wrong color. I tried to gather my composure enough to speak. "Uh ... I came to see ..." *Becka!* There was a tiny, heart-shaped birthmark on his chin. *Becka's birthmark!*

From inside came a woman's voice. "Tom? Who's at the door?"

"Becka?" I asked.

The man in the door nodded, then whispered in a deep masculine voice, "I'm so glad you're here, Kellie. It's terrible. I keep remembering things ... things about my father, except it's like ... from inside him. And I keep forgetting other things. And she makes me do bad things, like—"

Becka's mother came to the door and pulled Becka back. "Yes?" Her eyebrows went surprisingly high up her forehead as she spoke. She looked like a witch.

"I ... I came to see B-Becka," I stuttered.

"Becka is very ill, honey," she said in a sweet voice. Her eyebrows went back down. "She can't have any visitors."

Becka looked at me and opened her mouth to speak. Her mother smothered her words with a kiss, then kicked the door shut.

All the way home, I wondered: Who could I tell? The

police? My mom? Mr. Loftgren? Nobody would believe me.

Two weeks later my mother took me to Becka's funeral. Janet was there, and she cried and cried. I guess she thought she was supposed to do that at funerals. I didn't stand near her.

The coffin was closed, and I wondered what might be in it, because Becka was right there, next to her mother. Of course, no one else recognized her. Becka's mom introduced her as her "late husband's brother, Tom." I kept trying to make eye contact with Becka, but she was clutching her mother's hand and comforting her during the service.

After the coffin was lowered, people began walking back to their cars and offering kind words to Becka's mom. She was crying and shaking and clutching a ratty Kleenex—I was almost convinced she thought Becka was really dead. I crept forward.

When her mom turned for a hug from someone, I took my chance. I tugged on the sleeve of Becka's black suit. She turned and looked down at me.

"Becka!" I whispered.

She fitfully loosened her striped tie. "We all miss her terribly," she said in that deep voice. "My poor sister-in-law ... first my brother, then their daughter. Were you one of her playmates?"

"Don't you remember me?"

"I just came into town last week." This person resettled the glasses on that nose ... Becka's or her dad's, I didn't know anymore. Then the person who used to be Becka put an arm around Becka's mother's shoulder and said to me, "It's good to meet you." They walked away.

Six months later, my mother clucked her tongue as she turned the page of the newspaper. "I can understand a widow remarrying—but to her dead husband's brother? Having him in the house like that ... taking her husband's place. It's just as if he never went at all! How strange."

That was the end of Becka. She just didn't exist anymore, but her *father* did ... or something close enough to him. Becka held his place until he got back, and then everything was the same.

I was in a frenzy of guilt and terror: I could maybe bring back my own dad. What if that happened? What would happen to *me?* I didn't want to think about that, but I couldn't help it. The physical changes I'd seen in Becka were awful, but those weren't the worst. To become someone else, even my Daddy ... did you forget everything at once? One time Billy Chultez kissed me under the crabapple tree before he moved away; would that memory be just out of reach, like a word on the tip of your tongue? Would I remember filling out a tax form instead?

I began to avoid mentioning my father ... I avoided thinking of him. I never sat on his favorite end of the couch again. Since Mom didn't talk about him either, it was as if he'd never existed. Becka's dad had never gone, and mine had never been.

SOMETHING SHINY FOR MRS. CAULDWELL

by Fred Olen Ray

"I wouldn't put my hand in there," Mayweather said sternly.

"Neither would I," I heard myself say in return. "I was just looking at something shiny in the gravel at the bottom of the aquarium."

"A goldfish's head most likely," he mused. "Those piranhas are a vicious lot. They'll eat almost anything, but apparently they aren't too fond of the heads."

"Must be the eyes that bother them."

Mayweather let out a "Ummmph," and went back to work on his list. I stood up and arched my back. All this waiting around was getting on my nerves.

"How much longer you figure to be?" I asked.

The mousy beanpole looked up at me from his paper-noodling as if I had just screamed bloody murder in a library. "Please," he hissed, "I've only five pages of inventory left to verify if you'll just occupy yourself long enough."

That seemed fair enough and believe me there was plenty at Martin Cauldwell's house to get occupied with. Cauldwell had been one of those Explorer Club types that hunted the world over for his unusual tidbits. Here in his oversized estate was the total sum of a lifetime's worth of gathering, and none of it was in the least bit ordinary, including Mrs. Cauldwell, the most beautiful jewel in the collector's crown. Now the elder Cauldwell was presumed dead, and his grieving wife of twenty-nine was doing a little house cleaning. Everything was going to the

Yorktown Historical Museum. All the stuffed gorillas, human skull drinking cups, dinosaur femurs, varieties of primitive Indian weaponry and hundreds of other weird and bizarre doodads were being "lent out" to the museum for a small security deposit of two hundred thousand in cash. Even Cauldwell's tankfull of prized piranhas, his assortment of South American shrunken heads and his better-than-grandiose painting of himself as Napoleon (albeit with charcoal grey hair) were in the bargain. Yes sir, a kid could get lost in here for days.

I wandered around the cavernous old house, trying to leave Mayweather to his grousing, and wondered about the former Mr. Cauldwell. Did he in fact get lost in his own collection? One thing was for certain: The man *had* disappeared completely. His wife said he had gone out for an evening at his favorite gentlemen's club; the two of them never socialized much together—she too young, he too old, of course. The club said that he sailed out of there late in the evening after an agitated argument with another man—Mrs. Cauldwell's name being mentioned more than once—excitedly hailed a cab and was never seen or heard from again. His wife waits out the appropriate time, files her report. He's declared legally dead and she gets the keys to the palace, monkey's-tooth whistles and all.

Me, I was just hired to keep an eye on the creepy menagerie until every little piece of it could be carted off to Yorktown. It's not such a hot job, but like I said, you can get lost in it if you don't watch out.

The shrunken heads were extremely fascinating to look at. Strange little withered up things without too much expression. A kind of passive, sleepy look but not devoid of character. I wondered if there was a way to make them big again, but then, who would really want to? A little index card taped to the case front let me know all I ever needed to know about shrinking people's heads. All one had to do was remove the skull, sew up the eyes and mouth and roll some hot stones around inside until the whole damn thing shrunk up just right. Why, it was so simple even a primitive tribesman could do it, but I guess that was the general idea.

Mayweather was still squinting into the papers through his thick eye-glasses and scribbling a note every so often.

He seemed too content to be left alone, so I bothered him some more. "What do you figure really became of Mr. Cauldwell?" I asked him.

He stopped writing, pulled off his specs with an exhausted gesture and leaned back in his chair. For a moment he studied me closely. Closer even than I had studied the tank of man-eating piranhas and their shiny goldfish's head. After holding his breath for some time he spoke. "Martin Cauldwell was not extremely well liked, by myself or anyone else, but then I don't suppose you knew him at all."

I admitted there was truth in that.

"He was selfish and egocentric. Collecting was his life's work, and surrounding you are the trophies of just such a life. If he wanted something, it had to be his, no matter the cost."

"And Mrs. Cauldwell?" I asked.

"When he first met Annie in Ecuador a few years back, she was attending to her fever-struck father, Colonel Edwin March. Although smitten by her youth and simple beauty, there was nothing Martin could do or say that would sway her from her father's bedside."

"So what happened?"

"March died suddenly, unexpectedly, even though his fever was not thought to be fatal, and Cauldwell brought Annie back to the States along with his other objects d'art. His collection, seemingly complete in every detail, lacked only one thing."

Taking the bait, I asked what that might be.

"Love," he replied wistfully. "Martin Cauldwell had no love for his young bride. To him she was as any other piece of the collection. Something to admire and be admired for the possession thereof. To be handled sometimes, but not often. You see Martin had made up his mind long ago that the collection was something to be owned, not to be owned by."

"Sounds like you knew him pretty well."

"As a museum curator I have admired his achievements for many years. Mr. Cauldwell delighted in showing off his rare acquisitions to those of us he knew would envy them the most."

"And now they're yours," I said, fumbling in my pocket for a cigarette.

"Yes, thanks to the widow, Mrs. Cauldwell. God bless her."

"Well, two hundred grand's a lot of traveling money for a bunch of bear skin rugs and baubles," I grinned. "Think she's planning a quick trip or something?"

Mayweather dragged his thick glass poker-chips back onto his eyes and sighed. "I really haven't any idea. All I know is that Annie Cauldwell is as sweet as a summer's day and deserves a far better life than Martin had allowed her."

"Treated her poorly, eh?"

"Like a captive I'm told. And now," he spoke wearily, "I've still got forty-eight Sioux war bonnets and twelve shrunken Jivaro heads left to catalog before I can wrap this up, and you, sir, are stopping me. Please busy yourself with whatever it is you do and let me be."

I set fire to my cigarette and shuffled around the trophy room once more like a kid who's been told to go outside and play. I passed some odd but uninteresting looking rugs that were probably hand-knitted by a gaggle of pygmies or something, took another peek at the cold, staring pusses of the piranhas—they looked hungry—and at last came around to the glass bookcase with the shrunken heads.

"How many of these little noggins did you say you were getting, Mayweather?" I asked, disrupting him for the zillionth time.

"Why, twelve," he grimaced, looking up from his work. "Please don't tell me there's one missing."

"On the contrary, my friend. You've got one too many."

"Are you sure? It states here specifically that there are to be one dozen, no more, no less" he said, pointing at the inventory book.

"Sure I'm sure. There's this pale looking one at the very end of the row. The one with the gray hair and moustache."

Mayweather crossed the room and looked in the case. "So it is," he clucked resignedly and without another word he returned to his book, made a slight correction in his addition, and went on from there. As for me, I never said anything about my discovery; after all, who am I to say whether the Indians of South America part their hair

on the left side or the right side or if they even part their
hair at all? I'm not paid to speculate. I collected my
money from the lovely Mrs. Cauldwell, who was in fact
planning a lengthy trip with an unnamed member of a
certain gentlemen's club, and never mentioned how much
I thought that shiny fish's head at the bottom of the pira-
nha tank strongly resembled a mans gold-plated cufflink.

Mayweather said they didn't like heads, but biting the
hand that feeds you is just a matter of taste.

HOPE AS AN ELEMENT OF COLD, DARK MATTER

by Rick Wilber

Annie Lindsay watches out the tired glass of the narrow classroom window as a mountain peak emerges and then is hidden again in the drizzling rain clouds.

Hope, she thinks, would have loved a day like this. Hope always loved the rain.

Annie leans forward to look around the corner of the building and can see the long line of rowan trees that escort the path she walked along earlier from her room in the hostel. The trees look very tired; they drip with the moisture. Wet and gray day, official Scottish weather, just as her mother promised.

Annie tries to pay attention to the welcoming lecture; she can't allow herself to get behind right away. This is an astronomy class, and she's not sure her math is up to it, so she'll have to bear down. Annie knows she's bright enough; her PSAT showed it, and she's always made As in high school, but she hates science generally and would rather be writing poetry or playing some basketball. Still, this is the course that's paid for, so she's stuck with it.

So she's trying hard to concentrate, but she can't. Thoughts of Hope, thoughts that Annie wanted to leave behind, keep intruding. It's been nearly six months now and Annie still thinks about it, a lot.

There was no warning, that was the hardest part. They were supposed to be best friends, supposed to tell each other everything. Everything. And then that.

Annie found her. Walked across the street to see why the phone was busy all morning, if the line was down or

something. Hope's parents were gone every Saturday
morning, playing tennis. Really nice people, Hope's parents. Annie liked them, especially her father. Annie envied Hope on that score, having a father around who was
all tanned and handsome, full of friendly smiles.

The front door was unlocked. The door to Hope's room
was open. There was no warning, no hint, there was just
her father's gun to notice first, the small, silvery thing
that Hope and Annie had laughed about when they first
found it out in the garage, poking fun at a big guy like
her father having a little gun like this.

It looked like a toy, lying there next to Hope, who was
sitting cross-legged, back against the wall, in the corner
of her room, a grimace on her face, her eyes open. The
hole in her chest really wasn't very big, but there was
blood everywhere in the corner behind her.

Hope hadn't said anything, anything at all, about this to
Annie. No hints. She'd been fine the night before at the
basketball game, the season opener. Hope had scored six
points. Annie had scored eighteen. They'd won. They'd
both been happy. Pizza afterward, talking about boys,
about school, about the basketball team.

Little parts of the orientation lecture drift through to
Annie, snatches of information about Edinburgh's landmarks and some famous Scots—there's a place called Arthur's Seat, a Scott Monument, some writers like Burns
and Stevenson, some old hero named Bruce, some Bonnie
Prince, some dog named Bobby. It's all boring; they
haven't started on the real work yet.

Two months ago Annie actually managed to agree with
spacey Beth, her mother, about coming on this study trip.
A proud moment there, mother and daughter both quite
reasonable about something for a change. Annie thought
then that it might actually be fun, and at least it meant
getting away, finding some distance, from Hope.

Scotland, after all, is half of her heritage, as Annie and
Beth discussed, and Annie hasn't seen her father in ten
years, not since he and Beth divorced. Since he was willing to pay Annie's airfare and tuition for the college prep
classes she'll take, well, why not go? It means early college credit, a chance to see the country of her birth and
visit London and Paris while she is at it.

The price is the Big Meeting with Duncan, who, except for a vague childhood memory or two, is a distant tinny voice on the phone to her once or twice a year. No biggie.

Really, it *is* quite an opportunity. Hope would have loved it here, all gray stone and wet green grass. Together, Annie and Hope would have had a blast. Hope always knew how to make the best of bad weather. In the summers back home it was Hope who went jogging right in the blazing heat of the middle of the day and Hope who liked walking on the beach in the middle of a thunderstorm, ignoring the lightning, laughing at the sharp crack of close thunder.

But Annie is alone in this cold rain, and despite all the warnings about the weather she hadn't really realized it would be this damp and miserable. It poured in London as she started the tour that preceded the class. Drizzled in York. Poured again in Glasgow.

And now she is here, with people she doesn't know and with two months to go of what looks like a long, wet summer in this tired city of old stone, gray skies, and pale people.

There is a general shuffling of feet. The opening orientation lecture is over and Annie hasn't taken a note, almost hasn't heard any of it.

She sighs, rises. The rest of the American students are already pairing up and making plans for the day, but Annie has only a couple of hours and then Duncan is stopping by to pick her up. The Big Meeting, Day One: Getting to Know You. She says no thanks to two girls who ask her to come along and shop on Princes Street and instead opts for a walk on her own.

The rain is easing off as she walks up a steep street toward Edinburgh Castle—all stark and moody, very Robin Hood and Middle Ages. It seems to grow right out of the mountain of rock it is built on. The mist, she thinks, looks perfect, swirling around the battlements. What a weird place to live. She wonders how Duncan can bear it, rainy like this all the time.

Duncan—she can't call him Dad—is a scientist. She's never really figured that out. How could her mother, old weird New Agey Beth, ever have fallen in love with a scientist, an astronomer for god's sake?

You'd expect Beth, with her out-of-body experiences

and her pyramids and breathing sessions and channeling and all that, to be miles away (parsecs away, she thinks, and laughs at her own little joke) from a nerdy scientist-type like Duncan.

But fall in love they did, when Beth was a student on a one-year stay at Edinburgh University. The marriage lasted a few years, long enough for Annie to crawl into the world, and then slowly started to fall apart. By the time Annie was six, the long decline had ended in anger and it was over, mother and daughter leaving for the heat and Florida sunshine, about as far away from Scotland as Beth could take them.

Annie and Duncan talked on the phone for a good fifteen minutes just a few weeks ago, when her tickets showed up in the mail.

It was a clumsy, hesitant conversation, Duncan trying to explain what he did after she asked, telling her about looking for something that isn't there, searching for cold, dark matter.

Annie talked about basketball and her grades, said she was looking forward to coming over for the summer, and then, both of them out of words, lost for conversation, they hung up.

Later, Annie had looked up dark matter in the library, found out a few things about the search for the stuff. Now, at least, she had some better questions to ask Duncan, something worth saying, so maybe the conversation this afternoon wouldn't be so stupid.

Annie has a tickle of recognition as she reaches The High Street and looks downhill from the Castle to Holyrood Palace. From her vantage point the street looks long and dull, full of rickety old shops selling trinkets to tourists.

Boredom city. But it's all pretty familiar; she can almost see a toddler version of herself walking into the Camera Obscura building. Come to think of it, she remembers the place pretty well, how the big white bowl under the lens shows what's going on outside. She remembers standing at the rail that circles the bowl and watching the tiny images of the people outside walk by.

She's surprised by the memory, wonders how often that's going to happen here as she wanders around, and decides to check it out. She has nearly two hours to kill, needs the exercise anyway, and so starts walking hard, almost turning it into a jog, threading her way through the sidewalks full up with shoppers who showed up as soon as the rain slacked off.

She misses working out. Back home it was jogging on the beach, basketball and volleyball at school, waterskiing on the bay. There was always something. Here, in a week in Britain, all she's managed to do is walk. She promised Coach K that she would run a few miles every day just to stay in shape for her senior year. Coach has high hopes for her and for the team.

Things ended kind of poorly last season, after Hope's death. Coach gave Annie the standard We All Understand lecture and added the Anytime You Need to Talk Just Come By chat, but nothing really seemed to help. Annie saw ghosts every game.

She'd be fine in practice, usually, but every game she saw Hope, wearing that grimace, standing underneath the basket, waiting patiently for something as Annie ran down the court.

Of course she wasn't there, not really. Annie would blink, or look away and look back, and everything would be back to normal. Still, it kind of got in the way of winning.

The Barons had a chance to take the district title, too, and can do it this year if they can find a guard to replace Hope, someone who can get the ball to Annie in the middle. And if Annie Lives Up To Her Potential, as Coach put it.

On the one hand, walking down the wet bricks of the High Street, Annie hopes she won't get too rusty with two months away from the game. She's always loved it. No one has ever had to force her to play.

On the other hand, it feels good, really good, to not have practice, not have any summer league games. To "not," generally, just feels fine. This will be the most time she's spent away from basketball since the third grade.

She wonders, as she walks, why she isn't more excited about meeting Duncan. Shouldn't she be nail-biting nervous?

She isn't; she's calm. She thinks she's going to handle this whole Big Meeting thing just fine. Hello, Duncan, how nice to see you again. Handshakes, polite hugs. No static at all.

Annie hasn't really had a father and frankly hasn't missed the experience. She and Beth have done just fine, thanks. Annie always gets along well with Beth's various boyfriends, the Toms and Phils and Davids and even that one French guy from Canada, Claude with the attitude.

There's always that first excitement from Beth, then the Period of Closeness when the boyfriend tries to get to know Annie better, then the Big Break-up when Beth cools off and it all falls apart. It's all very dependable.

Annie has learned to keep a certain safe distance. She smiles, shakes hands, chats nicely and walks away. About twice a year is how it works out. She and Hope always had a great time making fun of the poor guys, giving them nicknames like The Jogging Suit for Phil, and Your Pal for the first David. Hope never really liked any of them, even the second David, a lawyer—a really nice guy, handsome in a soft kind of way—that Annie really got along with pretty well.

Hope hated him. She said the tall, good-looking nice ones were the ones you had to watch out for the most. The nicer they seemed, she said, the worse they were. Trust her, she knew. Annie wondered what Hope meant by that, worse in what way? But Hope wouldn't explain. She just hated him, that was all.

Annie tries to picture her father but can't. He's lost in the crowd of faces she's seen over the years. He sent photos last year, but they aren't real, they confuse the faded memories she has from a decade before. Can he be balding now, as the photos show? Can he have put on that kind of weight?

He was a good athlete when he was young; Beth told Annie about that, about watching him play soccer at the university, about how he used to be a serious runner, dashing around on the hilltops near the city, peak to peak in the rain and scattered sunshine.

But the photos from last year showed him filled out now, puffy. And the wavy hair that Mom talks about is nearly gone.

Beth has talked about how glamorous it was at first. Duncan at nineteen was the star of the soccer team and was also doing doctoral work in cosmology.

He'd read a paper on gravitational fields down at Oxford once, and Beth had gone to listen. Duncan talked about how there was mass hidden from view out there in the universe and how better detectors would allow astronomers to prove it, not by seeing it, really, but by seeing how much the dark mass bent light.

Beth told Annie that she'd found it all very metaphysical and mysterious, and, at first, the science had just added to Duncan's appeal. Then, finally—Beth always sighed when she said this—finally she had realized that all those stars didn't leave any room for her and her baby.

Annie wanders off the High Street and finds herself walking by a statue of a dog. Greyfriar's Bobby, it says on the stone, and talks about how the dog was loyal to its master, stood by his grave for years. Annie recalls hearing about it during the orientation lecture, but she can't recall the details.

There's a bench there, and the sun is shining for the moment. Annie sits, leans back against the cold stone of the bench and closes her eyes to soak up the thin sun. It feels good, warm on the face.

There is a rustling noise, like somebody else sitting down, and Annie opens her eyes.

Hope is there, sitting on the far end of the bench, legs crossed as usual, that grimace on her face, just staring at Annie. There is a hole in her blouse, in her chest, right between the too tiny breasts that she always complained about. She starts to raise her right hand in a greeting, is maybe going to say something.

Annie blinks, long and hard, and Hope is gone.

God, it's spooky. Annie wonders if she's going crazy. There was a shrink who came as part of the crisis team at the high school after Hope's death. Annie tried to tell her about Hope, about seeing her all the time, about how Hope's grimace seemed to carry a message. Maybe, Annie said, it answered why.

But the shrink just said Annie's mind was playing a few tricks with her, trying to cope. The why of it wasn't something they'd necessarily ever find out. And in time, the shrink said, these things would fade, Annie would get used to Hope being gone.

That was all a year ago. Annie gets up, starts walking

again, looking down at her feet mostly, afraid of what she
might see in the crowds on the street, who she might find
there.

There is a roundabout, cars whizzing by, and she walks
around it to find herself near the old palace at the bottom
of the High Street. The lecturer said there was something
important about the place—Mary, Queen of Scots,
maybe? Some murder?—but Annie can't recall it.

She starts to walk around the palace and hears the incongruous sound of a basketball against pavement. A rim
rattles, players shout instructions to each other.

She rounds a corner and there, wedged into a small
parking lot, is a half court and five players—all of them
about her age. She didn't know the Scots played the
game.

Annie watches them. The small mountain that she saw
out her classroom window serves as a backdrop here, rising in the middle of a park across the street from the
court. The lecturer called the little mountain Arthur's
Seat, said it was really just a steep hill, not even a thousand feet tall, and that people walked up it all the time.
Annie thinks maybe she has memories of being carried up
it as a kid.

She doesn't think she'd like to climb it now, though.
Annie gets a little dizzy when she's up high. Nothing serious, but she has a little bit of a problem with heights.
Including her own. There aren't a lot of boys interested in
dating the tallest girl in the school. And basketball, which
makes a boy all the more attractive, does the opposite for
her. Too intimidating. Tall, red hair, nice features, green
eyes. She knows she looks all right. Hey, looks good,
even. But not to the boys at RFK. Her straight As don't
help.

Hope, all curly blonde and cute, now there was someone popular with the boys. Too popular, maybe. She had
a reputation for that, but she just laughed it off when she
told Annie about her dates, the groping, the boys' clumsy
kisses. Hope and Annie giggled together for an hour,
sides hurting from it, when she told Annie about Bobby
Paschal and how hilarious it was when he took her out to
dinner at L'Auberge. He tried to order wine and got
carded, then tried to read the menu to her and got it all
messed up. The whole evening, right up to the panicky

good night kiss, was a stitch. Hope was so funny when she told that story.

Annie watches the Scottish girls play. Two of them, she decides, are pretty good. Two others are passable. The fifth is an athlete but just doesn't seem to know the game.

As Annie watches, that girl rolls off a screen and tries a clumsy jump shot, all air ball, misses the rim by a good foot.

Annie laughs out loud and the game stops.

They all turn to look at her. There is an embarrassing moment of total silence.

"Um. I'm sorry," she manages to blurt out. Great, first day in the city in ten long years and right away she manages to act nasty to the locals. "I shouldn't have laughed like that. It was just that, well . . ."

"So, you think you could better, do you?" the girl says. "Come on, then, get in here and prove it."

That sounds angry at first, but then the girl smiles, eases off. "Look," she says, "we need one more to even the sides, right? So join us." And she tosses Annie the ball.

Annie thinks for a moment about saying no; she's in that kind of mood. Besides, these girls aren't really at her level and she'll have to play down just to keep them in the game.

But it *is* hoops, and despite what she's been telling herself about having some time off, that's almost too good to be true. She smiles, takes off her jacket, watch, friendship ring from Hope sets them on the grass.

And plays the game.

It feels good. It feels great. She cuts backdoor for an easy layup, hits a pair of fifteen-footers, makes two sharp passes that turn into easy baskets for her teammates—the flow, the joy, is all there. It feels good. It feels great.

She loses track of time, just gets into the rhythm of the game instead. They have an odd way of doing things, playing brief but intense games to five instead of the games to fifteen that Annie plays back home. And they switch possession of the ball every time instead of make it/take it.

But these are minor details. The point is, it is basketball.

She is easily the best player on the court and knows it,

enjoys it, enjoys being good and being comfortable with herself. She's been lonely and homesick and insecure and out of place for a week, and here at last is a chance to do something familiar and fun.

In fact, if truth be known, she hotdogs it some; just for fun. A behind-the-back pass or two, an extra head fake to leave the defender hanging up there useless.

It is in the fifth game, with the scored tied at four all, that Annie is out at the head of the key, takes a pass from a teammate, looks underneath, and sees Hope standing there, starting to raise her hand in greeting, that deadly frown on her face, that stare.

Damn. Why here? Why now? Annie, in that moment, is angry, fed up with this. She throws the ball at Hope, hard, trying to knock it right through her, knock the ghost of her off the court, out of Annie's mind, out of her life.

A teammate, a girl named Mary, has pulled a beautiful spin move on her defender and gone backdoor toward the hoop. She reaches out to grab the ball as if it were meant that way all along, a perfect pass. The game ends with Mary's lay-in. Annie blinks, looks, and Hope is gone, was never there.

They take a break, the local girls gathering around Annie, the best player of their age they've ever seen. There's Mary, Caroline and Anthea, Alice and Anne. They all starting chatting with Annie, finding out about her classes for the summer, about basketball back in the States, laughing about Edinburgh's weather, about the schoolwork they all face.

Three of the girls are a little older, in their first year at university. The other two are in their version of high school. There's some talk about A-Levels and O-levels that Annie doesn't quite understand, but it doesn't matter; these are nice people. Not great basketball players, Annie thinks, but nice people.

When they find out Annie will be in town for the whole summer, they immediately ask her to play on a team they have in a summer league. Three games a week for six weeks, then the playoffs. Not great talent, of course, but loads of fun.

Annie begs off. She's not ready for that, not yet. They play pretty scraggly ball, she tells herself, and she doesn't want to mess up her game. But that isn't the reason, not the real reason. Hope was there again, big as life, staring, frowning.

The girls want to play another few games and Annie starts to say yes, but then thinks of the time, grabs her watch and discovers it's nearly noon. She has to get back to the hostel, clean up, change, and be ready by twelve-thirty.

The girls get back to playing as Annie jogs off toward the hostel. They were nice, she thinks. It would have been fun to play. She probably should have said yes. She wishes, in a way, that she had.

Only then, as she runs back toward her hostel, does Annie realize how she must have sounded, turning them down. What an ego. She must have sounded really conceited. But how can she explain about Hope? She hopes things go better than this with her father.

II

Things don't go better. An hour-and-a-half later, Annie sits in the mud with the rain pouring down on her. She is soaked to the skin, and when she looks up to see where her father is, the only person there in the rain is Hope, sitting a few feet away, staring at Annie, Hope's face tight with that death grimace. Damn.

Oh, Duncan has tried hard enough. He seems like a nice enough guy, and he's even slimmed down some from the pictures she's seen. It started out okay, really, the memories of good times they had shared when she was a little girl flooding back to her as soon as he drove up in his little Ford, said hello and gave her a hug.

But it didn't take long for things to start going down-hill.

Duncan wanted her to see the city from the top of Arthur's Seat; he had packed a picnic lunch so they could walk to the top and see the city while they ate their sandwiches.

There is a car park on the back side of the mountain. They parked there and started the long walk up to the peak. It was easy enough at first, and there were others doing it—a few young couples, several school-age boys, and one older couple, maybe in their seventies. It just

couldn't be that tough, Annie thought. She stayed right in
the middle of the path, away from any risky cliff edges.

Things seemed fine, but about halfway up the skies
opened and the cold rain poured down. The others all
seemed prepared, with rain repellent jackets and caps and
sturdy boots. But Annie was in sneakers and sweatshirt
and was soaked inside a minute.

With the wet wind in her face, the rain pelting down,
the turf slippery and muddy beneath her and Duncan a
good twenty yards ahead, Annie was miserable.

Then she slipped and fell, hard, onto her rear. It might
have been comic under better circumstances, but as it is,
she's a long way from laughing. She looks up and sees
Hope sitting there, frowning at her, shaking her head. Behind Hope, their backs to Annie, are the other people on
the mountain, all happily walking up toward the peak,
umbrellas out or rain gear on. Annie looks down at the
mud and cries.

Great, she thinks. Just great. She looks up again and
Hope is gone. But then, just like that, in a flash, the
whole weight of all that's happened comes crashing down
on her. She is five thousand miles from her home, family
and her friends, trying to ignore a ghost that won't go
away, trying nervously to get along with a father she can
barely remember and hardly understand in his thick accent, walking up a slippery slope in the driving rain with
months—months!—still to go before she can go home,
and it just all seems too much, way too much.

But Annie is not a quitter. In basketball, when the
game is on the line for the Barons, Annie is the one they
go to. They have an in-bounds play that starts—well, that
started—with Hope and ends with Annie taking a ten-foot
jumper. They use the play late in close games. Hope always gets the ball to her, and Annie always gets the shot
to fall. Annie always finds a way. Annie's never been a
crybaby, not even when Hope died. She gets to her feet.

Duncan finally realizes what has happened and makes
his way back to her. She is smiling when he gets there,
laughing at herself. She gladly takes his offered rain
slicker and tosses it over her shoulders. Side by side, they
give up the foolishness and trudge back down the mountain.

A couple of hours later Annie is warm and dry in the

front room of her father's house. She feels better but is still embarrassed about the mountain, though Duncan seems to have forgotten it. The two of them have been trying to talk, but it seems impossible to really say anything. His wife, Jane, should be home in a few minutes, and Annie dreads that, too. This whole thing is tougher than she thought.

Annie and her father have avoided all the really troublesome topics, like why he left her mother, or why he never comes to the States to visit, or why after all those years of nothing more than occasional phone calls he's sent the money for this summer's stay. Annie wonders if he even knows about Hope. She supposes not, since he doesn't bring it up.

They hear a car. Duncan's wife, Jane, has pulled her little Toyota into the drive, and Annie watches out the front window as Jane works her way out of the tiny car and then reaches back into it. She is dark-haired, tall, pretty. When she pulls back out of the car, she holds a baby in her arms.

The baby is a year old. The baby, little Sarah, has Down Syndrome. Retarded. Goofy smile in that round face, all the appropriate drool and coo, but when Annie holds her she seems droopier than Coach K's little girl that she sits for back home. And the eyes look Chinese or something.

The baby reaches out to hug Annie and smile, and Annie wants to cry for the second time in one day, which would set some kind of record. The baby is so sweet, and Duncan and Jane love her so much.

At one point little Sarah tries to stand, pulling hard on a chair, but she's too weak to manage it and never does quite get to her feet. Instead, a few minutes later, she struggles onto her hands and knees and crawls for a few feet.

Jane sees the crawl and yells out to Duncan, who comes to watch. The two of them laugh and clap, all happy for their baby, who's just crawled for the first time while Annie was there to see it.

Back home, the baby that Annie sits for is about a year old, too. And is walking. Crawled at five months. Stood at seven.

Annie feels terribly sad for Duncan and Jane. Sad, too, for the baby. The poor little thing.

The afternoon goes by and things get better, with Annie playing with Sarah and getting to know Duncan and Jane. They seem interested in Annie's life, her basketball skills and her grades, her boyfriends or lack of them, her plans for her future. It's all pretty warm, really, and after a while Annie, rolling a little ball toward Sarah, begins to forget about all the problems, hers and the baby's both, and just sees Sarah for herself, a happy little baby, all smiles and giggles.

Duncan and Jane are just great with Sarah. Duncan's face lights up when he holds her. Jane glows with parental joy. They seem to ignore the problem, as if the retardation weren't there at all.

A bit later, after dinner, while Jane is off changing Sarah's nappy, Annie gets up the nerve to ask Duncan about how it happened, about how they manage to be so great about it. He just looks at her for a second or two, thinking it over, and then puts it this way:

"Somewhere along the line I finally realized that you can't figure out a reason for everything, Annie. Sometimes you just have to accept things and get on with it, that's all—just do the best you can with what you have."

He sips his coffee, looks at his daughter. "Look, Annie, I must admit that we had a rough go of it at first. We even thought about giving her up for adoption, or putting her in some home. It was that difficult, that tragic, really. That's why I didn't, I couldn't, tell you or your mother about the baby.

"But then we started to just see her as she is. We quit trying to understand why, we quit feeling sorry for ourselves, and just got on with it."

He smiles. "She's great, really, in her own way. We've just decided to help her make everything she can of her life. Sarah will do the best she can with what she's got, Annie. It's all any of us can do."

There's a messy nappy in the next room; Jane calls to Duncan for some help, and he laughs, rises, says he'll be back in a minute or two.

Annie idly looks through the magazine rack that is next to the chair where she sits. There's a copy of the local paper on top, the Edinburgh Scotsman. It's folded to the

Scots' Personalities page, and there's a picture of Duncan, all serious-faced, standing with his arms folded in front of some building.

There is a story, an interview with Duncan, where he tries to explain the search for cold, dark matter. The latest data from a NASA satellite has picked up fluctuations in cosmic microwave background, he says, sort of gravitational ripples. The data seem to show that the ripples acted together with other forces as part of the Big Bang. Duncan thinks it's the cold, dark matter that added some push.

"It seems to follow quite logically that cold, dark matter is required for us to see this kind of information from the COBE satellite," Duncan says in the story. And then the reporter adds that Duncan Lindsay, her own father, the guy in there helping change messy diapers, is "one of the top cosmologists in the world in the study of the mysterious dark matter."

Whew. Annie knew he was important, and she's read up on this dark matter stuff. But famous? One of the best in the world? Her father?

What's spooky is how close this all seems to come to some of the stuff Beth talks about with her New Age friends—the unknowable cosmos, the invisible reality, the ripples in the fabric of time and space.

Duncan comes back into the room, sees Annie reading the paper, and laughs it off. "Rather overstates my importance, really. It was Smoot and Silk at Berkeley who are doing the actual work on this."

And he holds up Sarah, all clean and smiley and giggly. "Hey, you" he says to the baby, and rubs his nose into her belly. She squeals with delight. Annie laughs.

"You know," Duncan says to Annie, sitting down and bouncing little Sarah on his knee while Jane goes to put some coffee to the boil, "she's a great wee baby in her own way. We've just decided to help her make everything she can of her life. Like any parents would, with any child."

Later, as Duncan drives her back to her dorm room, Annie thinks about the day, thinks maybe she's beginning to understand a little bit why Duncan has paid for her to come to Scotland. That part he said about helping her be everything she can. Like any parent would. With any child.

The baby has changed things for him, and so for her. Duncan, better late than never, is trying to reach out to Annie, trying to climb back into her life a bit, back where he belongs.

Maybe that's what the trek up Arthur's Seat was all about, Annie thinks. Climbing together. Climbing toward something.

III

The next morning, Annie gets up, walks to class. It's a cool, sunny morning. She didn't get much sleep last night, thinking about things. This whole trip is a challenge, she realizes. Like a tough season in basketball. Like tournament time.

She thinks about cold, dark matter and Hope and that little baby. "You just get on with it," Duncan said.

The rowan trees have blossomed overnight, and there are white blossoms everywhere lining the path she takes. A few of them fall in the breeze to soften her path as she walks across the Meadows.

The lecturer talks about some basics, outlining the material they'll cover over the next few weeks. "From the Big Bang to ?" is the title on the hand-out he gives to all forty students. Annie, reading the syllabus, smiles. She knows a great tutor who'll help her through the tough spots.

By noon Annie is walking in bright sunshine back to the courts down by the park. By half-past she is back at the court. The girls are there again.

Annie asks the girls if she's still invited to play for them in their summer league and they laugh and say yes. Then they split up for some three-on-three. Annie's passing is perfect, her shooting is fine. Hope never shows.

A bit later, Duncan comes by the courts as he'd promised the night before, and an hour later Annie and her father are at the top of Arthur's Seat, the two of them, looking out over the city. The sun has shone the whole way up.

While they are up there, the weather turns; some clouds

blow through spitting rain. Duncan sits down to rustle through a backpack and pull out their rain slickers.

Annie smiles; she's prepared for it this time. She turns away from one gust of wind while he pulls the slickers out and there, standing on a rock outcrop, is Hope, that frown on her face, those eyes in their frozen stare, that hand coming up to wave hello.

Annie is worried for a moment. But then Hope's eyes slowly blink and the frown fades, becomes a slight, hesitant smile. The hand waves once, a good-bye, and Annie watches as Hope turns to walk away, steps down the slope, pivots once to wave again, and then disappears into the mist.

"Who was that?" Duncan asks her as Annie turns back to her father.

"A friend," she says, "just somebody I used to know."

Duncan, who is good at these things, understands without having to see. He opens his arms. Annie comes into them for a hug, and then, while the mist swirls around the two them, she finally cries her long good-bye.

MITTENS AND HOTFOOT

by Walter Vance Awsten

The day was bright and warm, and Mittens couldn't believe his humans would actually expect him to stay indoors. When the door opened to let the big human out that morning, Mittens slipped past his feet and hid in the bushes.

The big one didn't notice; he traipsed down the front walk utterly oblivious to the kitten crouching behind the azaleas, got in his car, and drove away.

Mittens was free!

He waited until the car was out of sight, then trotted out of the bushes and looked around.

Grass, flowers, trees—the whole wide wonderful world lay spread out before him!

Where to go, what to do?

He ran out onto the grass, wrestled with one blade, chewed on another, noticed his tail and gave a quick chase, then spotted a butterfly.

That was a worthy opponent! Mittens forgot about his tail and set out in pursuit of the fluttering insect.

It was a grand and glorious hunt, the butterfly flitting from place to place apparently unaware of Mitten's leaps and lunges, blithely ignoring the claws and fangs that passed within inches of its delicate wings.

The chase wound across the front lawn, around the side of the house, then down through the vegetable garden, between the stakes of a picket fence into the yard next door and into the neighbor's backyard flower garden.

Then, just as Mittens was closing in for the kill—or so Mittens told himself, at any rate—a jet of fire came from nowhere and fried the butterfly to a crisp.

Astonished, Mittens stopped almost in mid-leap and froze, back arched, paws braced.

Where had *that* come from? What had happened to the fluttery thing?

Leaves rustled, and a head emerged from a clump of tiger lilies—a little green, scaly head with smoking nostrils.

Mittens backed away, tail in the air.

A long, thin neck followed the head, and a long, thin body supported by four short legs, and finally a long, thin tail that dragged on the ground. The entire creature, though, was only a little over a foot long, and no taller than Mittens himself.

Mittens stared, wide-eyed, back arched. He'd never seen such a thing.

Of course, being only twelve weeks old, he hadn't seen much.

The two animals stared at one another; then the baby dragon turned away.

Mittens couldn't resist; he pounced.

Almost immediately, he decided that was a bad idea; the dragon writhed about and spat an angry flame at inoffensive air. The kitten leaped away sideways, back arched again, tail puffed up.

The dragon didn't pursue him; it just untangled itself, then turned to watch Mittens with those golden lizard-eyes.

Mittens didn't like that. He considered for a moment, then decided that whatever this thing was, it was best left alone. He turned and scampered away.

For the next hour Mittens had a wonderful time, running about the garden, chasing butterflies and other interesting creatures; he forgot all about that nasty lizard thing.

At last, tired and happy, Mittens decided it was time to go inside and take a nap. He clambered up the back steps to the kitchen door.

It was closed, of course. Somehow, Mittens had never thought about that—if he needed a human's help to get *out,* then he needed help to get *in,* too!

He mewed piteously; maybe a human would hear him and let him in. He mewed again, as loudly as he could.

The door didn't budge.

This was bad. Mittens wanted to curl up on his own little red cushion. He wanted to get inside where his food and water dishes were. Yards and gardens were fine for play, but the *important* stuff was in the house. It was getting hot out here, and the sun was too bright, and he didn't like it any more.

He mewed again.

The door didn't move. No one came. He couldn't hear anything moving inside the house.

Well, Mittens wasn't stupid, by kitten standards; he hopped down the steps and circled the house, trying every door and window he could reach.

All were closed tight.

How could this be? Hadn't the humans *noticed* that he was outside? Hadn't they realized he would want to come in? Where *were* they, asleep? Or had they all gone out without his noticing it?

Stupid, inconsiderate humans!

He tried clawing at the back door, but his tiny claws couldn't do much more than scratch the paint. He meowed as loud as he could—all to no avail.

He couldn't get in by himself; he needed help.

And if the humans weren't around, he'd have to find some other kind of help.

Bill Abbott waved farewell to his carpool and turned toward his house. Then he stopped, startled.

His next-door neighbor, a rather odd fellow named Cawley, was poking through the Abbotts' azaleas, muttering.

"Lose something?" Abbott asked.

Cawley looked up, startled. "As a matter of fact, I did," he said. "A pet. She must have gotten out somehow, I'm not sure how."

Abbott hadn't known Cawley kept any pets. "What sort of pet?" he asked. "A cat?"

"No, a . . . a sort of lizard," Cawley said. "Her name is Hotfoot."

"Odd name for a lizard," Abbott remarked. "What is she, an iguana?"

Cawley hesitated. "No," he said. "No, actually, she's a baby dragon."

Abbott blinked. "You mean, like a Komodo dragon? From Asia?"

"European," Cawley said. "If you see her, let me know, would you?"

"Of course," Abbott said. He walked on past Cawley and the azaleas, found his key, and let himself into the house.

He smelled smoke.

Janet or the kids had probably burned breakfast or something, but Abbott was a bit worried all the same. He peered into the living room.

There was Mittens, curled up asleep on his little green cushion. Nothing was burning.

Abbott hurried down the hall to the kitchen.

There he found the source of the smell—and as he looked at it, he remembered what Cawley had said, and he remembered that Mittens' cushion was *red,* not green.

He walked slowly back to the living room and looked again.

Sure enough, Mittens and Hotfoot were curled up together on Mittens' bed, both sound asleep. A thin wisp of smoke trailed up from Hotfoot's snout.

Abbott stared, then sat down abruptly on the nearest chair.

He shook his head.

He wanted to be a good neighbor and all that, and he didn't like to cause anyone trouble; live and let live was his motto. All the same, he was going to have to talk to Cawley about this. When Hotfoot made that foot-wide hole through the back door, she might have burned down the house.

He wondered what the local zoning regulations said about keeping dragons.

THE HOUSE AT THE EDGE OF THE WORLD

by Juleen Brantingham

A fly was buzzing in an upper corner of the phone booth. The sun shining through the glass had turned the little box into an oven. Leaving the door open didn't help; the air outside wasn't stirring. Diane felt sweat ooze from her scalp; the receiver was hot enough to raise blisters so she was holding it with the tips of her fingers, not letting it touch her ear, which made the receptionist's voice sound like the fly's buzzing. Her father's condition was unchanged.

She hung up in mid-buzz. She couldn't believe he was dying, could never forgive herself if she wasn't there to say goodbye, to tell him how much she loved him. She'd left the thruway, coaxed the car as far as this gas station, avoiding a hike through country that looked as though it hadn't echoed to the sound of a human voice since the last covered wagon passed through, but the mechanic said he couldn't get the parts to fix it before tomorrow. She should have had someone look at it before she left the city, but she'd been so anxious, so upset by the news from the nursing home, that it was a wonder she'd remembered to pack a bag and give notice at work that she would be gone a few days.

The view through the glass shimmered; there was no one moving near the houses she could just glimpse in the pools of shade beneath the drooping trees. This bump in the road wasn't a town; it was a graveyard, and all the spooks were haunting somewhere else.

Picking up her suitcase, she began to trudge in the direction the man at the gas station had indicated. Shade from the pecans and chinaberries didn't extend as far as the road; the sun fried her shoulders beneath her thin cotton blouse. On the far side of the rise there had been cattle grazing, birds wheeling in the sky, wind ruffling the grass, but here everything was so still it might have been a painting, veiled in dust, hanging in a forgotten corner of a museum. The houses seemed disdainful and secretive, hiding back there beneath the trees. Grass was tough and burned-looking, clinging in patches to the sandy soil. Diane heard nothing but the gritty crunch of her own footsteps. Desolation, loneliness, wilderness.

The mechanic had been helpful, mentioning someone named Miss Dita who sometimes took in overnight guests in her pink house at the edge of town.

She smiled at the memory. The heat must have addled her brain because for a moment she'd thought he said "at the edge of the world."

She could almost believe she was walking toward the edge of the world, the crumbling edge where life was precarious. What did these people do, how did they survive out here at the edge of a waste that was no better than a desert? In her long walk she didn't see a store, unless she counted the gas station; she didn't see a school or a post office or even a car after she'd left her own parked beside a pick-up suffering from terminal rust, its naked wheels set on concrete blocks. It was summer; where were the children? It was the middle of the day; where were the housewives hanging out laundry, washing windows, taking out the trash?

Diane had her father's love of cities, the liveliness, the independence. "Who wants to live in a small town where everybody knows everybody else's business?" he used to ask. "Give me a place where people have better things to do than watch the grass grow."

That certainly must be the primary pastime around here. She began to be frightened of the stillness, as if she were intruding in a place under a curse. Those houses couldn't be as empty as they seemed; perhaps she was being watched from behind those dark, unrevealing windows.

She'd only once been accused of having an overactive imagination and that was long in the past, but strange fancies began to prey on her mind. In spite of the heat and her fatigue, when her goal finally came into sight she broke into an awkward run, her suitcase bumping into her leg at every other step.

Miss Dita's house was a cottage of concrete blocks turned sideways to the road, its bright pink a splash of defiance against the faded landscape. Wilting petunias of the same shade snuggled up to the post that supported the mailbox and lined the path that curved around to the screened-in porch, sheltered by a pair of elderly pecans. She climbed the steps and rapped on the screen door, heard it rattle in its frame. There was a smell that wakened another hint of memory: standing with her nose pressed to a dirty screen while rain was falling. For some reason she associated it with someone very old, with hooded eyes, and lips folded over a toothless mouth. She dismissed the thought. She'd never known anyone like that.

A shape moved in the shadows. The screen was so dark Diane could only just make out the blur of a face topping a housedress of gaily printed cotton. She started to explain about her car, but the woman, presumably Miss Dita, interrupted to say she'd had a call from George at the gas station and her room was waiting to the left at the top of the stairs.

The screen door stuck in its frame, and by the time Diane wrestled it open, Miss Dita was a blur retreating from her like a stone falling into a murky pool. The woman said something about a supper of salad and cold cuts at six o'clock.

It was too dark to see anything of the front room, but an arch at the far end opened into a sunlit place, beyond which she could see a flight of stairs going up to the right. Miss Dita had disappeared. When she reached the arch, Diane paused, blinking, disoriented. To the left and right were uncurtained expanses of glass. An easel was set up in front of the left-hand window wall; the top of the table beside it was crowded with tubes, rags, and jars bristling with brushes. Everywhere she looked there were paintings: hanging on the wall beneath the staircase, leaning against a chair behind the easel, lined up against the sills of both windows. Diane had an impression of muted earth colors and images without much detail or shading, but somehow it seemed rude to examine them uninvited. Holding her suitcase in front of her so as not to bump the stacked canvases, she crossed to the stairs and went up.

The room contained the necessities and nothing more—a bed covered by a chenille spread, a wooden chair, a nightstand with a clock and a lamp, a window covered by threadbare curtains and a drawn shade. After a shower in the bathroom across the hall, as empty as the bedroom of personal or welcoming touches, Diane slipped into a clean blouse and a pair of shorts. Though she'd packed her suitcase only this morning, her clothes were badly wrinkled, as though someone had used a hot iron to set the creases. Without much hope she took her brown twill skirt and fish-print blouse and hung them in the closet—six wire hangers on an empty bar, empty shelf above. She would wear them tomorrow when she went to the nursing home—if nothing else went wrong, if it wasn't too late to go.

She'd packed a book. Her monthly visits had taught her that there was always some waiting time even in a weekend packed with activities and pleasurable talks about the past. She smiled, fondly remembering his slightly lecturing tone when he was being most self-consciously parental.

"Dee, don't ever waste a minute when you might be learning, improving yourself. Daydreams may be all right for artists and poets, but for the rest of us, life is too short."

Tears sprang into her eyes. He couldn't be dying. How could she bear to live without him?

She didn't think she was sleepy, but she'd no more than set the pillow against the wall at the head of the bed and opened the book before her eyelids began to droop. Sliding down, wondering if the window was open and whether or not she had enough energy to go and see, she dozed.

The air in the room became stifling. It had the effect of holding her back from the restfulness of true sleep but at the same time sapping her strength so she couldn't quite wake up. She drifted at the edge of the place where nightmares are born, sensing vague dangers, shapes that rose to menace her, then faded before she could bring them into focus.

Diane woke, dry-mouthed and exhausted, feeling the need of another shower. While she was in the bathroom splashing water on her face, she heard a clock chiming the hour of six. She suddenly realized she felt sick and faint with hunger. She'd been in such a hurry to reach the nursing home she hadn't even thought about lunch. Running her fingers through her hair, too impatient to look for her comb, she hurried downstairs.

The sun was low, filling the room at the foot of the stairs with an unearthly red light. Another small table had been brought in, the promised supper laid out with one plate, one set of silverware, one glass, and a pitcher of tepid lemonade. Diane was so thirsty she drank the first glass without tasting it. There was no sign of her hostess; the house was silent. Though she hadn't been looking forward to exchanging small talk with a stranger, she resented being shunned this way, as if she were a leper, so ugly and wretched no one could bear to be near her.

She picked up the plate to examine its twined flower-shapes, ran a finger along the curving pattern of the fork handle. These shapes and colors touched a memory, not strongly enough to bring it fully awake. Someone, somewhere in her past had had dinnerware with the same patterns, someone vaguely maternal and comforting, like a grandmother or an aunt. But that was impossible. She and her father had only each other, and his love for her had been so strong she'd never felt she was missing anything.

She didn't sit down to eat but strolled around the room examining the paintings, feeling Miss Dita's neglect excused this invasion of privacy. She knew nothing about art, but the paintings were almost cartoonish in their lack of detail. They were scenes of the waste she sensed must lie at the edge of the world, landscapes of cacti, bleached cattle skulls, and distant mountains, still-lifes of clay pots and desiccated ears of corn.

About to go back to the table for another helping of salad, she saw a small canvas turned to the wall, like a child hiding its face in shame. She couldn't resist the temptation. She picked it up and turned it over. The plate dropped unheeded from her hand.

Like the room, the scene of the painting was lit by an unearthly red light; slightly to the right of center was a crude stone altar; behind it rose a vaguely human shape, dark and blurred; the only clear detail was the knife in its bony, rotted hands.

Diane couldn't breathe; the air was dry as dust; she couldn't drag it into her starved lungs. The figure in the painting, the altar, the knife were features of her nightmare, forgotten until this moment. She'd had this nightmare before, many times before. She'd lived it. A certain smell was an integral part of it: the smell of a dirty window screen. And something else: hooded eyes, lips folded over a toothless mouth.

She whirled around. There was no one standing behind her, hovering over her. The room was empty.

By the time she found the back door, her panic had eased. She couldn't even remember why she'd panicked, unless it was the stress of the day, being told her beloved father was dying. What was it about the painting that could have frightened her? The light, the man-like shape, the altar? Surely they were too trite, the sort of thing one might expect from an artist with a morbid turn of mind. She knew now her first impression was wrong. She'd never dreamed such things before. She'd had a happy childhood, an adoring father. Her life now was busy, productive and successful thanks to his teachings, not filled with the kind of terrors that gave birth to nightmares.

Outside the air was cooling. Though the sky was not yet dark, the yard was thick with shadows. Somehow she wasn't surprised when Miss Dita spoke to her from those shadows, drawing her to a pair of metal lawn chairs at the far end of the yard. Miss Dita asked her if supper had been acceptable. Diane said it had been. They sat in companionable silence as the red-tinged sky turned to purple, then black.

"I hope you don't mind. I was looking at your paintings," Diane said after a while. Her resentment at being left alone now seemed unwarranted and childish, and she felt the need to say something complimentary. "They're very interesting." It wasn't a lie, only less than the truth. "Are you—a professional?" How *did* one ask, without giving offense, if people actually paid money for those cartoonish scenes?

"I've sold a few, but I don't do it for the money." For the first time there was a hint of life in Miss Dita's voice.

"Self-expression. Yes, I imagine it must be satisfying. I've often wished—"

"I've been painting since I was a child," Miss Dita went on with unmistakable though restrained eagerness. "I've never had a lesson, never had anyone who could tell me if my work was any good."

"I used to paint, too," Diane said, surprised by the memory of a week, her father away on business, her babysitter keeping her busy with stacks of paper and a box of watercolors, pleasurable hours that had produced washed-out blurs of color, empty cups holding only the remains of purple, black, and red.

"Did you? Then you know. There's nothing quite like it, is there? Time passes so quickly. It's as if you're in another world, a world where problems can't touch you. Whyever did you stop? I couldn't give it up even if someone threatened to cut my throat the next time I picked up a brush."

Diane's hand went to her throat. Why had she put it that way?

Why *had* she given up something she'd enjoyed so much? She remembered showing her father her pictures when he returned. He hadn't dismissed her efforts with unthinking praise as so many parents might have done. He'd studied them for nearly an hour. He'd even shared her new interest, going to the library for books on painting technique, teaching her the rules of color and composition, the real discipline required of an artist, helping her choose subjects for new paintings. It must have been lack of talent that had sapped her former enthusiasm.

In the darkness a child began to wail, heartbroken. Diane started to her feet.

"What's that?"

"A wild animal," Miss Dita replied. "Don't concern yourself. I hear it often. It's not what it sounds like."

Diane sat down again, aware as she did so that her hostess was getting to her feet.

"I hope you'll excuse me. I get up very early." Miss Dita started away, a vague shape in the darkness. Diane realized she had yet to see Miss Dita's face; she might pass her on the street and never know who she was. As the other woman walked away she called back, "Please don't leave the yard. It's desolate out there, easy to get lost."

The air was decidedly cool now. Diane shivered. Don't leave the yard. As if anything could lure her out there. It was a wilderness. She could easily imagine how someone might lose her bearings, wander for hours in the scorching heat, with predatory birds wheeling in the sky.

How could people bear to live out here at the edge of such emptiness, where there was danger, where anything might happen, where there was no one to hear a cry for help?

She was walking away from the house beneath a brutal red sun that burned her shoulders through her blouse. She'd lost her suitcase. She was aware she'd been following the sound of a voice calling her name, but she couldn't hear it now. Wiping the sweat from her face, she turned from the road and plunged off the edge of the world, into the desert, past a one-armed cactus, a bleached cattle skull. With no sense of transition she found herself climbing a rise toward a crude altar, a stone slab lying atop two uprights. The sky was the color of dried blood except where the sun had burned a hole in it. As she neared the altar, a shape rose from the puddled darkness behind it, a man-like creature holding a knife in its bony, rotted hands.

She was so tired—so tired and lost and all alone. She must lie down on the place that had been prepared for her, stretch her throat to meet the knife. Shame was an inner heat, the tears that spilled from her eyes. She was a child again, and this was the purpose for which she'd been born. She couldn't bring herself to look at the face of the man-like figure.

She woke with her gorge rising and barely made it to the bathroom in time. When she went to the sink to wash her face, she found she was weeping, weeping like a child, weeping as if her heart were broken. A nightmare. Only a stupid nightmare. Why was she weeping?

Afraid of a return to nightmare-haunted sleep, she went downstairs. The moon had risen, filling the artist's studio with clean silver light but for a faint, sullen red glow in one corner. Curiosity warred with dread. Her feet slapped the floor like those of a child dragged against her will.

". . . know what's best for you, Dee." A shamed child, turning her face to the wall.

She turned the canvas over.

Turned it over.

And she was lost.

The sound of a child's heartbroken weeping drew her to the place where the grass was thin and burned looking, then gave way to sand. That sound wasn't an animal's cry; it couldn't be. She knew a child's voice when she heard it, and didn't she hear it every night and day of her life, the inner cry of a shamed child afraid to weep aloud? She'd been warned about desolation and wilderness, but how could she ignore a lost child? With a last, despairing look at the house at the edge of the world and its false promise of safety, she plunged into the desert. Overhead the sky was the color of dried blood.

She was climbing a rise toward a crude stone altar. Now she knew the name of the weeping child. Now she knew the face of the man-like creature.

Dita had always enjoyed the view from her kitchen window, the lush grass and carefully tended flower beds giving way to the stark beauty of the desert. It had been a longing for scenes like this, this hint of wildness and danger beyond the edge of tidiness, that had made her flee the city years ago, shed her old life like a cast-off garment, even taking a new name, a name more expressive of her character. Her hands moved automatically in the dishwater, scrubbing dried egg from two plates, two sets of silverware. A knock on the back door startled her from her reverie. It was George from the gas station. Her guest's car must be ready.

She opened the door for him and poured him a glass of lemonade. "You drink this while I go and get her. You can run her back to the station."

She thought he gave her a strange look, but she'd learned not to mind what her neighbors thought of her.

She hadn't heard a sound from her guest since she'd gone upstairs after breakfast. She didn't hear her now. Strange woman. Most guests who came to stay with her liked to sit of an evening and chat, but this one kept to herself as though she felt she was too good for common people. The bathroom door was closed. Presumably she was getting dressed, combing her hair, putting on make-up. Women like her didn't go anywhere without make-up. Perdita smiled. She'd been like that herself once, overly concerned with rules and manners and appearances.

The door to the bedroom was half-open. Drawn by curiosity, she gave the door a nudge and it swung open the rest of the way. If the woman found her here, she could say she had to open the window, air out the room.

The woman's suitcase was open on the bed. Dita drew a breath, frowned. Her neighbors had warned her, taking in strangers the way she did she was bound to get a bad one now and again. But it had never happened, never until now. Clucking her tongue, she lifted her brown twill skirt and fish-print blouse from the woman's suitcase. A quick ruffling of the remaining contents revealed her nightgown, robe, blouses, and jeans. A thief. The woman was nothing but a common thief.

A piercing cry in the distance made her drop the blouse and cross to the window. She opened the sash and leaned out. Heat shimmered the air over the desert sands; the red of the rising sun lent an unearthly light to the familiar scene.

Perdita rubbed her eyes. For a moment she thought she saw, far away, a figure climbing a rise toward what looked like an altar, a man-like shape waiting behind it. She blinked and the image disappeared. Strange things happened out in that wilderness, people drawn into it by unexplained cries, images, getting lost not a dozen steps from their own back doors.

She turned back to the room, to the bed with its folded mattress, the nightstand, the broken clock, the lamp with the missing shade. The room was thick with dust, hadn't been used for years. She frowned, putting a hand to her head. Must be getting old. For a minute she couldn't remember why she'd come up here.

Oh, yes, the suitcase. She picked it up and went downstairs, where George was waiting to take her to the station.

When she got back, it might be a good idea to give that room a good cleaning. Maybe she'd take up her easel and paints, try to capture a few of the passing illusions to which the heat and the strong light gave birth. That one of a figure climbing to a crude stone altar, for instance, like a woman about to sacrifice herself to some primitive, hateful god. Interesting subject for a painting. Made her shudder to think of it.

George was on his feet, wringing his cap in his hands.

"That sound—it was the telephone, wasn't it? I thought it was an animal out in the desert." She found herself sitting at the table, strangely weak. George was hovering over her, looking upset.

"I'm sorry, Miss Dita. I'd have given anything not to be the one to give you the news, but you didn't answer when the phone rang or when I called up to you."

She reached up to pat his hand. "Never mind. I said what I had to say to my father a long time ago. Going to see him now wouldn't have proved anything." Neither love nor forgiveness.

It was finally over, and there were no tears. For the first time since her childhood, Dee felt whole and at peace.

BABY GIRL DIAMOND

by Adam-Troy Castro

My older sister died nameless after seven minutes of life, without ever knowing joy, or hope, or light less harsh than overhead fluorescents. She was a frail twisted thing, my sister, cursed with a heart that didn't want to beat and lungs that didn't want to provide her with air; and she would have died even earlier, but she clutched at those seven minutes with the simple rage of a creature born knowing that she'd been brutally cheated.

I was born two years later, two months premature in an era when that practically meant a baby could be given up for lost. My legs were black from poor circulation, my face cyanotic-blue, skin stretched thin as onionskin over unformed lemur eyes. My doctors gave me a ten percent chance of survival, which dwindled steadily as I lost weight every day for a full week. My mother, already shattered by one loss, refused to see me until my weight stabilized; my father refused to name me until the doctors pronounced me fit enough to go home. On that day, I became Abe. I returned to the hospital three times in my first year, as if wanting to follow my older sister wherever she had gone; my strength built only slowly and didn't become what it should have been until some years after my younger sister, Kate, entered the world strong and healthy, with no complications at all.

Kate and I grew up knowing there'd been an older sister before us, but we rarely spoke about her. Why should we? There were no baby pictures, no cute anecdotes, nothing that would turn her from a mythical abstraction into a human being. It was sad that a baby had died, of course, but it had all happened before we were born, so it had nothing to do with us. After all, life goes on. And so does death.

It wasn't until I was 23 that I put flowers on her grave.

The family had been to the site—a typically sprawling Long Island cemetery, criss-crossed by access roads—half a dozen times in the past few years, but never for her. As with any other extended family, we'd suffered funerals with monotonous regularity ... occasionally people close to us, but more frequently obscure relatives I may have met only once or twice. My distant cousin Estelle fit into that latter category. I couldn't remember what she'd looked like, I couldn't decipher the genealogy that related her to us, and for the life of me I couldn't decide whether the weeping fat woman was her sister or her daughter; either way, she was one of those embarrassing older relatives who remembers you from when you were five and insists on telling you at great length how cute you were then. She also said she couldn't believe I'd grown up so big and strong when for so long nobody was sure I'd live. I reacted to that statement about as well as any adult can be expected to, which is to say with silent mortification—all the while inwardly cursing the parental guilt that had bullied Kate and me into coming here in the first place.

We lowered Estelle's coffin into the earth, took symbolic turns dropping in individual shovelfuls of dirt, then filed back toward our respective cars. Some of the mourners were going to the usual post-burial feeding frenzy, but Kate and I were to be spared that ordeal as she had to get back to her apartment to study for finals, and I had been volunteered to drive her there. Relieved to be going, in the secret manner that people are always relieved to be done with the business of death, we gave our regrets and piled into the car for the long drive back upstate.

As the car crawled through the cemetery at five miles an hour, behind a traffic jam of other departing relatives, Kate lit a cigarette and said, "Godamighty. These things always make my head pound."

"You'll feel better when we get some food into you."

"Maybe." She snorted. "And maybe that's just nonsense. Maybe Mom and Dad and the rest of the family have just conditioned us to expect free food after funerals. You know, always laying out such a big spread for when we get back. That's kind of sick, you know that?"

"It's tradition," I said inadequately.

"Oh, please. You're turning into Mom."

I shut up. Kate had been next to impossible to talk to for the last couple of years, having recently adopted open hostility as a persona, after first experimenting with half a dozen others from distant to nurturing. It was a just a veneer, of course; but she'd worn so many veneers since the days when we actually liked each other that I sometimes wondered if there was still anybody of substance underneath. I shrugged, turned on the radio—Dylan, whom I venerated but she couldn't stand—and tried to breathe through her smoke as we waited for the cars ahead of us to move.

Eventually, just to make conversation, I said, "We must have three dozen relatives buried here by now."

"At least," Kate said. "Our sister's buried here, you know."

"What sis—oh. Her. Really?"

"Uh huh. Mom mentioned it to me last time we were here. You know, when Cousin Ruthie died? I don't think you were here for that one. Anyway, she said there's a special enclosed section off by the side somewhere where they bury unnamed babies. Our sister's there. She's got a stone and everything."

This blew me away. I had never actually realized that our older sister, the distant, ethereal, rarely mentioned ghost of our childhood, was buried somewhere. The revelation that she actually had a stone and a few feet of soil made her seem real for the first time. "Did Mom take you to see her?"

"What, are you kidding? Of course not."

"We ought to go sometime."

"Yeah, maybe. Not today, though."

I knew then that if we didn't go today, we'd never go. "Why not? What will it take, another ten minutes at most?"

Her eyes rolled. "Listen to that, God. He's actually serious."

"Come on, aren't you curious?"

"No. It's morbid."

My own enthusiasm for the idea was already waning,

but Kate had irritated me enough to make me defend it out of sheer spite. "It's my car," I said. "We're going."

It actually took a lot more than ten minutes. We first had to get away from the traffic, then we had to stop by the cemetery office to get the number and location of the lot, then we missed the turnoff, got lost, and drove around in circles until we got directions from a stoop-shouldered workman lugging dirt in a wheelbarrow. By the time we found the right place—a nondescript section of graveyard set apart by a stone arch and tall hedges—the whim was forty minutes old and was beginning to assume the dimensions of an epic quest.

I parked the car and stared at the great stone arch, which bore a legend rendered totally illegible by the ivy that had been permitted to grow over and hide the letters. There was a black iron gate, which was open, and a path of stones that led through the gateway and into the hidden places beyond. I tapped my hands against the wheel a few times, vacillating, then opened the driver's door. Kate got out when I did, which surprised me, since by that time I was sure she'd planned to remain in her seat and sulk. I glanced at her.

She shook her head. "Just getting some air. Go ahead, I'll stay with the car."

"You sure?"

"Absolutely."

I told her I'd be right back and followed the path through the open gate. The hedges on either side formed a corridor just wide enough to accommodate one person. The path turned left, then right, then left again, obscuring the exit behind me. I almost gave up when I saw another turn up ahead, but it turned out to be the last one; beyond it, I found the baby graveyard, a well-kept area about four acres square, entirely enclosed by hedges and filled with rows of little headstones separated only by the gravelly paths between them.

It was fancier than I'd thought it would be. The fountain in the center framed a cherub pouring water from a stone vase. Half a dozen marble benches were set against the hedges at regular intervals; one, right by the entrance, was even occupied, by a sleepy woman in white who kicked her bare feet absently as she stared at the cloud

formations. I nodded at her as I walked by, got no response, and walked along the graves, searching for Row
W, Plot 17.

The markings on the headstones were purely generic.
The child's sex, its last name, its birthday and the day it
died (which were, here, almost always the same day). I
saw Baby Boy Fein (May 19 1947), Baby Girl Wasser-
mann (April 23 1954), Baby Boy Posselvitch (September 9
1959), Baby Girl Shwarzmann (May 19 1962), and Baby
Boy Feder (November 17 1963), too self-conscious to feel
any sadness over all these truncated lives.

And then I found her:

Baby Girl Diamond. January 12 1964.

My heart thumped hard at the name. But after that, I
felt nothing. She was still an abstraction. I stood there,
staring at the cold, sterile letters and wondering why I'd
expected a great emotional rush. Kate had been right, after all. This was pointless.

After a few seconds of dutiful silence, I bent over, se-
lected a rock about the size of my fist, and balanced it on
the headstone to commemorate my visit. Then, the gesture made, I turned to leave, already thinking ahead to
lunch.

The woman on the bench watched me as I walked toward the exit. From this angle I got a much better view
of her. She was pale-skinned, and dark-haired, and thin to
the point of androgyny; she had a cool wistfulness easily
visible long before I approached close enough to spot the
Diamond family's trademark nose and chin. Her clothes
were white and shapeless—more like the suggestion of
clothes than an actual outfit. When she smiled at me, I
noticed how much she looked like an older version of
Kate, and my legs, while still carrying me forward, went
numb. I knew exactly who she was.

"That was nice of you," she said.

I froze in mid-step, wanting to run but knowing that if
I left now, I'd be reliving the inadequacy of this moment
every single day for the rest of my life. After a moment
I turned and approached her, which made her pretty
brown eyes widen with surprise. She'd expected me to
keep walking.

"Not really," I said, and the phrase sounded incomplete
without a name at the end of it, as if the most important

part had been amputated when I wasn't looking. "It was the least I could do."

"You see me," she said.

"Of course," I said, the words glib to cover my shock. "I came here to see you."

She covered her eyes with one smooth, unformed hand—a hand without wrinkles or lines, a hand that had never touched anything and had never been clenched in anger. "No one's ever seen me," she said. "I didn't think anybody ever would."

I sat down on the bench beside her, wanting to put my hands around her shoulders but fearing she'd burst like a soap bubble if I tried. "I'm sorry."

She refused to look at me. "When I was a little girl," she said, her voice straining at the edges now, gathering power as she expelled years of frustration one carefully considered syllable at a time, "maybe three or four years old, before I understood there had to be more to it, I thought I was just lost. I thought my mommy and daddy left me here by accident and they'd be back to get me as soon as they realized I was gone. That's what I thought, really. And I cried for them all the time, but nobody ever heard me. Then I got a little older, and I thought that I'd done something bad. The gardeners and the other families who came here sometimes, I thought they must have been in on it, because they never answered me no matter what I said to them. I thought I must have been the worst, most hateful, most evil little girl in the whole world. I needed somebody to tell me why I was here and why I wasn't allowed to leave."

My own voice broke: "It wasn't your fault. Don't think that. We just didn't know, that's all."

She buried her face in her hands. "It's been so long," she said. "And it's never going to end."

I sat there impotently and said nothing. What could I say? That things would be looking up tomorrow? Silence may have been inadequate, but anything beyond that was an out-and-out insult.

She said, "Please help me."

I said, "I can't."

"I'm stuck here. There's no way out. Help me."

"I'm sorry. I don't know how."

She bent her head. I almost reached out to touch her—

—and somewhere close behind us, Kate gasped.

I whirled and saw her, frozen with the shock of first recognition. Whatever had made her change her mind and follow me into this garden of dead children, she clearly regretted it now; her eyes were wide and her face white, and all her defining strength drained away by this, her first sight of the lonely woman beside me. I stood up just in time to see Kate fall to her knees.

The ghost gasped too. Before I could even think of stopping her—let alone wonder if there was any way I could have stopped her even if I tried—she leaped up and ran away with the bottomless terror of someone chased by demons. I stood there . . . watching her recede faster than her legs alone could have carried her, on a gravel path that made no sound beneath her feet . . . and stared helplessly at the empty place where she'd been, until I heard Kate call my name.

I turned and saw her still kneeling on the ground, her eyes closed and her shoulders shaking. It made no sense. Kate was way tougher than me, always had been. I couldn't remember the last time she'd been reduced to tears by anything. But her need gave me purpose. I went to her, held her, and asked a stupid question. "Are you okay?"

She shook her head. "N-no, I'm not. I don't know if I'll ever be okay again."

"Take it easy. She's—"

"Don't be dense! That was her, wasn't it? WASN'T IT?"

"Yes."

"And you saw her, too?"

"Yes, I did."

"Oh, God." She closed her eyes, made a fist, and pounded her forehead three times, just hard enough to make me wince from sympathetic pain. "Oh, God. Oh God oh God oh God."

"Kate—"

Her face was not a grown woman's anymore. It belonged to a lonely and miserable seven-year-old. "Take me away from here, Abe."

Predictably, we hit one of the worst traffic jams in living memory—miles and miles of frying pan steel, hope-

lessly snarled by construction creating a series of
bottlenecks six exits ahead. My head felt as though a railroad spike had been jammed through my temples; I
couldn't even begin to imagine how Kate felt, and I
didn't want to risk an explosion by asking her.

Eventually she said: "Abe?"

I had trouble recognizing the voice as hers. It was too
plaintive, too vulnerable to be hers. "What?"

She didn't face me: just continued staring out the passenger window, losing herself in the sunlight reflecting
off the other cars. "You really don't know why she scared
me so much, do you? You don't have the slightest idea."

"She's a ghost," I said evenly.

She winced. "Jesus. You don't know."

"Then tell me."

"No," she said. "I don't want to talk about it. I don't
even want to think about it. I want to forget this whole
day ever happened."

"But, Kate—"

"Put on your damn music," she said. And refused even
to speak to me for the next hour.

She made me promise I wouldn't go back. And I knew
she was absolutely right; neither one of us had any real
understanding of what had happened today. All we knew
is that we were alive, and our older sister was dead; that
I'd spent a few brief minutes straddling the boundary that
divided us; and that we'd have to be insane to blithely approach that invisible line a second time. I agreed with all
of that. Absolutely. Made perfect sense to me.

Except, of course, that it wasn't over.

Once I reentered the silence of my own apartment, surrounded by all the junk I'd ever accumulated, all the
books and records and snapshots and ten thousand other
stupid little things valuable to me only because they were
part of my life, it was impossible not to think of that
lonely woman who'd been so pathetically grateful just to
be seen. I thought of what she must have looked like at
seven, existing alone and unloved in that garden of dead
children, when I was five and taking the short yellow bus
to kindergarten, where I learned how to paint. I thought
of what she must have looked like at twelve, still alone,
still sitting on that bench waiting for something the world

had decided she would never have while I was with the family, vacationing in Florida and building sand castles on the beach. I thought of her changing from toddler to child to teenager to woman, suffering, instead of the oblivion that should have been hers, an endless succession of days spent in that same solitary place, where she grew and matured and aged without ever knowing even the simple pleasure of a deep breath.

I held out for two weeks. And then one night I went to my bedroom window and looked down upon the corner bus stop. There was a bench there, one of the wooden ones with bright green slats and iron dividers to prevent the homeless from lying down on them. Right now its only occupant was an old woman wearing a thick brown sweater that must have been broiling in this summer's heat. Even so, she hugged herself tightly, as if that were the only warmth she'd ever known, and when she peered down the street to see if her bus was coming, I caught a brief, possibly even imagined, glimpse of the despair hidden beneath her pale and wrinkled mask.

I imagined the woman at the cemetery someday looking like that, without ever having had a real life behind her to give her a reason why. I wondered what she'd look like when she was a hundred years old, or ten thousand.

I couldn't abandon her to that.

I drove back the next weekend hoping I wouldn't find her, that the long trip would have been for nothing, that her last appearance would turn out to be only the most fleeting exception to the way the world worked. But she was still sitting on the same bench, still idly kicking her heels as she watched the clouds drift across the afternoon sky. She glanced at me as I passed by, with the dull curiosity of a woman who didn't expect acknowledgement—then recognized me and smiled. "Hi."

I sat down beside her. "Hi."

"That . . . other girl didn't come with you this time, did she?"

"No. Why were you so scared of her, anyway? She's not as bad as all that."

She tensed. "Isn't she?"

"Her name's Kate," I said. "She's okay once you get to know her."

"I don't want to know her," the nameless woman said,

with a repulsed shudder . . . and there was plenty of Kate
in the way her eyebrows arced together at the thought.
"She scares me. I don't know where I know her from, but
I think she's always scared me."

"That's all right then," I said. "We won't talk about
her. I'm Abe, by the way."

"I thought that was your name. It seemed to fit you,
somehow. Almost like I used to know an Abe who was
just like you—except that I know I didn't because this is
the first time I ever knew anybody."

"You can't be the only one here," I said.

"I don't think I am. Sometimes when I get lonely, I
close my eyes and cover my ears and shut out all the
sounds, like the wind and the rain and that fountain and
even those motors I hear sometimes, past those hedges
where I can't go . . . and I think I hear others like me,
shouting and crying and trying to be heard. They sound
very far away; I can't understand them and they can't understand me. But I think they're all around us, trapped in
this place just like I am." She shrugged. "It's the same as
being alone, anyway. Worse, even. Because it doesn't
help to know they're crying too."

"No," I glanced at the neat rows of tiny headstones. "I
suppose it doesn't."

She sighed—the long, deep, expressive sigh of a
woman who'd been hoarding that sound for too many
years—and said: "Why did you come to visit me, Abe?"

I took out the long flat box I'd secreted under my arm,
placed it on the bench between us, and removed the
cover.

She stared.

Kate and I had played a lot of Checkers when we were
kids. Other kids had Chess, Backgammon, Chutes and
Ladders, Monopoly—and we'd experimented with each
of those, along with all the other board games that rose
and fell in local popularity—but for some reason having
to do with the way our minds were wired, none of them
had appealed to us the way Checkers did. We hadn't
played since high school, in part because we'd finally
grown bored of it but mostly because the teen years had
inevitably changed us from good friends to mock-adults
who rebelled violently at the very thought of being seen
spending time with each other. The set Kate and I had

played with had long since gone out with the trash; I'd
had to buy this one on the way here, at a neighborhood
toy store whose proprietor hadn't understood my relief at
finding the very last box.

I unfolded the board and set up the plastic pieces in
standard checkers format: twelve pieces facing each other
across a battleground of sixty-four squares. "Do you
know how to play?"

She picked up one of the black pieces. I'd expected her
hands to pass through it, but she had no trouble holding
it; whatever other limitations her existence might have set
for her, checkers were easily as real for her as I was. "I
don't know how, but . . . I think I'm a better player than
you."

I'd expected that. It seemed right. "Yeah, right. You
forget you're dealing with the world champion here."

"In your dreams," she said, surprising herself enough
to raise a blush.

And as she made her first move, I watched the way the
thoughts flickered across her face and the smile played at
the corners of her lips. It was not a stranger's face but
one so familiar, from some hidden country just around the
corner from the life I'd lived, that I could almost believe
we'd both grown up eating breakfast at the same table
and riding to school on the same bus. It was a face that
could very easily have teased me about the embarrass-
ments of my childhood, even as I gave her merry hell
about the secrets of hers.

Ghost-memories poured in, like home movies from a
life I hadn't lived: the year she went to summer camp and
I didn't because she was old enough and I wasn't; the
time we played hide-and-go-seek in the house and she
picked a spot so cunning I was sure she'd disappeared for
real; the time we had that fight, vowed never to speak to
each other again and by dint of incredible will power
managed to keep it up for three days, as we each waited
for the other one to apologize first. Hundreds of scenes
just like that, ranging from high drama to low comedy
and sitcom-banal, and they were neither better nor worse
than the scenes I'd lived with Kate: just different. Because she would have been a different person. She would
have had a sillier sense of humor but also a nastier and
more unpredictable temper. She would have been more

generous with favors but also more prone to depression.
She would have had more trouble making friends outside
the home and been more prone to poetic turns of phrase
in everyday speech. And I would have known who she
was now, as opposed to Kate, who had become, in all too
many ways, a familiar stranger.

The thought made me leap to my feet in a panic.

"What's wrong?" she asked.

Kate barely existed for me at that moment. She was an
abstraction, just like pi, or absolute zero, or a perfect vacuum. I searched for the memory of her face or her voice
or the sound she made when she laughed and found none
of them; they were hidden behind a heavy fog that had
swallowed her up when I wasn't looking.

"Abe?"

The voice, so near, so real, so easy to accept as something I'd been hearing my entire life, scared the crap out
of me. "I forgot the time. I . . . have to go."

She blinked. "Will you be back?"

I couldn't say no, because even then I knew it would
have been a lie. So I just ran.

I didn't stop at a phone or go straight home—just drove
like a maniac through two hours of mercifully light traffic
to Kate's tiny off-campus apartment. I didn't have to
press the buzzer to get in because another lady who lived
in the building was already in the vestibule using her key;
even so, Kate knew I was coming because she was in her
bathrobe and slippers waiting for me to get off the elevator. I only had a second to note her red eyes and tear-
streaked cheeks before she seized me by the collar and
pulled me into the hallway.

"I'm sorry," I said.

She spun me around and pinned me against the corridor
wall. "You sorry bastard," she said. "You went back,
didn't you? After I asked you not to! You went back and
you talked to her again!"

"I know, I'm sorry, I didn't think there was any
harm—"

Her eyes widened. "No harm? Do you have any idea
what I've been through today? Do you?"

"I'm sorry . . ." There wasn't anything else to say.

The strength went out of her all at once. She released

me and trudged back toward her apartment. I rubbed my neck gingerly and followed her.

Her place was a cramped studio, which accommodated her furniture only because she kept her bed on stilts. The kitchenette was a closet that had somehow been persuaded to hold a refrigerator, table, sink and stove that would have stuffed a room twice the size. The similarities to a coffin did not escape me—especially since the reek of Kate's two-pack-a-day cigarette habit had become a permanent fixture of the air. I sat down at the little table and stared at the checkerboard tablecloth until she placed a glass of ice water before me as her concession to hospitality. I sipped at it as she sat down and waited for me to say anything that would give her the chance to explode again.

I outwaited her. She said, "What gets me is that you knew better. We talked about it. We agreed that there's some things you just don't fuck with. And you went anyway. What the hell did you think you were doing?"

"I don't know. Correcting a wrong, maybe."

"And did it ever occur to you that some things can't be fixed without breaking something else?"

"No," I said.

"I didn't think so," she said. She pulled the last cigarette from a crumpled pack and lit it after three trembling attempts. "Meanwhile, I spent the past several hours trying to hold on to myself. You ever have that feeling? When you can see the wall right through your hands? When you look in the mirror and your face looks like a bad caricature, with all the details slightly off, and your eyes the wrong color? When you can feel the cold creeping up your arms and legs, turning them numb, eating you a piece at a time? When you keep thinking that you really ought to call a doctor because you might be dying? When you know a doctor's not going to be able to help you because when you close your eyes, you can see your only brother in a graveyard feeding the days and nights of your life to some spook?"

"I don't understand. I was just talking to her—"

"Don't talk, just listen. Mom and Dad only wanted two kids, right? Remember? Every time we said we wanted another brother or sister, they said no, two was enough. And that was you and me. But if that—other girl—had lived, then *you* would have been number two. Get it now, dummy? I'm alive only because she's dead!"

The sympathetic pain made my toes curl. "How long have you felt this way?"

"All my life. And don't get carried away, Abe, because it's not exactly a deep psychological complex; it's just something I live with. All it means is that the only times I ever wished she'd lived, were the days when I wished I'd never been born. The rest of the time, I never thought about her, never wished she'd been a little stronger, never wondered what she would have been like, and sure as hell never hoped to meet her. And the more you . . . fuck . . . with her, the more I feel like the ghost I almost was."

I couldn't look at her. "I came pretty close to being a ghost myself."

"I remember. The folks tell the story of your miraculous recovery every time they get an excuse. I'm sick of hearing it, already. But don't you understand, Abe, it's different for you? It didn't matter whether she lived or died, you would have still gotten your fair chance. With me, my whole life rests on her death."

"It could have been you and her alive and a dead brother between you . . ."

"Don't be stupid. I'm not about to wish you dead. You're already my brother. But her—she's not my sister, she's just something I narrowly escaped. And you're *changing* that."

Neither of us spoke for a long time.

Eventually, I said, "Why did you even mention her that day? Why did you follow me in?"

Kate opened her mouth to answer, then clamped it shut, clearly disturbed by the answer she'd just rejected. "I don't know. I think . . . somehow . . . she wanted me to."

The silence between us was as thick and suffocating as river water. I found I couldn't face her anymore and turned my attention back to the checkered tablecloth. For a moment I wondered distractedly if it was new; I seemed to remember eating dinner here, not too long ago, when the table was covered with some silvery material that caught the light with distorted reflections of our faces. Then I probed the memory further and realized that Kate had never owned anything like that; I was recalling some apocryphal meal at my other sister's place. Terrified, I looked at Kate again and saw her flickering like a TV picture spoiled by bad reception.

She felt it and paled. "Oh, God. It's not over."

I touched her hand and almost recoiled from the cold, distant feel of her flesh, which was more like the distorted memory of skin than skin itself. "Yes, it is. I won't go back—"

"She won't need you to," Kate said, in a voice that sounded like an old record worn through with scratches. "You've already given her all she needs."

I spent that night by her bed, watching her fade away an inch at a time, then pulling her back by sheer force of will.

As she tossed and turned and cried out in voices that were not always recognizable as hers, I concentrated on everything I remembered about her; everything I'd loved and everything that drove me crazy; everything I'd understood and everything that remained a mystery; everything that had made us family and everything that had conspired to turn us into strangers.

I remembered her refusing to go to the circus because she was so frightened of the clowns. I remembered her best friend in grade school, Wendy something, who had loved painting and had infected Kate with the same passion. I remembered how that had gone the way of all Kate's great enthusiasms, flaring briefly and then fading away as soon as the next big thing came along. I remembered her on a horse, in love with the animal, wearing the expression of someone who'd been born to ride; I remembered her tiring of horses after six months and never setting foot in a stable again. I remembered the way she laughed when something really got past her defenses: a high-pitched, girlish whoop that dissolved into fragments of shallow breath. I remembered that time in junior high when she saw two older girls pushing around the dull-eyed, heavy-lidded, slow-talking girl who had spent months being the school's designated victim; how, though I'd seen Kate be as cruel to her as anybody else, something about this particular bullying had seized her protective streak and driven her to wade into the situation with fists swinging. I remembered her declaring again and again that she had no interest in going to her senior prom

and then changing her mind at the last minute to go with
a painfully earnest kid whose name still escaped me. I remembered the killer depression that had come over me
for a full week when I was seventeen, how I'd spent days
on end hiding behind false smiles, fooling everybody but
her; how she'd canceled plans with friends one Saturday
night to stay home and watch TV with me, pretending she
just didn't feel like going out. I remembered how, on the
other hand, when I came home for my first vacation from
college, she refused to talk to me and refused to explain
why; how I finally confronted her, demanding to know
what she thought I'd done and how she said that if I
didn't know there was no use telling me. I remembered
never finding out the answer because she'd inexplicably
turned friendly again by the next time I came home.

I thought about the way brothers and sisters are like
people married from birth on and how sometimes they
don't really know each other all that well, even when they
think they do. I thought about how that gulf would only
widen as we lived our separate lives. And I thought about
how little that really mattered. Because she was still my
sister, and I didn't want to lose her.

All that night, as I scraped the bottommost wells of
memory for the times we'd shared, she flickered in and
out of existence like a TV image during a lightning storm.
I watched her turn transparent, then solid; I felt her skin
burn with fever, then turn cold as death; I listened to her
breath and heard the familiar rasp give way to a distant
echoing whistle of something forever tumbling from my
reach.

It was the worst night of my life.

And in the morning, she was not all the way back. But
neither was she all the way gone. She was white as chalk
and covered with beads of cold sweat, but when she
opened her eyes to discover me beside her, she grinned
sardonically. "Whaddaya know. My hero."

I didn't smile back. I didn't think I had the right. "Are
you okay?"

Kate said nothing, either unwilling or unable to give
me an answer. She turned away from me, looked at the
ceiling, blinked several times, then closed her eyes, sat up,
swung her legs over the side of the bed, and spent a good
minute silently facing the floor between her feet. Then

she dragged herself to her feet and shuffled off to the bathroom, without acknowledging me in any way. A moment later, the shower started to run.

I stared at the closed door, wondering if she'd ever forgive me for what I'd done to her.

In five minutes she came out, wearing a green terrycloth bathrobe. The shower had revived her somewhat; she was still pale, still clearly washed-out by everything she'd been through, but the color had begun to return to her face. She said, "God, I feel funky. Like I've been erased and then redrawn. I bet if we could put this feeling in a pill, there are any number of trendy assholes who'd want to buy it."

I grunted. "Do you hate me now?"

Whatever glib thing she almost said next vanished as soon as she saw the expression on my face. Instead, she heaved a sigh and sat down on the edge of her bed. "I don't hate you. I never did."

"You just don't like me very much."

She simulated the sound of the wrong-buzzer on a TV game show. "The last couple of years, I've been through some deep depressing shit that I don't want to talk about, and I haven't been in any mood to like anybody. But, no, I don't hate you. Especially not now, after the way you stayed with me and kept me here. That means a lot."

"I almost killed you."

"Only because you tried to be a brother to somebody else." When I didn't answer at once, she used the tip of her finger to tilt my face toward hers. "In case I haven't told you this, recently, Abe—you're good at that."

"Thanks," I said. "You're not so bad yourself."

The silence between us was a solid thing. For a moment there I felt certain she was angry after all, that she was readying some kind of verbal grenade, to start off a fight that would end with me fleeing out her door and neither one of us speaking to the other for weeks; but the threatened anger didn't come, and the only clue that anything was going on inside her head was the telltale scent of possibility I'd noticed before, wafting all around us like a heady perfume. "And her?"

I hesitated.

"Don't waste my time with bullshit. You're the one who's talked to her. Tell me."

I considered telling her something falsely reassuring,
then realized she'd know at once if I was lying. "I like
her. I think . . . that if she had lived, I would have liked
her a lot. And when I'm with her, I think about how close
I came to being where she is . . . and I know that if our
places were reversed, she wouldn't have wanted to leave
me alone either."

Kate chewed on that. "Does that mean you're going to
see her again?"

"No. I wish I could. But not if it means hurting you.'

She spent several seconds studying an invisible spot on
the ceiling. A dozen conflicting emotions played on her
face. The most powerful among them was anger—and
though I couldn't help bracing for an explosion, I knew
almost at once that it wasn't directed at me but at something between us, that wasn't just a ghost glimpsed in a
graveyard. I thought about that deep depressing shit she'd
mentioned, knew that must have been part of it, and was
reminded anew, to my shame, how little I knew her; but
when she turned toward me again, she was spookily calm.
"It's Monday, right?"

I blinked. "Yeah."

"Can you get out of work?"

"If I have to."

"Uh huh. And I don't have my last test till Wednesday;
I can do without another day of cramming."

"So?"

"So," Kate said, "let's go help her."

Circumstances had neatly reversed our initial positions:
This time, I was the one who didn't want to go, and she
was the one who insisted. She said she should be okay as
long as we went together. I wasn't sure I bought that, but
letting her go alone—as she threatened to do—was impossible.

And so it came to pass that several hours later, on an
unseasonably cold day, damp and overcast and altogether
too appropriate for the exorcising of ghosts, we stood together before the familiar stone arch, armed with nothing
but a floral arrangement and the knowledge gained from
a single phone call. We didn't go in immediately; instead,
we stood there, thinking our own private thoughts, which
in my case was simple awe at Kate's self-control in mak-

ing it even this far without showing a single sign of panic.

I said, "You don't have to do this."

She raised an eyebrow and held eye contact until I looked away. It had been a stupid thing to say.

We walked in side by side, though the closeness of the hedges made that a tight fit; when we turned corners too quickly, the leaves brushed against our shoulders, leaving damp streaks on our clothes. With almost every step I glanced at Kate to make sure she was still there. She conscientiously avoided glancing back: she just kept walking, her spine rigid, her eyes carefully fixed on the path ahead.

When we entered the garden of dead children, our older sister was nowhere to be seen. The only sign that she'd ever been there at all was the checkerboard I'd abandoned yesterday; it was still sitting on the bench, with a game still in progress exactly the way I'd left it: five kings against three, facing down in the middle of the board.

Kate gave me a wry look that let me know she knew I'd been playing the losing side. I shrugged and peered down the rows of headstones, searching for the wan figure we'd come here to find. I would have had to be blind, deaf, and dumb not to know she was here somewhere, just outside the limits of my perception, watching us, waiting to see what we would do, refusing to come out because Kate was here with me. I turned to Kate, once again to suggest that maybe this had been a bad idea.

But Kate was smiling slyly. "Bet I beat you two out of three."

"What?"

"Checkers, stupid. It's been ages since we played. As long as we're here . . ."

I hesitated, then began to see it. "I call black."

"No fair. You're always black."

I shrugged. "I called it first."

The childhood ritual, reinacted.

We circled the bench like gladiators looking for a perfect moment to strike, sat down on opposite sides of the board, placed the pieces at their starting positions, and started to play. No idle conversation passed between us.

There hadn't been any when we were kids, either; we'd taken Checkers way too seriously for that. The only words we passed were the occasional cries of "King me!" signaling that one or the other of us had reached the other side and found there the strength to come back.

We played one game. Two. A dozen. I won half, she won half. We sped up, played a dozen more and stopped pausing to think between turns, instead just moving on impulse, letting our hands decide which piece to move. Eventually we stopped paying attention to who won or lost and just concentrated on keeping the pieces in motion, slide-slide-slide, jump-jump-jump, king-me, some moves pointless, others suicidal, none of them mattering except as the first necessary step toward the next move after that. The games themselves sped by in blurs, some over in minutes, others exhausting their possibilities in seconds, none of them bearing any resemblance to the quiet, contemplative, zen-of-childhood matches we remembered; the memories not nearly as important as the sensation that chance itself was being rearranged around us with every move we made.

And then a cold wind raised the hackles on the back of my neck. Kate must have felt it too, because she looked up the same instant I did, to meet my eyes over a game about to self-destruct between us. Then we both turned our heads and saw her.

Our older sister stood silently about ten feet away. For the first time since we'd met, she actually looked like the phantom she was; there was absolutely no color to her skin, no life in the way she looked at us. The pretty brown eyes I'd known were just deep black circles on a pale white face, and when she spoke, the dirt of the grave sounded like gravel bubbling in her throat.

"Why did you bring her here, Abe?"

My first attempt at speech failed. I cleared my throat and said, "Because I wanted you to meet her."

"I don't want anything to do with her. Why can't you make her go away?"

"Because she's my sister, and I won't choose between you."

"She scares me."

"She's here to help you," I said.

The ghost's head swiveled, her black eyes burning like

coals as they focussed on Kate. I looked at Kate to see how she was handling it, saw from her stiff posture that she was terrified but fighting it. She even managed a smile, or something that might have resembled a smile if it hadn't taken all her self-control just to keep it on her face.

Our older sister didn't smile back. She just shuddered, like a child offered a plate of food she couldn't finish, and turned her attention back to me. "It's not fair. Please, Abe. Make her go away. She doesn't have anything I want."

"Yes, she does. Ask her."

Reluctantly, our older sister turned.

Kate took a deep breath. We'd called our parents that morning, hiding the real reason for our question behind idle curiosity, unsure whether there'd be any answer at all but wholly unsurprised to discover that there was. Beyond that, there hadn't been any debate—we'd both known, instinctively, that she would have to be the one to give it:

"Your name would have been Rachel."

Our older sister stiffened. "What?"

"Specifically," Kate went on, "Rachel Elizabeth. Rachel Elizabeth Diamond."

Our older sister covered her eyes with one hand—a hand, I noticed, that now had some definition to it, that bore the wrinkles and creases of a real hand used by a real person who had really lived—shuddered, and shook her head slowly, as if struggling to deny that which had been denied her for so long. Then she faced me, searching for confirmation.

I nodded. "I'm glad I got to meet you, Rachel."

She stood there motionless, as if the words were boulders, too heavy to carry.

Kate glanced at me, bit her lip, and rose from the bench to approach Rachel in the slow measured steps of a woman approaching a skittish animal. Rachel made no attempt to run away—just stood there, wide eyed and trembling, as Kate stopped before her and wrapped her in a hug. It looked pretty solid, as hugs go: nothing ghostly or insubstantial about it. For that moment, they were real to each other.

"Abe?" Kate said. "Would you mind leaving us for a

few minutes? I think Rachel and I have a few things to talk about."

I hesitated, said "All right," grabbed the flowers we'd brought, and abandoned my sisters to their privacy. I was too scared, even now, of letting Kate out of my sight, so I just followed the gravel path past the neatly kept graves, reading the names on each stone I passed, noting how many of them were anonymous, wondering how many of these children were wandering the landscape around me. I wished I could do something to help all of them, but I knew I couldn't even if I dedicated my entire life to that and nothing else. The only thing I could do was try not to imagine I heard their voices in the whispers of the wind.

When I found the stone for Baby Girl Diamond, I turned around and looked for my sisters. They were sitting together. Rachel was talking; Kate was listening intently. I faced the stone again, making a mental note to talk with Kate about having it replaced with one bearing Rachel's full name. Then I knelt, brushed aside a couple of dried leaves, and placed the flowers on Rachel's grave.

I knelt there a long time.

It was over an hour later that Kate made me jump by placing her hand on my shoulder. I looked up and saw that she was alone. And though her eyes were moist, she was smiling.

I stood. "Rachel?"

"She's gone," Kate said. "She told me I should say good-bye for her. She was sorry she couldn't stick around to say it herself, but she's been waiting a long time. She said you'd understand. And that she's glad she got to meet you, too."

I swallowed. "What did you talk about?"

"Mostly? Stuff that sisters talk about. But we wished each other luck, I can tell you that."

I nodded—enjoying the renewed freshness of the air and the sudden warmth that seemed to break through the clouds—and took one last look at the dead slab of stone that by itself had nothing to do with anybody I'd ever known. Then I smiled and let Kate lead us out.

We left the checkerboard behind. And despite years of wind and rain and snow and the interfering hands of all the caretakers assigned to keep that place respectfully clean, it has remained there ever since, looking as new as the day I bought it ... the only noticeable change from one visit to the next the positions of the pieces and which side seemed to be winning.

This one's for Jill.

LINDEMANN'S CATCH

by Rod Serling

The fog and mist that rose up from the sea drifted over the wharves, spindly docks, and broken-down jetties, to mix with the gaslight over the cobblestoned streets. It slipped through the reefed sails and riggings of shabby little fishing boats, as if beckoned to by the distant frog-call of a foghorn and faraway ship's bells that rang out nervously as they groped through the night.

There was a big, orange, roaring fire in the hearth of the Bedford Village Inn, and the sporadic crack of burning logs mixed with the clatter of mugs and low voices of the men in the room. They were mostly local fishermen and a few sailors on leave from whalers—all men of the sea who sensed the tension of the fog-shrouded night and sought out each other's company in an unspoken thanksgiving that on that particular night they could anchor themselves to a tankard of rum instead of peering with aching eyes from a crow's nest, wondering at what death-filled moment they would strike a reef or a hidden shoal.

Mordecai Nichols, the town doctor, stood near the bay window of the inn, looking through a spyglass toward a distant promontory that angled out from the shore in a clawlike curve. He saw the faraway sails of a ship just moving past the farthest spit of land. He lowered the spyglass just as the inn's owner, a wooden-legged former sea captain named Bennett, moved past him with a tray of mugs.

"Looks like a lugger, doesn't it?" Nichols asked, pointing toward the window.

Bennett picked up the spyglass and briefly looked through it. "Too square in the stern," he announced, "and she's ketch-rigged. Trawler of some kind. And she better put some water between her and the coast, or she won't be seeing Boston this trip."

"She'll not make Boston."

Both men turned to look at Abner Suggs, who, as always, played solitaire at a distant table. Suggs had an emaciated, skeletal face and a look of perpetual worrying disapproval. He returned the look of the two men with intense, challenging eyes.

Nichols took a step toward him. "Who says?" he asked.

Suggs pointed to the cards and shrugged. "The cards."

The doctor winked at Bennett. "Where do they put her down, Master Suggs? I mean—those cards." He moved closer to the table. "Will she hole her bottom on a reef, or strip her sails in a gale?" He picked up one of the cards and looked at it. "Don't any of these damned cardboard squares offer anything but disaster?" He flipped the card back onto the table. "Cross-seas, swamped hulls, and man overboard—I swear, Suggs, that's all we hear from you." He pointed to the cards. "Is there not one single cheerful prediction in that net of doom you weave every night? Is there no good fishing? Light winds? Maybe a keg of treasure washed into this benighted little place to make our lot a little easier for a change?"

Suggs's head seemed to hunch down into his shoulders. "I simply tell what the cards say," he said glumly; then he blinked and tried to lighten his voice. "What about your fortune, Doctor? In the cards—or in your palms. For just the price of a short brandy or a spot of rum. Maybe I'll see a fortune coming for you."

Nichols laughed. "A fortune for me? Most likely you'll see a bony rider on a pale horse coming for *me*." He coughed and pounded on his chest. "Fog and damp and chill! Ask your cards how I survive my patients?"

He moved back over to the window, staring out at the fog. " 'Physician, heal thyself,' " he said softly, "or so it is said. But not in this bloody place!"

There was a sudden quiet when the door opened and Hendrick Lindemann entered. He carried with him an unspoken command into the room, only barely acknowledging with a slight nod the greetings of the men clustered around. He was a big man, well over six feet, his strength and bigness not even remotely hidden by his bulky

slicker, now wet with fog and sea spray. He moved over
to the bar, throwing back the hood of his slicker, to reveal the gold stubble of a light beard on a face in which
wet, cold, and sullen bad humor gave battle to handsome-
ness. He moved directly over to the bar, nodding to
Bennett, who stumped over on his wooden leg to serve
him.

"Just coming in?" the innkeeper asked him.

Lindemann nodded and pointed to a bottle of rum.

"How was your catch?" Bennett asked as he poured the
rum.

"Too light," Lindemann said. "Some undernourished
cod and a few dead shiners. Filthy catch—filthy night."
He took the rum and downed it in a series of noisy,
thirsty gulps, then held out the mug for Bennett to refill.

"See a ship out there?" Dr. Nichols asked him, coming
up to sit alongside.

Lindemann nodded. "Two-master. Too shallow of draft
and too big of sail. And badly skippered—too busy shifting ballast to look where she was going. Almost ran me
down." This time he finished half the rum, then placed
the mug down. "But in keeping with the night's sport," he
said thoughtfully, "hopeful idiots like myself—to be
killed by fearful fools."

"Captain Lindemann." Sugg's voice, shrill, unpleasant,
and persistent, snaked across the room. "Perhaps the
cards offer up a better future for you." He rose from the
table, and with a smile that oozed from him like snake
oil, walked diffidently toward Lindemann. "Or on the
palms of your hands," he continued, "maybe a windfall
on the way. Or the tea leaves, Cap'n. Let me read the
leaves for you. Now, there's many a pretty picture painted
for a man in the bottom of a cup. Or would a potion of
a sort interest you? I've got ancient bottles that are the
perfection of the soothsayer's art." He stood there like a
famished little gnome—lips wet, hands twitching, his
eyes hungry little orbs that seemed desperate to devour
anything they saw. He placed the cards on the bar.

Lindemann looked at them for a moment, then very
slowly scooped them up. "Mr. Suggs," he said in a soft
voice, "I have to live with the fog, because it's hell's
blanket, and it creeps up through the earth to bedevil sea-
men like me. And there's nothing I can do about that.

And I have to sail on that leaking rat catcher of mine because there's not a damned thing on heaven or earth that'll change that. I'll go out every freezing morning and I'll come back every wind-screaming night with just enough in my net to keep me alive." He held the cards out in front of him. "Now, all this is my miserable lot, Mr. Suggs, and it will be until God decides to cut bait, turn my sail into a shroud, and throw me back into the sea. But what I *don't* have to do"—he dropped the cards into the cuspidor at his feet—"is to come in here night after night and look at that wormy little face of yours and listen to that bilge about potions and palms and tea leaves."

He reached out, grabbing Suggs by his dirty shirt front, and yanked him off the floor with one incredibly strong hand. With the other he pointed toward the spittoon. "That's where *your* fortune is, Mr. Suggs. Where men spit."

He held Suggs out at an arm's length, while the little man wiggled like a speared fish and the onlookers laughed and exchanged winks. Then he slowly lowered him to the floor, where he stood, eyes averted, face burning.

Sugg's voice shook in a combination of rage and fear. He looked down at the cards spread around the floor, some of them still protruding from the spilled brass pot at his feet. "You had no call to do that, Cap'n . . ."

"Didn't I now?" Lindemann's voice was steady and almost gentle. "Well, now, Mr. Suggs—now I'll tell *your* fortune. No charge to you. With my compliments. For taking up my time, you're going to wind up on your back with a bloody mouth."

His big hand left his side, the back of it connecting with Sugg's cheek, the sound of it like the sharp crack of a rifle.

Suggs was propelled backward, hitting his back on the side of the bar then rebounding off of it, to land face first, crunchingly spreadeagled onto the floor, one hand knocking over the cuspidor, which spilled over him as he lay there dazed—blood, drool, and tobacco juice a stinking porridge rolling down his face.

It was Dr. Nichols who helped raise him to a sitting position. The doctor's voice was ice-cold when he looked

up at Lindemann. "Not an act to be proud of, Captain
Lindemann—to take your miseries out on harmless little
men who'd do you no harm."

Lindemann raised his mug and drained the rum, not
even looking at the doctor. "On whoever, my good
Doctor—if he throws his line in my waters during the one
free hour I've got to get drunk and *forget* those miseries."

He pounded the mug on the bar, and Bennett hurried
from the opposite side of the bar back over to him, his
peg leg thumping on the wooden floor. As he poured out
more rum, Suggs rose slowly to his feet, his face the
color of a fish's belly. He wiped the wet off his face and
looked up at the big man in the slicker. "You're an evil
man, Cap'n," he said in a shaking voice. "You've no
heart in your body. You can't love. You can't give. You
can't share."

Lindemann very deliberately emptied the mug, the rum
coursing through him like some kind of medicinal lava.
Then he very slowly turned to look down at Suggs. The
men closest to them made nervous movements, as if to
get between them. Lindemann had a murderous rage, well
known and frequently experienced in the village. But the
look on the captain's face froze them.

He reached out and touched Suggs's shirt, then flicked
his fingers across the buttons, as if dusting. His voice was
so soft as almost not to be heard. "You've just taken a
share, Mr. Suggs; just a spoonful of the hate I've got in
me for the place, the time, the company, the weather, and
the night's catch." He reached into his pocket and took
out a handful of coins, which he flung onto the bar; then
he turned and surveyed the silent men around him. "And
the rest of you half-frozen cod catchers—what would Mr.
Suggs have you love?" He moved away from the bar, but-
toning up his slicker as he walked. He stopped at the
door, staring out of its window at the fog, then listening
pensively to a distant foghorn. "The sea, maybe?" he
asked. "Should we love the sea? It ties up our bowels
with fear. It ages us, and it finally kills us. And still each
morning we sail out for an embrace." He turned to look
at the men at the bar. "We are such damned fools that we
don't deserve any better."

With this, Hendrick Lindemann opened the door and
walked out onto the cobblestoned street, past the dirty lit-

tle lofts and shops that huddled along the street front facing the sea. He went in and out of the little pools of gaslight that shone so weakly through the layers of fog, until he reached the wharf where his little ketch was berthed. He was halfway down its length when he noticed three men of his crew gathered at the far end, murmuring, whispering, and pointing toward the net at their feet.

When Lindemann emerged from the fog, it was Granger, his first mate, who rose to his feet and faced him. "Cap'n," Granger began, "either we're out of our minds—"

Lindemann curtly cut him off. "Likely. Or full up on some bad grog. Or maybe you can tell me why three full grown men kneel around a fish net and shiver."

The smallest and oldest of the sailors, a gnarled little Pole named Bernacki, kicked at the net, "Lookee here, Cap'n. Lookee at what's in that net. If you see what we see, maybe *you'll* shiver."

Lindemann picked up a ship's lamp from off the wooden planking of the wharf and held it over the net, peering down through a maze of seaweed and dead fish until what he saw chopped off his breath. He straightened up and dropped the lantern. At the same moment, the light went out and there was nothing but darkness, mixed with the breathing of the frightened men and the sound of some flapping thing inside the net.

Granger thumbnailed a match and relit the lantern. His voice was a whisper. "Do you . . . do you see it Cap'n?"

He started to bring the lantern back over to the net. Lindemann grabbed his arm and held tightly to it. "There's no need of light," he said through his teeth, "to look at an illusion."

The third sailor, a young harpooner named Doyle, pulled the lantern from Granger's hand and slammed it down on the plank next to the net. "Take a look at that illusion, Cap'n. Just take a look at it."

Lindemann, with an almost desperate reluctance, let his eyes focus on what he knew he had already seen.

Through the mesh of the net there was a woman's face—white, cold, the lips a shade of purple, but the face incredibly alive and also incredibly beautiful. The folds of the net covered the outline of her body from face to waist, but protruding out of the net on its other side was the lower half of the woman's body—a long, fin-tailed protuberance that flapped weakly from side to side.

Lindemann closed his eyes briefly. "Kill it," he said in a strained voice, "then throw it back into the sea."

His first mate let out a gasp. "Cap'n—it's part woman."

Lindemann wrenched his eyes away from the net. "It's all monster."

Old Bernacki scratched at his seamed face. "Fifty years I've sailed, Cap'n, and I've never seen the likes of this." He shook his head back and forth. "It would be sacrilege to harm this creature."

"And you're suggesting what?" Lindemann roared at him, trying to disguise his fear with a semblance of rage. "Take it home? Fondle it from the belly up and fry it from the waist down?" He pointed to the net. "That goddamned thing isn't from Davy Jones—it's from the devil."

The men on the wharf turned toward the sound of voices and footsteps. Approaching the moorings were at least a dozen figures, some of them carrying lanterns, their voices full of growing excitement. The village was like a stagnant pool, desperate for some kind of tidal wave to break the killing monotony. Obviously some of Lindemann's crew had hurried over to the inn with news of the catch. Onto the wharf they came, tramping feet on the wooden plankings, until they stopped at the periphery of the ship's lamp and stared down at the net.

One of the crew members looked around proudly, challengingly, as if vindicated. "There she is," the sailor said loudly. "It's the creature, just as I described her."

It was Dr. Nichols who pushed his way through the knot of men, to move over to the net and kneel down beside it. He shook his head in disbelief. "I wouldn't believe it if I weren't . . . if I weren't seeing it with my own eyes. He looked up at Granger, the first mate. "Cut her loose out of there," he ordered. "She looks half frozen."

Doyle, the former harpooner, took out his skinning knife from his belt and started to chop at the netting.

Lindemann, in a quick, sudden motion, twisted the boy's wrist, sending the knife falling to the ground; then he turned, facing Nichols. "This your catch, is it, Doctor?

Or are you just confiscating it in the interest of public health?"

"She's half-frozen—" the doctor started to explain.

" '*She*,' " Lindemann interrupted, "is a finned and scaled nightmare, and that knife would be better used ..." He stopped abruptly, noting that Nichols was not looking at him but over his shoulder at the thing in the net, as were all the others.

Through the mesh the thing's hand had pushed its way out and was stretched out toward Lindemann in a gesture unmistakably supplicating.

There were hushed, whispered voices, and then silence.

"You call her a nightmare," Dr. Nichols said, "but the gesture, Captain Lindemann—the gesture is human."

"Cap'n," Doyle said, "think a bit. We could keep her alive. We could put her on exhibition. I've seen men pay good money to look at doughy things floating in alcohol." He pointed toward the net. "What would they pay to see a mermaid? A *real* mermaid."

Peg-legged Bennett stepped out into the lantern light. "To that end, Cap'n," he said, "count this an offer. Let *me* take her. I'll feed her and care for her, and I'll put her on display. And what's more—one-half of the take will go to you and your crew. And I have no doubt but that that take won't be minnow-sized, either. Doyle's right. Barnum himself couldn't come up with anything like this."

The crew members smiled hopefully and looked toward Lindemann. Four dollars a week and keep—that's what they sweated for, froze for, risked their scrawny, perpetually bone-tired bodies for daily, casting nets into the always quixotic and frequently menacing sea. And there in the net was one of the few gifts ever offered up in return. They held their breaths, waiting for Lindemann's response.

The captain looked around the circle of faces, and then, for a reason he couldn't explain, he knelt down and very tenderly touched the hand stretched out through the net. The hand, in response, enclosed his, and Lindemann yanked his away as if touching fire; but he did look at the face that stared at him through the mesh and weed; and the face was undeniably beautiful.

He slowly rose to his feet. "I'll think it over," he said.

"Cap'n," his mate Granger said in a tremulous voice,

receiving encouraging nods from the rest of the crew, "we've got ourselves a gold mine here. Woman or fish— she's a gold mine. I'd be thinkin' we should take her aboard—"

"You'd be thinking too much, Mr. Granger," Linde- mann answered. "You're not master of this ship, and the catch isn't yours. It belongs to me. Now, I said I'd think about it. And while I'm thinking—please to leave the wharf, all of you."

"Captain," Dr. Nichols said, "you just can't leave her in the net there and—"

"No more, Doctor," Lindemann barked out at him as if ordering him up a mast. "No more from any of you. Just go back to your houses or that pig trough Mr. Bennett calls an inn. Or lie in the gutter, for all of me. But I want all of you out of here."

Reluctantly, still whispering and murmuring, the group started backing off the wharf, Lindemann's crew the most reluctant.

He waited until the lights of their lanterns disappeared into the fog and night and their voices could no longer be heard. Left alone, he stared down at the apparition, then picked up the skinning knife and took it over to the net. It glinted in the light of the lantern.

The face of the thing inside the net looked directly into his.

Lindemann cut away some of the strands, then held up the knife and in a quick, sudden motion sailed it through the air until it embedded itself in a post.

The thing in the net looked toward the knife, then back to Lindemann—the eyes wide and frightened; one of its hands touched the side of the newly cut hole.

Lindemann caught the wrist in a vise. "No, my dear," he said evenly, "not back into the sea. Not yet. The sea *gave* you to me. Now I'll ponder it a bit—as to your value to me. Maybe there *is* a breed of gawker who'd pay money to gape at you. Maybe that's the case."

He moved over to the gangplank of the ketch. "But while I ponder this, my dear, I'll have to take away any temptations you might have." He moved quickly across the gangplank to the deck of the ketch and picked up a coil of heavy rope. He carried it back across the gang- plank, unfurling it as he moved back toward the net.

"Now, don't look so frightened," he said. "I'll not mistreat you." He waited for a moment, seeing the unspeakable fear in the thing's eyes. "Can you talk?" he asked. "Do you have a language of a sort?"

The eyes just stared back at him.

Lindemann laughed. "I expect too much. Talk from you yet. Conversation." He knotted one end of the rope. "But you might consider your blessings. As cold as that wood is, and the air—the water is much colder."

Then quickly and expertly he had the line around the net, imprisoning the thing inside, as he drew the free end of the rope through the knot and pulled it taut. He pulled the net off the planking, flinging it over his shoulder like a sack, and started back across the gangplank, feeling the creature struggle and thresh about as he did so. At last, he thought, as he crossed the gunwales onto the dirty, greasy deck—at last, a catch that had some worth; at last, that murky bastard of a sea had rewarded him with something other than bleeding hands and bent back.

He lifted up a hatch cover with the toe of one of his boots and started below, carrying the squirming thing over his shoulder.

The crew members of Lindemann's ketch stood on the wharf like a silent, disapproving jury, occasionally whispering among themselves, then looking toward Granger, waiting . . . expecting . . . hoping.

The first mate took a step away from the group, cupped his hands around his mouth, and called out. "Cap'n Lindemann?" He waited for a moment. "Cap'n Lindemann!"

On the ketch the door to a small cabin opened. Lindemann came out, walked the length of the small ship over to the stern, and looked out at the men.

"Cap'n," Granger called out again, "the men wanna know when you plan to take her out again. It's been three days."

"When I'm ready," Lindemann shouted back. "Did anyone go get Doc Nichols?"

"On his way, Cap'n," old Bernacki called back in a cracked voice. "But what about the fishing, Cap'n? Three days without a catch, sir . . ."

"Tell Nichols to come right on board into my cabin,"

Lindemann said over his shoulder as he turned and started back toward the cabin.

The crew members looked expectantly again at Granger. The first mate was their voice, and under the complex but unwritten protocol of ships and men, he was their link to the throne of that wet little kingdom called the Sea.

"Cap'n," Granger called out, reluctance softening his voice. "Begging your pardon, sir, but the men wanna know if . . . if you don't plan to fish . . . what about the . . . the creature? She came in the catch, sir. And by agreement, we're owed a percentage . . ."

Lindemann paused at the cabin's door. "You'll get a percentage," he said through his teeth. "You'll get a percentage of a pike staff across your heads. Now, clear the hell out of here, all of you—all of you." With that he disappeared into the cabin.

Moments later Dr. Nichols approached the wharf and was immediately enclosed by the men, all talking at the same time, all protesting and explaining, until Nichols held up his hand.

"Hold it," he said. "You, Granger. You tell me. What's it all about?"

Granger looked toward the ketch. "Three days he's stayed aboard, Doc. He'll not see or talk to anyone. And our last catch rotted right where we put her. At least, the fish did."

Nichols looked at him through narrowed eyes. "What about that . . ." He stopped, unable to identify by name or description the thing they all knew had been put on board.

"You tell us," Granger said meaningfully. "You know the Cap'n. With that raging northwind temper of his—he could've cut her up for bait by now."

"What does he want to see me for?" Nichols asked.

"Tell us that, too," the first mate answered. "He said to come right on board and go to his cabin."

Nichols nodded, hoisted up the little black bag that he carried, and walked the rest of the length of the wharf to the rotting gangplank spread from pier to vessel. He walked across it onto the deck, looked briefly at the crew members who remained there, then took a step over to the cabin door.

"Captain Lindemann," he called out.

The cabin door opened. Lindemann was silhouetted against a lantern light from inside. "Come in," he said.

Nichols, with another look toward the men, moved through the cabin door.

It was a tiny, low-ceilinged little cubicle, sparse of furniture save for fishing equipment and a few navigational aids.

Nichols looked briefly around the squalid interior as if expecting to find something other than the cot that was the only piece of furniture in the room. "What's it all about, Captain?" Nichols asked.

Lindemann handed him a pewter mug. "Warm yourself." It was more a command than an invitation.

Nichols took the mug, nodded his thanks, then sipped at the rum. "Your crew tells me," he said, "that you haven't shipped out in three days."

Lindemann's face looked inexpressibly tired. "A little shore leave for them," he said tightly.

"What about you?"

"What *about* me?"

"Captain," the doctor said, "the creature caught in your net—no one's seen her since you took her in."

He waited for a response. Lindemann just turned his back.

"Bennett is willing to pay cash for her," Nichols persisted, "or work out any arrangement you think fair."

There was a silence for a moment; then Lindemann said, "Shove her in a tank someplace while the bumpkins stand around drooling out a lot of filth at her."

Something in Lindemann's tone made Nichols stare at him. There was an emotion deeper than anger, a quality of desperation that Nichols had never heard before.

"Captain," the doctor began softly.

Lindemann turned abruptly. "She's sick, Doc," he said, his voice nakedly placating. "She's not eaten in a day and a night. She just . . . she just lies there on the floor."

"Where?" Nichols whispered.

"In the hold. She seems to be . . . just wasting away." He took a step toward Nichols, both his hands held out. "Look at her, Doc," he implored, "and treat her. Give her medicines. Keep her alive."

Nichols stared at him.

"She's . . . she's more human than anything. We can communicate together."

"She speaks to you?" Nichols asked, astounded.

"Not in words," the Captain answered. "Not in any language. But she makes herself understood. And I to her. Please, Doc—see what you can do."

Lindemann moved across the small cabin to another door that led to a passageway to the hold below. He stepped aside and pointed.

Nichols started slowly and carefully down the rickety steps. Lindemann held up a lantern behind him. At the foot of the steps Nichols stopped and stared, his eyes wide, unbelieving, full of both pity and horror.

Lying on the floor, half-covered by a filthy blanket, the thing threshed about weakly. Her finned tail protruded from the foot of the blanket.

Both men moved over to her. Again Lindemann held up the lantern. Nichols stared, then looked at Lindemann. "Captain," he said, "it . . . that is to say . . . *she* is amphibian, and she's been without water too long."

Lindemann didn't answer. But again Nichols looked at his face. Twenty years he had known the sea captain. And he'd known him as a cold, emotionless, taciturn, frequently cruel man; silent, ungiving, unsharing, full of secret anguish that, with so much rum, would hiss out in a steam of rage and then be bottled up again in his own special, unpeopled hermitage. But there was want on Lindemann's face now—a raw, naked desperation that went beyond language.

Nichols put a hand on Lindemann's arm. "You've got to throw her back," he said gently but firmly.

Lindemann shook his head. "Give her medicine, Doctor. Something to get her strength back."

"Her strength comes from the sea, Captain."

"Save her, Doctor." The intensity of Lindemann's voice almost charged the room.

"I'm sorry," Nichols said softly. "I wouldn't know how. I treat only . . . humans."

"She *is* human."

Nichols let his eyes move down the prostrate form, from the closed eyes in the pale, wan face, down the length of the blanket to the fins; then he looked up at Lindemann. "Three nights ago you called her a nightmare

. . . a monster. I'll tell you something, Captain. She's a little of both. But I'll tell you what she *isn't*. She's not a companion to man. Any man."

He started back toward the steps, picking his way carefully over piles of flemished rope and buckets, reaching for the rail.

Lindemann's voice was more a cry than anything else, more a deep sound of pain. "Help her," the captain said.

Nichols turned at the foot of the ladder. "Help her? No, Captain. I can't help her. You must. Give her back to the sea."

He started up the ladder, suddenly conscious of a cold and dampness that ate into his body, like the moisture-laden air of a tomb underneath water; but as he reached the entrance to Lindemann's cabin, he heard the unmistakable sound of the big man's sobs. Lindemann was crying. Good God, he thought, as he walked through the cabin and out through the door onto the deck—there was no mountain that could not be scaled. And there was no man, no man on earth, who in some way at some time could not be torn into.

Inside Bennett's inn, Lindemann's crew mixed with the usual nightly coterie of rum drinkers. Doyle pounded his tankard on the bar. "Crazy," the young sailor said. "Turned crazy is what he did."

Bernacki nodded and wiped the rum off his mouth. "Keepin' her down there in the hold. And plannin' on sellin' her—that's what he's a mind to. And that's the last we'll have seen of him. And of the thing, as well."

Suggs was in their midst, looking left and right— nodding, smiling, his rat eyes blinking, shining, and moving from one to the other. "Did you expect different?" Suggs asked. "It's what I've told you a thousand times about Lindemann. He's got no heart. He's built out of iron, timber, and ship's tar—"

Nichols' voice from the door, though quiet, cut off the other voices and made all eyes turn to him. "But with sufficient heart, Master Suggs," Nichols said as he moved into the room, "to call me out in the middle of the night to help that creature."

Sugg's lips twisted. "For what purpose, Doctor? To keep it alive so he can torment it?"

There were several nods and more than one whispered assent.

"To keep it alive," Nichols said, "because he's a lonely man."

"That lonely, Doctor?" Bennett asked from behind the bar.

"As lonely as is possible," Nichols responded, "for a human being to be."

Bennett looked around the faces. "But," he began hesitantly, "it's a creature. It's not human."

Old Bernacki crossed himself and nodded.

"Whatever it is," Nichols said, "it won't survive too many more hours."

First Mate Granger, deep in his cups and brave with rum, slammed one fist into a palm. "We could go over there—all of us—a boarding party. Tie up the damned thing and take her up to Boston and sell her while she's still alive."

He looked around hopefully, as if expecting a reaction. There was silence. The men were still looking toward Nichols.

"You do that," the doctor said very quietly. "Pick up pikestaffs and rifles, if need be. But best draw lots as to the first half-dozen men to start down the ladder. They'll be dead before they reach the hold." He looked from face to face. "Understand? Captain Lindemann, in the manner of solitary, friendless men, has found something to care about. Reptile, apparition, specter from the seaweed—whatever it is—it's given him something to love."

He made a motion to Bennett, who poured a tankard full of rum and handed it over to him. Nichols slowly sipped at it, savoring its biting heat, and thinking to himself of the bleakness of Lindemann's voice and the hollow desolation on his face as he stood in the dank dungeon of the ketch trying to hold back death with a lantern and a gnarled fist and his own unused, untried heart. Nichols shook his head and drained the rum from the tankard. The Lord did, indeed, work in mysterious ways; to pluck an object of love for Hendrick Lindemann out of the wet and endless cemetery that he had despised, hated, and feared all of his life.

* * *

Like an undersized scarecrow, Suggs stood on the wharf, a ragged pea jacket billowing away from his gaunt body, and felt the razor-sharp wind come off the water to slice against him. He lifted up his face, listening intently at the sound of footsteps on the deck of Lindemann's ketch. Then he peered through the darkness and saw the big outline of the captain's body leaving the cabin. He heard the footsteps move over to the gunwales, and then the sound of a bucket hitting the water.

Reluctant and yet intense, Suggs forced himself to move down the length of wharf toward the ketch. "Cap'n Lindemann," he called out.

He saw the big figure bolt upright, still clutching to the bucket rope and trying to carve identity out of the darkness.

"Who is it?" Lindemann asked.

"It's Suggs, Cap'n. But that bucket of water you're filling—that won't do it."

"What will, Suggs?" Lindemann asked. "Tea leaves?"

Suggs moved over to the wharf end of the gangplank. "The trawler that almost ran you down, Cap'n . . ."

"What about it?" Lindemann asked.

"She went aground off Carney's Cape. Just as I said she would. Eleven hands lost."

Lindemann lifted the water-filled bucket up to the deck. "That must have pleased you, Mr. Suggs."

Suggs put one foot on the gangplank. "Not a bit, Cap'n. I may cry doom, but I don't take pleasure from it."

Lindemann looked at the hunched-over dwarf figure. "What do you take pleasure from, Mr. Suggs?"

"From helping," Suggs said softly. "You can believe that, Cap'n. I take pleasure from offering up a hand when I can."

Suggs could almost see Lindemann's face freezing in the darkness.

"Put that hand in your pocket," the captain said. "I'd sooner take my lunch in a bilge bucket."

"You don't understand, Cap'n," Suggs said. "I've come to help you. As only I can."

Suggs heard Lindemann's footsteps moving over to the cabin door.

"Help yourself, Mr. Suggs. By putting distance between yourself and me. Or have you lost track of how many times I've put you on your back and how many of your teeth I've loosened?"

"All forgotten, Cap'n," Suggs said, his face contorted into a gargoyle smile. Then, from inside his moth-eaten, ragged shirt he produced a bottle. "Cap'n," he whispered, as if sharing the most important secret on earth, "I told you I had potions. Powerful nostrums with miraculous properties."

Lindemann lowered the bucket to the deck, then moved over to the gangplank. The one ship's lantern hung from a stanchion and threw out a weak, pale ray of light to illuminate Suggs. Lindemann looked from the bottle into the other man's face.

"To burn my insides, no doubt, Mr. Suggs."

Suggs shook his head. *"To change a half-woman into a whole woman."*

Suggs could hear Lindemann catch his breath. "Watch your talk, Suggs . . ."

"I mean it, Cap'n. The contents of this bottle poured into the mouth of that creature you have below—and by dawn she'll walk on two legs."

Suggs felt an impulse to run when he saw Lindemann step onto the gangplank and walk its length toward him, the figure vast, bulky, and imposing; but he forced himself to stand his ground, and allowed Lindemann to reach out and take the small bottle from his hand, studying it.

"Two bells now, Cap'n," Suggs said, almost breathlessly. "And by seven bells, the miracle will have occurred."

The bottle was almost obliterated by Lindemann's giant hand. "I'm a desperate man, Mr. Suggs," he said softly. "They call my desperation insanity; I know that. But it's sufficient to tear you to pieces if this is your idea of a joke."

"Cap'n . . ." Suggs sensed his advantage, the only advantage he could have over any man—to find another being more desperate than he, more frightened than he. "It's a scrawny, brandy-soaked carcass I carry around with me, but it's all I've got, and I value it. Would I come here in the dead of night so you could break me in half?" He pointed to the bottle. "Have her drink it. Then leave her alone. And in five hours, give or take a few minutes— you'll see the change."

It was then that he noticed Lindemann's hand shaking as he held out the bottle.

"If it's as you say," Lindemann said in a strained voice, "if it's as you say"—he looked up—"I'll bless you, Suggs, and I'll not forget it."

Suggs studied the big man, noting the strange, strained quality in the voice and the look on his face.

"She means something to you."

Lindemann nodded. "She means life itself." He turned and moved back across the gangplank onto the ketch.

"She'll have life itself, Cap'n." Suggs's voice followed him. "A gift from me to you. With my compliments."

Then he turned and shuffled back into the darkness, disappearing at the far end of the wharf. He felt his feet touch the cobblestone, the coldness reaching through the thin leather to move up his skinny legs. The cold. Always the cold. But as he moved down the street toward the inn, he felt one elusive spot of warmth. The hate. The burning, flaming, all-consuming fire of hate for Hendrick Lindemann. For the slaps across his face, for the bloody mouths, for the stinking contents of spittoons splashed across his face, for the multiple hours of animal humiliation—God in heaven, what a debt had been incurred! And God in heaven, now it would be repaid that night!

Captain Lindemann sat alone in his cabin, staring at the empty bottle on the small table in front of him. The creature below had gulped it down thirstily. Liquid. Any liquid. She was like some desert flower, baked by the sun, disintegrating from dryness. No matter how much water he poured over her, no matter how many glasses he placed to her mouth, she seemed to wither and dehydrate in front of his eyes. And those eyes. Those pained, aching eyes. How they stared at him and beseeched him; how they pleaded with him and begged him; how they spoke in her soundless language and asked for release. But the eyes had captured Lindemann. The face had captured him. The soft blond hair. The white skin. He was as much a prisoner as the gasping, threshing thing down below in the hold.

For Hendrick Lindemann had never known love. He had never known a possession that came with passion.

And the thought of the creature (he thought of her as "woman") escaping him—this was simply beyond bearing. It was as Dr. Nichols had perceived. Something had breached his loneliness; something had crossed over the frontiers of his self-imposed exile from other humans, and to the extent that he could feel passion, he felt it for that captive being whose metamorphosis from freak to woman he now waited for.

He pulled out his pocket watch for perhaps the twentieth time during the course of the night, and noted the gray, filtered light of dawn illuminating the face of it. Five hours had elapsed since administering Sugg's potion. He rose on unsteady legs, feeling a debilitating weakness that incredibly came with the surge of excitement. He moved over to the door leading to the ladder and opened it, then slowly descended toward the hold.

The same dawn light came through the grating on the deck above the hold and revealed the figure of the woman, now standing. It took a moment for Lindemann to assimilate what he saw, and sort out from both what he had feared and what he had hoped for. But gradually the realization came that the creature had legs—long, perfectly formed woman's legs. And then he realized that her back was to him and that her long blond hair partially covered her naked back. Her hands were at her sides, and she seemed no longer to be struggling. And as the component fragments took form and moved into place, Lindemann realized that the body was beautiful—beautiful beyond anything he could describe. He felt his throat constrict and knew that he was crying.

"You're a woman now," he managed to blurt out. "Understand? Magic or miracle or whatever—you're a woman now!" He shouted it out again, "You're a woman now!" as he started back up the ladder. "Suggs," he screamed as he ran through his cabin and out onto the deck. "Suggs, it worked. It's happened. You turned her into a woman."

Beyond the gangplank on the wharf were the members of his crew and some of the people from the village.

"She's no creature," Lindemann shouted at them. "She's no reptile. She's a woman!"

The sailors stared at him.

"You don't believe me?" Lindemann's voice carried

over the early-morning silence. "Well, I'll tell you what, gentlemen. I'll *walk* her out onto the deck. That's what I'll do. I'll walk her out here so you can see her!"

He turned and moved back over to the grating covering the hold, then yanked it open as if it were a layer of tissue paper. "Come up! Come up the ladder and show them!" He turned toward the wharf. "She'll not lie gasping below in that filthy hold anymore! She'll live with me at my side from now on!"

He heard the creak of the ladder behind him, and he felt the tears running down his face. But it didn't matter. Let the bastards gape at him. Let them see him cry like a baby. Let them for the first time in their lives—and his—witness the birth of joy! But look at them stare! Look at their mouths drop open! Look at their eyes pop!

"You've not seen Lindemann cry before, have you, you mother's sons," Lindemann roared out at them. "Well, I'll show you my tears without shame, lads. Without any shame at all. And you can gape and pop and swallow your tongues, and you'll get no apologies from me! I have a woman now! I have the most beautiful woman on earth, who will stay by my side now until . . ."

It was then that Lindemann realized they weren't looking at him at all. They were looking past him to the hatch cover, and there was no admiration on their faces, no sudden contemplation of beauty, not even a touch of the lustful awe that men show for the unclothed woman thrust in front of them.

Lindemann turned.

He saw her only briefly as she swept by him, racing toward the bow of the ketch. Briefly. Just a flash of her as their eyes met. Then she had flung herself off the bow and into the sea.

Her eyes.

Unblinking, cold fish eyes popping out of the scaled fish face—the overlapping rows of fins. The pulsating slits on either side of her green throat that struggled for air. The puckered fish mouth that rounded out the horror that sat atop the beautiful white neck and the shapely white shoulders.

But Lindemann's scream was not one of horror. The men on the wharf could perceive words to it even as he ran from them toward the bow. "No," he was screaming, "no, please. Wait."

He was still screaming the words as he threw himself over the rail and into the water. "Wait . . . please . . . come back . . . please . . ."

And then there was silence. Far off in the distance the men could see a small ripple of movement and just a flash of one white arm breaking the surface, then disappearing, followed by a thin white wake. But in the spot that Lindemann had disappeared, there was nothing to be seen. The sea had enclosed him. It had swallowed him. It had taken body and voice into its confines as completely and permanently as only the sea can do.

In a fog-cloaked twilight the people of the village stood alongside the wharf and looked toward Dr. Nichols, who had just thrown a wreath into the now quiet sea. It floated serenely away from the shore, small pitiful-looking early-spring blossoms that bobbed in and out of sight and finally disappeared.

Nichols' voice was very soft as he opened the book in his hands and read from it. " 'We have fed our sea for a thousand years and she calls us, still unfed, though there is never a wave of all her waves . . . but marks our dead.' "* He closed the book and stood there.

It was Suggs who broke the spell and the silence by shifting around and clearing his throat.

Nichols looked at him. "Master Suggs? Anything to add?"

Suggs smiled, the cadaverous, rodent little face shining. "This needn't be *your* lot, Doctor," he said. Then he took Nichols' elbow. "What about a palm reading, Doctor? Or let me look at the tea leaves for you."

*Rudyard Kipling, "The Song of the Dead" (1893), II, Stanza 1.

Here, for your careful consideration . . .

THE TWILIGHT ZONE ANTHOLOGIES

edited by Carol Serling

☐ **JOURNEYS TO THE TWILIGHT ZONE**   UE2525—$4.99
The first of the Twilight Zone anthologies, this volume offers a wonderful array of new ventures into the unexplored territories of the imagination by such talents as Pamela Sargent, Charles de Lint, and William F. Nolan, as well as Rod Serling's chilling tale "Suggestion".

☐ **RETURN TO THE TWILIGHT ZONE**   UE2576—$4.99
Enjoy 18 new excursions into the dimension beyond our own. From a television set that is about to tune in to the future . . . to a train ride towards a destiny from which there is no turning back . . . plus "The Sole Survivor," a classic tale by Rod Serling himself!

☐ **ADVENTURES IN THE TWILIGHT ZONE**   UE2662—$4.99
Carol Serling has called upon many of today's most imaginative writers to conjure up 23 all-original tales which run the gamut from science fiction to the supernatural, the fantastical, or the truly horrific. Also included is "Lindemann's Catch," written by Rod Serling.

FANTASY ANTHOLOGIES

Science Fiction Anthologies

Welcome to DAW's Gallery of Ghoulish Delights!